PURE LUST

Ignoring the whispers of warning in the back of her mind, Myst placed her hands on his chest, exploring the satin heat of his skin.

"I want this," she assured him. "I want you."

Myst's breath tangled in her throat as his burning bronze gaze swept slowly over her naked body. Good Lord, he was spectacular. His shoulders were broad. His chest was sculpted and his abs formed a perfect washboard. He had a narrow waist and hips that led to long, muscular legs.

It'd been so long.

So painfully long.

"I don't know what you do to me," she whispered.

"I assure you the feeling is mutual, *cara*." He threaded his fingers through her hair. "I've never wanted anyone like I want you."

His words melted any lingering hesitation. Who knew what the future would bring? For tonight she wasn't going to let it rule her.

Easily sensing the last of her barriers had crumbled, Bas bent his head to brand her lips in a kiss that demanded utter surrender. . . .

Books by Alexandra Ivy

Guardians of Eternity
WHEN DARKNESS COMES
EMBRACE THE DARKNESS
DARKNESS EVERLASTING
DARKNESS REVEALED
DARKNESS UNLEASHED
BEYOND THE DARKNESS
DEVOURED BY DARKNESS
BOUND BY DARKNESS
FEAR THE DARKNESS
DARKNESS AVENGED
HUNT THE DARKNESS
WHEN DARKNESS ENDS

The Immortal Rogues
MY LORD VAMPIRE
MY LORD ETERNITY
MY LORD IMMORTALITY

The Sentinels
BORN IN BLOOD
BLOOD ASSASSIN
BLOOD LUST

Ares Security
KILL WITHOUT MERCY

Historical Romance
SOME LIKE IT WICKED
SOME LIKE IT SINFUL
SOME LIKE IT BRAZEN

And don't miss these Guardians of Eternity novellas

TAKEN BY DARKNESS in YOURS FOR ETERNITY
DARKNESS ETERNAL in SUPERNATURAL
WHERE DARKNESS LIVES in
THE REAL WEREWIVES OF VAMPIRE COUNTY
LEVET (eBook only)
A VERY LEVET CHRISTMAS (eBook only)

And don't miss these Sentinel novellas

OUT OF CONTROL in PREDATORY
ON THE HUNT in ON THE HUNT

Published by Kensington Publishing Corporation

BLOOD LUST

ALEXANDRA IVY

ZEBRA BOOKS
KENSINGTON PUBLISHING CORP.
http://www.kensingtonbooks.com

ZEBRA BOOKS are published by

Kensington Publishing Corp.
119 West 40th Street
New York, NY 10018

All Kensington titles, imprints, and distributed lines are available at special quantity discounts for bulk purchases for sales promotion, premiums, fund-raising, educational, or institutional use.

Special book excerpts or customized printings can also be created to fit specific needs. For details, write or phone the office of the Kensington Sales Manager: Attn.: Sales Department. Kensington Publishing Corp., 119 West 40th Street, New York, NY 10018. Phone: 1-800-221-2647.

Zebra and the Z logo Reg. U.S. Pat. & TM Off.

First Printing: June 2016
ISBN-13: 978-1-4201-3759-0
ISBN-10: 1-4201-3759-X

eISBN-13: 978-1-4201-3760-6
eISBN-10: 1-4201-3760-3

10 9 8 7 6 5 4 3 2 1

Printed in the United States of America

Prologue

It had been over a century since the high-bloods revealed themselves to the norms.

In that time they'd established Valhalla, the main compound for the high-bloods, and built it smack-dab in the middle of the United States, as well as several satellite compounds around the world.

It was a way to try and convince the mortals that the witches, healers, psychics, necromancers, telepaths, and clairvoyants were just like them . . . only with special powers.

And that the monk-trained warriors called the Sentinels could be trusted to maintain order among the high-bloods.

What they didn't bother to share was that there were several high-bloods with rare, sometimes dangerous powers who were kept hidden from sight. And that while the guardian Sentinels—who were covered in intricate tattoos to protect them against magic—and the hunter Sentinels—who remained unmarked to be able to travel among the people unnoticed—had been revealed along with the other high-bloods, there was another sect of warriors . . . the assassins.

The faction of ruthless killers had been disbanded years ago, but a few had managed to survive.

And a rare few had managed to prosper.

Chapter One

Bas had retreated to his penthouse suite in the luxury Kansas City hotel after fleeing from the clusterfuck that recently destroyed his highly profitable business.

Not that he gave a shit about the money.

He had enough wealth stashed in various properties around the world to last him several lifetimes.

And he gave even less of a shit about ending his role as the leader of a renegade band of mercenary high-bloods who defied the laws of Valhalla to sell their various talents for an indecent price.

It'd been fun, not to mention highly profitable, to create his merry band of misfits, but he'd made more than his fair share of enemies over the years. A fact that had come back to bite him in the ass when a former employee had kidnapped his precious daughter and used her as leverage to try and gain control over a volatile high-blood who could have started Armageddon.

Now all he wanted to do was find someplace safe to raise Molly.

He could, of course, have gone underground. Keeping a low profile was easy for a man who had his talent for altering his appearance. But he wasn't going to drag Molly from one seedy location to another.

She needed love and peace and stability in her young life.

Things he fully intended to give her. Once he figured out how to avoid being arrested and thrown into the dungeons of Valhalla.

He was in the process of plotting his future when he heard the pitter-patter of tiny feet.

He turned to watch Molly enter the salon, her stuffed hippo, Daisy, clutched in her arms.

Joy pierced his heart as he studied his daughter's sleep-flushed face surrounded by her silvery curls. Christ, he still got up a dozen times a night to make sure she was safely tucked in her bed. Molly, on the other hand, barely seemed to remember her time as the witch's captive. Thank God.

"What are you doing out of bed? Did you have a bad dream?"

She flashed a smile that could light up the world. "Mama called me."

Bas swallowed a curse. Molly often spoke about Myst. Almost as if she was a constant companion instead of the woman who'd given birth to her and then promptly disappeared.

"Called you?" He gave a teasing tug on a silvery curl. "On the phone?"

She giggled, the dimple he loved appearing beside her mouth. "No silly. In my head."

"It was a dream," he gently assured her.

Her bronze eyes, which perfectly matched his own, widened. "No. It was real."

"Molly."

"She talks to me all the time."

Bas bit his tongue. He couldn't tell his daughter that five

years ago he'd had a one-night stand . . . no, it hadn't even been that.

Myst had come into his office, desperate for a job. She'd claimed to be a clairvoyant, but she hadn't been capable of providing even one reading of the future.

He hadn't had much choice but to tell her that he didn't have a place for her on his payroll.

Not only because she didn't bring the skills that could make his business money, but because he'd been rattled by his intense reaction to her fragile beauty.

He was nearly three centuries old. He'd had countless lovers. Some had been passing acquaintances, some he'd enjoyed for several years.

But none of them had ever come close to making him a conquest.

Which was why he hadn't been prepared when Myst had stepped into his office, nearly bringing him to his knees with the force of his instinctive, gut-wrenching desire.

Even now the memory of her beauty haunted him.

Her pale, exquisite face that was dominated by a large pair of velvet-brown eyes. And the long, silvery blond hair that looked as if it was spun silk.

She was danger. Pure female danger wrapped in the warm scent of honeysuckle.

Unfortunately, before he could get rid of her, Myst had caught him off guard when she'd burst into tears.

He might be a bastard, but he'd been unable to toss a sobbing woman out on her ass. So instead he'd given her a good, stiff drink to calm her nerves. And then another.

And the next thing he knew they'd been naked on his couch and he was lost in the spectacular pleasure of her body.

Bas gave a sharp shake of his head, his hand reaching into the pocket of his slacks to touch the locket he'd carried for the past five years.

He'd wasted too many nights recalling just how good it'd felt to have Myst pressed beneath him, her legs wrapped around his waist.

The only thing that mattered was that she'd disappeared from his office the second his back was turned. And then, nine months later, slipped through his security to abandon Molly in his private rooms.

What kind of woman did that?

"Okay," he murmured, fiercely attempting to disguise his opinion of Myst. "What does she say?"

"That she has something she has to do, but she misses me," Molly said. "And that soon we'll be together again."

"I don't want you to be disappointed if she can't come," he said gently. He tenderly smoothed her silken curls. "You have me. And I'm never going away."

"But she is coming." Molly bounced up and down at the sound of the door to the suite being opened. "See? I told you."

Bas surged upright, his hand reaching for the gun holstered at the small of his back.

What the hell? How had an intruder gotten past his security system?

"Molly, go to your room."

"But it's Mommy."

There was the unmistakable scent of honeysuckle drenching the air before a silver-haired female stepped into the salon, her yellow sundress swirling around her slender legs. Bas hissed, feeling as if he'd been punched in the gut.

Christ.

She was just as beautiful as ever.

Perhaps even more beautiful.

"Myst." The name was wrenched from his lips.

Her delicate features were impossible to read. "Hello, Bas."

He gave a shake of his head, trying desperately to dismiss his potent, intoxicating response to the sight of her.

"What the hell are you doing here?"

Her gaze shifted to the tiny girl standing beside him, a luminous smile lighting her fragile features.

"I've come for my daughter."

Myst had learned to endure living in a constant state of terror.

It wasn't like she had a choice.

For years she'd attempted to avoid her inevitable fate, always on the run, always looking over her shoulder.

Stupidly, she assumed that she'd become so accustomed to her sense of dread that nothing could rattle her.

Until five years ago.

The day she'd first met the man who was standing in front of her like an angel of retribution.

Not that she'd felt dread when she'd walked into his office. She only wished she had.

No. If she wanted to be brutally honest, she'd tumbled into instant lust. Who could blame her? Bas Cavrilo was a stunningly beautiful male.

His features were carved by the hand of an artist. A wide brow. A narrow, arrogant blade of a nose. Full, sensuous lips that hinted at a passionate nature beneath his stern facade.

His skin was a pale ivory and satin smooth unless you counted the small eye-shaped emerald birthmark on the side of his neck, and the thin horizontal lines tattooed beneath it.

In contrast his hair was as black as midnight and cut short to emphasize his male beauty.

And his eyes . . . Lord, those eyes.

A tiny shudder had raced through her at her first glimpse of the metallic bronze eyes that held a cunning intelligence.

She'd felt as if something vital had been switched off in her brain. That would explain why she'd so recklessly chugged the scotch he'd offered after refusing to give her the job she so desperately needed.

And then another scotch had been chugged. . . .

The next thing she knew she was giving in to the passion that had exploded between them with electric force. Once sanity had returned, she'd slipped away, hoping to put the crazed incident behind her.

Of course, she couldn't be so lucky.

Instead she'd discovered that she was pregnant, and she'd learned the true meaning of terror.

Now she licked her lips, her heart thundering like a freight train in her chest as she forced herself to meet the scorching bronze glare.

"How did you get past my security?" Bas snapped.

Before she could speak, Molly was darting forward, ignoring her father's biting fury with the confidence of a child who knew that she was well loved.

"Mommy, Mommy!" she cried.

Myst fell to her knees, enfolding the wiggling bundle of sunshine in her arms.

For a perilous second she closed her eyes, savoring the pure joy that briefly drove away the nightmares that were Myst's constant companion.

"Hey, baby," she murmured softly.

A shadow fell upon her as the tall, lethally dangerous assassin moved to tower over her. "I asked you a question."

She pressed her cheek to the top of Molly's soft curls, staring at the original Renoir painting that was hung on a far wall.

"I heard you."

"Then you have no excuse for not answering."

"You didn't hire me, remember?" she muttered.

There was a startled silence. "I remember everything," he at last said, the words oddly husky.

Myst shivered. Heavens. His voice was magic. Low, and

whiskey smooth. Sometimes she woke in the middle of the night, imagining she could still hear him whispering words of pleasure in her ear.

"You're not the boss of me."

He snorted, unimpressed. "And?"

"And I don't have to answer to you."

Tiny arms wrapped around her neck as Molly smacked a moist kiss on her cheek. "I missed you, Mommy."

Her arms tightened around her daughter, tears filling her eyes. "I missed you too, baby. More than you could ever imagine."

She heard Bas swear beneath his breath.

"Molly, go back to your bed so Mommy and I can have a little chat."

"No, I don't want to go to bed," Molly pouted, burying her face in Myst's neck. "I want to stay with Mommy."

"Molly." The edge in Bas's voice warned that he was at the end of his patience.

Keeping her arms around the fragile little girl, Myst rose to her feet and carried Molly toward the door that led to the back of the suite.

"It's okay." She brushed her lips over Molly's forehead. "I'll tuck you in."

Molly gazed up at her with shimmering bronze eyes. "I don't want you to leave."

Pain sliced through Myst. She'd known this was going to be difficult. But she hadn't realized it was going to feel as if her heart was being ripped out.

She forced a smile to her lips. This was for Molly.

After everything her daughter had been forced to endure over the past week, a visit from her mother was the least she could do for her.

"I'm not leaving," she said, pretending to ignore the large male form prowling behind her like a panther shadowing its prey.

The hair on her nape stirred, her mind urging her to flee as she walked down the short hall that led to two bedrooms. She chose the nearest, heaving a silent sigh of relief at the sight of the toys piled in the corner of the elegant black and gold room.

The last thing she wanted was to accidentally intrude into Bas's privacy.

Not that she feared he would toss her on his bed and strip off her clothes. Her lips twisted. His expression when she'd entered the suite had revealed what he thought of her.

And it was nothing good.

But it would have been . . . unnerving.

"You swear you won't leave?" Molly pleaded as Myst crossed the lush black carpet to settle her daughter on the bed. "A pinkie swear?"

She gently tugged the gold comforter over Molly's tiny body. "I swear."

"You shouldn't make promises you can't keep," Bas growled from behind her.

"We can discuss it later," Myst muttered, concentrating on her daughter, who was snuggling into the mattress with her stuffed hippo pressed to her chest.

Although they'd been in constant mental contact, she'd never had the opportunity to savor Molly's delicate beauty or the pure innocence of her soul, which glowed around her with a golden aura.

She was . . . perfect.

And worth every sacrifice that Myst had to make.

"Will you tell me a story?" Molly pleaded.

Myst gently pushed a silver curl off her daughter's cheek. "Of course."

Molly flashed her a dimpled grin. "I want to hear the one about the princess who saves the troll and he turns into a prince. That's my favorite."

"Her favorite?" Bas growled, abruptly grabbing Myst by

the arm to tug her away from the bed. "What's she talking about?"

Myst made a sound of impatience as they halted near the doorway. Okay, Bas had every reason not to trust her. She got that. She truly did.

But she only had a limited amount of time with Molly.

She couldn't afford to waste a minute.

"It's a fairy tale that I made up," she confessed, forcing herself to meet the bronze male gaze even as tiny shudders raced through her body.

Who wouldn't shudder when an assassin was scowling at her as if he was considering where he intended to dump the body?

It had nothing at all to do with the fingers that had loosened their grip and were absently stroking up and down the bare length of her arm.

"Fairy tale?" he snapped.

She shrugged, wishing she wasn't such a shy, timid mouse.

If she was one of those beautiful, sophisticated women that seemed born with the knowledge of how to manipulate men, she could use her wiles to convince this man to let her stay.

As it was . . . she had no flipping idea how she was going to perform that particular miracle.

"It's a harmless story."

The stunning metallic eyes narrowed, the air heating. Bas was not only a witch, he was a born Sentinel, which meant his body temperature ran hotter than other people's. Especially when they were pissed off.

Or in the throes of passion . . .

She slammed shut the door on that agonizingly vivid memory, watching as the bronze eyes narrowed, his heat spiking.

Almost as if he'd managed to catch her wicked thoughts.

"Myst—"

"Mommy," Molly called from the bed.

Myst released a breath she didn't know she was holding. Thank God for a timely interruption.

"Coming." She moved to step around the male only to come to a halt as his fingers tightened on her arm. She tilted back her head to glare at his painfully beautiful face. "Let me go, Bas."

He refused to release his grip, but his fingers instantly eased. She blinked in confusion. Was he afraid he was hurting her?

That seemed very . . . unassassin-like.

"Have you been sneaking in to see Molly?" he growled.

She shook her head. "No."

"Then how did you tell her a fairy tale?"

Myst hesitated. She wanted to lie, but she feared he would sense she wasn't telling the truth.

Probably not the best way to convince him that she could be trusted with their daughter.

"We're psychically connected."

His dark brows lifted in surprise. "You told me that you're a clairvoyant."

"That's one of my gifts," she agreed, her voice carefully devoid of emotion.

"One?"

Her lips twisted in a wry smile at the disbelief in his tone. She was used to being dismissed as a mere scribe with meaningless powers.

"Yes."

He looked . . . offended.

"You didn't tell me you were a telepath."

She shrugged. "You didn't ask."

"You applied for a job. I assumed you would have shared your complete resume." He leaned down, wrapping her in the scent of clean male skin and scotch. "Or were you keeping secrets even back then?"

His lips brushed the top of her ear, sending streaks of lightning through her body.

Danger, excitement, and pure lust twisted her stomach into a knot.

Dammit. She'd spent the past four years isolated in the bowels of a Russian monastery. She wasn't prepared to deal with the cascade of sensations.

She struggled to suck air into her lungs. "I wasn't a telepath when I applied for the job," she said in hoarse tones.

He frowned, his fingers resuming their absent path up and down her arm. Was he even aware of what he was doing?

Her skin shivered with delight.

"Is that supposed to be a joke?" he demanded.

She grimaced, understanding his annoyance. High-bloods were born with their mutations, even if some didn't reveal themselves until after puberty. Most people only had one, but a rare few could claim a combination.

Like Bas, who'd been born with both the magic of a witch and the superior strength of a Sentinel. And even more rare were those powers that appeared later in life, seemingly out of nowhere.

None of the healers had an explanation.

It simply happened.

"The talent didn't reveal itself until I was pregnant," she grudgingly confessed.

He lifted his head, genuine amazement in his eyes. "A spontaneous manifestation?"

"Yes."

He studied her with a searing intensity. "Fine. You should have told me you were in contact with Molly."

She forced herself to hold that raptor gaze. Bas was a

natural leader with a male confidence that easily intimidated others.

In other words . . . an arrogant ass.

He would run her over completely if she didn't try to stand her ground.

"As I said, you're not my boss."

"No, but I am Molly's father."

"I know that—" she started to snap, only to bite her tongue. Well, hell.

He was right.

"And?" he prompted.

She grimaced. It was true he was an arrogant ass, but he'd taken in a baby that he hadn't known existed, without question and without hesitation, and surrounded her with the sort of love every little girl deserved.

As much as it might pain her to stroke his bloated ego, she owed him her eternal gratitude.

"I'm truly appreciative that you've done such a wonderful job with Molly." She managed to force the words past her stiff lips. "She's a very special little girl and I know that you had a very large part in that."

He blinked, a flare of color staining the sharp line of his cheekbones.

Had she managed to knock him off guard?

Amazing.

Then his lips abruptly thinned. "You're very good at deflecting my questions," he accused.

She dropped her gaze to his thousand-dollar Italian shoes.

"Then stop asking them."

"Myst." His finger curled beneath her chin, tilting her head up. "Why didn't you let me know you were in contact with my daughter?"

A fresh pain sliced through her heart. "*Our* daughter," she corrected in fierce tones.

His lips parted, but before he could deny her right to be

a mother, Molly's plaintive voice interrupted their tense confrontation.

"Daddy, I want Mommy to tell the story."

Myst glanced toward the tiny girl who was perched on the edge of the bed before returning her wary gaze to the predator who was nearly vibrating with the urge to toss her through the nearest window.

"Let me go to her, Bas," she said in low tones. "Please."

Frustration tightened his stark features, but dropping his hands, he forced himself to take a step back.

"Tell her the story. Then we talk," he warned, turning his head to send his daughter a smile that held uncomplicated affection. "Good night, pet."

Bas stalked from the room, his phone pressed to his ear as he reached the main room of the suite.

"Kaede," he snapped as soon as his enforcer picked up. "I need you in Kansas City. I'll explain when you get here."

He shoved the phone back into his pocket and paced to the bank of windows that overlooked the Kansas City skyline.

Unfucking believable.

After five years of paying a fortune to trackers, witches, and even a human private investigator to hunt down Myst, she waltzes into his penthouse as if she had every right to be there.

Worse, he discovers that she'd been in constant contact with Molly.

A short, humorless laugh was wrenched from his throat.

No, that wasn't the worst.

The worst was the undeniable fact that he found her just as damned exquisite as the first time she'd sashayed that tiny body into his office.

His fingers had twitched with the urge to run through

the moonlit silk of her hair. To yank off her pretty sundress and explore the pale ivory skin that had haunted his dreams. To crush the soft curve of her lips until they parted in helpless surrender.

Emotions are the enemy.

He'd been taught that by the monks who'd honed him into the perfect killer.

But Myst managed to shatter a lifetime of training, stirring his passions with an ease that was frankly terrifying.

He needed her gone.

Now.

Pacing toward the long bar that was set near the leather sectional couch, Bas grimly poured himself a scotch. Tomorrow he would have the suite cleaned from top to bottom. Maybe that would get rid of the lingering scent of honeysuckle.

He was on his second drink when he heard the sound of approaching footsteps and he whirled to study the woman who came to a hesitant halt in the center of the room.

His brows snapped together. He told himself it was because she was an unwelcome interloper and not because she looked as delicate and ethereal as a moonbeam.

A very sexy moonbeam.

She wrapped her arms around her slender waist, making a visible effort to meet his gaze.

"There's no need to glare at me," she chided.

He set aside his empty glass, smoothing his face to an unreadable mask.

It was something that should have come easily. He was a cold, ruthless assassin, wasn't he? Unfortunately, this woman had a unique talent of getting under his skin.

In more ways than one.

"You've been screwing with my daughter's mind," he said between clenched teeth, still unnerved by the revelation that this woman had been speaking with Molly without his knowledge.

Her chin jutted to a defensive angle. "I'll admit that I've often communicated with Molly, but I was hardly screwing with her mind. We talked like any other mother and daughter."

He narrowed his gaze. "You knew very well that I was unaware of your telepathic powers. You deliberately used that lack of awareness to take advantage."

"Molly was the one to reach out to me."

His scowl deepened. "How? You're not trying to claim she's a telepath?"

"No, but I could sense her," Myst muttered. "She needed to know that her mother loved her."

"A mother who loves her child doesn't abandon her."

She flinched at his deliberate attack. "I didn't . . ."

"Didn't what?"

"Nothing."

He studied her pale face.

She was hiding something. But what?

"Why are you here?"

"You know why." She hunched a shoulder. "I'm here to see my daughter."

"Why?" he pressed again. "Four years ago you left her on my bed and walked away without looking back. Surely you can understand my confusion as to why you were struck with a burning need to see her now."

Her lovely face, which looked far too young to be a mother, flushed at his accusation.

"Molly was traumatized when she was kidnapped."

His breath hissed between his teeth.

The memory of Molly's kidnapping was still a raw wound that made him think about killing things.

"You don't have to remind me," he snapped. "We were all traumatized when she was taken."

The velvet-brown eyes widened with something that might have been confusion.

"I'm not blaming you."

"Then what are you doing?" he asked.

"Trying to explain that after Molly was taken she reached out to me in terror," she said, her voice trembling as if she'd been as tormented as he'd been by her abduction. "She couldn't tell me where she was, or who'd taken her, so all I could do was try to give her comfort and swear to her that I would come and visit if she would be a good girl and do everything they told her to do until you could come for her."

Her soft words should have infuriated him. What right did she have to make promises to his daughter?

Instead, he went hunter-still. "You were so certain I would find her?"

"Yes," she said without hesitation.

Shit.

He struggled to keep his face devoid of emotion at the insane flare of pleasure that raced through him at her absolute confidence in his skills.

What the hell was wrong with him?

It wasn't as if this woman's opinion mattered, did it?

"Is that why it took you a week to get here?" he snapped, angered by his ridiculous reaction to this female. "Or were you just too busy to care that your daughter was in danger?"

Her head snapped back, an unexpected fury tightening her delicate features.

"Don't ever say I don't care about Molly," she spit out, her hands clenched into tiny balls. "I left the second I knew she'd been taken. If I hadn't had to make sure I wasn't being followed I would have—"

She bit off her impulsive words, stiffly turning to walk toward the bank of windows.

"Followed?" he instantly pounced. Was this a trick? A lame excuse for not rushing to help in the search for Molly? "By who?"

"It doesn't matter."

Bas kept his gaze locked on the fragile profile reflected in the window.

"It does if you're in danger."

She hunched her shoulders, a visible shiver shaking her body.

"All I'm asking is a few days to spend with my daughter," she said in low tones.

Bas was moving before he could halt his forward progress, grabbing her shoulders so he could turn her to meet his searching gaze.

"I want to know why you think you're being followed," he insisted.

Her ridiculously thick lashes lowered to hide her expressive eyes. A sure sign she was about to lie.

"You're always in hiding," she muttered. "I didn't want to accidentally give away your location."

"Bullshit."

Her jaw tightened, but her gaze stayed lowered. "Can I stay?"

His grip eased on her shoulders, his fingers compulsively stroking the satin-soft skin of her back.

"For how long?" he demanded.

"A few days."

"And then you intend to disappear into the ether once again?"

"Yes."

Some undefinable emotion clenched his stomach at her

blunt admission that she couldn't be bothered to spend more than a handful of hours with her child.

His hand moved from her shoulder to grasp her chin, tilting back her head so he could study her delicate features.

So innocent.

The face of an angel.

How the hell could she be so cruel toward her only child? Unless . . .

"Do you have another family?" he abruptly demanded.

She blinked, as if confused by his question. "Do you mean parents or siblings?"

His lips thinned. "I'm asking if you have a husband and pack of kids. Is that why you treat Molly like a dirty secret?"

"Of course not," she breathed, a genuine outrage darkening her eyes. "And I don't treat Molly like a dirty secret."

Dropping his hands as if he'd been scalded, Bas took a step back.

He didn't want to feel a sharp-edged relief that he'd been wrong in his suspicion that Myst was already claimed by another male.

He didn't want to feel anything for this woman.

"No," he said abruptly.

"No what?" she asked in bewilderment.

"No, you can't stay," he informed her, retreating behind his icy composure. "It isn't fair to Molly."

She sucked in a sharp breath, her expression stricken. "A visit from her mother isn't fair?"

"You can't just appear and disappear from her life whenever you want." He shrugged. "It's too confusing."

"All I'm asking is a few days."

"No."

"Bas . . ." She held out a slender hand. "Please."

Her soft, pleading expression didn't touch him, he fiercely assured himself.

He was turning away and heading out of the room because he needed to check on Molly, not because he was trying to avoid the blatant yearning on her beautiful face.

And the strange emotion that was currently twisting his gut into tight knots wasn't guilt.

Or regret.

No way.

"Lock the door on your way out," he commanded, refusing to glance at her.

"I'll return in the morning," she said, the words soft but stubborn.

His steps never faltered. "You're wasting your time."

"It's my time to waste," she muttered. "I'll be back."

Bas had reached the end of the short hallway when he heard the sound of Myst's retreating footsteps, followed by the closing of the door.

Coming to a sharp halt, he pulled out his phone and made a swift call to his security team.

"There's a silver-haired woman leaving the building," he said in clipped tones. "I want her followed."

Keeping the phone in his hand, he quietly entered his daughter's room, standing beside her bed to savor the sight of her tiny body curled beneath the blankets.

Usually he loved these moments. When the world was quiet and he could enjoy the knowledge that his daughter was safe in his care.

But tonight his peace was disrupted by the lingering scent of honeysuckle that stirred sensations he hadn't felt in far too long.

Damn, Myst.

Damn her to hell.

His phone vibrated and with long strides he headed out the door and into his bedroom across the hallway.

"You got her?" he demanded as he pressed the phone to

his ear. He stiffened as the hunter Sentinel shared the bad news that Myst had somehow managed to slip past them unnoticed. "Shit."

Throwing the phone across the room, Bas watched with satisfaction as it shattered in a spray of worthless technology.

Chapter Two

Bas's mood wasn't improved the next morning.

It could have been the thunderstorm that rolled through Kansas City just before daylight. Or the bottle of scotch he'd consumed before tumbling into bed.

But if he was honest, he'd admit that it'd been the erotic dreams that had left him achingly unfulfilled and tangled alone in his black silk sheets.

Taking a long, cold shower, he'd promised himself that he was going to make a discreet phone call later in the day. He knew any number of women who would be happy to ease his current needs.

By seven o'clock he was dressed in a pair of dark slacks and a white French silk shirt with the cuffs rolled up and the collar left open to reveal the witch mark on the side of his neck, along with the horizontal tattoos. His hair was smoothed from his freshly shaved face and he had a new phone that'd been delivered at the crack of dawn.

Leaning against the walnut desk in the corner of the main suite, Bas sipped his coffee and watched the man who was seated next to him pull up the security footage on the top-of-the-line laptop.

Kaede was a slender man with dark eyes and liquid-smooth

black hair that reached his shoulders. He had the Asian features of his ancestors and a whip-cord build that made most people underestimate him.

An advantage that Kaede was happy to exploit.

As a fully trained Sentinel, the younger man was a lethal killer who'd been Bas's enforcer for over a century.

Or he had been until Molly's kidnapping and the unfortunate revelation of Bas's illegal activities.

The few mercenaries who'd managed to escape the Mave's command to have them rounded up and taken to the dungeons of Valhalla had scattered and disappeared like wisps of smoke.

His people were extremely talented at melting into a crowd.

Bas knew he was taking a risk in calling Kaede to the hotel. But after Myst's appearance last night, he felt the sudden urge for backup.

"Here." Kaede broke into Bas's dark thoughts, pointing toward the computer screen. He'd stopped the footage at the spot where there was a glimpse of silver hair that briefly shimmered in the overhead lights as Myst slid out of the lobby, completely unnoticed by his highly paid hotel employees.

Bas set aside his coffee, leaning to the side for a better view as Kaede allowed the footage to roll forward in slow motion.

"Damn," Bas breathed, grudgingly impressed by her graceful ease as she flowed through the shadows, disturbingly skilled in keeping her back turned toward the camera. "How does she do that?"

"She's good," Kaede murmured. "Almost as good as me."

Like all Sentinels, Kaede had the ability to mentally . . . *encourage* . . . people not to see him, although the enforcer took his to another level.

Kaede had once walked into the Oval Office of the White House just because he could.

"A thief?" Bas guessed. Why else would a low-grade clairvoyant develop the ability to slip around unnoticed?

Kaede shrugged. "It's possible."

"Did you find out anything about her background?"

Kaede closed the laptop, rising to his feet.

"Not yet," he admitted, his tone revealing his opinion of his lack of information.

Bas grimaced, not particularly surprised.

He'd spent five years trying to track down the elusive woman.

She was well named. . . .

Myst.

"Keep digging," he commanded, instantly turning as he caught the pitter-patter of tiny feet.

Entering the room like a miniature tornado, Molly ran into Bas's open embrace, wrapping her arms around his neck as he pressed a kiss to her tousled curls.

"Morning, Daddy."

"Good morning, pet," he murmured, lowering her back to the ground as she gave a cry of pleasure at the sight of his companion.

"Kaede" She hurled herself forward, no doubt the only creature in the world who wasn't terrified of Sentinels.

Kaede chuckled, lowering himself to his knees so he could enfold the child in a tight hug.

"Hey, precious. It's good to see you."

Molly tilted back her head to regard him with a puzzled gaze. "Why weren't you here?"

"I had some work I had to take care of." He tapped the end of her nose before he reached into the front pocket of his faded jeans that he'd matched with a plain black tee. Kaede had never shared Bas's love for fine clothing. "But I brought you something."

Molly's eyes widened with wonderment as Kaede held up a silver bracelet that dangled with exquisitely carved jade figurines.

"For me?" she breathed.

"Just for you," Kaede assured her, wrapping the bracelet around her wrist with tender care.

Going on her tiptoes, Molly planted a wet kiss on Kaede's cheek before she skipped away, her arm held over her head so the charms danced in the morning sunlight.

"Very nice," Bas murmured in soft tones, his gaze glued to his daughter. "But it looks expensive for such a little girl."

Kaede straightened, his fists planted on his slender hips. "The amulets are tracking devices."

Bas cocked a brow. He'd expected as much. Kaede had always enjoyed carving jade figures, but over the past few years he'd developed a skill for hiding tiny GPS devices in his works of art.

They'd used them more than once to track both friends and foes.

He pointed out the obvious flaw. "It won't do any good if someone takes the bracelet."

Kaede allowed a rare smile to curve his lips. "It's spelled. Only Molly can remove it."

Bas laid a hand on his friend's shoulder. His work as an assassin had meant a lonely, barren existence for most of his life. But after becoming a rebel, he'd discovered the undeniable benefit of surrounding himself with associates who could assist his obsessive need to gain power.

Most stayed because he offered the opportunity to make serious cash, the protection of a high-blood community, and the freedom to use their talents without the tedious rules that Valhalla demanded.

A rare few stayed out of sheer loyalty.

Kaede was one of those few.

"Thank you," he said with unmistakable sincerity.

Kaede nodded his head toward the little girl who twirled in the center of the floor, dancing to music no one else could hear.

"We all love her."

Coming to a halt midtwirl, Molly sent Kaede a dimpled smile.

"Are you staying for breakfast? Mommy's bringing donuts." She clapped her hands together. "The ones with sprinkles are my favorite."

Bas sucked in a sharp breath. God. Dammit.

Had Myst spoken to Molly telepathically? Or had she promised the little girl sprinkled donuts last night?

Not that it mattered.

This was ending.

Now.

"Molly. I need you to listen to me."

She smiled at him with absolute trust. "'Kay."

He stepped forward with a grimace. Christ, there was no easy way to do this.

"I don't think it's a good idea for Mommy to come back."

Molly's bottom lip quivered. "I want her."

"Of course you do, pet," he soothed, "but she can't stay."

"I know, she told me." Her tiny face settled in stubborn lines. Just like her mother. A strange tightness wrapped around his chest. "That's why we have to make this time extra special."

"Molly . . ."

The bronze eyes widened before Molly was running toward the door.

"She's almost here."

"Dammit," Bas muttered, his teeth clenching in frustration.

Kaede moved to stand at his side, his voice pitched so it wouldn't carry.

"Do you want me to take care of this?"

Bas knew what his friend was asking.

Assassins had one way of getting rid of problems.

He jerked in horror, the mere thought of Myst being tossed in an unmarked grave making his blood run cold.

"No." He paused to regain his composure as Kaede sent him a questioning glance at his outraged tone. "Molly's too happy," he muttered. "I can't take that away from her. Not now." His heart missed a beat at the sound of Molly pulling open the door. "Return to your search. I want to know every damned detail about Myst," he ordered his enforcer. "Down to the size of her shoes."

Kaede gave a small shrug. "You know the most important thing."

Bas frowned. "What's that?"

"She makes a beautiful baby."

Bas's expression melted.

He'd committed a thousand sins that stained his soul to black. But somehow the moment he'd held that bronze-eyed baby in his arms, he'd been cleansed of his past.

Which was why he was so determined to become a better man for his future.

It might have taken Molly being kidnapped to kick-start his enlightenment, but better late than never.

"That she does," he said softly.

They heard Molly's happy chatter a few seconds before she came out of the foyer, tugging the woman who had haunted his dreams for years.

This time he was braced for her entrance. Which meant he shouldn't have felt anything but annoyance when she walked into the suite. Instead the air was jerked from his lungs as if he'd just been kicked in the gut.

She was wearing another floaty sundress, this one in a soft lavender that had thin straps and a neckline that revealed far too much of her small but perfectly rounded breasts, and ended just above her knees.

The amazing silver hair was left loose to float over her shoulders and down her back, emphasizing the delicate beauty of her face and contrasting with her velvet-brown eyes.

She looked like something straight out of a male fantasy.

"My . . . God," Kaede breathed, clearly stunned as he caught his first look of Myst in the flesh. "Now I know why she makes such beautiful babies."

Bas tensed before a wry smile twisted his lips.

He couldn't blame his friend. There wasn't a male who wouldn't be dazzled by this female.

"Don't you have something to do?"

Kaede kept his gaze focused on the woman who'd come to an uncertain halt, a box of pastries in her hands.

"Aren't you going to introduce me?" the enforcer demanded.

"No."

Kaede turned to meet Bas's warning glare, his lips twitching with an unexplainable burst of humor.

"She looks like an angel."

"Which only makes her more dangerous."

"True."

Bas heaved a resigned sigh, keeping his voice pitched low to make sure Myst couldn't overhear.

"Kaede, are you going to do the background search or not?"

The man continued to stare at him with that amused expression. "I get it," he at last admitted.

"Get what?"

"Why you've never forgotten her."

Bas stiffened. He didn't want to discuss his weird-ass obsession over Myst with Kaede.

Not with anyone.

"She's the mother of my child," he snapped.

"And that's all?"

"I won't know until you've finished your job, will I?" he countered, the warning in his voice unmistakable.

"Fine." Kaede glanced back at Myst. "If you need someone to keep an eye on her—"

"Christ, just go," Bas snapped.

Myst stood in the center of the room, one hand holding the box of donuts and the other gently stroking through Molly's curls as the little girl leaned against her leg.

When she'd awoken this morning, she'd cursed herself for being so easily routed.

She'd traveled halfway around the world to see her daughter, only to be tossed out by Bas.

Today, however, was a new day.

She was going to beard the lion in his den, whatever the hell that meant, and demand that she be allowed the privileges any mother deserved.

Her fierce determination had carried her to the nearby pastry shop and back through the hotel lobby, where she'd deftly avoided security. It'd even allowed her to sweep through the door that Molly had pulled open for her.

But the second she'd caught sight of Bas and his companion, her courage had faltered.

It was bad enough to endure Bas's condemning glare without the piercing scrutiny of the handsome man at his side.

What did they see when they looked at her?

A heartless female who would abandon her own child?

A dangerous stranger who couldn't be trusted?

A failure as a woman and a mother?

She stiffened her spine as the slender, dark-haired man

strolled across the room, his gaze sliding down her tense form as he passed by.

It didn't matter what Bas or his mysterious companion might think of her. Nothing mattered but Molly and this all-too-brief time they could spend together.

Waiting until she heard the door close behind the unknown man, Myst leaned down to place the box of pastries into her daughter's hands.

"Here, baby, why don't you put them on the table?" she murmured.

"'Kay."

Skipping toward the small kitchenette in the corner of the suite, Molly was blissfully unaware of the tension in the air. Myst, on the other hand, felt as if she was about to jump out of her skin as Bas strolled forward, his movements smooth and economical.

A predator stalking his prey.

"Did you think the donuts would sweeten me in the hope I'd let you stay?" he demanded in low tones.

Her lips twisted at the sensation of lightning dancing over her bare skin.

It was something she'd noticed from their first meeting. She didn't know if it was his magic that caused the electric awareness, or his raw male magnetism.

Hoping to disguise her reaction, she deliberately turned to watch as Molly meticulously arranged the donuts on the glass table. Even then she was acutely aware of Bas towering over her.

If she was a normal woman she would have worn a pair of Christian Louboutin heels so she wouldn't have to tilt back her head to talk to people. But she wasn't normal. And the need to quietly disappear when necessary kept her in soft leather slippers that didn't make a sound when she walked.

"I doubt it's possible to sweeten you," she muttered.

"I think we both know that's not true." He lowered his head to speak directly in her ear, his finger tracing a path over her bare shoulder. "You managed to sweeten me just fine when you put your mind to it."

The air was sucked from her lungs at his light touch.

Holy crap.

"I didn't put my mind to it," she croaked, vividly reminded of their first meeting and how she'd been so dazzled by this man that she couldn't think straight. One kiss and she'd melted. "I wasn't using my mind at all or I would never have . . ."

"Seduced me?"

She gave a short, humorless laugh. She'd never seduced a man in her life.

Certainly not a gorgeous, sophisticated male who clearly had his choice of women.

"I think you've got that backward. You're the one who gave me the scotch," she said, shivering as the heat of his body wrapped around her. "How was I supposed to think clearly?"

His fingers abruptly tangled in her hair, tugging her head around to meet his blazing bronze glare.

"Are you trying to imply that I got you drunk so I could take advantage of you?"

She blinked in surprise.

This man was an assassin.

He'd killed without mercy, flaunted the authority of Valhalla, and sold the services of other high-bloods, but he was offended that she implied he'd liquored her up so he could get her naked?

"Not intentionally," she admitted, oddly reluctant to pretend their sex had been anything but consensual. Almost as if she didn't want to taint the memory. "You couldn't know I'd never had alcohol before."

His brows lifted, his fingers easing to stroke through the loose strands of her hair. "Never?"

"Never." She shrugged. "I'm always a very cautious person."

His brooding gaze lowered to her lips. "Not always or we wouldn't have a daughter."

It was her turn to stiffen, her hand lifting to touch the small tattoo behind her ear.

The magically enhanced mark should have kept her from conceiving a child.

She still didn't know how or why the spell had failed.

"I was protected," she said defensively. "I didn't deliberately get pregnant."

"I never thought you did." His chiseled features abruptly tightened. "You wouldn't have regretted having a child if it'd been intentional."

She flinched, feeling as if he'd slapped her. "I don't regret Molly."

"Then why did you leave her?"

"Stop saying that," she rasped.

"It's the truth."

She jerked away from his touch, barely noticing that he had swiftly loosened his hold on her hair to make certain he didn't hurt her.

Probably because no pain could be greater than his brutal accusation that she regretted giving birth to her own daughter.

"Do you think I wanted to leave her?" she snapped, her voice bitter. "It was only because—" She bit off her impetuous words.

Good Lord. What was wrong with her?

"Because why?" The bronze eyes narrowed.

She shook her head. "Nothing."

"Dammit, Myst, I'm sick of your secrets." He studied her with a seething frustration. "Tell me what's going on."

Her lips parted, but before she could conjure some reasonable excuse Molly appeared at her side, her little face creased with concern.

"Are you fighting?" she demanded.

Myst squatted down, allowing her hair to slide forward to hide her heated cheeks.

"Of course not, baby."

Molly glanced toward the man who was heating the air with the force of his annoyance.

"Daddy has his scowly face on."

"Scowly face?" Myst inquired, wrapping her arms around her daughter.

Molly nodded. "He makes it when he has a fustation."

It took Myst a second to decipher the childish word. "You mean when he's not getting his way?"

Molly gave another nod. "Uh huh."

"Then I would think it would be a permanent fixture," Myst muttered, cradling Molly in her arms as she straightened and headed toward the table. "It's time for donuts."

Molly tossed her arms around Myst's neck. "I want one with sprinkles."

Myst relished her daughter's pure, uninhibited affection, breathing deep of her sweet scent.

"First, a glass of milk," she murmured.

Molly wrinkled her nose. "I want soda."

Myst reached up to tug a silver curl. "Milk."

Molly heaved a deep sigh, but made no protest when Myst settled her on one of the chairs before opening the small refrigerator in the built-in bar, where she found several individual containers of milk.

"'Kay," Molly grudgingly agreed, glancing toward the man standing as still as a statue in the middle of the room. "Aren't you going to eat a donut, Daddy?"

"Later, pet," Bas murmured. "Daddy has some work to take care of first." The bronze gaze shifted toward Myst, his expression unreadable. "You." He pointed a finger toward her. "Don't even think about leaving."

Myst rolled her eyes.

Bossy bastard.

Chapter Three

Bas understood there were several reasons for his success.

His hunger for power.

His ambiguous moral code.

His ruthless discipline.

His natural ability to lead.

But he knew his greatest asset had always been his patience.

While most Sentinels charged into situations with guns blazing, metaphorically speaking, Bas hid in the shadows, cunningly waiting for the perfect moment to strike.

Which was why he retreated to his desk in the corner of the suite for the majority of the day. Pretending to work on his computer, he kept a close watch on Myst as she interacted with his daughter. She read to her, patiently taught her to play some complicated game of solitaire, and watched some dreadful show that included lots of dancing and jumping around. After sharing a nap they braided each other's hair, painted toenails, and watched yet another show that made Molly giggle.

Bas didn't know precisely what he was looking for.

Perhaps a sign that she was there to use Molly for some

nefarious purpose. Or that she was angling to try and get her hands on his considerable fortune.

Or hoping to crawl back into his bed . . .

But all that he could see was a tender affection between mother and daughter that couldn't be faked.

Waiting until he heard Myst telling the sleepy Molly some outrageous fairy tale that seemed to include a number of bumbling trolls and a princess who was armed with a sword and the habit of saving the world, Bas rose to his feet and strolled toward the windows.

Outside, the skyline of Kansas City was bathed in deepening shades of amber and lavender as the sun dipped over the horizon. It was a magnificent view, but Bas was far too focused on the sound of Myst's soft voice and the pervasive scent of honeysuckle to notice.

Enough was enough, he abruptly decided.

He'd assumed for years that Myst had dumped her newborn baby because she couldn't be bothered to take care of Molly.

Now he not only knew that Myst had kept in constant contact with her daughter, but she obviously possessed her fair share of maternal instincts.

Which meant that there had to be some desperate reason for abandoning her newborn baby with a male she barely knew.

And she wasn't leaving until he knew what that reason was.

Holding himself completely still, he waited until he heard Myst leave his daughter's room and enter the main area. She briefly hesitated, then, catching sight of him by the windows, she hurried toward the door.

Bas felt an intoxicating anticipation flow through him as he moved with supple speed to stand directly in her path. He might have trained to become a cold-blooded assassin, but at heart he was still a predator. There were few things he loved more than being on the hunt.

Especially when his prey was as sweet as this silver-haired, velvet-eyed female.

"Going somewhere?" he asked in low tones.

Myst glanced toward the door, almost as if considering the futile effort of trying to make a run for it. Swiftly coming to her senses, she heaved a deep sigh and met his smoldering gaze with a tight smile.

"Molly's asleep."

He took a step closer, savoring the sight of her tiny shiver of excitement.

Awareness feathered over his skin.

It might have been five years since they'd come together, but neither of them had forgotten just how glorious it had been.

"Good," he murmured, his hand reaching to trace the line of her shoulder.

Christ. He could spend the next century stroking that satin skin.

"So I'll return tomorrow," she said, taking a step back.

A dangerous smile curled his lips as he took two steps forward, deliberately intruding even farther into her space.

"What's your hurry?"

Belatedly realizing that she'd stirred his primitive instincts, Myst visibly forced herself to halt her retreat.

Smart woman.

"It's late," she said.

"It's not that late." He nodded toward the small table that room service had discreetly covered with a white cloth before unloading the dinner that was hidden beneath the silver covers. They'd also added a bowl of fresh flowers and tall candles that flickered in the fading light. "I ordered dinner."

She blinked in confusion. "Dinner?"

"We both have to eat," he pointed out smoothly. "We might as well do it together."

"I don't understand."

His gaze lowered to the lush temptation of her lips before returning to meet her wary gaze.

"Sharing a meal is a fairly simple concept."

Her eyes sparked with a hint of that temper she attempted to keep hidden from him.

"You've been hoping to get rid of me since I arrived. Now you want to have dinner with me?"

Unable to resist, he allowed his fingers to brush the pulse that hammered at the base of her throat.

"I'm a mercenary, Myst."

Her wariness deepened. "I know what you are."

"Then you realize I never do anything for free."

She searched his face, clearly sensing the trap but unable to avoid her inevitable fate.

"What does that have to do with me?"

"You asked for a favor," he reminded her in soft tones.

"Favor?"

His fingers drifted down to explore the prominent line of her collarbone. Inwardly he frowned.

She was so ridiculously fragile. Why the hell didn't she take proper care of herself? For some reason, her too-slender body pissed him off.

"The day with your daughter."

Genuine shock widened her eyes. "You want me to pay for spending time with Molly?"

His fingers found the deep dip of her neckline, skimming over the swell of her upper breasts.

"In a manner of speaking."

"I see." With a gesture of disdain she slapped his hand away. "I don't have much money, but you're welcome to—"

"I'm not asking for money," he interrupted, his smile never faltering.

"Then what do you want?"

He leaned forward, brushing his lips down the curve of her neck before he was whispering in her ear.

"A dangerous question, *cara*."

She sucked in a sharp breath, unable to halt the flush of arousal that stained her pale cheeks.

"Bas."

Without warning a sharp-edged desire twisted his gut. Instantly he was hard and aching. Oh . . . hell. He'd intended to use Myst's reaction to him as a weapon to cloud her thoughts.

An assassin knew that questioning his target was always easier when they were distracted. But he should have known better than to play those sorts of games with this female.

They were destined to bite him in the ass.

Needing to hide the visible sign of his fierce arousal, he turned to stroll toward the nearby sideboard, pouring himself a glass of red wine before opening a bottle of sparkling water that had been chilling in the fridge.

Waiting until he was certain he had his expression smoothed to a polite mask, Bas poured the water into a glass and turned to press it into her hand.

She took a careful sip before meeting his brooding gaze. "You haven't told me what you want."

"You know my price, *cara*," he said, lightly grasping her elbow to lead her toward the table. Placing his wineglass on the table, he pulled out a chair. "I want answers."

She instantly tensed. "I need to go."

With a gentle insistence he pressed her into the chair. "Sit down, Myst."

"You have no right to bully me," she muttered, glaring at him as he rounded the table to take his seat.

He studied her stubborn expression, his lips twitching.

For such a tiny thing she could radiate disapproval at a hundred feet.

"You got what you wanted. Now it's my turn," he reminded her.

The dark eyes narrowed with frustration. "Fine, but no dinner. I'm not hungry."

Bas placed his hand flat on the table, leaning forward to allow the heat of his body to flood the air.

"Myst, you've had one donut and nibbled on half a grilled cheese sandwich," he said in stern tones. He didn't give a shit that he was revealing just how closely he'd watched her throughout the day. If she wouldn't take care of herself, then he damned well would. "Eat."

Her lips parted, no doubt to tell him what he could do with his dinner, but she forgot what she was going to say when he pulled the lids off the chafing dishes to reveal the crisp green salad, bowls of creamy squash soup, and the portabella mushrooms stuffed with wild rice.

"Did you order this?" she demanded.

"I did." He arched a brow. "Why?"

She studied the meal with a faint frown. "I assumed you would be a steak and potatoes kind of guy like most Sentinels."

Bas shrugged. Sentinels tended to burn through enormous amounts of energy and needed high doses of protein to keep up their strength.

"I used to enjoy a fine steak, but like you, Molly prefers a vegetarian diet, so I've learned to adapt," he said.

Her head snapped up, something that might have been fear tightening her features.

"How did you know I'm a vegetarian?"

He held her gaze. She needed to know just how ruthless he could be when he wanted answers.

"Five years ago you had lunch at a small diner near my office in St. Louis before you came in for your interview."

She looked confused. "Were you having me watched?"

"Unfortunately, no." He filled a plate with the lightly dressed salad and placed it in front of her before serving himself. "After your disappearing act I went in search of you."

"Why?"

His lips twisted as he recalled his reaction when he turned from his untimely phone call to discover the warm and welcoming female he'd left sated and drowsy on his couch had done a vanishing act. His furious disbelief had lasted for days.

"Because I wasn't done with you." He deliberately paused. "Not even close."

There was no mistaking the meaning of his low words, and a pretty blush stained her cheeks.

"I . . ."

"Eat," he commanded as she floundered for a response.

Clearly rattled, Myst picked up her fork and attacked her salad. Keeping a close watch, Bas instantly had the soup placed in front of her the second her plate was clean, sipping his wine as he shared amusing stories of Molly when she was just a baby.

He waited until she'd polished off the mushrooms and rice before he leaned back in his seat and studied her with an expression that warned that he was going to get answers from her.

One way or another.

"Now." He tapped his finger on the table, his gaze taking in every nuance of her body language. He didn't have the ability to read minds, but he'd been trained to sense a lie. "We start at the beginning. Your name isn't Myst, is it?"

There was a tense silence as she wavered between answering his questions and trying to make a dash toward the door. Perhaps realizing there was no way she could outrun him, she heaved a sigh of pure resentment.

"Not originally," she admitted between gritted teeth.

He ignored the scent of charred honeysuckle. The search for the truth had gone from a casual itch to a relentless quest.

"What's your real name?"

"I won't tell you."

The words and her expression were uncompromising. Bas didn't press.

For now.

"Why did you change it?" he instead demanded.

"Because my family sold me to the Brotherhood."

Bas froze. If she'd meant to shock him, then she'd succeeded. Beyond her wildest dreams.

He silently studied her tiny face.

"You're serious?" he at last demanded.

She grimaced. "It's not something I would joke about."

His fury heated the air as he shoved himself to his feet. Her family sold her to their enemies?

It was . . . inconceivable.

He paced to refill his wineglass, struggling to leash his emotions.

"Humans," he growled, wanting to punch something. His own uncle had skinned him when he'd barely been out of the nursery. He'd claimed he was trying to rid Bas of his demons. "They will never accept us."

"It wasn't about acceptance," she corrected, the words clipped. "It was a financial decision."

"Financial?"

"Yes."

Bas drained the wine, sensing he hadn't heard the worst.

The Brotherhood was a secret organization of humans who devoted their lives to the elimination of high-bloods. For years they'd hidden in the shadows, forgotten by Valhalla.

But recently they'd started to make pests of themselves again.

"Bastards," he hissed.

Her expression tightened. "My parents never wanted me once they found out I was a high-blood."

His brows snapped together. "If they knew you were a high-blood why didn't they send you to Valhalla?"

Many high-bloods were sent to Valhalla so they could be raised by foster families. Some because their human parents were unable to give them the proper care, and some because they were abandoned.

And overall the system worked well.

"They lived off the grid in a remote community in Alaska," she said, the words obviously painful. "The colony believed that Valhalla would come and round them all up if they discovered they had a high-blood child."

Bas made a sound of impatience. "So instead they put you up for sale?"

She hunched a shoulder. "As a group, the colony had always sympathized with the Brotherhood. They believed in their cause."

"What about your parents?" he demanded. "It didn't matter to them that they had a daughter who was a high-blood?"

"They just wanted to forget they had me." She lowered her gaze, but not before Bas could see the savage sense of betrayal in her dark eyes. "Until I had my vision and they realized I could make them a lot of money."

The table nearly shattered as Bas slapped his hand on the glass surface.

"I'm going to kill them."

Myst bit back a curse.
Dammit. She was handling this all wrong.

Not that it was entirely her fault.

How could she have known that Bas would react as if he was personally offended by the fact her parents would see her as a means to an easy paycheck? He'd been determined to drive her out of Molly's life from the moment she showed up in Kansas City.

Or was this just another act to try and keep her off guard? Just like the perfect dinner and the charming baby stories about Molly?

He was an assassin.

They were infamous for playing games with people's heads.

Setting aside his empty wineglass, Bas glared at her as if she was to blame for being hunted like an animal.

"I don't even know if they're still alive," she muttered, giving a shake of her head. She'd never felt more than an obligatory sense of duty toward her parents and the small community, but she'd never dreamed they would actually be willing to barter her like a piece of property. "They were both older when I was born."

"Tell me what happened," he commanded.

She wanted to condemn him to hell. He had no right to probe into her past. Unfortunately, he had every right to keep her away from Molly if he wanted. She'd give him anything he demanded for the opportunity to spend these few precious days with her daughter.

Her gaze lowered to where her fingers were twisted in her lap.

"I told you I'm a clairvoyant."

"So you said, but you were unable to give me a reading."

Most clairvoyants were able to touch a person and witness a brief glimpse into their future. It was usually no more than a slice in time that offered little information.

"I'm not a seer," she admitted.

She could sense his surprise.

"You're a foreseer?"

She gave a grudging nod. She couldn't see the future of individuals. Instead she was given visions that affected the entire world.

"Unfortunately."

There was a blast of heat as Bas moved to stand next to her chair. She shivered. Yow. He always ran hot, but this was . . . intense.

"It's a rare gift," he murmured.

"Not a gift." She gave a short, humorless laugh. "A curse."

Without warning Myst found her chair being turned to the side so Bas could crouch in front of her. She blinked, unnerved to discover his fiercely beautiful face only inches from her own.

"Why?"

Her heart raced as she met the bronze gaze.

Annoyance? Fear? Excitement?

Probably a combination of all three.

Grimly squaring her shoulders, she pretended she wasn't acutely aware of the erotic chemistry that smoldered between them.

"Because on my fifteenth birthday I foresaw that I would create a powerful weapon that would be used by our enemies."

"A weapon?" His brows pulled together. "What does that mean?"

"I'm not sure," she admitted. The vision had come without warning. One minute she'd been standing in the community center preparing for dinner, and the next she'd fallen onto the floor, the prophecy wrenched from her lips as her mind had exploded with horrifying images of the future. "I just saw blood and death being spread through Valhalla."

She braced herself, prepared for Bas's shock, or even revulsion, at her revelation.

Instead it was anger that tightened his aquiline features. "And your family decided that the answer was to sell you?"

She blinked.

She'd just told him she was destined to bring blood and death to Valhalla and his response was to be angry at her family?

That was . . .

Myst sternly squashed the flare of tenderness that threatened to destroy the barriers she'd built around her heart. She was vulnerable enough where Bas was concerned, thank you very much.

"They understood that the Brotherhood would pay a great deal for such a lethal weapon," she tried to explain.

The bronze eyes narrowed. "And the Brotherhood agreed?"

She didn't miss the hint of disgust in his voice.

"Of course." She shrugged. "They've been waiting forever for a chance to destroy the high-bloods."

The bronze eyes flared with fury. "Your parents should have protected you. They were your family."

Her lips twisted. Her definition of family was considerably different from most people's.

Not that she intended to share the raw sense of betrayal. Or the stupid wish that things had been different.

"I'm not the only person to have a crappy childhood," she said, keeping her tone deliberately light.

Almost as if sensing she felt disturbingly exposed, he leaned forward, wrapping her in the heat of his body.

"True," he murmured, his tone wry. "Shortly after I was born my uncle tried to skin me, and when that didn't kill me, my father tried to drown me. Tough to top that."

She blinked. Was he joking?

"Why would they try to kill you?"

Bas shrugged. "They saw my birthmark and assumed I'd been spawned by the devil."

She gave a tiny gasp. Good Lord. She thought her parents were horrible for selling her to the Brotherhood. At least they hadn't tried to murder her when she was just a baby.

Instantly she forgot her unease, unconsciously lifting her hand to touch the eye-shaped mark on the side of his neck. God. The thought that he might have died before they'd ever met . . .

It made her heart clench with an unexplainable pain.

"How did you survive?"

"My mother fished me out of the river and ran off with me clutched in her arms." His jaw tightened, his eyes revealing an ancient wound that he swiftly disguised behind a humorless smile. "She left her home and family with nothing more than me in her arms and the clothes on her back."

"She must have loved you very much," Myst said, thinking of her own mother, who'd barely hidden her joy the day Myst had been picked up by the Brotherhood.

Myst never knew if that happiness came from the pile of cash in the middle of her floor, or the sight of her daughter being hauled away by complete strangers.

And in the end, it didn't really matter.

"She did," he said, his expression bleak. "Unfortunately, in those days a female had no way to make her own money. She either married or became a prostitute."

"Oh my God." Her hand skimmed to cup his cheek. It was in her nature to offer comfort, she told herself. It had nothing to do with an overwhelming urge to savor the abrasive scrape of his five o'clock shadow and the searing heat of his skin. "The poor woman."

Holding her gaze, he reached up to press her hand tightly against his face.

"I was barely eight when she was killed by one of her patrons."

"Bas," she whispered. "I'm so sorry."

For a breathless moment they stared at each other in silence, something intense passing between them.

The world faded away, narrowing until there was nothing but this fiercely gorgeous man. Then, with a sharp curse, Bas was surging upright, his face smoothed to an unreadable mask.

"I was lucky enough to be taken in by the local monks," he said with a lift of his shoulder. "You, however, weren't so lucky. What happened after you were sold to the Brotherhood?"

Myst blinked as he abruptly turned the conversation back to her own childhood. Clearly he'd said all he intended to say.

End of story.

Her lips parted before she abruptly snapped them back together. There was no need to be told that Bas had just revealed more about his past than he ever had before. There was no way she was going to disrespect his trust in her.

She grimaced, reluctantly recalling that god-awful day. "I don't know how my parents contacted the Brotherhood, but one night four men came into our house and tossed a bag of money in the middle of the floor. My mother told me to pack a few things, and the next thing I knew I was in a truck headed to Wyoming."

Something dark and scary flared through the bronze eyes. "Did they hurt you?"

She gave a swift shake of her head, startled as the floor trembled beneath the force of his fury.

"Not in the way you mean," she assured him, unconsciously wrapping her arms around her shivering body. When the men had tossed her into the back of their truck she'd been terrified they intended to rape her. Thankfully they considered high-bloods as little better than animals. That protected her from a sexual assault. Of course, that didn't keep them from dragging her by the hair or kicking her like a dog when she didn't move fast enough. "Once we reached the ranch where they lived I was tossed down a mine shaft."

His brows snapped together in confusion. "A mine shaft?"

She wrinkled her nose. At the time she hadn't understood either. If they truly believed her vision enough to buy her from her family, then it didn't make sense to keep her in a hole in the middle of nowhere.

It was only after she'd overheard a conversation between two of the Brotherhood that she'd understood their delusional plot.

"They assumed by keeping me isolated and in constant discomfort, I'd use my magic to create the mystical weapon from my vision."

"What magic?"

She snorted. "The Brotherhood assumes that every high-blood has magic."

"Idiots," he growled.

He wasn't wrong. Most of the jackasses who had brought her meals and occasionally clean clothes had clearly been incapable of original thought. They were sheep that had to be herded or they would have spent their lives wandering in aimless circles.

Still, they'd been deeply indoctrinated by their leaders, and had fully signed on to the crazy-train.

"Not only idiots, but true fanatics," she muttered.

His nose curled with disgust. "A lethal combination."

"Yes."

"How did you escape?"

"Nothing very exciting," she admitted, grimly fighting back the memories. What was the point of reliving the nagging terror that she would die alone in that dark, desolate prison? "I spent most of my days digging a small tunnel into an adjoining cave." She lowered her head, her gaze locking on her clenched hands. "Once I was free I stole one of the trucks they kept near the stables and took off."

She heard him suck in a sharp breath. "Christ. You had to dig your way out?"

"There weren't a lot of choices," she muttered.

Bas knelt in front of her, his hand cupping her cheek as he studied her with a brooding gaze. She quivered, tiny tingles racing through her body.

"I can't imagine how much courage that must have taken."

Her lips parted. Was this lethally dangerous assassin actually implying that she was brave?

Good Lord. Something warm spread through her heart.

Something that was treacherously close to pride.

It was stupid. What did it matter what this male thought of her?

But abruptly she recognized that it did. She didn't want him thinking of her as the spineless female who'd abandoned her own daughter.

Then just as quickly her pride was smothered by the heavy sense of destiny that followed her like a constant cloud.

"No." She gave a sharp shake of her head, knocking away his hand. "I'm a coward."

His eyes narrowed. "Why would you say that?"

Somewhere in the back of Myst's brain was a voice warning her to shut her mouth.

She'd already put herself at risk just by admitting the truth. For all she knew, Bas might be plotting to get rid of her by hauling her to Valhalla.

After all, if the Mave discovered she was destined to harm Valhalla, the powerful leader would most certainly try to lock her away. Then Bas would never have to worry about her bothering Molly again.

But now that she'd revealed her dark secret, she couldn't seem to stop herself from sharing the fear that had plagued her since she'd first had her vision.

"If I had true courage I would do what was necessary to ensure that I never create a weapon that could be used against our people," she pointed out.

It took a second before Bas realized precisely what she was saying. Then his eyes blazed with a bronze fire.

"Stop." His tone was hard, uncompromising.

She ignored his warning.

"I told myself that I could alter the future," she continued, the words spilling over each other in a need to get them out. "That I had time to discover what my vision meant before I had to do anything drastic. But there are days when I think I'm just being a selfish coward. If I truly cared about our people, about Molly, I would . . ."

"I told you to stop." He leaned down until they were nose to nose. "If I hear those words again I'm going to chain you to my bed."

She licked her dry lips. "We'll see."

His jaw tightened, the heat in the air so intense it caused a thin layer of sweat to coat her skin.

"No, we won't," he informed her, his voice harsh even as his thumb tenderly stroked the curve of her lower lip. "I'm not going to let you hurt yourself. We're going to figure out what the vision means."

For a crazed moment she allowed herself to be swayed by the fierce certainty in his voice. As if this male could actually offer her the promise of a future.

Then she gave a sharp shake of her head. No. There was nothing more dangerous in her life than false hope. It blinded her to the painful decisions that had to be made.

"What do you care?" she demanded, deliberately reminding herself that this man wasn't her friend. Hell, he considered her the enemy. "I thought you wanted me out of your life?"

His lips thinned. "You're the mother of my daughter."

"But—"

"You were fifteen when you were taken by the Brotherhood." He overrode her words. "How long did they hold you captive?"

She swallowed her fierce demand to know why he was willing to help.

Dammit, she was exhausted. The sooner she answered his questions, the sooner she could return to her hotel room and get some sleep.

She'd never realized how arduous spending the day with an active four-year-old could be.

Not that she would have missed a single second.

"Three or so years. I lost track of time."

His anger only deepened. "They held a baby for three years in a mine shaft?"

Baby? She resisted the urge to roll her eyes.

"I don't think I was ever allowed to be a baby," she assured him in dry tones. "From the minute my parents realized I was . . . different, I was expected to take care of myself." She shook her head. "I think they were afraid I might contaminate them."

He pulled back enough to sweep his gaze over her upturned face, lingering on her mouth.

"How old are you now?"

She blinked at the unexpected question. "How old?"

"It's a simple question."

She made a sound of annoyance. Most humans assumed that she was in her early twenties, but she was over thirty.

Not very old by high-blood standards, but that didn't mean she was going to reveal the truth to Bas.

It was none of his damned business.

"I'm socially awkward and even I know that's not a polite thing to ask a woman."

"Tell me," he commanded.

Knowing he wasn't going to let it go, she sent him a glare.

"I'm older than I look and that's all I'm saying."

"I hope to God that's true," he muttered, a strange smile twisting his lips.

"Why?"

"Because there are occasions when I look at you and feel like a perv."

She shivered as his hand reached out to cup her cheek, his thumb teasing her lips apart.

"What are you talking about?"

The bronze eyes darkened, his entire body tensing before he was abruptly shoving himself away.

"Nothing." He studied her with a smoldering gaze, the air suddenly thick with an electric awareness. "What did you do next?"

Myst struggled to think as her body shuddered with a need she hadn't felt since the last time she'd been in the presence of this male.

"I changed my name and went on the run," she managed to say. "I never stayed in the same place more than a few months. Then I heard about you."

He lifted a dark brow. "How?"

"I was doing fortune-telling out of the back of a tattoo shop in St. Louis when one of your psychics came in," she said. Before Valhalla had been established, many clairvoyants had made their living by telling fortunes, although her inability to read personal futures meant she could only offer vague promises of love and happiness. Barely good enough to allow her to scrape by. She lifted her hand as Bas's expression tightened with disapproval. The last thing she wanted was to get the psychic who'd tried to help her in trouble. "He didn't tell me anything about you, I swear, except that you hired high-bloods like me who wanted to keep a low profile." She shrugged. "I made an appointment to meet with you in the hope I could stay in one place."

He folded his arms over his chest. "You should have told me the truth."

"I couldn't risk it." She tilted her chin, silently warning him that her trust wasn't something she offered. Not to anyone. "For all I knew you could have sold me back to my family. Or even Valhalla."

His face smoothed to an unreadable expression.

Her heart skipped a beat.

What was he trying to hide?

"Where did you go after you left St. Louis?" he demanded.

"I went to New Orleans for a few weeks," she answered. There was no point in trying to lie. "That's where I realized I was pregnant." She gave a small shiver, still able to recall her disbelief when she grasped why she'd been so tired. "I couldn't believe it."

"Why didn't you let me know?"

She shrugged. "I was terrified the Brotherhood would track me down before I could give birth. Then once I had her . . . once I held her in my arms . . ." Myst was forced to halt and clear the lump in her throat. No one would ever know the price she'd paid to protect her precious daughter. "I knew I couldn't condemn her to sharing my life. As much as it hurt to think of living without her, Molly deserved so much more."

Chapter Four

Bas ground his teeth, belatedly wishing he'd never started this damned conversation.

Twenty-four hours ago he was quite content to assume Myst was some unfeeling bitch who'd been too self-absorbed with her own life to give a shit about her daughter.

It made it easy to hate her for crashing into his life, turning it upside down, and then disappearing like a whiff of smoke.

Now he was forced to accept that she'd truly been trying to protect Molly. And that he wasn't going to be able to simply toss her out the door and forget about her.

Shit.

"Did you go back on the run?" he demanded, leashing the urge to pace around the suite like a caged panther.

Trained Sentinels learned to conserve their energy. And since he was slowly coming to the conclusion he was going to have to reach out for allies among people who wanted him dead, he was going to need every ounce of his strength to survive.

"I traveled enough to cover my tracks," Myst said, unaware of his dark thoughts. "I didn't want anyone to realize that I did anything but pass through St. Louis on my way to Chicago."

"And then?" he prompted.

Her fingers absently toyed with the tiny bow that held together the neckline of her dress.

"Then I traveled to Russia."

Bas studied her with a flare of curiosity. "Why Russia?"

"Because the monastery there has one of the best libraries in the world."

"True." He deliberately allowed his gaze to skim over her slight form, lingering on the tempting swell of her breasts. Surely it was a sin against nature to have her shimmering beauty hidden in a dark, musty library? Of course, if he was going to be completely honest, he didn't actually want to see that beauty anywhere but in his bedroom. Her hair spread like liquid moonlight over his pillow and her bare skin glowing like satin in the firelight . . . Hell. He was going to have blue balls if he didn't get a grip on his fantasies. "Are you a big reader?"

Easily sensing his X-rated thoughts, Myst straightened her spine and sent him a chiding glare.

"As a matter of fact, I am. The monks were kind enough to train me to become a scribe."

"Why?"

"After I had Molly I was tired of running." She wrinkled her nose, her expression unconsciously wistful. "I wanted to see if I could find some clue to the meaning of my vision among the other prophecies. I hoped—" She bit off her words with a sharp shake of her head. "It doesn't matter."

Bas was moving before he could halt his impetuous need to touch this female, crouching down so he could grasp her hands in a tight grip.

"What did you hope, *cara?*"

Her thick fringe of lashes lowered in a futile effort to hide her vulnerable emotions.

"That I could discover how I was going to create such destruction."

His thumbs pressed against the pulse fluttering beneath the skin of her inner wrists.

"If you knew what the weapon would be, you hoped you could change the future?" he asked in soft tones.

"Or at least minimize the damage," she admitted. "After I had Molly it was no longer my life I was worried about. If I can't find a way to stop the vision, then I'll have to—"

"Last warning, *cara*," he growled, his fingers tightening on her hands. "Unless you actually want to be tied to my bed? Because that can be arranged."

There was no way in hell that he was going to let her even consider the possibility of harming herself.

No. Way. In. Hell.

He heard her breath catch. "You wouldn't dare."

"Try me."

The dark eyes flashed with a spirit that helped to ease the coldness that had lodged in the pit of his stomach.

She wasn't going to give up without a fight.

That's all he needed to know.

"It's not your decision, Bas," she snapped.

"It is now."

"No. It's not." She tried to pull her hands from his grip, only to concede defeat with a muttered curse. Frustrated, she glared into his stubborn expression. "Can you even imagine how I felt when I found out Molly had been kidnapped? I thought my family had found her and intended to use her as bait to force me out of hiding."

His lips twisted. He'd bordered on the edge of insanity when he'd discovered that Molly had been snatched from her bed.

"Instead she was taken because of me," he said dryly.

Something that might have been regret fluttered over her

face. As if she wished she hadn't reminded him that it'd been his fault Molly had been terrorized.

"It just proved that I'm running out of time," she said in husky tones. "Either I find the answers I need or I make sure Molly is never hurt."

"Damn." He abruptly straightened and pulled his phone out of his pocket. "Give me the name of the hotel where you're staying."

She was instantly wary. "Why?"

"Because I'm sending Kaede to get your things."

"My things?" She pushed herself out of her seat, her muscles tensing as she prepared to flee. "I don't understand."

He selected Kaede's number and waited for his friend to answer.

"Hold on," he said into the phone, meeting Myst's shocked gaze. "You're staying here," he told her.

"Here?"

"I thought you wanted to be close to Molly?"

"I do, but . . ." Her words trailed away as she caught sight of his grim expression. "Fine." She wrapped her arms around her waist. "I'm staying on the third floor."

His brows snapped together. "Of this hotel?"

"Yes."

Bas recalled the tape he'd watched that had caught her slipping out of the lobby and down the street.

"Why did . . ." Realization hit, making him feel like an idiot. Dammit. He better than anyone knew the worth of a good diversion. Once she'd shaken his guards, she'd obviously doubled back. It was no wonder she'd managed to stay hidden for so long. "You knew I would try to have you followed."

She shrugged. "So you see, there's no need for me to stay here."

"What room?" he pressed.

"I just told you. . . ."

"What room?"

He heard her suck in a sharp breath. "You are a pain in the ass."

"So I've been told," he murmured.

"Shocker," she muttered before grudgingly conceding defeat. "Three eighteen."

"Three eighteen," Bas repeated to the waiting Kaede, his gaze savoring the sight of Myst's sparkling eyes and flushed cheeks. She looked like she was considering the pleasure of kicking Bas in the nuts, while all he could think of was tossing her onto the nearby couch and kissing away that prickly annoyance. "Get her things and then bring them to my rooms. Be prepared to stay. I need to take off for a few hours."

Her eyes widened as he shoved the phone back into his pocket.

"You're leaving?"

He headed toward his desk, pulling out the keys to his silver Lamborghini parked in his private lot. Then, moving across the room, he placed his hand against the electronic scanner, waiting for the hidden panel to slide open so he could pull out a handgun.

He closed the panel before he turned to meet Myst's confused frown.

"I should be back by morning."

Her delicate features hardened with a mounting suspicion. "Where are you going?"

"For reinforcements," he promised.

"Bas."

Realizing there was no time to give her the reassurance she desired, he contented himself with crossing the floor to wrap an arm around her shoulders. Yanking her tight against him, he waited for her lips to part with an indignant protest.

Only then did he lower his head to claim her mouth with a brief kiss that seared through him like wildfire.

"Trust me," he whispered against her lips, stealing one more kiss before he was forcing himself to release his hold on her and head toward the door.

The Mave's office in Valhalla had been designed to intimidate.

Decorated in pure white with contrasting black accents, it had built-in bookshelves on two walls and low, leather chairs that were set opposite the heavy ebony desk.

The floor was covered by a white carpet with a black geometric pattern. And the far wall was made of floor-to-ceiling glass to provide a perfect view of the formal rose gardens.

It'd been carefully chosen by the current leader of the high-bloods, just as she had carefully honed her reputation as a ruthless leader who would do whatever was necessary to protect her people.

Not that Lana Mayfield had ever dreamed she would one day be the ultimate leader of the high-bloods.

Actually, she'd rarely allowed herself to dream at all.

She'd been born nearly four hundred years ago, a time when the eye-shaped birthmark on her upper breast meant she was condemned as a demon.

Her entire life had been a fight for survival.

Since becoming the Mave she'd tried to use that grim endurance to lead her people.

She didn't want the children to ever endure the same prejudices that she had. Or to ever think they were freaks because they were different.

They still had a long way to go, but she hoped she was making a difference.

Unfortunately, becoming the Mave wasn't without cost.

Most of her life had been lived in isolation. When she'd been young it had been a simple matter of necessity.

But there'd been an all-too-brief time when she'd been a part of a larger group who'd banded together to form a safe place for all high-bloods. They'd shared their lives, their dreams, and occasionally their hearts as they'd tried to build a place that was worthy to be called Valhalla.

She'd been happy during that time, despite the turmoil and danger. For once, she hadn't been alone.

Then the previous Mave had proven unworthy to be a leader and Lana had found herself thrust into the role.

Which meant she was once again isolated.

Unless she counted the tall, whip-cord lean man who was standing in the center of her office, studying her with a scowl that would make most people tremble with fear.

Wolfe, the current Tagos and leader of all Sentinels, was barely civilized under the best of circumstances.

Oh, he could play the part of a politician when necessary. He was a hunter, so he didn't have the tattoos of a guardian Sentinel, and he could lay on the charm when it suited his purpose. And Lana was well aware that he wasn't opposed to using his intoxicating sexual magnetism to manipulate others.

But there was no mistaking the fact that he was a lethal predator.

Leaning against the edge of her desk, she absorbed the impact of his male beauty.

In ancient times he would have been worshipped as an Egyptian god, with his rich, copper skin, his proud, hawkish nose and sharply angled cheekbones. His arched brows were heavy and set over eyes as dark as ebony. His lips were sensuously carved along generous lines.

It was the sort of intensely masculine face that made women swoon when he walked past.

If that wasn't enough, he had thick, satin-smooth black

hair that fell past his shoulders with a wide streak of shimmering silver that started at his right temple.

Tall, dark, and dangerous wasn't just a cliché when it came to this man.

He was also bossy, arrogant, and fiercely overprotective.

For the most part, Lana appreciated his constant concern, and the knowledge that he always had her back. His loyalty was priceless.

But there were times when he was convinced he knew what was best for her.

And more than willing to let her know.

Like tonight.

Dressed in black jeans, shit-kickers, and a white tee that was painted over the chiseled muscles of his chest, Wolfe planted his fists on his hips and gave a shake of his head.

"No."

She rolled her eyes at his blunt response.

"I was informing you of my decision, not requesting your permission, Tagos," she said, deliberately using his formal title.

"It's my duty to protect you, Mave," he snarled in return.

Her lips parted, only to snap shut as she forced herself to draw in a deep, steadying breath.

No one else could stir her temper like this male.

Hell, most of Valhalla referred to her as the Ice Queen behind her back.

And that was a problem.

If Wolfe was merely bossy she could handle him with ease.

She'd spent most of her life dealing with pushy males.

But their perfect working relationship was increasingly threatened by a smoldering awareness that neither had been able to purge over the years.

If anything, it'd only grown sharper, more intense.

More than once she'd toyed with the idea of giving in to

her explosive need. Maybe if they got it out of their systems it would go away.

Thankfully she'd come to her senses before she did anything stupid.

Allowing Wolfe into her bed would screw up everything.

And worse, she was terrifyingly certain that giving herself to Wolfe would only intensify her need, not end it.

So they both danced around the elephant in the room, trying to pretend it wasn't waiting for the perfect moment to go on a rampage.

Lana straightened from the desk, managing to meet Wolfe's glare with a bland smile.

"If Bas wanted to hurt me he wouldn't have requested to meet me," she pointed out. "He would have just crept into Valhalla and done his business."

"He could have tried," Wolfe growled.

"He did it before," she said with a grimace, recalling Bas's ability to sneak in and poison Serra.

Only one of many reasons she'd issued an arrest warrant for the assassin.

The room prickled with the heat of Wolfe's temper. "If you're trying to piss me off, you're succeeding."

Hardly a difficult task. Anything connected to Bas managed to piss off the Tagos.

Not only because Bas had slipped past the considerable defenses of Valhalla and compelled Serra to search for his kidnapped daughter, but because Lana had been forced to admit she had a past with the assassin.

"Bas is an assassin. He works in the shadows," Lana said. "Your point?"

"My point is that he doesn't conduct his business at public diners."

Wolfe's lips thinned, unimpressed by her logic. "He's a wanted criminal."

"And a father," she countered.

"What the hell does that have to do with anything?" Wolfe demanded, the intensity of his personality consuming the office until it felt far too small.

"He's managed to elude us for days." Lana held the dark gaze, one of the few in the world that wasn't intimidated by the lethal Sentinel. "There's no way he would be willing to risk being separated from the daughter he nearly destroyed the world to retrieve." Her brows drew together as she tried to imagine what would be so important that Bas would contact her. Nothing good. "Not unless it was important."

"Then he can come to Valhalla and speak with you."

Lana arched a brow. "So you can arrest him?"

Wolfe didn't bother to lie. "He belongs in the dungeons."

Lana couldn't argue. Not after she'd been the one who'd issued the orders to have him tracked down and brought to justice.

But a part of her remembered Bas when they'd both been young and idealistic. Before their paths had parted into two very diverse directions.

"Perhaps, but first I want to discover why he contacted me."

Wolfe muttered a curse, taking a step toward her. "You're allowing your emotions to cloud your judgment."

She narrowed her eyes. The male was treading toward dangerous territory.

"My emotions?"

Predictably he ignored the warning edge in her voice. "You have a history with this male."

She conjured her frostiest expression. The last thing she wanted was to discuss her old lover with the male who routinely played a starring role in her sexual fantasies.

"A history that included me trying to kill him," she reminded her companion.

Bas had a habit of living on the wrong side of the law. This wasn't the first time he'd earned her punishment.

Wolfe folded his arms over his chest, his body vibrating with male outrage.

"Which only makes it worse."

She frowned in genuine confusion. "Makes what worse?"

Wolfe ignored her question, his lean face set in lines of grim purpose.

"If you insist on meeting him, then I'm coming with you."

"Wolfe—"

"That's nonnegotiable." He overrode her instinctive protest. "You're too important, especially now." He held her gaze, silently daring her to deny the truth of his words. "Our people need a sense of stability. If something happened to you it might fracture Valhalla."

Their gazes clashed, Lana's chin tilting even as she conceded he was right.

Over the past weeks the high-bloods had endured a crazed necromancer followed by the near catastrophe of having one of their most dangerous high-bloods released to cause chaos among the humans.

The last thing they needed was the sudden loss of their leader.

"Fine," she muttered, heading toward the door. "You can come, but I speak to Bas alone."

Grabbing her arm as she tried to sweep past him, Wolfe tugged her against the hard length of his body. Slowly, bending his head, he spoke directly in her ear.

"Do you still have feelings for him?"

Lana shivered, the bittersweet desire clutching her stomach.

"I'm the Mave," she said, her voice husky with the need she couldn't entirely disguise.

His lips brushed her temple, the caress so light she might have imagined it.

"And?"

For a crazed second she leaned against his solid strength, absorbing the raw power that pulsed around him. It'd been so long since she'd allowed herself to be a woman.

So very, very long.

She trembled, tendrils of desire curling through the pit of her stomach. Dammit. She desperately wanted to turn, to forget who she was so she could melt into his arms.

But there was no forgetting. Not when this male threatened to destroy the hard-earned barriers she'd built around her heart.

With a smile that didn't reach her eyes, she firmly pulled away and continued toward the door.

"And I'm not allowed to have feelings for anyone."

"The destiny I have promised is at hand," Stella Newcombe announced, a hidden microphone allowing her words to be easily heard by the gathered crowd. "Soon we'll have what we need to bring an end to the mutants." She paused for the predictable cheer. Really, it was like shooting fish in a barrel. "Valhalla will become nothing more than an empty shell and the Brotherhood will triumph over the high-bloods."

Standing on the balcony, Stella gazed down at her faithful followers, keeping her disdain hidden behind a charming smile.

She knew what they were seeing. A woman with thick auburn hair that tumbled down her back and wide eyes that were so dark blue they looked purple in the Wyoming sunlight. Her face was heart shaped with lush lips and skin that had a faint copper tint. She'd chosen to wear an ivory robe that was modest enough to appeal to the male-dominated Brotherhood while emphasizing her seductive curves.

Stella had discovered at a young age that her sexual appeal was a potent weapon. One she could use to climb out of the trailer park on the edge of Vegas.

Not that her dream had been to be in charge of a bunch of fanatical whackadoodles. But power was power, and she understood that she was in a position to use the idiots to create the life she'd always dreamed would be hers. And at long last her plans were falling into place. With any luck she would soon have all she'd ever desired. And that she so richly deserved.

Giving her soldiers a last wave, Stella turned to reenter the lavish A-frame house she'd recently had constructed to resemble a French chalet. Gilbert, the former leader of the Brotherhood and her longtime lover before his death, might have been content to live in a squalid cabin in the middle of nowhere, but she demanded luxury.

Ignoring the chants that filled the air as her followers celebrated their soon-to-be victory, Stella entered the large bedroom that had polished wood floors, open-beamed ceilings, and a stone fireplace that blazed with a welcoming heat. In the center of the room was a four-poster bed where a middle-aged man was leaning against the heavily carved headboard wearing nothing more than a pair of boxers.

Stella managed to keep her smile intact.

Peter Baldwin wasn't a man that a woman would willingly choose as a lover. He was short, pudgy, with a chubby face and rapidly thinning hair. His eyes were an unremarkable brown and his charm nonexistent.

On the other hand, he had the benefit of being a psychic with a rare talent. He could touch an object and get a glimpse of a precise location where the person who owned the item would be on a certain date at a certain time. It might seem like a harmless talent to most, but from the second the Brotherhood had kidnapped the high-blood with the intention of sacrificing him, Stella had instantly recognized the man's potential.

Unfortunately, her need for his skills meant that she had to keep him loyal to her, and the easiest, most efficient way to accomplish that goal was to give him endless orgasms. Really, men were so simple.

Now that he was addicted enough to her body, he'd become yet another tool she could use to achieve her goals.

Crossing the room, she stood in front of the floor-to-ceiling windows that overlooked the distant mountains. They'd been tinted to keep out the sun, as well as to prevent any of the Brotherhood from getting a peek inside.

They would lynch her if they discovered she had a high-blood in the house, let alone in her bed.

"Have you done any further research?" she demanded.

"I've read a dozen prophecies, angel," Peter said in a languid tone. "None of them refer to the mysterious weapon."

Stella turned, her eyes narrowed as she took in the man's smile of anticipation. Obviously he assumed she'd returned to the bedroom to give him a quickie.

She shuddered in revulsion. Damn. The things she had to do to rule the world. Okay, she didn't want to rule the world. She just wanted enough money to buy it.

Arching a brow, she held his hopeful gaze. "Was that the question I asked?"

He blinked. "I'm just saying—"

"We both know our future depends on that weapon." She overrode his stumbling explanation. God Almighty, the man was a weak, spineless fool. Still, until she got what she needed, she had no choice but to endure his presence in her home. That didn't mean, however, she had to like it. "If we can't use it for some reason, I'm not going to be pleased."

He reached a chubby hand toward her. "I'll do more research later today."

"No." She gave a sharp shake of her head. "You'll do it now."

"Fine. I'll do it now," he muttered, climbing off the bed to pull on a robe. He sent her a pleading glance. "Then maybe we can have a late breakfast in bed."

"Maybe." Which translated to "not fucking likely." Stella gave a dismissive wave of her hand. "Go do as I ask."

"Stella—"

"Peter, don't piss me off," she once again interrupted, turning away to head toward the walk-in closet.

"Dammit," he muttered, moving to the secret doorway that led to his private rooms.

"Putz," Stella growled, shedding the robe, moving to study her perfectly curved body in the full-length mirror.

Soon she would be in a position to rid herself of Peter, just as she rid herself of Gilbert. Then she would take a lover who was worthy of her.

She smiled, her hands skimming over her body before cupping her full breasts.

She couldn't wait for that day.

Chapter Five

The diner just north of Columbia, Missouri, had gone through more than one reincarnation.

It'd started as a prime destination for truckers who enjoyed their food cheap and plentiful. Then the bypass had been built for the local interstate and it'd slowly faded into a greasy spoon. A few years ago some investor with more money than sense had tried to reopen the restaurant as a karaoke bar. It'd thrived for a few months, but now it was once again a shabby dive that attracted the late night drunks and early morning hunters.

Which meant there were a dozen or so customers inside the restaurant despite the fact it was nearly four in the morning.

Standing in the shadows, Bas watched as the heavy SUV pulled up beneath the lone streetlight.

There was a short hesitation before the tall, slender woman slid out of the automobile and headed toward the diner.

Bas's lips twitched.

The Mave of Valhalla was still as regally beautiful as ever with her silky black hair pulled into a smooth knot at her nape and her classically perfect face. But the dark gray eyes held a power that had gone from impressive, when he'd known her, to downright intimidating.

His gaze lowered to the slender body that was shown to advantage in a pair of black jeans and a sleeveless sweater that was cut low enough to expose the birthmark on the upper curve of her breast.

Even in the darkness the shimmering emerald color revealed that her magic was off the charts.

Once they'd been friends and casual lovers, thrown together by their fierce need to protect the high-bloods being hunted by the previous Mave.

But while he still found her beautiful, he wasn't surprised when his body failed to react.

Since Myst had crashed into his life, his taste in the opposite sex had been fully consumed with a tiny, silver-haired woman.

Silently waiting near the edge of the lot, Bas watched as Lana came to a sharp halt. She was one of the very few with acute enough senses to pick up the presence of an assassin.

She turned in his direction, her head tilting to the side.

"Bas?"

He immediately stepped forward. Tonight wasn't the time for games.

This female had already tried to kill him. The last thing he needed was to give her yet another reason to want to see him dead.

Or in the dungeons of Valhalla.

"Hello, Lana," he murmured, a faint smile curving his lips as she moved with elegant grace to stand directly in front of him. "As beautiful as ever."

"Bas," she murmured, facing him without fear.

Of course, she had enough magic to destroy him and everyone in a hundred-mile radius. There wasn't much this woman had to fear.

Especially when she had her private Sentinel standing at the far side of the diner.

Bas had sensed his arrival five minutes ago.

He had to admit to a stab of surprise. Not that Lana had sent a hunter. She'd be a sucker not to make sure this wasn't a trap. But he hadn't expected Wolfe to make an appearance.

Bas had never met the current leader of the Sentinels, but there was no mistaking the thunderous power signature. Only the Tagos could make the ground vibrate just by the power of his temper.

And he was in a temper.

Bas had assumed it was because he was forced to waste his night escorting the Mave to meet with a wanted criminal. But as Lana walked ever closer the vibrations increased, revealing a barely restrained fury.

Hmm . . .

That sort of reaction only came from a territorial male who considered a particular female his own.

Interesting.

"It's been a long time," Bas murmured.

She gave a regal nod of her head, her beautiful face unreadable. Only a fool would play poker against this woman.

"Yes."

His gaze shifted in the direction of the SUV before moving toward the empty street.

"How many Sentinels did you bring with you?"

"Just one."

His lips twisted. "I don't know whether to be pleased that you realize that I would never hurt you, or offended that I'm so easily dismissed as a threat," he drawled, his gaze covertly darting in the direction of the shadowed figure near the diner. "Of course, I suppose you only need one when you bring the Tagos."

"You know Wolfe?" she demanded in surprise.

"By reputation." He returned his attention to the female standing directly in front of him. "Is he house-trained?"

Her lips twitched. "Barely."

"He's your lover?"

She stiffened, an emotion darkening her eyes to a stormy gray before she was giving a sharp shake of her head.

"No."

"He wants to be."

The air became frosty and pinpricks of magic pressed against his skin as she planted her hands on her hips. She was no longer Lana Mayfield, his friend and lover, but the Mave in her full glory.

"I have an arrest warrant with your name on it."

He shrugged. "So I heard."

"Did you want to meet so you could turn yourself in?"

"You know me better than that," he drawled.

A humorless smile curved her lips. "I thought I did, but it became obvious I didn't know you at all."

Bas grimaced. He didn't regret leaving Valhalla. He wasn't the sort of male who played well with others. But he did regret the knowledge that his decision to become a mercenary had destroyed any hope of a relationship with his old friends.

Reaching out, he ran a finger down her throat in an intimate gesture. A silent apology, and deliberate challenge to the Tagos watching him with murder in his dark eyes.

Win-win.

"We had the same goals, just different paths of getting there," he murmured softly.

Knowing his love for living on the edge, Lana rolled her eyes and took a step back.

"Are you trying to get killed?"

Bas gave a sudden laugh. "Your guardian does look a tad homicidal."

"You are—"

"A pain in the ass?"

Lana sucked in a deep breath, as if needing to regain command of her temper.

"What do you want from me?"

Bas's mocking smile vanished. He'd done enough provoking to prove that Lana was truly willing to listen to his plea, even if her companion was ready to rip out his heart.

Time to get down to business.

"I want you to take my daughter."

She jerked at his blunt admission, her eyes widening. "Your daughter?"

"Despite our"—he paused to consider his words—"interesting past, there's no one I would trust but you to take care of Molly."

Her expression instantly softened.

Lana might be one bad-ass leader of the high-bloods who could destroy entire towns, but she was notoriously protective of children.

"What's going on, Bas?" she asked in gentle tones.

He turned so the watching Sentinel couldn't read his lips. "Molly's mother is a clairvoyant," he said, his voice barely above a whisper. "A foreseer."

"Oh, Bas." Lana lifted her hand to her mouth, genuine horror in her expression. "Not Molly?"

"No," he swiftly assured her. "Myst had a vision, but it wasn't about Molly."

"Myst." Lana frowned. "The scribe?"

Bas narrowed his gaze. "You know her?"

"I never met her personally, but I know she helped when we were searching for information on the necromancer," Lana said, referring to the recent battle with a crazed diviner. "I've heard she's beautiful."

"She's exquisite," Bas corrected before he could halt the revealing words.

Lana arched a brow even as Bas grimaced. This female

was too perceptive not to have sensed his relationship with Molly's mother was . . . complicated.

"And her vision?" She thankfully kept focused on his reason for demanding this meeting.

"She foresaw that she's going to create a weapon that will end up in the hands of our enemies."

Lana nodded. She was familiar enough with clairvoyants not to waste time asking if Bas was certain it wasn't a dream or a figment of her imagination.

Thank God.

"Any specifics?" she instead demanded.

"Blood. Death. Mayhem."

She wrinkled her nose. "The usual?"

"Exactly. She's determined to discover what the vision means. Or—" His voice broke at the mere thought of Myst ending her life. Even when he didn't know where she was, or why she'd abandoned Molly, he'd always known she was out there, just as he'd known that one day he'd track her down. To think of a world without her in it was . . . unbearable. "Fuck."

"Or she'll ensure she destroys herself before she can create the weapon?" Lana finished for him.

His jaw clenched, the air heating with the force of his flare of fury.

"I'm not going to let that happen."

Lana studied him for a long moment before giving a slow nod of her head.

"Bring her to Valhalla."

He grimaced. "She won't come."

"Why not?"

"Her family decided she was a stroke of fortune." There was another blast of heat. One day he intended to introduce himself to the bastards who'd sold their own daughter. It wasn't going to be pretty. "They handed her over to the Brotherhood."

The gray eyes turned silver as Lana's temper threatened to escape her firm leash.

She'd spent decades trying to forge a peace between the humans and Valhalla.

The knowledge that there was a group of fanatics out there intent on purging the world of high-bloods was the sort of thing custom-made to get on the Mave's shit list.

And you didn't want to be on this female's shit list.

He knew firsthand.

"Damn," she snapped, holding up a slender hand as Wolfe took several steps in their direction. The Tagos obviously sensed her distress. "I assume the Brotherhood is desperate to get her back?"

He shrugged. "I'd say that was a legitimate guess."

Lana grimaced. "I'd like to dismiss them as a bunch of wackjobs. Unfortunately they've started to become far more organized and they've managed to get their hands on a large stash of illegal weapons."

Bas nodded. He'd learned just a few days before that the Brotherhood had been making large purchases on the black market.

"Which means that the sooner we can figure out what the hell the vision means, the sooner she'll be safe," he said.

"The sooner we'll *all* be safe," the Mave smoothly pointed out.

He shrugged. Right now all he cared about was Myst. "True."

"Where does she intend to start her search?"

"She's used the traditional methods and found nothing," he said, angling his body so he could keep Wolfe in his sight. The Tagos was nearing the edge of his patience. Bas wanted to be prepared in case he snapped. "It's time to think outside the box."

Lana narrowed her gaze. "I'm afraid to ask."

She should be.

Only desperation would prompt him to seek out the strangest, most secretive, most unstable high-blood ever born.

"Boggs," he said in a resigned voice.

It was a rare occasion for Myst to wake with a smile on her lips.

Okay, it wasn't rare, she silently conceded.

It was never. As in never-ever-ever.

Oh, she wasn't one of those miserable, wretched women who went through life in a fog of self-pity.

She tried her best to remain optimistic.

But her childhood had been one of lonely isolation, followed by years of utter terror as she tried to avoid being captured by her enemies. And worst of all was the constant ache at the knowledge she could never be a true mother to her beloved daughter.

This morning, however, she was waking with the scent of baby powder tickling her nose and the soft touch of tiny fingers patting her cheek.

Tears stung her eyes.

Oh . . . God, her sweet daughter.

Slowly lifting her lashes, she discovered Molly's sleep-flushed face only inches away.

"Morning, Mommy," she muttered in a husky voice.

Myst reached up to gently brush her fingers through Molly's tangled curls, pressing a kiss to the tip of her nose.

"Morning, baby."

"Why are you in my bed?"

Myst kept her smile pinned to her lips, refusing to recall Bas's abrupt disappearance the night before. She intended to savor every single second she had with her daughter.

"I thought it would be fun to have a sleepover."

Molly wrinkled her brow as she considered Myst's explanation.

"But mommies are supposed to sleep in bed with daddies."

"An interesting proposition, wouldn't you say, Myst?" A male voice sliced through the air, as lethal as a rapier.

Myst glanced over her shoulder, her mouth going dry at the sight of Bas still in the black slacks and white silk shirt he'd been wearing the night before.

His dark hair was ruffled, as if he'd been running his fingers through it, and his jaw was shadowed with a hint of his heavy whiskers.

He didn't look at all like a sophisticated business tycoon, but his rumpled appearance only emphasized his savage beauty.

Dammit.

It wasn't fair.

"You're back," she muttered, acutely aware she was a hot mess.

Unlike Bas, rumpled wasn't a good look on her.

His lips twitched, as if aware of her utterly feminine embarrassment. Then, strolling forward, he held out his arms to catch the tiny bundle of Molly who was throwing herself off the bed.

Myst felt her heart melt.

Molly would never know how lucky she was to never doubt for a second that her father would be there to catch her.

"Daddy," she squealed, lifting her face for a kiss. "Did you come to share our sleepover?"

"It's already morning," Myst hastily muttered, scooting until she was leaning against the headboard, the covers pulled to her chin. "Time for the sleepover to be over."

Twin pairs of bronze eyes studied her flushed face.

Molly with innocent happiness.

And Bas . . . with mockery, of course, but also something darker. Something that made her heart flutter and a heat pool between her legs.

"Spoilsport," he taunted before pressing a kiss to the top of Molly's curls. "Time for breakfast, pet. I brought you a surprise."

"Surprise?" The tiny girl widened her eyes with excitement. "What is it?"

"Why don't you go see?"

He lowered her to the ground and Molly was darting out of the room on bare feet.

Bas watched her retreat with a fond smile before he closed the door and crossed toward the bed.

Acutely aware she was wearing nothing more than a tiny pair of silk shorts and matching camisole, Myst cleared her throat, glancing toward the robe she'd left on a chair near the window.

When she'd crawled into bed with Molly last night she hadn't considered the fact that Bas would actually stroll into the room before she had a chance to get dressed.

"I should—"

"No more running, Myst," he interrupted, sitting on the edge of the bed.

She pursed her lips. "I wasn't running. I need a shower and change of clothes."

He shrugged, turning on the mattress so he could stretch out beside her, one arm cocked beneath his head.

"You can have both after we talk," he assured her.

Myst sucked in a shocked breath. Even with the thick

comforter between them she could feel the heat of his body searing against her bare skin.

"What are you doing?"

"Making myself comfortable," he said. "It's been a long night."

She studied his pale face, belatedly noticing the shadows beneath his eyes. Despite his restless power that pulsed through the room it was obvious he was exhausted.

"You haven't slept?" she asked, annoyed to realize she was actually concerned about the aggravating male.

"Not yet."

"Why don't you rest?" She tried to scoot toward the edge of the mattress. "We can talk later."

He rolled to the side, throwing his arm over her waist to keep her pinned in place.

"No."

She stiffened, telling herself it was outrage that was making her heart race.

"Bas."

"I didn't return alone."

"What?" Myst closed her eyes, struggling to sense who was in the outer room with her daughter. At last she opened them with a stab of surprise. "A witch?"

"The Mave," he corrected in soft tones.

"You bastard," she breathed in shock, shoving at his arm as she struggled to escape. Dammit, why hadn't she asked more questions last night? She'd suspected he was plotting something devious, but she'd allowed her desperate desire to spend time with Molly to overcome her common sense. "I knew I couldn't trust you."

"Easy, *cara*," he murmured, grunting when she managed to knee him in the upper thigh. Growling out a low curse, he moved with the speed and strength that marked him as a Sentinel. Yanking her flat against the mattress, he rolled his large body on top of her and glared down with smoldering frustration. "Dammit, listen to me," he commanded.

She went rigid. Why waste her energy on a battle she couldn't win?

Instead she gazed into his beautiful face with a pleading expression.

"Let me go. . . ." She grimaced, forcing the words past her stiff lips. "Please, Bas."

His hand moved to cup her cheek, his touch gentle although his heavy body remained lodged on top of her.

"She's not here for you, Myst," he said, his thumb brushing her bottom lip. "She's here to take Molly to Valhalla."

She made a sound of distress. Did the bastard think she would be any happier seeing Molly being handed over to the Mave?

"You're giving her our daughter?" she breathed.

His brows snapped together, his head lowering until they were nose to nose.

"Don't be a fool," he growled. "She's going to protect her."

Myst forced herself to think through the panic that was clouding her mind.

Of course Bas would never hand over Molly. Not to anyone. She might not trust Bas with her own welfare, but she never doubted that he loved Molly with all his heart.

"Protect her from what?" she demanded.

"From the Brotherhood." His lips twisted. "The bastards wouldn't hesitate to hurt a little girl, no matter how innocent she might be."

She winced, feeling as if he'd just slapped her. Did he think she didn't realize her presence was a threat to Molly? Why else would she have walked away from her?

"I told you I would only stay a few days," she said in husky tones. "I would never put Molly in danger."

He continued as if she hadn't spoken.

"I also need her to protect Molly against my own enemies." His lips twisted into a humorless smile. "Shockingly I've managed to acquire quite a few over the years."

"Yeah, big shocker," she muttered.

"Careful."

Without warning he closed the small distance to crush his lips against hers.

It was short, and intense, and so unbearably sweet she felt her entire body melt beneath him.

"Bas," she rasped, not sure if she was chiding him to stop or pleading for him to rip off her clothes and ease the brutal need that refused to leave her in peace.

"You shouldn't provoke me," he whispered against her lips, the hard length of his body pressing her deeper into the mattress.

For a crazed minute Myst became lost in the molten bronze of his eyes, her hands lifting to grip his shoulders.

She hadn't been with a man since Bas. She told herself it was because she didn't have the time or the interest. It was enough to concentrate on saving the world.

Now she realized it was because she didn't want another male to touch her.

Only Bas could make her shiver with anticipation by just being near. Or send jolts of electric excitement through her body with a brush of his lips.

Or make her wish she could wrap her legs around his waist while he surged deep inside her.

She shivered, her hands sliding so she could tangle her fingers in the satin softness of his hair. Then the moment was shattered as the sound of Molly's laughter floated through the closed door.

Myst turned her head to the side, drawing in a deep breath.

"All I'm asking for is the opportunity to spend time with

my daughter," she said, her voice strained as she tried to battle back the urgent need that thundered through her body. "Why are you determined to take her away from me?"

His lips brushed her cheek, the faint tang of male cologne teasing at her senses.

"I told you to trust me."

She swallowed a moan, tiny sparks of pleasure exploding through her.

Dammit. How was she supposed to think when he was sending her up in flames?

He nuzzled the corner of her mouth, his thickening erection pressed against her inner thigh.

She desperately wanted to spread her legs. To let the madness consume her.

Instead, she forced herself to turn her head back to meet his smoldering gaze.

"Don't send her away," she implored.

"Listen to me, *cara*," he murmured softly. "I'm trying to give you a future with her."

She frowned in confusion. "Future?"

"We're going to find the answers you've been looking for," he promised.

It wasn't what she was expecting.

Bas wanted to help her?

That seemed . . . unlikely.

"In Russia?" she demanded, wondering if he intended to take her halfway around the world while he hid Molly someplace she would never be able to find her.

"No." He shook his head. "We're going to speak with the Keeper of Tales."

Her eyes widened. She'd tried for the past twelve years to locate the mysterious Boggs.

The elusive high-blood had a rare talent. He was capable of touching objects to see the future, as well as catching glimpses of the past. It was also said that he could decipher some of the most obscure prophecies.

"You know how to contact him?" she asked in disbelief.

He grimaced. "Not me, but the Mave has promised to set up a meeting."

A dangerous hope began to bloom in her heart.

If Boggs could actually reveal the weapon she was supposed to give to their enemies, she could avoid her fate.

And be a real mother to Molly.

Of course, she'd prefer to accomplish this goal without becoming indebted to the male who was watching her with unnerving intensity.

"There's no need for you—"

"We're doing this together, *cara*," he interrupted, his tone warning his decision wasn't up for debate.

She blew out an exasperated sigh. "Why?"

His bronze gaze lowered to her lips, his expression impossible to read.

"When I figure that out I'll let you know."

Chapter Six

It took four hours for Bas to finally convince Myst that he wasn't leading her into some devious trap, and to pack Molly a suitcase.

The little girl was at first reluctant to leave, terrified she wouldn't get to see her mother again. But once they'd promised that it was only for a short time and they would be reunited after Myst returned to Kansas City, she was eager to see Valhalla.

Plus, it didn't hurt that Lana had tumbled instantly in love with the little girl, and even the cold-eyed Wolfe had melted at Molly's first dimpled grin.

Bas was resigned to the knowledge that Molly would be utterly spoiled before he could return her home.

Then he'd had to wait for the Mave to spread the word that he wasn't on the top of the most-wanted list before he and Myst were headed toward the nearest monastery.

Now they were standing in the small antechamber built of gray stone with narrow windows that allowed a glimpse of the early afternoon sunlight.

Like most of the public areas of the abbey, it was a stark room with nothing beyond a few wooden benches and a woven rug on the stone floor. The monks didn't provide comfort because they didn't want visitors to linger.

And even the sections used by the acolytes tended to be barren. Sentinels-in-training were fortunate if they were given a cot and a blanket to sleep with at night.

But deeper in the abbey were beautiful libraries, exquisite woodwork and stained glass windows, as well as galleries filled with artwork created by the Sentinels. Each warrior was trained in some craft to teach him that he had more than mere violence to offer the world.

All except assassins like Bas.

They'd been the baddest of the baddest.

The secret weapon of the monks who'd been disbanded years ago.

He was honed for death.

And the only thing of beauty he'd ever created was Molly. Of course, he hadn't created her alone. No. He had to thank Myst for her very vital role in Molly's birth.

Bas glanced toward the woman who was standing at his side, ensuring she was fully covered by the heavy robe he'd demanded one of the monks provide for her.

When she'd emerged from the bedroom of his hotel wearing nothing more than a floaty white sundress, he'd wanted to protest. The dress revealed far too much skin for his peace of mind. Her beauty was startling enough to cause talk without adding in a sneak peek of her perfect body. The fewer people who knew where she was, the better.

Or at least that was the reason he'd given Myst when he'd wrapped her in the heavy material.

Ignoring her puzzled gaze, he turned to watch a bald man in a robe similar to Myst's poke his head out of a narrow opening at the back of the room.

"The guardian is prepared to travel."

The monk disappeared and Bas reached to capture Myst's fingers in a tight grip.

"Wait here. I want to have a last word with Kaede," he told her softly.

He sensed her surprise.

"He's not coming with us?"

"No, I need him to take care of another project," he said. "He'll be travelling with a different guardian."

She tilted back her head, her expression troubled. "Does it have anything to do with me?"

Bas hesitated. His instinct was to lie. The last thing he wanted was for Myst to be distracted when they were about to meet with the Keeper of Tales.

But logically he knew it was unfair to try and keep her out of the loop. Besides, they would need her help.

"Wolfe mentioned that they've been trying to keep a close eye on the Brotherhood," he admitted, his tone pitched to make sure it wouldn't carry.

"They have a spy in the Brotherhood?" she demanded.

"He wasn't willing to share any specifics," he admitted, his expression wry. "You would think he didn't trust me."

She rolled her eyes. "Imagine that."

He shrugged, not particularly concerned with the Tagos's opinion. He was, however, extremely concerned with the intel Wolfe had grudgingly passed along.

"According to their . . . informant, there's been an increase in chatter over the past twenty-four hours."

Myst frowned. "I don't know what that means."

"From what Wolfe could figure out, it seems as if the Brotherhood is buzzing with word that some long-awaited prophecy is about to be fulfilled."

She stiffened, the color draining from her face. "It doesn't necessarily have anything to do with me."

"I would usually agree." He grimaced. Shit, he hated

having to add to her fear. "The Brotherhood is full of crazy-ass prophecies and predictions. But Wolfe specifically mentioned that the center of the talk was coming out of Wyoming."

"Crap," she breathed, her eyes suddenly haunted with memories she'd never fully escaped.

Bas's jaw tightened. Someday soon he was going to take pleasure in introducing himself to the people who'd traumatized this female.

Starting with the Brotherhood and working his way back to her family.

"Kaede will find out either way," he smoothly assured her.

She gave a startled blink. "Kaede?"

"He's headed to Wyoming." Bas's lips twisted. His enforcer had been the one to volunteer to travel to the Brotherhood compound to discover what the chatter was about. "He intends to infiltrate the Brotherhood and discover what prophecy they think is going to be fulfilled. It would help if you have the exact location of the compound," he said, an abrupt edge to his voice. "Do you remember?"

"You can't let him." Her gaze briefly flickered toward the younger man before returning to Bas. "The Brotherhood can sense a high-blood. He'll be caught the minute he gets close enough to set off their mutant-sensors."

He studied her with an unexpected surge of amusement. "Mutant-sensors?"

She shrugged. "Do you have a better name?"

His lips twitched as he considered the strange ability of the Brotherhood to tell a high-blood from a normal human. They'd go to their graves denying that it was magic, preferring to claim it was some mystical gift from their God.

"No," he murmured, his lips twitching.

"Please, Bas." She reached out to lay her fingers on his arm. "I don't want him to be hurt."

He studied her in surprise. "Are you worried about Kaede?"

"Of course I am," she said, as if it was the most natural thing in the world.

Despite his tension, Bas couldn't help a sudden laugh.

Kaede was a trained Sentinel who'd willingly sold his skills to become Bas's enforcer. He was calculating, wickedly skilled, and willing to kill when necessary.

Not the sort of male whom most women fussed over.

He gave a wry shake of his head. "I doubt Kaede has ever had anyone worry about his safety."

Her expression unconsciously softened. "Everyone should have someone who worries about them."

Bas grimaced, his heart twisting as he studied her delicate face and the velvet-brown eyes that had never appeared more vulnerable.

"How the hell have you survived with that soft heart?" he murmured.

She leaned forward, almost as if she was about to sway into his arms, which were ready to catch her. Instead, she took a step back, her expression smoothing to an unreadable mask.

"I can be ruthless when I have to be." She shivered, her eyes dark with all she'd had to sacrifice.

He resisted the urge to reach out and halt her retreat. This wasn't the time. Or place.

"It's okay," he reassured her. "He's trained as an assassin. Like me."

"What does that mean?"

"Assassins are capable of casting illusions." He held her gaze as he called on his inner magic, subtly weaving an image of an elderly man with a bald head and deeply lined face. "See?"

"Oh," she breathed in disbelief as he became a different

man right before her eyes. Her hand lifted to touch his face, as if assuring herself he was real. "That's amazing."

He turned his head, pressing his lips to the center of her palm.

"I can be whatever you want, *cara*."

There was a breathless second as they both froze, the air vibrating with a white-hot awareness. Bas could taste the warm silk of her skin lingering on his lips, the sweet scent of honeysuckle filling the air.

Then, with a tiny gasp, she was tugging her hand free and wrapping her arms around her waist.

"Fascinating, but I don't think it will fool the Brotherhood," she muttered. "They use some weird instinct to detect if someone is a high-blood."

Bas abruptly released the illusion, studying her with a brooding expression.

"Kaede's specialty is masking his presence," he explained, trying to concentrate on anything other than his hunger for this female. "Not even another high-blood would know what he is."

She looked confused. "He's invisible?"

"Nothing quite so dramatic. He passes as human," he explained. It was a talent the enforcer had used on countless occasions to infiltrate the human world, not to mention to enter Valhalla without alerting the Mave that he was anything more than a common petitioner there to seek the services of the healers. "To everyone," he emphasized. "The Brotherhood won't suspect a thing."

She bit her bottom lip. "You're sure?"

"Absolutely." He held her gaze. "Okay?"

"Okay." She gave a slow nod. "But he still needs to be careful. That group is isolated," she said, her concern for Kaede completely sincere. "They're suspicious of strangers and they fully embrace the motto to shoot first and ask questions later, even if they do assume he's a human."

Dammit. His heart gave an odd twist, and he lifted his hand to rub his thumb over the plush softness of her lower lip.

Just a few hours ago she'd been pressed beneath him, her cheeks flushed with an arousal she couldn't hide. In that moment he hadn't cared that his daughter was in the next room, not to mention the Mave and the Tagos. Or that he'd considered this woman the enemy for years. Every fiber of his being was desperate to wrench aside the heavy comforter and run his lips over every inch of her satin skin before he was spreading her legs and entering her with one deep thrust.

And now she was sabotaging his cynical belief that he was more likely to find a unicorn in this world than a truly good person. . . .

He abruptly dropped his hand, feeling as if he'd been burnt. This was dangerous. He'd spent a lifetime honing his iron control over his reactions. It was the only way an assassin could survive.

She wasn't supposed to be an irresistible sexual temptation. Or a loving mother. Or a tender female who could be concerned about a male she barely knew.

Christ.

Warily she watched him, no doubt wondering if he was about to bite. She should be worried. He wanted to sink his teeth into her. The tender curve of her throat, the soft curve of her breast, the silky skin of her inner thigh . . .

He clenched his hands as the truth struck him with the force of a cement truck.

He had to have her.

Not here. Not now.

But soon.

Very, very soon.

Realizing she was studying him with a growing concern, Bas gave a sharp shake of his head.

"Can you give me the directions to the compound?" he forced himself to ask, handing her his phone.

After typing in the coordinates to the compound, Myst shoved the phone back into his hand.

"There," she muttered.

"Stay here, I won't be long."

He glanced around to make sure no one could approach her without going past him before he crossed the annex to stand beside his enforcer. He held up his phone to show the map that Myst had pulled up.

"Here are the coordinates."

Kaede used his own phone to study his target, his brows drawing together as he plotted his strategy.

"It won't be easy to slip in and out unnoticed," he said with his typical understatement. The compound was sixty miles north of Casper in the middle of nowhere. It would be *impossible* to get near the place without alerting the natives. "I'll travel to the nearest monastery and go in as a Brother who wants to join the commune."

Bas absently shoved his hands into his pockets, his fingers automatically wrapping around the small locket he'd tucked into his slacks before leaving the hotel.

"Myst wants you to be careful."

Kaede glanced toward the slender female who was swathed in black robes.

"She's not the woman you thought she was," he said in low tones.

Yet another epic understatement.

Bas grimaced. "No, she's not."

Kaede shifted his attention back to Bas. "Are you sure you want to take her to the Keeper of Tales?" he demanded.

"There are rumors that he likes to play nasty games with people who petition for his services."

Bas had heard the same rumors.

Along with wild tales that he kidnapped human women to fill his harem, performed blood sacrifices, and ate small children for breakfast.

It made it impossible to sort the truth from the fiction.

All he knew for certain was that the strange creature was an expert in the history of their people, and had the rare ability to decipher prophecies.

"If anyone can help Myst it will be Boggs."

Kaede gave a grudging nod. "Don't let him screw with her head."

Bas swallowed a curse as a renegade anger clenched his muscles.

Christ, was he jealous at Kaede's obvious concern for Myst?

What the hell was wrong with him?

"You worry about your own head," he warned, attempting to disguise his lunatic reaction. "I prefer that it remain attached to your neck."

Kaede gave a slow lift of his brows. "It will take more than a bunch of inbred yokels to decapitate me."

Usually Bas would agree.

There were few people who could match Kaede in strength, speed, or cunning.

But he also understood there were few people more dangerous than fanatics.

"They're trained soldiers who've proven a willingness to kill, and it's rumored they own a stash of illegal weapons that were created specifically to destroy high-bloods," he reminded the enforcer.

"Worry about your woman, Bas," Kaede said. "I can take care of myself."

His woman. Bas gave a sharp shake of his head. He didn't want to consider just how right the words sounded.

Not now.

He reached out to clap a hand on his friend's shoulder. "Keep in touch."

After waiting for Kaede to nod, Bas turned and retraced his steps to where Myst was standing. He tugged her hood forward, making sure nothing could be seen of her face before he wrapped a possessive arm around her shoulders and led her into the octagon-shaped room.

Unlike the outer chamber, the stone walls of this room were covered in elaborate carvings that matched the tattooing on the massive Sentinel who was standing by the copper post in the center of the floor.

The history of the pathways the guardian Sentinels used to travel had been lost in the mists of time, but the recent discovery of an ancient temple in the Middle East had revealed hints that the early high-bloods had been forced into a desperate escape from the Brotherhood.

It was suspected that was the start of traveling.

"We're ready," he said to the robed monk.

The monk gave a low bow, motioning toward the guardian Sentinel who was well over six feet and as thick as a tree trunk.

The Sentinel moved to touch the post with a tattooed hand, waiting for Myst and Bas to join him before he spoke a low word of power.

Bas grimaced. It didn't matter how often he'd traveled the pathways, it always unnerved him.

Holding tight to Myst, Bas touched the post, feeling the world melt away. His stomach lurched, his knees threatening to give way, before there was a blur of light and they were suddenly standing in the center of a room that was identical to the one they'd just left.

Myst gave a small moan, landing against his chest as she lost her balance.

Instantly concerned, he wrapped her in his arms. "Are you okay?"

"I will be," she muttered, sucking in a deep breath. "I've only traveled the pathways a few times."

Bas grimaced, glancing toward the Sentinel who'd moved to the edge of the room, his stoic face impossible to read.

"It doesn't get easier with practice," he admitted, keeping her in his arms as he guided her out of the room, his senses on full alert.

The monastery should be safe, but he wasn't taking any chances.

Not with Myst.

"Where are we?" she asked as they crossed the antechamber and entered the Great Hall.

His gaze took in the vaulted ceiling and the line of arches along one wall that opened into the public receiving rooms. On the opposite wall were heavy tapestries that were faded with age.

"France, near the border of Switzerland," he said, pleasantly surprised by the heavy silence that surrounded them.

Usually the monastery was bustling with activity, but Lana had promised to send word that their visit was to be kept hush-hush.

The monks had clearly taken her words to heart.

Bas and Myst had reached the nearest archway when a gray-haired man wearing a simple brown robe stepped into view.

"Welcome to our monastery," the stranger said with a small bow, his voice thick with a French accent. "I am Brother Jean-Luc."

"Thank you, Brother." Bas released his hold on Myst, covertly stepping in front to hide her from the view of the monk. "We have a meeting later, but I requested that the Mave pass along word that we would need dinner."

"Of course. If you'll come with me." The monk beamed with obvious pleasure, waving a hand toward the end of the hallway. "I think you will enjoy our cuisine. We have the best chef in all of Europe, if I do say so myself."

Bas followed the monk, not surprised when Myst grabbed his arm and hissed beneath her breath.

"I don't want dinner. I want to find"—she hesitated, aware the walls might have ears—"the man we came to speak with."

Bas never slowed. "He will contact the Mave when he's ready to meet with us. Until then we have to wait," he said. "Besides, you barely pecked at your breakfast." He sent her a chiding frown. "If you won't take care of yourself, I will."

He felt her stiffen, her lips parting to tell him what he could do with his concern. Thankfully they were stepping through an arched entryway and into an inner courtyard.

They both came to a startled halt, stunned by the sight of the formal gardens.

Framed by classic marble statues were wide swaths of grass that had been cut into intricate patterns lined by blooming roses, hollyhocks, and pansies. Flagstone pathways led to the center of the gardens where a vast fountain sprayed water into the air.

Bathed in the rich purples and pinks of the encroaching dusk, the courtyard possessed a magic that had nothing to do with witchcraft.

"This is . . . exquisite," Myst breathed.

Jean-Luc urged them toward the small table that was draped with a white linen cloth.

"Our acolytes tend to the gardens as well as the vineyards. I will let them know their work is appreciated."

Bas was swift to step past the monk, pulling out Myst's chair so the older man didn't have a reason to be near her.

Overly protective?

Hell, yeah.

But there didn't seem to be any way to stop himself.

"You've spoken to the Mave?" he asked as Myst settled on her chair and he rounded the table to take his own seat.

"Oui." The monk moved to pour them each a glass of wine from the bottle in the center of the table, before pulling a serving cart from behind a small hedge. "Everything is arranged."

Bas had requested the dinner to make sure Myst ate something before their meeting with Boggs, but as the scent of warm onion soup and freshly baked bread teased at his nose he found his stomach rumbling with hunger.

"What cover did you give for us being here?" he demanded of the monk.

Although the monks and Sentinels would rather have their tongues sliced off before they gossiped about two mysterious guests enjoying dinner in the gardens, there were a number of servants who were hired to perform various tasks around the monastery.

Jean-Luc efficiently served them the soup and bread, placing a pot of fresh butter and honey in the center of the table.

"The servants have been told you're a businessman from America who is here to purchase several bottles of our finest wine." He sent Bas a satisfied smile. "It seemed a . . . beneficial story."

Bas gave an abrupt chuckle.

The monk might look like a harmless grandfather, but he was a shrewd negotiator who'd just ensured that Bas was obligated to buy several thousands of dollars' worth of wine.

"Vous êtes trop gentil, merci," he murmured in wry tones.

"Bon appétit."

With a bow toward Myst, the monk turned to exit the courtyard.

Once they were alone, Myst shook out the linen napkin, tucking it in her lap before lifting the earthenware bowl to take a sip of the soup. Instantly, her eyes closed in appreciation.

Bas buttered a piece of bread and set it in front of her, wise enough to hide his smug smile as she consumed the meal she'd insisted she didn't want.

He had just polished off his own bowl of soup when she leaned back in her chair and arranged her hood so her expression was effectively hidden.

"Why is the Mave helping you?" she abruptly demanded.

Bas refilled their wineglasses. "She's not helping me," he corrected her. "She's protecting Molly."

"Why?"

He shrugged. "Lana has a soft spot for children."

"And for you?"

Ah. Bas sipped his wine, heat licking through his veins. Was that the sound of jealousy he could hear in her voice? "What precisely are you asking, *cara?*"

Myst loved the gardens.

The clean, elegant lines. The vibrant blooms that perfumed the gentle breeze. The cool spray of water from the fountain.

The sense of being isolated from the world.

After one of the best meals she'd ever tasted and a fine glass of wine, she should be savoring this rare moment of peace.

Instead she'd found her thoughts dwelling on the

stunningly beautiful female who'd returned to Valhalla with Molly.

She wanted to believe it was because she was concerned for her daughter. After all, the Mave had a reputation as a ruthless leader who would do whatever was necessary to protect her people. And she hadn't been alone. The Tagos was every bit as intimidating as the woman he was there to protect.

His lean features had looked as if they'd been chiseled from granite, and the entire room had trembled beneath the force of his power.

But Myst wasn't an idiot.

At least not a *complete* idiot.

The two might be the most dangerous high-bloods in the world, but they'd been utterly bewitched by Molly. She didn't doubt for one second that both of them would lay down their lives to protect the enchanting little girl.

No, her interest in the Mave had more to do with the older woman's obvious comfort in Bas's company.

The two had a history together.

And if she had to guess, she'd say it'd been a very *intimate* history.

But while she wanted to know what had happened between them, she didn't want Bas to know she wanted to know.

Yeah, it was crazy.

"Nothing," she muttered.

A tiny smile tugged at his lips. "Are you asking if she's my lover?"

Arrogant ass.

"No." She ignored the glass of wine, sipping at the ice water that she'd poured from a pitcher on the serving tray. The one time she'd had alcohol in this man's presence she'd ended up in bed with him. She wasn't going to let that happen again. "I saw how the dark-eyed Sentinel watched her. He would kill any male who tried to touch her."

He shrugged, clearly indifferent to Wolfe's blatantly possessive attitude toward the Mave.

"True." He continued to watch her with an aggravating smile on his lips. "But . . ."

She heaved a frustrated sigh. Dammit. She couldn't stand it. Her curiosity was going to eat her alive if she didn't know what Bas's relationship was with the exquisitely beautiful witch.

Oh, he didn't have to say they'd been lovers.

It'd been obvious when she'd seen them together at the hotel. Wolfe had known it too. The very air had prickled with violence whenever Bas had been near the Mave.

Her interest was in whether Bas was hoping to use this opportunity to remind the older woman what she was missing.

Why she cared was something she didn't intend to ask herself.

"But it's obvious the two of you know each other."

He hesitated, and she assumed he intended to torment her by refusing to explain. Then he gave a small shrug.

"We once fought against the previous Mave."

Myst gave a startled blink. "The woman who just took my daughter was an outlaw?"

His lips twisted. "Not in the way you think," he assured her. "We worked together to save the high-bloods who'd been targeted for death."

"Why would the previous Mave target high-bloods?"

He grimaced. "She thought the humans would be more willing to accept us if she eliminated the more extreme mutations. Especially the ones who had powers that tended to be unstable."

Eliminated? Myst was genuinely shocked. Although she'd spent the past four years as a scribe in the Russian monastery, she'd concentrated most of her time on prophecies, not the history of Valhalla.

"She killed her own people?" Myst breathed in horror.

Bas's expression was unreadable. A certain sign that he was hiding some intense emotion.

"She called it a necessary purging."

Myst shuddered. It'd been easy to think of the Brotherhood as evil. They were the enemy. And even her parents were dismissed as humans who were too weak to resist the temptation of money.

But the thought that there were high-bloods who could commit genocide made her stomach twist with horror.

"Good Lord."

He nodded. "It was an ugly time in our history."

Myst began to understand why she'd so easily sensed the bond between this man and the leader of the high-bloods. It was obvious they'd shared the sort of experience that would forever bind them together.

For some reason the realization made her stomach clench with regret, but still she couldn't halt herself from pressing for more information.

She had to know . . . what?

If he was still in love with the beautiful witch?

"And then Lana took over the position as Mave?" she abruptly demanded.

He gave a slow dip of his head. "She did."

"Why didn't you join Valhalla?"

"Because I don't take orders from anyone," he answered with blunt honesty, a wicked hint of amusement in his eyes. "And I like the finer things in life." His gaze did a slow, lazy survey of her tense body. "Being a mercenary pays a lot better than being a Sentinel."

She tried to ignore the shiver of utter pleasure that raced through her body as his heat wrapped around her like a teasing caress.

"Mercenaries are against the law," she said, as determined as a bulldog with a bone.

His smile widened, as if sensing she wasn't going to be satisfied until he'd confessed his feelings for the older woman.

"So I've been told," he murmured, giving nothing away. "Thankfully I'm too smart to get caught."

She rolled her eyes. Did he have to be so smug?

"Then why didn't the Mave or Wolfe arrest you?"

He glanced down at the wine he was swirling in his glass. "Because Molly is an innocent who deserves to have her mother in her life."

Myst's heart missed a beat.

Dear Lord, she so desperately wanted the opportunity to be a mother to Molly.

A real mother who could be in her life every day.

But she wasn't going to allow herself to be distracted. "And that's the only reason she's helping us?" she demanded.

"The primary reason," he said, a strange expression settling on his intensely beautiful features. "Although I suspect there's a part of her that's delighting in the sight of me being led around on a leash."

A leash? Was that some slang word for having to ask for help?

"I don't understand."

"That's the only thing that makes this situation bearable," he muttered in wry tones.

She shook her head, not for the first time aware that she didn't seem to speak the same language as everyone else.

"Do you always have to talk in riddles?"

"Let's enjoy our meal." He abruptly drained his wine and reached toward the serving tray where two dishes of crème brûlée were waiting. "I have a feeling we're not going to be in the mood to eat after we speak with Boggs."

She grimaced. "That's fine with me," she said, grabbing her spoon.

She had better things to do than worry about whether or not Bas was jonesing for the beautiful Mave.

Right?

It didn't matter to her.

Not. At. All.

Stabbing her spoon into the creamy dessert, she forced herself to clean her dish before she rose to her feet and strolled around the lovely garden. Right now nothing mattered but finding Boggs so he could . . .

Well, she wasn't entirely certain what he could do.

Translate her vision?

Share other prophecies that might give her a better understanding of what weapon she was supposed to hand over to their enemies?

She'd heard he was capable of both.

She could only pray it would be enough to help her alter the future.

Chapter Seven

It took less than two hours for Kaede to reach the sprawling ranch. He'd traveled directly to the monastery in Casper and then used a small plane to land on the private airstrip.

There'd been a tense moment when a couple of the Brotherhood had greeted his landing with AK-47s and a bad attitude. He'd resisted the urge to rip out their hearts and instead risked using a small burst of magic to cloud their minds long enough to convince them that he was an expected recruit arriving from Hawaii.

Killing them would have been far more satisfying, but it would have been a pain to have to deal with the bodies. And as a bonus, the entire compound now was ready to accept him as a welcomed member of their group.

He'd been forced to take a tedious tour of the eighteen hundred acres of barren prairie surrounded by a large lake to the south and a rim of rolling hills to the north before being given an empty cot in one of the wooden bunkhouses close to the lake.

He'd intended to slip away once he was left to settle in. He wanted to investigate the house he'd spotted from the air.

The rest of the property was exactly what he'd expected.

Isolated. Plenty of space to practice their fighting skills. Stark living conditions. The only thing that struck him as odd was the sleek A-frame house built in the center of the land.

It was large and elegant and the sort of house that belonged to country music stars who were looking to get away from their adoring fans.

Or Wall Street moguls who were hiding from the IRS.

Not a fanatical leader of a cult of killers.

But before he could shake off his newfound friends he was being hustled toward the long log building that was set away from the bunkhouses. Kaede grimly allowed himself to be shoved inside, his gaze swiftly taking in the small obstacle course that was set at one end and the gun range constructed at the other end.

It was clearly a training center where he was no doubt expected to prove he was worthy to join the group.

He moved forward, his attention captured by the man who was stepping out of a side room where Kaede could catch sight of two cells with heavy iron bars. The local jail? Or something more sinister?

Kaede folded his arms over his chest and waited for the man to approach. He'd deliberately dressed in the traditional loose pants and long tunic of the Brotherhood, a fake arrow tattoo prominently displayed beneath his right eye. The man who walked forward to greet him, on the other hand, was wearing a pair of faded jeans and a wifebeater that revealed the numerous prison tattoos that covered his arms.

"You the new guy?" the stranger demanded.

"Kaede," he said. He'd never been a big believer in using fake names.

They were too easy to screw up.

"Hester," the man said, jerking his chin toward the obstacle course. "Let's see what you got."

Peeling off his shirt and kicking off his shoes, Kaede headed toward the course of ropes, tunnels, and a tall wall that was meant to be scaled. It was laughably easy for a trained Sentinel, but he deliberately slowed his pace and managed to take a fall from the wall before finishing the course.

Hester's resigned expression had shifted to a grudging respect as he walked up to Kaede and shoved a gun into his hand.

"Not bad. Not bad at all," he muttered, giving another jerk of his chin. "Let's go to the firing range."

Kaede obediently moved to take his place in front of the targets, casually emptying the clip into the center of the bull's-eye.

"You're good," Hester said, taking the gun from Kaede's hand and tossing it onto a nearby table. Then, planting his fists on his hips, he studied Kaede with a suspicious frown. "Too good to choose this bumfuck of a ranch. Which means you're running from something or looking for someone."

Kaede shrugged. "I've done my share of running in the past, but this time I'm following the word on the street," he said, his tone casual. "They say you're getting ready to take on Valhalla. I want in on the action."

The man snorted. "Get in line, boy. I've waited fifteen years for the action to start."

Kaede didn't bother to hide his frown. Was this some wild goose chase?

"Are you warning me that I'm wasting my time?"

There was a strange hesitation before the man was glancing over his shoulder, as if making sure they were alone in the building.

"Are you serious about wanting to take on Valhalla?"

Kaede didn't miss the sudden glint of barely suppressed excitement in the male's pale eyes. He had information he was dying to share.

The question was whether it was worth the time to listen or if Kaede should find an excuse to leave so he could try his luck sneaking into the main house.

In the end, it was the knowledge he would have to wait until dark to try and see what was hidden inside the A-frame that kept him standing in place.

"Why wouldn't I be?" he demanded.

Hester shrugged, his expression hard. "Ninety percent of the recruits that come here are posers."

"Posers?"

"They're happy to beat on a high-blood that's sedated and chained in our fun house." The male glanced toward the side room where Kaede had caught a glimpse of the cells. "But they'd shit their pants if they thought they had to face a high-blood in hand-to-hand combat."

They'd held high-bloods in the cells and tortured them?

God. Damn. He was going to . . .

Kaede slammed down his shields, knowing an explosion of fury would fill the air with heat if he wasn't careful. And he wanted to ensure that no one guessed who or what he was. Not until he had the opportunity to make each and every one of the bastards pay for what they'd done.

"Trust me, I like killing things." A humorless smile twisted his lips. "A lot."

Easily sensing Kaede's lust for violence, even if he didn't have a damned clue he was in the crosshairs, Hester gave a slow nod.

"I believe you." The man turned his head to spit on the floor, acting like he was some sort of bad-ass. Kaede wondered if the male would be so cocky when he ripped his heart out of his chest. "I'm going to give you the inside scoop."

Kaede moved to grab the shirt he'd removed before entering the obstacle course, pulling it over his head. He needed to keep his hands busy if he didn't want to accidentally do something he was going to regret.

"I'd appreciate that," he managed to mutter.

Hester leaned against a long table, blissfully unaware he was hovering on the edge of death.

"Fifteen years ago a clairvoyant had some sort of vision. According to our leader she was going to invent a weapon that would allow the Brotherhood to defeat Valhalla."

Kaede pretended to be confused. "You've had a weapon that could defeat the high-bloods for fifteen years?"

"No." Hester grimaced. "The moron who was running this band of misfits brought the clairvoyant here and tossed her into one of the mine shafts."

Kaede felt another surge of anger.

He barely knew Myst, but he adored her daughter, Molly. The tiny girl had stolen his heart from the second he'd held her in his arms. Which meant he'd do anything necessary to protect her mother.

And just as importantly, he'd seen how his friend and employer watched the pretty clairvoyant when he thought no one was looking.

Bas might claim he wasn't completely obsessed with the female, but Kaede knew it was only a matter of time until the older man gave in to his need to claim her.

The knowledge that these worthless jackasses had dared to lay a hand on her made him once again consider the pleasure of ripping out a few hearts.

"Any reason he chose a mine shaft?" he asked, his tone stripped of emotion.

Hester grimaced. "He thought it would force her to magically create the weapon."

Kaede cocked a brow. It never failed to amaze him just how stupid their enemy could be.

"She didn't?"

"Hell no." The man gave a sharp bark of laughter. "She escaped and our jackass of a leader wasted years and fuck knows how much money trying to track her down."

"A shame," Kaede said, leaning over to put on his shoes. "That weapon would have come in handy."

He straightened to realize the man was studying him with a smirk.

"You mean it *will* come in handy," he corrected.

Kaede tensed. Hester was a common street thug who depended on muscle, not brain, to survive. But there was a brash certainty in his tone that warned Kaede this wasn't an empty boast.

"You have it?" he asked.

"Not yet." Hester took another look around the long room before leaning forward, his voice pitched low. "Our leader died a few weeks back and his woman took over the position."

Kaede arched a brow. That was the big secret?

Not that it wasn't a shock that these renowned misogynists would actually allow a woman to give them orders.

"You let a female become your leader?"

"It wasn't my choice. I think that bitches should know their place." He shrugged. "But Stella swore she'd received word from God."

"She has a direct line to God?"

Hester smiled with nasty glee. "Yep."

"How . . . convenient." Kaede resisted the urge to roll his eyes. Where did they get these yokels? If they weren't so well armed and well funded he would enjoy watching them stumble around like idiots.

"Did she share any of the intel she's supposedly getting?" he instead asked.

"She knows exactly where the missing clairvoyant is going to be," Hester said, his voice edged with anticipation. "I've heard rumors that it's someplace in Europe."

A cold chill blasted through Kaede. What the hell? Could they truly know where Myst was going to be?

Or was this some sort of trick being played by the

mysterious Stella to keep her position as leader of the Brotherhood?

"When?"

"Soon." Hester's smile widened. "Maybe even today."

"Shit." Kaede knew that Stella was more than likely manipulating her followers with false promises. After all, Europe could just be a stab in the dark. But he couldn't shake the ominous fear that Myst was in danger.

"Yeah." Hester reached out to slap Kaede's back. "You got here just in time."

"Or too late," Kaede muttered.

Leaning against one of the marble statues, Myst was gazing over the low hedge at the vineyard basking in moon-light when the air heated and the force of Bas's presence wrapped around her.

She shivered as his fingers brushed her cheek, tucking a curl behind her ear.

"I'm afraid it's time," he said, an edge in his voice sending a warning chill down her spine.

She turned, studying his guarded expression.

"You sound reluctant," she said. "Is there something you're not telling me?"

"I don't entirely trust Boggs," he said, his chiseled features indecently gorgeous in the fading light. "From what I've heard, he's unpredictable and he likes to play games."

She frowned. "What kind of games?"

He shrugged, his expression abruptly hardening. "It doesn't matter. I'm not going to let him bother you." Reaching out to grasp her hand, he gently tugged her toward the small gate at the side of the garden. "Let's get this over with."

She didn't argue.

The sooner they found Boggs, the sooner she would know if she had a future with her daughter.

If that meant dealing with a crazy doppelganger, that was fine with her. She'd fight a tiger bare-handed for the chance to spend her life with Molly.

Or risk her heart to an assassin, a voice whispered in the back of her mind.

She stiffened, fiercely squashing the renegade thought. No way. This had nothing to do with her heart. Bas was helping her because he understood how much Molly needed her mother.

She'd be a fool to forget that for a second.

She silently repeated the words over and over even as she covertly studied Bas's finely sculpted profile as he led her to the nearby stables.

God. It was so unfair.

Bas was fiercely intelligent, an assassin with the magic of a witch and the benefit of Sentinel training, plus a financial whiz.

Did he also have to be so ridiculously beautiful?

Pondering the fickleness of fate that gave so many blessings to a few and so little to others, Myst followed Bas into the nearby stables, which had been converted to a garage that stored a dozen different automobiles.

Bas chose a Peugeot SUV, politely holding the door as Myst climbed in and pulled on her seat belt before he crawled behind the wheel. Minutes later they were headed out of the stables and down a narrow dirt road.

Neither of them spoke as they drove through the darkness. Bas was no doubt preparing for the upcoming encounter with the doppelganger. No matter what his motive was in escorting her to Boggs, he would take it as a personal insult to his honor if something happened to her on his watch.

Myst closed her eyes and concentrated on her connection with Molly.

For an indulgent moment she allowed herself to savor the sense of sweet, childish joy that shimmered through the telepathic connection. Clearly Molly was enjoying her time in Valhalla.

Torn between relief that her daughter was being suitably spoiled and regret that they had to be parted, Myst sent a psychic kiss before she firmly shut the doorway between them.

She hated the feeling of being cut off from Molly, but she didn't know the extent of Boggs's powers.

What if he could rummage around in her mind? Being telepathically linked to Molly might put her daughter at risk.

Besides, there was the off-chance that she might not survive the encounter. If the mysterious Keeper of Tales decided she was a threat to the high-bloods, he might put an end to her.

She had to make sure Molly wasn't connected if that happened.

Feeling the SUV come to a halt, Myst opened her eyes and peered out the side window.

"Are you sure this is the right address?" she demanded, seeing nothing through the gloom beyond a narrow, three-story home built of white stone. The roof was steeply sloped and constructed from red tiles and the wooden shutters were in dire need of a fresh coat of paint.

It looked like a typical French farmhouse.

Not the sort of place she would expect to find a powerful high-blood.

"Certain," Bas said, his expression distracted as he studied the overgrown garden and the fence that leaned at a drunken angle.

She bit her lower lip. She had a bad feeling.

A really, really bad feeling.

It wasn't just the air of neglect that blanketed the area. With a little attention the property could be as charming as ever. Or even the sense of isolation. If the sun had been shining and there was a light summer breeze stirring the trees, this place could be a haven of peace.

No. What she was feeling was perilously close to a premonition.

Something was wrong.

Unfortunately, the vague sense of wrongness didn't change her need to meet with the doppelganger. In fact, it only made it more vital.

"Aren't we going to go inside?" she demanded.

Bas scanned their surroundings, his face tight with tension. "I want to have a look around," he at last muttered, pushing open his door. "Stay here."

She reached to grasp his arm. "No," she protested. "You can't go in there alone."

He turned his head to send her an impatient glance. "Something doesn't feel right."

She frowned. "All the more reason for both of us to go."

He blinked, a strange expression spreading across his face. "I'm an assassin, *cara*," he said in gentle tones. "This is what I do."

"But . . ." Her words trailed away as she realized he was right.

What was wrong with her? This man had been trained by the finest warriors in the world. He was strong, fast, lethal with his bare hands, and capable of hiding in plain sight. A perfect weapon for the high-bloods.

She, on the other hand, had zero fighting ability, which meant she would only be in the way.

"Fine," she muttered, trying to pretend the thought of watching him walking into the house alone wasn't making her heart pound with panic.

Without warning, he leaned to the side and captured her lips in a brief, searing kiss. Heat curled through the pit of her stomach, easing her fear, although it did nothing to slow her thundering heart.

"Lock the doors," he commanded before slipping out of the SUV and melting into the shadows.

She instinctively reached to hit the lock button, her hands curling in her lap as she nervously kept her gaze focused on the house.

"Please, be careful," she whispered softly, unable to bear the thought he might be hurt.

It wasn't that she cared. It was just that . . . Molly would be heartbroken.

The minutes slowly passed, the darkness thickening until she could see nothing beyond the nearby fence. At the same time, her sense of unease continued to deepen.

Dammit. What was taking so long?

Bas had blazing speed. He could have run to Paris and back by now.

Myst grimaced. Okay. That might be an exaggeration.

But jeez, how long did it take to look through one medium-sized farmhouse?

She was on the point of going to search for him when the unmistakable sound of gunfire exploded the silence. Oh God. She reached to open the door, desperate to reach Bas and make sure he wasn't hurt.

But before she could do more than grab the handle the windshield shattered, several stray pieces of glass slicing through her cheek.

Stunned by the unexpected attack, Myst lunged to the side, trying to get out of the path of the flying bullets. But even as she hit the leather seat, she heard more shots and felt a blow to her shoulder.

She gave a low grunt, sharp pain piercing through her.

Oh hell. She'd been shot.

Weirdly it hurt, but not as much as the cuts on her face.

She awkwardly turned her head, glancing down at the small piece of metal sticking out of her skin.

Oh. She hadn't been shot with a bullet. It was a tranq dart.

Her mind went fuzzy even as she heard the door to the SUV being pulled open. Fingers dug into her hair, roughly jerking her head up so a flashlight could be shoved in front of her face.

"Hello, freak," a male voice taunted, his foul breath nearly choking her. "We've been waiting for you."

Chapter Eight

Bas heard the buzzing in the back of his head. He groaned, trying to block out the aggravating noise.

"Bas," a female voice spoke directly in his ear. "Wake up."

With an effort, Bas turned his head to gaze through the cloaking shadows. Was he in his bedroom? Why was it so dark?

His fuzzy thoughts were distracted as he caught sight of the tall, dark-haired witch who was standing just a few feet away wearing a sleeveless jade sweater and jeans that clung to her long, slender legs.

"Lana?" Bas frowned. He could see her, but he couldn't actually sense her presence. The knowledge disturbed him. "What the hell are you doing here?"

"I'm not there." Her voice was edged with impatience. "I'm speaking to you telepathically."

Well, that would explain why he hadn't known she was sneaking up on him. He glared at her pale, perfect face.

No doubt any number of males would be happy to have their dreams interrupted by this gorgeous witch. Hell, they'd probably be eager to weave her into their fantasies.

Bas, however, had no interest in any woman beyond his silver-haired clairvoyant.

"Hasn't anyone told you that it's rude to intrude into a person's mind?"

Her lips twitched. "On several occasions."

"Then go away."

A shocking blast of power slammed into him without warning as Lana's voice vibrated through his brain with painful intensity.

"Wake up."

Bas winced. Christ. What was wrong with the woman?

"Why?"

"I think Myst is in danger."

"Myst?" Bas sucked in a sharp breath, a sudden fear squeezing his heart. "Where is she?"

"I hope she's with you," Lana said. "What happened to you?"

"Shit."

Bas fought against the sleep clouding his mind, belatedly realizing he wasn't safely tucked in his bed at home.

So where was he?

Grimly ignoring the panic that fluttered at the edge of his fuzzy mind, Bas forced himself to reconstruct his memories with cold precision.

Right now, emotions were the enemy.

If Myst needed him, he had to be able to think clearly.

He conjured the image of traveling to the monastery with Myst and Kaede and then arriving in France. They'd had dinner. Soup and crusty bread, right? Yes. Then they'd had to wait for several hours before they'd finally left for the meeting with Boggs.

He remembered the feeling that something wasn't right when they'd arrived at the remote farmhouse. A strange sense of foreboding that had thickened the air until he could taste it on his tongue.

So what'd happened after they arrived?

His thoughts went blank for a second, struggling against the fog that continued to cloud his mind.

Then abruptly he had a vivid image of creeping up the dark staircase, scouting for the hidden source of danger. He'd been on the upper landing when he'd felt a pinprick on the back of his neck.

Less than a half a heartbeat later he'd been tumbling onto his face, his body shutting down just before his mind had gone blank.

"I've been drugged," he abruptly growled.

Lana nodded, clearly already having suspected what'd happened to him.

"Do you have the magic to burn it out of your system?"

"We're about to find out," he muttered, concentrating his energy on one powerful blast that seared through his veins, cleansing it of any lingering toxin.

A gasp was wrenched from his lips as the heat nearly boiled his blood. Damn. It was rare that he had to use his magic on himself. He'd forgotten how much it could hurt.

The last of the heat reached his toes, and slowly Bas battled his way through the clinging darkness.

He was lying face down on a nasty carpet that reeked of stale tobacco and thick dust. Unfortunately, his body wasn't yet on board with actually moving, so he was forced to try and use his senses to ensure there was nothing near that was about to attack.

"Bas?" Lana sharply broke into his focused search. She no longer looked as if she was standing directly in front of him, but instead he could see she was seated at her desk in Valhalla. Lana was the only telepath he had ever met who could implant her image in another's mind. It was as unnerving as hell. "Are you awake?"

"I'm conscious," he muttered, concentrating on regaining command of his limbs.

"Where are you?" she demanded.

"The farmhouse where we were supposed to meet Boggs."

"Were you attacked?"

"Yeah." He managed to move his arms far enough to plant his palms on the carpet. "It must have been a tranq gun."

Lana frowned, her slender fingers tapping on the glossy top of her desk.

"You didn't sense them?"

"Only an overall feeling of . . ." Bas searched for the words to explain what he'd felt the minute they'd arrived at the farmhouse. "I don't know . . . wrongness."

The Mave gave a slow nod. "It could be some sort of human technology. I've heard the Brotherhood has been seeking weapons that can disrupt our powers."

"Great," he muttered.

That's all he needed. Humans who could cloak their presence.

Lana grimaced. "Is Myst with you?"

"No." Desperation clawed at him, even as he tried to straighten his arms. "I made her wait in the vehicle." He managed to shove himself onto his knees before he swayed to the side and crashed into the nearby banister. "God dammit."

"Easy, Bas," Lana tried to soothe.

He reached to grasp the heavy wooden balustrade that edged the upper foyer, ignoring the sweat that beaded his upper lip as he ruthlessly pulled himself to his feet.

"I have to get to her," he growled between clenched teeth.

"You're not going to do her any good if you collapse," Lana warned.

Bas muttered a curse, clinging to the smooth wood as his knees refused to hold his weight.

"Does Wolfe know how annoying you can be?" he snarled.

Lana arched a brow. "You only think I'm annoying when I'm right."

True. In the past they'd usually gotten along well.

It was only a silver-haired, dark-eyed minx who set off his temper.

"Why did you contact me?" he demanded, relieved when he managed to regain his balance.

He glanced around the empty house, taking in the peeling plaster and dust that covered the forgotten furnishings like a funeral shroud.

He couldn't detect anyone nearby, but he no longer trusted his senses.

"Your enforcer was worried when he couldn't get ahold of you," Lana explained.

Bas felt a stab of surprise. The younger male hated anything connected to Valhalla. Bas had never asked why.

A man's secrets were his own.

"Kaede called you?"

"Yes." A hint of amusement flickered over Lana's face. As if she was aware of Kaede's revulsion toward her authority. "He managed to infiltrate the Brotherhood in Wyoming."

Bas smiled wryly, inching his way toward the stairs. At least something had gone right.

"Did he discover anything?"

She nodded. "That the new leader claims to have some way of knowing where Myst is going to be."

Bas came to an abrupt halt, shock reverberating through his body.

They'd walked into a trap?

"How?" He asked the obvious question.

"The female says she's talking with God, but Kaede is

convinced she's getting her intel from a less holy source," Lana said in dry tones. "He's working to figure it out."

Bas might have been astounded by the news that the idiotic group had a female leader if he hadn't been so infuriated that someone had passed along information that'd put Myst in danger.

"The Brotherhood has to have a spy in Valhalla," he snapped, forcing himself back into motion.

"We're looking into it," Lana promised, her beautiful face smoothed of emotions. "But it's extremely unlikely the leak came from here."

He headed down the staircase, one painful step at a time.

"Of course not," he muttered. He didn't think Lana could be entirely unbiased when it came to her beloved Valhalla.

He heard her heave an exasperated sigh. "Think, Bas. The Brotherhood isn't large enough to have their followers based in every city. How could they have time to set up a trap and get it in place when none of us knew the coordinates until Boggs contacted me?" she said.

He scowled. "Maybe we were followed from the abbey."

"Only Wolfe and I knew you were traveling to France."

Shit. She had a point.

He didn't believe for a second that Lana or Wolfe would betray them.

He reached the bottom of the stairs and weaved his way across the small foyer like a drunken human.

"Could Boggs have set us up?" he asked, managing to reach the door without collapsing.

Grasping the handle, he held onto it with a death grip, his breath a loud rasp.

Christ. He felt as weak as a newborn pup.

What the hell had they shot into him?

"Doubtful," Lana murmured, her brow furrowing as she

considered the question. "He's unpredictable, but he's fiercely loyal. I don't think he's a traitor."

Neither did Bas.

Which meant he had to hope Kaede could discover how the Brotherhood had gotten their information.

Accepting that it was a question he'd have to deal with later, Bas pulled open the door and stepped out of the house. It was dark, the front garden bathed in shadows, but Bas had the ability to easily see at night. Which meant he was still several feet away from the SUV parked at the gate when he realized the front window had been shattered and Myst was no longer in her seat.

An icy fear clutched his heart, his mouth dry as he stumbled forward.

"Shit," he breathed in horror.

In his mind, Lana shoved herself to her feet, the feel of her magic a tangible force.

"What's going on, Bas?"

"She's gone," he rasped.

"Wait there and I'll send hunters from the monastery to help you search for her," she commanded.

"Screw that."

Bas didn't hesitate to slam her out of his brain. Lana wasn't the only one with power. And if she thought for a second he was going to wait around for backup, she didn't know him at all.

Moving toward the SUV, Bas paused long enough to retrieve the gun he'd hidden beneath the seat and to lock on to Myst's scent.

"Hold on, *cara*, I'm coming," he whispered softly, heading down the narrow path with a lethal determination.

* * *

Kaede had been forced to wait until dinner was being served in the main bunkhouse before he could at last slip away from his new bestie.

Hester had refused to leave his side as they'd finished up at the training center and taken a tour of the abandoned mines now known as the "pit." For a while Kaede thought he might have to scrape the man off like a barnacle. Or he might just kill him and dump his body in one of the deep shafts where they'd left Myst when she was barely more than a baby.

The idea had poetic justice.

Unfortunately he couldn't risk attracting unwanted attention, so he'd bided his time, waiting for Hester to grab a tray and get in line before he silently slid out a side door.

From there he'd casually strolled toward the A-frame house, taking careful note of the various guards who stood on duty, as well as the number of doors into the private residence. His only intention had been to get a feel for the security that surrounded the house and the easiest point of entrance. But he'd been passing along the back edge of the swimming pool that looked grossly out of place in the barren landscape when he realized he was being watched.

He'd deliberately dropped his phone, giving him the opportunity to covertly glance toward the outdoor bar near the back of the house.

Lying on a recliner was a woman with long auburn hair and a lush body shown to advantage in a red halter top and white shorts. Her gaze had followed him from the time he'd stepped around the house.

At first he'd sensed her burst of fury. No doubt she preferred to keep her loyal followers from realizing she lay around the luxurious pool sipping a glass of wine and enjoying a private meal while they stood in line for some slop tossed on a plate.

But as he'd slowed his pace to a leisurely stroll, he'd instantly realized the second her anger had transformed to a sharp-edged interest. He hid his small smile as he straightened and deliberately flexed his muscles.

Yeah, it was cheesy, but it worked.

With a slow, sinuous movement the female rose from the recliner and sashayed her way around the pool.

"Are you lost?" she demanded in a voice that had been trained to sound like a low, sensuous invitation.

It went perfectly with her whole sex-kitten image.

Kaede turned to meet the dark blue gaze, casually leaning against the wrought iron gate that was clearly intended to keep out the riffraff.

"Just getting familiar with my new home," he murmured, discreetly allowing his heat to fill the air.

As a human she would be susceptible to the pheromones he'd been trained to use as a weapon.

"Your home is on the other side of the property," she informed him, waving her hand toward the side of the house even as her nose flared and her eyes darkened with excitement. "This area is off-limits to recruits."

"I can see why." He deliberately took a slow, thorough survey of her lush curves. "The Brothers would never get anything done if they had you as a distraction."

She lifted a mocking brow. "Does that actually work?"

Kaede shrugged, his gaze returning to her heart-shaped face, which was flushed with an awareness she was trying to disguise.

He leaned forward, lifting his hand to trail a lazy finger down her heated cheek.

"Sometimes."

She licked her lips, unconsciously swaying forward. "Let me give you a clue. . . . Your technique is lame."

Kaede chuckled, his fingers grasping her chin so he could tilt back her head.

"You prefer a more direct approach?" he demanded. "I can do that."

Leaning down he took her lips in a rough, demanding kiss. She gave a low moan, the scent of her fierce arousal spicing the air before she was placing her hands against his chest.

"Brute. Let me go," she muttered, making no actual effort to push him away.

Kaede allowed his fingers to skim down her neck, resting them over the pulse at the base of her throat.

"Your heart is racing."

"Because I'm pissed off," she tried to bluster out. No doubt she was accustomed to being the one using sex as a weapon.

"I don't think so." He wrapped his arm around her waist, yanking her against him. "I know when a woman is hungry for a man."

She released a shaky breath, her body softening as she leaned against his chest.

"Who are you?" she rasped.

He tightened his grip, watching her eyes dilate. The female liked an edge of pain.

He could do that.

"Kaede," he readily answered.

"Where did you come from, Kaede?"

He gave a lift of one shoulder. "I started in Hawaii, then moved to Vegas, then to Dallas, and now here." He dipped his head down to nip her lower lip. "I like it here."

She hissed in pleasure, her nipples hardening to tiny pebbles.

"Stop."

"Say it like you mean it, sweetheart," he taunted, kissing

her with expertise if not enjoyment. He sincerely hoped he was going to be able to lure her into the privacy of her home without having to do the actual deed. He wasn't sure he could muster the enthusiasm to actually have sex with the bitch. "We need to take this someplace more comfortable," he muttered as her hands began to run an impatient path up and down his back.

She dug her nails into the muscles of his shoulders. "I don't sleep with my recruits."

His lips twitched at her protest.

Hell, she was nearly climbing up his body in an effort to get closer.

"Then I quit," he countered, his hand lowering to squeeze her ample ass.

She gave a low groan of pleasure. "What?"

"I'm a believer in our cause, but I'm willing to trade my immortal soul for an opportunity to warm your bed," he assured her.

"I might consider your offer once. . . ." She pressed her hips forward and Kaede hastily moved back.

He didn't want her to discover his lack of arousal.

"Once?" he prompted.

Her lips parted, but before she could speak there was the sound of a door opening and a male voice floated across the pool.

"Stella?"

With a muttered curse, Stella wrenched herself out of Kaede's arms and sent him a frustrated glare.

"Return to the barracks."

Kaede glanced toward the house, jolts of alarm racing through him. Although the male remained lost in the shadows of the house, he'd caught the unmistakable prickles in the air.

"You already have a lover?" he rasped, disguising his shock behind a pretense of annoyance.

Stella thinned her lips, giving him a sharp shove. She clearly didn't want him knowing she wasn't alone in the massive house.

"Did you hear what I said?"

"Yeah, I heard."

"Then go away," she commanded.

"I won't be far when you're ready for a real man," he assured her as he casually strolled away.

Kaede forced himself not to look back as he rounded the corner of the house, his hand already reaching for the phone he'd tucked in his pocket. He didn't know what game Stella was playing with the Brotherhood, but there was one thing he was certain of. . . .

Her male companion was a high-blood.

Stella struggled to contain her explosion of fury as she marched toward the house.

Not only had Peter risked exposing them both, he'd interrupted her very enticing encounter with the scrumptious Kaede.

Dammit. It'd been years since she'd been in a position to take a lover who was more than a tool in her obsession for power. Now that she was near to achieving her goals, she wanted to savor her success. Starting with a few sweaty nights in bed with the new recruit.

Instead she was stuck dealing with a moron whose idea of foreplay was a fumbled kiss and trying to get his cock in her before he came.

Stepping through the open door, Stella placed her hand in the center of the man's chest and gave him a violent shove.

"I've told you never to leave my private rooms," she

hissed. "If one of the Brothers discovers I have a freak as my personal companion they'll kill both of us."

A petulant expression settled on Peter's chubby face. "Your phone was ringing. I thought it might be important."

Shit. She'd left her phone next to the bed when she'd decided to enjoy her dinner by the pool. The last thing she'd expected was to be distracted by the sinfully sexy Kaede.

"You have to be more careful," she muttered, brushing past her unwelcome companion to head toward the nearby staircase.

Peter scurried to keep pace. "Who was that man?" he asked.

She grimaced at his hot breath on the back of her shoulder, climbing the steps at a brisk pace.

"A new recruit."

"What's his name?"

"What does it matter?" she snapped.

"There was something strange about him," Peter groused.

Stella rolled her eyes as she reached the upper landing and turned to head into her bedroom. Where Gilbert had tended to be a blustering bully, this high-blood whined like a child.

"There was nothing strange."

"There was," Peter insisted, trailing behind her as she crossed to pluck her phone off the nightstand. "I can't put my finger on it. I just don't trust him."

"You're being a fool." She dismissed his concern, far more interested in the missed call.

The number belonged to Roy. The Brother she'd sent to capture the clairvoyant in France.

"He was touching you," Peter continued to press, too stupid to realize he was doing nothing more than digging his own grave. "I should have—"

"Be very careful, Peter," she warned in icy tones, pressing the CALL button on her phone. "You're standing here because I put a knife in Gilbert's back. If it wasn't for me you'd still be locked in that cage."

He folded his arms over his chest. Predictably he disliked being reminded he'd been a helpless victim until she'd decided he could be of use.

"I know what you did for me."

"Then understand you have no rights over me or my body. Not now, not ever," she said, holding his gaze before she deliberately turned her back on him as she concentrated on the voice that eventually picked up her call. "Do you have her?"

Chapter Nine

Myst knew before she opened her eyes that something was wrong.

It wasn't just the fuzziness that clouded her brain. Or the leaden lethargy that made it impossible to move her muscles.

It was in the malevolent vibrations that filled the air.

Careful to remain perfectly still, Myst absorbed her surroundings. She was lying on a low, uncomfortable cot in some sort of small structure. A cottage, maybe. She could catch the scent of a thatch roof. Outside she could hear the sound of the muted conversations of several males. At least a dozen. Probably more.

And unnervingly, there was the unmistakable stench of an unwashed human who was standing directly over her.

He intended her harm. She could feel it in her very bones.

Dammit. She'd been careless for the first time since climbing out of that mine shaft. Sitting in the SUV, she'd been concentrating on the farmhouse instead of keeping watch on any intruders trying to sneak up on them.

She'd let down her guard and now she was in the hands of her enemy.

Grimly, Myst battled through the fog in her mind,

preparing herself to strike out. She was more than capable of dealing with a human even if she wasn't as strong as a Sentinel . . . or an assassin.

Oh Lord.

Her heart gave an abrupt squeeze as she was abruptly reminded of Bas. Where was he? She'd heard the shot before she'd been attacked. Was he injured? Or captured?

Dangerously distracted, she dwelled on her dark thoughts until they were interrupted by the sound of a door opening and loud footsteps crossing the wood-planked floor.

"What are you doing?" a male voice demanded.

She felt a hand reach down to grab the narrow shoulder strap of her sundress. Damn. Where was the thick robe she'd been wearing?

It'd been hot and scratchy, but it would have kept her from enduring the rough touch of the stranger.

She held her breath, sheer determination keeping her from reacting.

"I've never been this close to a freak," the man next to her said. "I wanted to see if she had any weird mutations."

"Christ," the first man muttered. "You're the freak. Get away from her."

"She's tiny, but she has all the right parts. We could have some fun before Roy gets back."

"She's our prisoner, not your toy."

"No reason she can't be both," the man muttered, his hand tightening on the strap. As if he was debating the pleasure of ripping off her dress.

She covertly tensed. She'd fight them both if she had to, but no one was going to treat her as a toy.

"You're an insult to the Brotherhood," the first man said with blatant disdain.

"And you're a dried-up pissant," the nearest man snapped.

"We've been camped out here for two weeks. I'm tired of my hand."

There was the sound of footsteps again as yet another male entered the room.

"Is there a problem here?" he asked, the edge of authority in his voice revealing he was the leader.

Her strap was abruptly released. "No problem."

"Good, then you can take a turn on guard duty."

"But, Roy, I—"

The whining came to an abrupt end as Myst sensed Roy move forward. There was a small scuffle, then a pained grunt as the male who'd tried to strip her was tossed from the cottage and the door slammed shut.

"Did he hurt her?" Roy demanded of the first male.

"No, but he's untrustworthy."

"Damn. He might have to have an unexpected accident before we return home."

"You've spoken to the leader?"

"Finally," Roy muttered. "It took her long enough to return my call."

Her? Myst felt a stab of surprise.

She'd assumed it was the Brotherhood who'd kidnapped her, but she'd never heard of them allowing a woman to become their leader.

"What did she say?"

"We're supposed to bring the clairvoyant back to the ranch," Roy answered, making Myst cringe. The ranch had to be the compound in Wyoming where they had kept her trapped in the mine shaft. No way in hell she was going back there.

"Thank God," the first male muttered. "I'm tired of sharing a tent with half a dozen Brothers who haven't showered in two weeks."

"But first she wants us to kill her companion."

Myst felt a jolt of sheer terror before it was abruptly replaced by sharp-edged relief. Bas was still alive. That knowledge was all that mattered.

After all, she fully intended to escape. She could warn him of the danger before they could track him down.

"Why bother with him?" the first male demanded. "He didn't see us."

"He was a high-blood, probably a Sentinel. It's possible he might be able to track her."

"A warrior?" There was no missing the edge of fear in the male's voice. Which proved he wasn't stupid. "Do you think it's possible?"

"I don't intend to take any chances," Roy muttered, not sounding any more excited than his companion at the thought of facing a Sentinel. "I have double guards on duty for tonight. We'll leave for Paris at first light. I'm not going to breathe easy until we have the woman locked in a cell at the ranch."

There was a long silence, as if the male was carefully considering his words.

"I have to admit I'm surprised," he at last said.

"Why?"

"I thought the new leader was sending us on a wild goose chase when she told us the clairvoyant would be at the old farmhouse," he said, thankfully too consumed with his own thoughts to hear Myst's tiny gasp of shock. "I never dreamed we would gain such a mighty prize."

They knew. . . .

Myst forced herself to accept the stunning realization that someone had told the Brotherhood she was traveling to meet Boggs.

But who?

Before she could even begin to guess who had betrayed her, Roy was speaking.

"She won't be mighty until she gives us the weapon," he muttered.

"There's been no word on what the mysterious weapon is supposed to be?"

"Not to me." Roy gave a sharp laugh. "Of course, I'm just a lowly soldier."

Myst clenched her teeth. God. She wished they did know what the weapon was. Once she understood the danger, she could work to avoid her fate.

"It's odd the leader knew where to find the clairvoyant but can't tell us how the high-blood is going to help us defeat Valhalla," the first male muttered.

"Maybe you should ask her when we get back," Roy suggested.

The companion sucked in a horrified breath. "I don't think so."

"Wise choice," Roy muttered. "The leader may be a female, but she's more ruthless than Gilbert could have ever hoped to be."

There was another awkward pause. Then the first male cleared his throat.

"Do you think the rumors are true?"

"Rumors?"

"That Stella was responsible for Gilbert's—"

"Don't say it," Roy interrupted in harsh tones. "Don't even fucking think it. Not unless you want to end up in the pit." There was a stark pause. "Or worse."

"Fine," the male muttered. "I'm going to pack my things. The sooner we can get out of here, the better."

"Agreed," Roy said as they walked across the floor and out the door.

Left alone, Myst continued to feign sleep. She couldn't be sure the males wouldn't return. Or that they wouldn't send in another guard to keep watch on her.

She was still lying there when she heard the soft sound

of a footstep from the back of the cottage. She stiffened before she caught a familiar scent.

Her eyes snapped open, her heart lodging in her throat. "Bas?"

"I'm here, *cara*," he whispered, moving to crouch beside the cot. In the dim light she could make out the grim expression on his finely chiseled features and the bronze eyes that abruptly flared with a combustible fury. "You're hurt."

"Just my face," she hastily assured him, not bothering to analyze her acute joy at the sight of him.

She could tell herself it was relief that she was going to be rescued, but she knew without a doubt that wasn't true. She was a strong, independent woman who'd been taking care of herself her entire life. She didn't need any male to rescue her.

Which meant her joy was something far more dangerous.

And this wasn't the time to worry about it.

Thankfully unaware of her crazy thoughts, Bas reached out to gently touch her cheek where one of the pieces of flying glass had sliced through her skin.

"I'm going to fucking kill them," he rasped.

"No." She reached to grasp his wrist, her heart squeezing with fear. What'd happened to the cold, always logical Bas? Right now he looked angry enough to take on the entire Brotherhood. Even if that meant putting his life in jeopardy. "I just want out of here."

The air vibrated with his barely leashed hunger for violence, but with a visible effort he relaxed his coiled muscles and gave a slow nod.

"First, I need to check for guards," he murmured softly.

"Be careful," she ridiculously warned. As if the assassin needed to be told how to do his job. "They're expecting you to try and rescue me."

He straightened, a hard smile of anticipation curling his lips.

"Good."

She gave a shake of her aching head as Bas silently moved across the room and slid out the door.

"Men," she muttered, managing to push herself to a seated position on the cot, her glance taking a quick inventory of her surroundings.

She'd been right to guess she was being held in a cottage, although that was a generous term for the shabby one-room building with peeling plaster and a warped floor.

There was also a decided lack of handy weapons.

Not that she needed one, she wryly acknowledged, watching as the door opened just far enough for Bas to toss an unconscious human on the floor before disappearing back into the dark. Less than ten minutes later he'd repeated the process three more times.

Then, stepping over the pile of bodies, he crossed the floor to bend down and scoop her into his arms.

"Let's go."

Even aware that he was a trained Sentinel, Myst had to admit she was impressed. He'd neatly disposed of four guards and now he was carrying her out of the cottage and jogging toward the thick line of trees.

And he wasn't even breathing hard.

Keeping a watch over his shoulder, Myst could see several humans seated around a large campfire while others were cheering on two males who were taking pleasure in punching each other in the face.

None of them seemed aware that their prize was slipping from their grasp.

She waited until she and Bas had become lost in the darkness of the trees before she broke the silence.

"I can walk," she said in soft tones.

"Not as fast as I can," he countered, his body stiffening as there was the sudden sound of footsteps behind them. "Shit," he growled, tightening his arms around her. "Hold on."

Darting forward, Bas weaved his way through the trees with a liquid grace that the humans could never hope to duplicate. Unfortunately, they had the benefit of weapons they didn't hesitate to use.

"Bas," she cried out as the peaceful night was shattered in an explosion of gunfire.

"Keep your head down," he commanded, leaping over a narrow stream as the bullets whizzed past them.

She wrapped her arms around his neck, burrowing close as she sent up a silent prayer he wouldn't be hit. A bullet might not kill him, but he could bleed to death like any mortal in this remote area.

Her prayer was answered only seconds later.

"Stop shooting, you idiots," Roy ordered in a pissed-off voice. "He has the clairvoyant. We need her alive."

For the first time in fifteen years, Myst was happy the stupid Brotherhood needed her.

After running through the woods for over an hour, Bas knew he was nearing his limit.

Despite his formidable strength, the drugs in his system were taking their toll, not to mention his intense fury as he'd followed Myst's trail into the Brotherhood camp.

He'd wanted to destroy each of them with his bare hands. To rip them apart for daring to attack his female. Not at all the calm, cool, and collected assassin he'd trained to be.

As if sensing his weariness, Myst lifted her head from his chest to study him with a concerned frown.

"We have to stop, Bas."

He nodded his head toward the distant lights he could see through the tree trunks.

"There's a town just ahead," he assured her, pressing his lips to the top of her head.

Despite the danger they'd been in, he'd taken a savage pride in carrying her in his arms as they'd escaped. Idiotic, of course. He wasn't a teenage human with the childish need to prove his manhood. Or even a self-sacrificing Sentinel who'd sworn to serve and protect.

He was a killer. Pure and simple.

But with Myst he wanted . . . what?

He gave a sharp shake of his head as he cautiously made his way down a steep slope and followed the bank of a river toward the sleepy village. He wasn't going to worry about his illogical responses when it came to this female. Not until the danger had passed and he could return to his life as a ruthless mercenary.

Keeping to the shadows, he easily spotted the three-story house that had been transformed into a bed and breakfast. Entering the side garden, he lowered Myst to her feet and briefly closed his eyes, using his finely honed senses to assure him that no one was near.

Not that he could fully trust his instincts. He'd only sensed a vague disturbance in the air as a warning before he was attacked at the farmhouse.

Still, he didn't have any choice but to hope they were alone.

"I need you to stay here and wait for me," he murmured softly.

She tilted back her head, the moonlight playing over her pale, perfect face.

"Why?"

He was abruptly seized by an almost uncontrollable urge to lean down and capture her lips in a searing kiss. As if to assure himself she was safe and once again in his care.

Madness.

Myst was clearly still weakened from the drugs she'd

been given and in need of a bath and a warm place to sleep. Not to mention the fact that there was the smell of impending rain in the air.

The sooner he had a room the better.

Taking a step back, he forced himself to concentrate on his magic, weaving a spell of illusion. With practiced ease he altered his features, making them pleasantly plump and lined with age. He thinned his hair and turned his eyes to a pale blue. His body was equally transformed into a dumpy shape that was covered in clerical black pants and black shirt with a white collar tab.

To the world he suddenly appeared to be an elderly priest.

"When the Brotherhood comes looking for us they won't ask about a lone, elderly priest," he answered her demand to know why he wanted her to wait in the garden. "I'll let you in the back door once I have a key to the room."

"Okay," she muttered.

He arched a brow. No argument? She truly must be ready to collapse.

Giving one last glance toward the empty street, Bas entered the building, forced awake the manager to request a key. There was a brief delay as he was told that the rooms were all filled, but at last accepting that Bas wasn't going away, the manager gave him the key to the attic.

Tottering out of the lobby, Bas waited until he was certain the manager was once again snoozing in his chair. Then, moving through a small parlor, he pulled open a door and gestured for Myst.

Not hesitating, she hurried across the garden and slipped through the door. Bas wrapped an arm around her shoulders and urged her toward the nearby stairs. In silence they climbed to the top floor.

There were a few squeaky steps, and the scent of old furniture polish was thick in the air, but the owners had maintained the old-world charm with the original wooden paneling on the walls and an ornately carved banister.

Thankfully, they'd also had the attic converted into a comfortable space with a small sitting area at one end that had a brocade couch and matching chair. And at the other end of the long, narrow room a brass bed was tucked beneath the eaves. There was also a detached bathroom with a claw-foot tub and small washstand.

Most guests would no doubt find it charming, although it could hardly match his own elegant chain of hotels in America, and the steeply slanted ceilings were most certainly not intended for a man well over six foot.

Glancing down at Myst's pale face, he gave her a gentle push toward the bathroom.

"Take a hot bath," he murmured. "It will help to ease the cramps in your muscles."

She frowned. "But you were the one who carried me. . . ." She allowed her words to trail away with a sigh, no doubt catching sight of his uncompromising expression. "Never mind. I'm too weary to argue."

He reached to grasp a silver curl that nestled against her cheek, giving it a light tug.

"A miracle."

With a roll of her eyes she entered the bathroom, firmly closing the door behind her.

For a crazed moment Bas lingered in the middle of the room, listening to the sounds of water filling the tub and the subtle whisper of Myst's sundress sliding down her body.

He instantly hardened, his feet taking a compulsive step toward the bathroom before he was jerking back and swiftly forcing himself to leave the room.

Christ, where was the iron control he'd always taken

such pride in? His cool, aloof ability to smirk at the lesser creatures at the mercy of their emotions?

Right now he'd give his vast fortune for one night with Myst in his arms.

Covertly slipping out of the building, he headed down the main street. He paused long enough to borrow clean clothing from an elegant boutique. Okay, some might call it stealing. Bas didn't care as long as Myst had something clean and comfortable to wear. Then, he headed to the bakery on the corner where there was already a light burning.

Within half an hour he was back in the converted attic, tossing aside the clothing and setting out the warm croissants, fresh butter, honey, and hot tea on a small table in front of the couch.

He'd just finished when the door to the bathroom was pulled open and Myst warily stepped into the main room. Bas sucked in a sharp breath, feeling as if he'd been slugged in the stomach.

Holy hell.

Even though her slender body was covered from neck to toe in the large guest robe, her face was rosy from her recent bath and her hair was left free to tumble down her back, shimmering like moonlight in the shadowed room.

Their gazes locked, both acutely aware of the desire that smoldered just below the surface. The air heated with the intensity of his need, but even as he was calculating how quickly he could wrestle her out of the robe, she was jerkily moving past him to settle on the sofa.

"This smells amazing," she murmured, busying herself with slathering a croissant with the butter and honey before sipping the tea. "Where did you get it?"

Heaving a rueful sigh, he settled on the cushion beside her. The warm bath and the food were clearly restoring her flagging energy, but she was still trying to pretend they weren't both on the edge of going up in flames.

"The small bakery down the street was willing to take mercy on a poor old priest," he said. "It's fresh out of the oven. I will reimburse them and the boutique that supplied your clothes eventually."

She polished off two croissants and her cup of tea before leaning back with a small yawn.

"That was delicious, thank you."

He was reaching toward her before he could halt the movement, tucking her hair behind her ear.

"How do you feel?"

"Better." Her cheeks heated as his fingers brushed down the curve of her neck, lingering on the pulse that beat at the base of her throat. "I think the drugs are almost gone."

"They should be completely out of your system in a few hours," he assured her, his hand cupping her delicate cheek as a blast of fury trembled through him. "Bastards," he hissed, once again consumed by a fierce urge to track down the Brotherhood and destroy them.

Slowly, painfully.

Her lashes lowered in a belated attempt to hide the hunger that flared through her dark eyes.

"I overheard my captors talking," she said, no doubt hoping to distract him. As if anything less than a nuclear bomb could divert the increasingly painful need. "They had some way to know that we were going to be at the farmhouse."

"Yeah, Kaede heard the same thing," he muttered, his brooding gaze locked on her mouth. "He called Valhalla to warn the Mave when he couldn't get ahold of us. Unfortunately, it was too late."

She shivered as his thumb brushed her lower lip. "How did they know?"

"They have a new leader who claims to have a direct connection to God."

She abruptly glanced up, her eyes wide. "She speaks to God?"

He gave a dismissive shrug. "It's a predictable tool to keep her followers loyal to the cause. Kaede's working to discover the truth of how she's getting her information."

Her brow furrowed as she considered the various possibilities, easily coming to the same conclusion he had.

"It had to have come from Valhalla," she breathed.

"Lana swears it couldn't have come from there," he said, his voice distracted.

He didn't want to waste their time alone talking about the Brotherhood or the potential betrayal of Valhalla.

Hell, he didn't want to be talking at all.

Without warning, Myst stiffened. "You spoke with the Mave?"

Bas frowned at her unmistakable annoyance. Then, realizing what had caused her irritation, he felt a burst of smug satisfaction.

His beautiful clairvoyant was jealous.

"Briefly," he murmured.

"She—"

"It's a worry for another day, *cara*," he interrupted, done with the conversation. In this moment they were alone, and safe, and conveniently close to a bed. He was done waiting. Rising from the sofa, he grabbed her hand and gently tugged her to her feet. "We should get some rest."

Her tongue peeked out to wet her lips. Bas swallowed a groan, his cock pressing against the zipper of his slacks.

"We're staying here?" she demanded.

"Yes." His thumb brushed her inner wrist, covertly tugging her closer. "The Brotherhood will expect us to be on the run. It's safer to stay here until the initial search moves on."

She hesitated, as if trying to consider the flaw in his plan. Then, at last, she gave a slow, grudging nod.

"I suppose that makes sense."

His lips twitched. "Then why are you so nervous?"

She glanced toward the far side of the room. "There's only one bed."

"It's big enough for both of us," he murmured, his fingers skimming up her arm. "We might have to squish together, but . . ."

She tried to glare in outrage, but he didn't miss her tiny shiver of pleasure, or the leap of her pulse as he traced the gaping neckline of her robe.

"That's not funny," she breathed.

The tips of his fingers rested against the gentle swell of her breasts.

"Are you afraid you won't be able to keep your hands off me?" he teased.

Her dark eyes narrowed. "I'm afraid your oversized ego might smother me in my sleep."

He chuckled, lowering his head to brush his lips over her forehead and down the narrow length of her nose.

"My ego isn't the only thing that's oversized," he said in soft tones. "Do you remember?"

She sucked in a sharp breath. "No."

"I do." He pressed a slow, lingering kiss on her mouth. "I remember every second. From the moment you stepped into my office until you groaned in pleasure as I emptied myself in your body."

"Bas," she breathed, the scent of honeysuckle drenching the air.

"Nothing has ever been so perfect." He lifted his head to study her flushed face with a brooding gaze. "It's no wonder no other woman could capture my interest."

"You shouldn't say that."

He studied her with a curious gaze, not missing the fragile tension that shimmered around her.

"Why not?"

"Because it's a lie," she breathed, her arms wrapping around her in a defensive motion. "I was nothing more than one more female in a very long line."

Anger stabbed through Bas as he abruptly framed her face in his hands.

"Oh no, you don't," he growled, glaring down at her startled expression.

"Bas . . ."

"What we shared was special." He lowered his head until they were nose to nose, the air prickling with the heat of his temper. He might have been pissed for the past five years that this female would dare to walk away from him, but he never, ever underestimated the power of what'd happened between them. "I'm not going to let you ruin it. Admit the truth." His hands slid so he could tangle his fingers in her hair, breathing deep of her honeysuckle scent. "Say it, *cara*."

Her hands lifted, her fingers curling around his wrists. He narrowed his gaze, prepared for her to deny the truth.

For whatever reason, she was determined to believe he was a villain. Maybe it was the same reason he'd tried to convince himself she was a heartless bitch.

Survival.

But she managed to throw him off balance when she licked her lips and breathed out the words that eased the empty ache that'd plagued him since her disappearance.

"I . . . it was special."

"That's better," he whispered, brushing her lips in a light kiss before pulling back far enough to gaze deep into her eyes. "When I say there's been no one else, I mean it."

Her hands tentatively lifted, fluttering like butterflies before they finally came to rest on his chest.

"You haven't been with another woman?" she asked.

His lips twisted. He wasn't sure why he'd confessed that little tidbit of information. It wasn't something a male went around bragging about, but her brittle attempt to view him as some sort of ruthless sex addict had struck a nerve.

Now, catching sight of the vulnerable fear she was so desperately trying to hide, he was glad he'd told her.

"Not since a silver-haired clairvoyant disappeared with my desire," he admitted, stepping forward so her hands slid up to his shoulders and he could feel the sweet press of her breasts against his chest. Instantly his cock hardened, a fierce hunger twisting his gut. "Now I intend to make up for lost time."

She shivered, her nails unconsciously digging into his flesh. Not that Bas objected to the pinpricks of pain. Desire curled through the pit of his stomach, heating his blood.

"I thought we were going to rest," she breathed.

His hands traced the delicate line of her shoulders before smoothing down her sides.

"Is that what you want?" he demanded, tugging the sash that held the robe together.

Her eyes darkened, her breath leaving her lips on a tiny sigh. "No."

"Thank God," he rasped, already feeling as if he was on fire.

He didn't know what it was about this female, but she set off a chain reaction within him that was impossible to combat.

Hell, if he was honest, he didn't want to combat it. Why would he? The excitement that seeped through him by just having her near was addictive. Now that he held her in his arms it was saturating him in sheer lust.

He was a junkie and Myst was his high.

Skimming his hands up her back, he burrowed his fingers beneath the robe and slid it over her shoulders. On cue the garment fluttered down the length of her body to pool at her feet.

Oh . . . hell.

His heart forgot to beat as his gaze slid over the slim curves that were perfectly formed.

Holy shit.

She was stunning.

Her milky skin shimmering in the low glow of the lamp. The small, perfectly formed breasts tipped by rosy nipples. And a narrow waist he could span with his hands.

Just as he remembered every night in his dreams.

Not that there weren't a few changes. There was an added curve to her hips that came from carrying their beloved daughter, and a newfound maturity in the way she carried herself.

His cock twitched. If she'd been gorgeous five years ago, now she was staggeringly beautiful.

Half afraid he might be jerked awake to discover that this was just another fantasy, he gently palmed her breasts.

"You are exquisite," he rasped, molding the small globes as he sucked in a deep breath drenched in honeysuckle. "I ache for you."

Her lips parted on a tiny gasp, her face flushed as she quivered beneath his touch.

"Bas."

He slowly dipped his head, allowing his tongue to touch the pulse fluttering at the base of her throat. He smiled as he felt her jerk in surprise at the electric pleasure that jolted between them.

He traced his lips up her throat, finding a sensitive hollow beneath her ear before at last covering her mouth in a kiss that hinted at pleasure yet to come.

"No more talking." He nuzzled the corner of her mouth, his fingers finding the hardened nubs of her nipples. She gave a soft groan. He used the tip of his tongue to trace the sumptuous curve of her lower lip. "I've waited far too long to have you back in my arms."

Her mouth parted in an unspoken invitation even as she pulled back her head to meet his smoldering gaze with a frown.

"You should know that I still have the same spell I had when I got pregnant with Molly," she murmured.

He frowned at her strange words.

"And?"

"And I can't be certain it isn't faulty."

Without warning a savage surge of satisfaction raced through him.

There was no way she wouldn't have seen a witch to ensure her birth control was working properly if she had taken another lover.

"Good," he said, his voice thickening as he continued to tease her sensitive nipples, watching her eyes darken with hunger that matched his own. "I hope it is faulty."

She blinked, clearly having difficulty following his conversation.

"What?"

"We make beautiful babies, *cara*."

Taking swift advantage of her dumbfounded reaction to his blunt admission, Bas reached down to scoop her off her feet, heading toward the narrow bed tucked beneath the sharply angled ceiling.

It was going to be a wonder if he didn't knock himself out on one of the open beams.

Leaning forward, he gently laid her on the mattress before crouching beside the bed.

"Your hair fascinates me," he murmured, allowing his fingers to run through the silver strands, carefully spreading them over the pillow. "And your skin." His fingers drifted over her cheek. "I've never seen such flawless perfection."

She watched him with dark, hungry eyes, unconsciously licking her lips.

His cock twitched in instant response. Christ, what he wouldn't do to have her take him in between those lush lips.

"I thought we weren't talking?"

A beat passed before he tilted back his head to laugh with rich enjoyment.

The first time they'd been together it'd been all about heat and need and swift gratification. This time there was a far deeper connection.

Not only because they shared a child whom they both loved, but because now he knew what caused the haunted shadows in the velvet depths of her eyes, and the boundless courage beneath her fragile appearance.

He not only lusted after her, he actually admired her.

Holding her gaze, he slowly tugged his shirt out of his pants and unbuttoned it. Peeling it off, he tossed it aside before he was moving to perch on the edge of the mattress. He kicked off his shoes and pulled off his socks, then, careful to stand where he wouldn't whack his head, he slid down the zipper of his trousers.

Acutely aware of her heated gaze, he shoved them off his legs along with his silk underwear. Instantly his erection throbbed in anticipation.

He'd gone so long without giving thought to his sexual needs, he'd forgotten how intense the anticipation could be. Now he felt as if he were under some strange compulsion as he leaned a knee on the mattress, gazing down at the female stretched below him like a pagan sacrifice.

Myst stirred restlessly beneath his unwavering scrutiny.

"Is something wrong?" she asked in husky tones.

"I want to take it slow," he muttered. "I want to savor every second." He leaned down to claim her mouth in a deep, searching kiss. He shuddered. Her lips tasted of honey and pure womanly temptation. An intoxicating combination. "Last time, I assumed we would have as long as we desired to explore one another." He brushed his lips over her cheek, her temple, and her forehead, memorizing each finely molded feature. "I'm not making the same mistake again."

"I couldn't stay," she muttered, sounding as if she was speaking more to herself than him. "You refused to give me a job."

"I didn't want you as my employee," he chided, his hand wrapping around her throat in a gesture that was pure possession to a high-blood. "I wanted you to be my lover."

Chapter Ten

Myst stared up at the magnificent man poised above her, the mere thought of creating another baby with him making her heart twist with a bittersweet longing.

It was impossible, of course. She'd already been forced to give up one child. It would destroy her to have to walk away from another.

Still . . .

"Bas."

"Shh." He leaned down to press a kiss to her lips before skimming his lips with a heart-stopping gentleness to the small design tattooed just behind her ear. The mark was the visible display for the spell that was supposed to keep her from getting pregnant. "We'll deal with any repercussions together."

Myst groaned as he dipped his tongue into her mouth, shutting out the whispers of warning.

After all, what were the chances of the spell failing again? Any risks were virtually nonexistent.

Right?

Shoving aside the fear, she instead relished the erotic sensations that reverberated through her as he used his tongue to trace the shell of her ear.

For five long years she'd tried to deny the needs of her body. Something that'd been remarkably easy. At least it'd been easy until she'd walked into Bas's hotel room.

Now she vividly recalled why she'd so eagerly tumbled into his arms the first time.

In this moment she didn't want to think about unplanned pregnancies, or being on the run from the Brotherhood, or the fear that she was just a meaningless body to this male.

No other male could make her feel like this, and if it was only for this one night, she intended to seize the moment.

Her thoughts shattered as he stretched out beside her, his fingers gently stroking down her arm. She shuddered, her body clenching with anticipation.

She'd been ridiculously innocent the first time she'd shared her body with Bas. She hadn't been prepared for the overwhelming pleasure that had exploded through her. This time, she was able to fully appreciate Bas's skillful touch.

Not that there wasn't still overwhelming pleasure.

It was shimmering through her with a sharp-edged need that was demanding satisfaction.

Ignoring the whispers of warning in the back of her mind, Myst placed her hands on his chest, exploring the satin heat of his skin.

"I want this," she assured him, relishing her power as he shuddered beneath her touch. "I want you."

He lifted his head to study her with a fierce need.

Myst's breath tangled in her throat as his burning bronze gaze swept slowly over her naked body.

Good Lord, he was spectacular. His shoulders were broad. His chest was sculpted and his abs formed a perfect washboard. He had a narrow waist and hips that led to long, muscular legs.

Her gaze was abruptly captured by the thick erection that made her clench in anticipation.

It'd been so long.

So painfully long.

"I don't know what you do to me," she whispered, unaware she was speaking out loud.

"I assure you the feeling is mutual, *cara*." He threaded his fingers through her hair. "I've never wanted anyone like I want you."

His words melted any lingering hesitation. Who knew what the future would bring? For tonight she wasn't going to let it rule her.

Easily sensing the last of her barriers had crumbled, Bas bent his head to brand her lips in a kiss that demanded utter surrender.

He rolled on top of her, molding her into the mattress. She groaned in bliss.

The scorching heat of his skin branded her with a shattering pleasure, the graze of his fingers down her throat sending erotic sparks in their wake. A near-painful arousal rushed through her as his fingers traced the line of her collarbone, the scent of his male power clouding her mind.

"This is what I've been waiting for." He cupped one breast in his hand, taking her nipple into his mouth.

Myst hissed in shock at the feel of his teeth closing over the tip, the tiny pain arrowing straight between her legs. His touch was magic.

Pure magic.

Sliding her hands up and over his shoulders, she explored the hard muscles of his back. Satisfaction pierced her heart at his muttered growl of pleasure. She wasn't alone in her madness.

Bas wanted her just as desperately as she wanted him.

Somehow that fact was intensely important to her.

"I didn't expect this to happen again," she muttered.

He lifted his head to smile with rueful humor.

"Neither did I . . . until you walked into my hotel room." He held her gaze. "Then it became inevitable."

"Yes." A craving she hadn't experienced for five long years squeezed the air from her lungs.

But it wasn't the intensity of her reaction to Bas that she found unnerving. It was the odd sense of homecoming she felt in his arms.

As if this was the place she was destined to be.

No. She couldn't let herself think that way. Not unless she wanted a broken heart on top of everything else.

"Bas—"

"It's my turn to remind you that we're not supposed to be talking, *cara*." He kissed her, thrusting his tongue between her lips. Myst moaned, arching her body in greedy pleasure as his hands stroked over her naked body with a possessive boldness. "Just enjoy."

Anticipation licked through her like wildfire, the sheer force of his demands overriding her annoying inner voice.

Enjoy . . .

She allowed her eyes to slide shut, intent on the feel of his fingers circling her tightened nipples, and the thrust of his erection that pressed against her lower stomach. With every caress he was spiking her desire higher and higher, making her ache for completion.

Scoring her fingernails up his back, Myst concentrated on making this night one that she could dream about for years to come.

"You taste of honeysuckle," he whispered, thrusting his thigh between her legs to press at her most sensitive flesh. "So sweet."

"I'm not always sweet," she husked.

"Good." He pressed a soft kiss to her nipple that still tingled from his small bite, then slid his mouth downward. "Tonight I want you wicked."

Her heart thundered in her chest. She felt wicked. And utterly wanton.

She lifted her hips in a silent invitation. "How wicked?"

"We're about to discover," he promised, kissing a path down the center of her stomach.

Myst rubbed against the hard muscle of his thigh. "Bas, I need you."

She tugged on his hair, trying to urge him up so she could kiss him. He refused to budge. Lifting his head, he studied her flushed face with a brooding gaze.

"I want to taste you, Myst. Last time I was too impatient. Tonight I want to explore every satin inch of you."

A violent surge of excitement exploded through her at the thought of him crouched between her legs, his tongue sliding over her swollen clit.

Oh, yes. That's exactly what she wanted.

As if reading her X-rated thoughts, Bas slid lower, keeping careful watch on her expression. She shivered at the raw tenderness that lurked in the depths of his bronze eyes.

As if he . . . cared.

She squashed the dangerous thought. Tonight was about pleasure and need, not emotions.

He settled between her legs, his hands gripping her inner thighs as he ran his tongue through her damp heat. She nearly jerked off the bed at the powerful shock of bliss that cascaded through her.

Her entire body was on fire. She needed more.

She needed him buried deep inside her.

"Please, Bas."

He chuckled, swiping his tongue over her tender bud. "Patience, *cara*."

Her toes curled, a delicious force swelling beneath the stroke of his tongue. "It's too much."

"I'm just starting," he muttered, pushing his tongue deep inside her.

Myst made a sound of dazed need, her gaze riveted to the sight of him lying between her legs. He continued to tongue her even as he watched the emotions flicker over her face.

Nothing had ever, ever felt so good.

"Come for me, Myst," he commanded, pressing his tongue deep inside her body. On cue, a brutal orgasm burst through her, making her body shake from the sheer joy.

She cried out, trembling from head to toe at the glorious release.

Still, Bas wasn't done. His tongue pushed in and out of her body, swiftly teasing her back toward another climax.

She groaned as he turned his attention to her swollen nub and gently sucked it, at the same time sinking a finger deep into her body.

Myst hissed out a groan. It was too much. He was wrapping her in his sensual possession. How would she ever be free again?

He turned his head to nibble at her inner thigh, his voice a low growl. "You're ready?"

"Yes. I want you inside me."

He chuckled, giving her one last, lingering lick before he was sliding upward. He paused to kiss the tip of each tightly budded nipple before he reached down to tug her legs apart, his gentleness not hiding the grim urgency that clenched his features.

Dazedly feeling as if this was yet another fantasy, Myst grounded herself by grasping his shoulders, and concentrated on the stark beauty of his face. The elegant features that were flushed with passion, the satin darkness of his hair that fell across his forehead, and the bronze fire of his eyes.

There would never be another male who could replace him.

The thought had barely formed when he plunged into her wet channel with one hard surge of his hips.

She made a sound of shock at the sensation of being conquered. Possessed with a ruthless intimacy.

As if they were one.

He held perfectly still, their gazes tangled as something seemed to pass between them. An emotion she refused to name.

"You are so perfect," he finally groaned, slowly beginning to thrust in and out of her. He watched her face, his sweat-drenched body trembling. "Are you okay?"

She nodded, unable to speak.

He muttered beneath his breath as he spread her legs even wider. Then, surging forward, he impaled her with a fierce, unrelenting pace.

She sank her nails into his back, arching to meet his hard thrusts. A swelling hunger raced through her as her body easily accepted his invasion. He dipped his head down to claim her mouth with an openmouthed kiss.

He was dominating and raw and intense in his passion.

And she loved it. Myst wrapped her legs around his pistoning hips, astonished to discover another massive orgasm was rapidly clenching her lower muscles.

"Christ, I've missed you, *cara*," he muttered against her lips, their bodies moving together with a primitive force.

Her fingers tangled in his hair as his hands slipped beneath her butt to tilt her to an angle that allowed him to thrust even deeper.

His cock hit a magical spot she didn't even realize she possessed, sending her vaulting over the edge, the orgasm ripping through her as she cried out his name in stunned pleasure.

Lana ignored the weariness that made her feet feel oddly clumsy as she walked down the long corridor. It was an unfamiliar sensation. Usually her power made her feel so buoyed with energy that she could barely sit still.

Of course, considering the amount of magic she'd used over the past few hours, it was amazing she had the strength to move at all. Most other witches would already have collapsed.

Concentrating on placing one foot in front of the other, she took the elevator downward, a file folder held in one hand. The bulk of Valhalla was hidden below the surface of the large pentagon-shaped structure above ground. The lowest level was reserved for the secretive Sentinels as well as the large stash of weapons they kept hidden from prying eyes. The levels in between were taken up by private apartments, offices, a hospital, gym, and a vast library.

Lana was headed to the second level where the Master of Gifts had claimed a dozen offices.

Calder, the current Master, was in charge of tracing highbloods around the world. His people had a rare ability to sense even the smallest spark of power in others. Usually all they did was log the person in to a database that included their name and talent. There was no law that said a high-blood had to live at Valhalla or a satellite compound.

There were times, however, that a high-blood had to be brought in if their powers were a danger to themselves or others. Or if they'd broken the law.

When that was necessary, Calder would send a hunter Sentinel to track down the high-blood.

Almost as if the thought of Sentinels had conjured up their aggravating leader, Lana heard the sound of approaching footsteps and caught the unmistakable scent of raw male power.

Ridiculously, she kept moving forward, as if she could ignore the male rapidly gaining ground on her. She'd have better luck trying to ignore an impending avalanche.

Proving her point, she felt slender fingers grasp her

upper arm, pulling her to an abrupt halt and turning her to confront Wolfe's grim expression.

Treacherous heat spiked through her body at his touch even as she fiercely kept her face smoothed of all emotion. Every day it seemed harder and harder to control her reaction to this male.

"Wolfe." She arched a brow. "Do you need something?"

The Tagos narrowed his eyes to ruthless slits. A sure sign he wasn't happy. As if the heat that sizzled against her skin wasn't warning enough.

"We need to speak."

"Perhaps later."

"Now."

With an arrogance shocking even for this male, Wolfe was tugging her across the corridor and into an empty office. He closed the door behind them, reaching to snap on a small lamp on a nearby table.

Lana barely noticed the tidy room with the oak desk and two deep leather chairs set near the floor-to-ceiling book-case. She was far too busy glaring at her companion.

She was furious at being manhandled.

That's why her heart was racing and butterflies fluttered in the pit of her stomach, right?

It couldn't be because her fingers ached to trace the copper features that reminded her of an Egyptian deity. Or to thread through the silky black hair with the striking silver streak that had always fascinated her.

No.

Dammit. She was the Mave. She wasn't allowed to notice a male as anything more than a tool to be used for her people.

Tilting her chin, she deliberately pulled her arm from his lingering grasp.

"Do I have to remind you who I am?"

Wolfe stepped forward, invading her space and allowing his power to wrap around her like a physical force.

"You can if you want to, but it would be a waste of your breath."

She scowled. Wolfe enjoyed getting under her skin. He was a male who lived on the edge. In every aspect of his life.

But he rarely pressed beyond the barriers she'd firmly established.

"What's wrong with you?" she demanded.

"You," he growled, leaning down until they were nose to nose. "You're what's wrong with me."

She blinked in shock. "What?"

"When was the last time you ate?"

"Excuse me?"

"It's a simple question."

His breath brushed her cheek, sending tiny jolts of awareness down her spine.

This was dangerous. So . . . dangerous.

Instinctively she took a step away from the disturbing male, her back hitting the glossy paneling.

"I don't remember," she muttered.

His hand landed on the wall next to her head as he once again leaned into her.

"I do," he growled. "It was over twenty-four hours ago."

Her brows snapped together. Had he been spying on her? Or had her personal chef been tattling? Neither possibility made her happy.

"How do you know?"

Predictably he ignored her question. "It's also been forty-eight hours since you last slept."

Dammit. He *had* been spying on her.

She lifted her free hand to press it against his chest. "You're not my father, Wolfe," she snapped.

His lips twisted, his heat pounding against her palm as his gaze lowered to the low-cut neckline of her sleeveless sweater. She deliberately chose clothing that revealed the witch mark, which shimmered with a brilliant emerald sheen. It never hurt to remind her people of her power.

Only Wolfe could make her feel soft and feminine and sexually vulnerable.

"I have never once, in all the time I've known you, possessed any fatherly feelings toward you." His low words sent a renegade awareness tingling through her body.

She clenched her teeth. "Then stop fussing."

"It's my job to protect you," he reminded her in stark tones. "Even if it's from your stubborn refusal to take care of yourself."

Lana grimaced. He had a point. The Tagos was directly responsible for ensuring the well-being of the Mave. And she might have appreciated his attempt to play the mother hen if it didn't threaten to undermine her icy command over her emotions.

She couldn't allow herself to become addicted to Wolfe's unwavering concern.

She couldn't rely on anyone.

"I will eat and rest after my meeting with Calder," she said, holding his gaze until he took a reluctant step backward.

He glanced toward the file folder in her hand. "Why are you meeting with the Master of Gifts?"

"Kaede contacted me earlier."

Wolfe was on instant alert. "What did he discover?"

The constriction that was making it difficult to breathe slowly eased as Wolfe deliberately leashed his raw, male power.

"He thinks the leader of the Brotherhood is hiding a high-blood."

Wolfe's jaw tightened. "A captive?"

Lana gave a slow shake of her head. None of them

wanted to believe that one of their own could be anything but completely loyal.

Unfortunately the past months had proven that high-bloods were just as likely to betray their people as humans.

"He didn't think so," she admitted.

The ebony eyes smoldered with revulsion. "A traitor?"

"It's possible."

"Shit," Wolfe bit out.

Yeah. That about summed it up.

"Kaede managed to take a picture on his cell phone and send it to me," she said.

His brows snapped together. "Why didn't you tell me?"

She didn't take offense at his annoyance. She rarely kept information from him.

"It was at a distance and the man was standing in the shadows," she explained. "Thankfully I had enough to work with to conjure a clearer image."

Unexpectedly his finger reached up to brush the delicate skin beneath her eyes.

"That explains these shadows," he murmured.

She struggled not to react to his light touch, instead recalling the complicated spell that had not only demanded total concentration, but had taken a physical toll.

In the end it'd been worth it.

The fuzzy, too-dark picture had slowly been transformed into an image she hoped would give them a lead on the mysterious high-blood working with the Brotherhood.

She held up the file folder. "Now that I have something to work with, I want to see if Calder can find him in the database."

"Fine." He nodded his head toward the door. "Let's go."

"There's no need for you to—"

Her cool dismissal came to an abrupt end as he wrapped

a hand around her nape and tugged her against the hard length of his body.

"Don't press me, Lana," he warned her in low tones. "I'm very close to carrying you to your rooms and handcuffing you to your bed."

She stiffened in outrage. Or at least she was telling herself it was outrage.

There was no way in hell she was going to admit there might be a traitorous thrill of excitement at his rough grip.

"You think handcuffs could hold me?" she demanded, allowing a hint of her thunderous magic to flicker through the air.

Despite the promise of pain, his fingers tightened on her nape, his eyes smoldering with a barely concealed hunger.

"There are other ways to keep you there." His voice softened to a low whisper, his head lowering until his lips hovered just above her mouth. "Do you want me to explain?"

Desire slammed into her with the force of a freight train, nearly sending her to her knees.

God Almighty, she couldn't remember the last time she'd felt a man's touch. And even then it'd never been like this.

No man could ever compare to Wolfe.

But while her heart raced and her stomach twisted with need, she forced herself to shake her head in denial.

"Wolfe," she softly protested.

The air hummed with the awareness that sparked between them.

"Yes?"

She had to force the words past the lump in her throat. "You have to stop this."

"And if I don't want to?" he murmured.

Time seemed to halt as they stood poised on a knife's

edge, their gazes entangled. Lana understood the danger. One brush of his lips, one caress of his hand, and she would combust.

Her desire for this male had been churning just below the surface for years.

And if she was honest, she'd admit there was a huge part of her that wanted to give in to the madness. Why not? She was a female with the usual needs, no matter how often she tried to deny them.

But she'd made a promise to herself when she'd accepted the position of Mave. A promise that she couldn't toss aside just because it was inconvenient.

"This will never be possible," she whispered.

His fingers tightened, his heat flaring around her. "Never is a long time."

"Don't—"

Her protest didn't have the opportunity to leave her lips before he was abruptly dropping his hand and heading toward the office door.

"Let's show your picture to Calder," he said in smooth tones.

Lana swayed at his sudden withdrawal. Then, with a silent chastisement at allowing Wolfe to knock her off balance, she was stiffening her spine and forcing her feet forward.

"Stubborn," she muttered beneath her breath.

Of course Wolfe heard her. Stupid super-hearing. His lips twitched as he placed his hand on her lower back and urged her out of the office and down the hallway.

"That's why you hired me."

She snorted, recalling the day Wolfe had strolled casually into her office. She'd known from the start he was going to be trouble.

"Actually I think you arrived at Valhalla and told me you were taking control of the Sentinels," she said.

"Someone had to," he assured her. "The monks were willing to accept the philosophy of Valhalla, but they wanted to make sure their warriors had a voice in the decision-making." His thumb brushed intimately against her lower back. "And you have to admit I've been useful."

"On occasion." She sent him a narrow-eyed glare. "You can also be a pain in the ass."

He flashed a wicked smile. "I try."

Chapter Eleven

Bas was lying on his side next to Myst, aimlessly stroking his fingers through her hair as he closely monitored her distracted expression.

They'd had a few hours of sleep, but he was in no hurry to leave the bed. Hell, if it was up to him, they might stay there for the next month.

His lips twisted at the irony.

He'd spent three centuries enjoying transitory relationships with the most beautiful women in the world. They came, they went, and while he was always faithful during their time together, he'd never wanted to simply lie in bed with them and . . . snuggle.

Kaede would laugh himself sick if he could see him now.

Or maybe not, he wryly admitted. His enforcer had been bewitched by Myst. The younger male would no doubt thoroughly appreciate Bas's reluctance to leave the bed.

There was a tiny movement at his side as Myst blinked and slowly turned her head, meeting his unwavering gaze with a hint of surprise.

"I didn't know you were awake," she murmured, a flustered blush staining her cheeks.

His breath lodged in his throat as he was struck again by

her beauty. The early morning sunlight shimmered in her silver hair and deepened the darkness of her eyes. She looked like an angel.

Young and fragile and unbearably tempting.

His fingers trailed down her throat, tracing along the sheet she had clutched to her breasts. As if he hadn't kissed every silky inch of her.

More than once.

The memory instantly had him hard and wanting more.

Yeah, he was a greedy bastard, but who knew when he would have this woman all willing and naked in his bed again?

"Did you speak with Molly?" he murmured.

She stiffened in surprise. "How did you know?"

"Your face gets all soft and gooey."

"Gooey?"

"Yes, gooey." He leaned down to plant a tender, lingering kiss on her mouth. "Is she okay?"

"Yes." A wistful smile touched her lips. "She misses you, but she's enjoying her adventure."

"I feel like a piece of me is missing," he admitted with blunt sincerity. He never tried to hide the fact that his daughter was the center of his world. Not that he was opposed to sharing his attention. Not when it was with the beautiful woman lying next to him. "Of course, there are a few benefits to having a night alone with her mother."

"We should—"

"Finish up what we started?" he interrupted her soft words. He didn't want to hear any sensible suggestions about getting up to shower or eat or contact Valhalla. Instead, he slid his leg over hers, his thickening cock pressing against the side of her hip. "I couldn't agree more."

Her eyes widened, her heart racing loud enough for him to hear it in the silence that cloaked the room.

"That's not what I was going to say," she breathed.

He chuckled, bending his neck to stroke his lips over her heated cheeks. Would there ever come a day when he wasn't utterly beguiled by this female?

History assured him that he would eventually tire of her. It always happened. The initial rush of lust would wear down to tedious boredom. But gazing down at her exquisite face, he couldn't deny a whisper of warning telling him that Myst was so deeply engraved on his soul he would never be rid of her.

"Are you sure?" he teased, using his tongue to trace the line of her stubborn jaw.

A groan was wrenched from her lips. "What are we doing?"

His hand gently tugged the sheet from her clenched fingers, revealing the pale perfection of her slender body. The breath was wrenched from him at the intensity of his need.

He'd made love to her over and over, but he still craved her like she was a drug.

"If you have to ask, then I'm fairly sure I'm doing something wrong," he muttered, planting a line of kisses down the length of her collarbone.

With a shiver she lifted her hands to grasp his shoulders, her nails digging into his flesh with delicious pinpricks of pain.

"I can't afford to waste time," she said.

"Wasting time?" Bas lifted his head, studying her flushed face with a lift of his brows. "I have to admit that's the most original insult a woman has delivered when she's lying in my arms."

She lowered her lashes, no doubt hoping to hide the desire that was darkening her eyes. A wasted effort. Her arousal spiced the air with honeysuckle heat.

"Bas, you know what I mean."

"Where do you suggest we go?" he demanded, his hand skimming up her hip to rest on her lower stomach.

He wasn't praying that she was pregnant. Myst had suffered enough when she'd been forced to be separated from Molly. And until they'd rewritten her future, she would be in constant danger.

But there was a part of him that was already preparing for the day when she was no longer in peril and he could convince her to create another miracle.

Together.

"We need to go back to the farmhouse," she insisted. "We have to speak with Boggs."

His hand moved upward, over her too-prominent ribs, before gently cupping her breast.

"Think, *cara*," he urged in soft tones, smiling as her rose-topped nipple hardened to an enticing nub. "That's exactly where the Brotherhood will be expecting you to go."

She trembled, her tongue reaching out to wet her dry lips. "We can't stay here."

His gaze locked on her lush mouth, spikes of need shooting through him. It shouldn't be possible to want her with such brutal need. Not after he'd sated his passion just a few hours ago.

But he was discovering that Myst shattered all his preconceived ideas of how a relationship should be between a man and woman.

Rolling on top of her naked body, he hissed in pleasure as her legs instinctively parted, allowing the tip of his cock to rest against the entrance of her body.

"It's as safe a place as any to wait for Kaede to discover how our enemies knew where you were going to be," he said, his mouth seeking the racing pulse at the base of her throat.

He fiercely wanted to devour her. To shove deep inside her welcoming heat and lose himself in raw, mindless pleasure. At the same time he wanted to take it slow, savoring each touch. Each kiss.

He decided on the slow, savoring route.

His head lowered to brush a light kiss over her lips. A promise of things to come.

She struggled against the passion that was rapidly spiraling out of control.

"And if Kaede can't discover anything?" she managed to ask.

He kissed the tip of her chin, the seductive dip beneath her ear, and the curve of her upper breast.

"Then we'll have Lana arrange another meeting with Boggs," he murmured against her skin. "Someplace where we can have Sentinels in position to protect you." His exploration at last led him to the puckered tip of her nipple, and, deliberately holding her darkened gaze, he gave it a slow lick. "Okay?"

She shuddered, her back arching in silent invitation. "Okay," she muttered.

He closed his mouth over her nipple, using his teeth and tongue to wrench a cry from her lips.

Lifting his head, he studied her with a blatant hunger. "Any other objections?"

"I . . ." Her breath was released on a low groan as he slowly penetrated her, tilting his hips forward until his cock was buried deep inside her moist channel. "No," she rasped, her arms wrapping around his neck. "No objections."

Lana stood in the center of the Master of Gifts' office with every appearance of serene patience. It was the image that she'd perfected over the years and no one looking at her would ever guess that beneath her calm exterior she was seething with emotion.

Of course, her aloof composure was made considerably

easier by the fact that Wolfe had chosen to remain in the hallway to prevent them from being interrupted. The mere thought of having to share cluttered space with the sizzling dominance of his presence was enough to make her shudder.

It was difficult enough to maintain the barrier between them when they were in their roles of Mave and Tagos. But when he was determined to remind her that she was very much a woman despite her responsibilities, it became almost impossible.

And right now, she needed to concentrate on the threat to her people.

Pretending she couldn't sense the aggravating male who was pacing the floor just outside the closed door, she instead watched the tall, painfully thin man with long gray hair that he'd scraped back into a tail at his nape. He was wearing a pair of dark pants that were wrinkled and a loose cardigan beginning to fray around the edges.

He looked like a typical absentminded professor, although she was well aware there was a brilliant mind beneath his shabby appearance.

At the moment, he was threading his way through the tunnels of books and papers stacked on the tables, desks, and shelves that lined the room as he headed toward the computer beeping loud enough to make Lana flinch.

Thankfully pressing a button on the laptop that brought an end to the alarm, Calder hunched over the desk, a smile of triumph softening his sharp features.

"Ah," he murmured. "I think we have a match."

Lana felt a surge of relief. When she'd given the image to Calder she hadn't been sure the unknown high-blood would be listed in the database. There were far too many of her people who remained fearful of revealing their gifts and preferred to live as a human. Unless one of Calder's staff managed to locate them, they could remain lost in the shadows.

"Who is it?" she demanded, remaining in the center of the room as Calder printed off the information and headed in her direction.

She felt like she was standing in a maze of dominos where one wrong move would send everything toppling into chaos.

"Peter Baldwin," Calder said, coming to a halt at her side. "A clairvoyant."

Lana ignored her regret at the thought that a high-blood would betray his people to join with the Brotherhood.

"He can do individual readings?"

"I think . . . no, wait."

Lana grimly struggled to hold on to her patience as Calder shuffled through the stack of papers.

"You found something?" she at last prodded, knowing her companion well enough to realize he might very well have forgotten her presence.

"He's very specialized," the older man at last muttered.

"Specialized?"

Calder lifted his head to reveal pale eyes and a small tattoo of a triangle within a circle that was placed on his temple. The mark was a powerful spell that increased his ability to sense high-bloods.

"He can touch an object and sporadically see where the owner of that object will be in the future."

Lana pressed her lips together. Had Myst left behind some personal possession when she managed to escape? That would certainly explain how the Brotherhood had managed to be waiting for her in France.

Abruptly the fear that Bas wouldn't reach the young, vulnerable female in time threatened to distract her. She clenched her teeth. For now she had no ability to help her old friend track down the clairvoyant. All she could do was concentrate on the things within her power to control.

"How far into the future?" she asked.

"It's never the same," Calder said, returning his attention to the papers in his hands. "One vision could be years in the future and some only a few hours away. It was too unpredictable to be of much value."

Lana felt a small sense of relief. If Bas managed to rescue Myst, then it was possible the Brotherhood wouldn't be able to use the traitor clairvoyant to find her again.

"Do you have other information about him?"

"Let's see." He shuffled through the documents, his brow furrowed. "He was born in San Francisco sixty years ago and abandoned by his parents when he was ten. He worked at Valhalla until last year when his wife left him for a Sentinel."

Lana grimaced. Was that the reason he'd become a traitor? Was he bitter at his wife's betrayal?

"Where did he go when he left Valhalla?"

More shuffling. "Denver," Calder finally announced. "He worked for an accounting firm for a few months and then he simply disappeared."

"He didn't marry again?"

"No."

"No children?" she pressed.

Calder shook his head. "None that he claimed."

"So no one would have raised the alarm when he vanished?"

"Probably not." The older man glanced up, realizing Lana had more than a passing interest in Peter Baldwin. "Has something happened to him?"

Lana grimaced. She didn't know if the clairvoyant had deliberately sought out the Brotherhood or if they'd somehow managed to brainwash him, but it did seem increasingly likely that he was a traitor.

"We think he might be working with the Brotherhood," she admitted.

Shock widened Calder's eyes before he was clicking his tongue in disgust.

"A shame."

"It will be more than a shame if we can't prevent him from helping our enemy to acquire a weapon to destroy Valhalla," Lana informed her companion, a heavy sense of dread lodged in the pit of her stomach.

She planned to use everything within her power to halt the Brotherhood, but she'd discovered over the past months that sometimes her best efforts weren't enough.

Calder tilted his head to the side, easily sensing her tension.

"What weapon?"

"I don't know." She gave a frustrated shake of her head. "And that's the problem."

"How can I help?" Calder instantly offered his services.

"Will you try and find anyone who might have kept in contact with Peter?" she asked. "There could be someone who knows what happened to him in Denver."

"Of course."

"Thank you."

On the point of turning to tunnel her way out of the office, Lana was halted as Calder reached out to lay a hand on her shoulder.

"If you have a minute, Mave, there's another matter I would like to discuss with you."

She stifled an exhausted sigh. She was weary to the bone and she still had a dozen things to do before she could finally eat and go to bed.

"Is it important?"

The pale eyes abruptly glittered with a hectic excitement. "Actually, it's a most astonishing breakthrough."

Lana had known Calder for over fifty years. She'd never seen him so animated.

"Now you have me curious," she wryly admitted. "What's happened?"

Calder tossed the information onto a nearby stack of books, allowing him to rub his hands together. The unconscious gesture sent tiny sparks of magic into the air, emphasizing the male's excitement.

"It started with the child you recently brought to Valhalla."

Her brief amusement was forgotten. "Molly?"

"Yes."

She stiffened, a band of fear clenching around her heart. "Is there anything wrong with her?"

"No, she's fine," Calder hastily reassured her. "In fact, she's more than fine."

"What does that mean?"

Turning, the male began to pace from one end of the office to the other, amazingly not disturbing so much as a piece of paper.

Magic?

More likely years of practice.

"As you know it's common practice for one of my staff to test any new residents," he said.

Lana resisted the urge to roll her eyes. It'd actually been her command that all high-bloods be tested. Some possessed gifts that were unstable, or downright perilous.

Valhalla needed to be prepared for any potential threat.

"Is Molly a high-blood?" she asked in confusion. She hadn't detected any spark of talent in the little girl, but she didn't have Calder's refined senses.

Calder paced back in her direction, his brow furrowed as if considering his words.

"She had a resonance," he said slowly. "But no discernable talent. At first we dismissed it. There are a number of humans who carry an echo of power without ever being able to use it."

"So she has a spark." Lana shrugged. She assumed her old friend had a point, but as usual he was taking the scenic route to get to it. "Does it matter?"

"It wouldn't have, but early this evening I decided to see the child for myself." Calder stopped directly in front of her. "I entered the nursery to discover two of the older children had spontaneously acquired new gifts."

Lana studied the thin face with an increasing confusion. "What gifts?"

"A young healer developed a talent for kinetic energy," he said, referring to the ability of a person to move objects with his or her mind. "And a healer accidentally crushed a toy truck he was playing with. I assume the young boy has the potential to become a Sentinel."

"Spontaneous manifestation has happened before," Lana pointed out, even as she was grappling with the information that two of her children had acquired new gifts.

"Yes, but they're extremely rare," Calder retorted. "To have two happen at the same time"—Calder lifted his hands—"the odds are astronomical."

He was right. Lana had heard of fewer than twenty in the past three hundred years.

"What are you suggesting?"

Calder was back to rubbing his hands together, the air vibrating with the force of his enthusiasm.

"We tried for years to discover how spontaneous manifestation occurs. Unfortunately, all our information has come from secondhand stories. None of us have actually witnessed a manifestation firsthand."

"And?"

"And I think Molly was the catalyst," the older man

announced, oblivious to Lana's dark frown. "I think that's her gift."

Lana clenched her hands, feeling oddly protective of the little girl.

It wasn't because Molly was Bas's daughter. Lana didn't have any emotion toward her one-time lover. At least nothing beyond a fond irritation and the knowledge that he should probably be locked in her dungeons.

Instead it was because Molly had managed to touch some maternal instinct deep inside her. A knowledge that was frankly terrifying.

Annoyed with herself, Lana slammed the door on her ridiculous broodings and concentrated on what Calder's hypothesis might mean for her people.

"You believe she can stir latent powers?" she asked.

He gave a vigorous nod. "It makes perfect sense."

"Maybe to you," she said, her tone dry.

"Okay." No doubt accustomed to having to explain his convoluted ramblings, Calder sucked in a deep breath and visibly organized his thoughts. "Let's say there are these catalysts. They seemingly have no obvious skills, but when they are put into contact with someone with dormant powers, they are capable of creating a chemical reaction that transforms them into high-bloods. Or if they've already manifested a talent, the catalyst will ignite any secondary powers they might possess."

Lana stilled, trying to visualize what he was claiming.

There were some high-bloods who had mutations that were obvious from birth. Necromancers, or diviners, as they preferred to be called, had faceted eyes that were unmistakable. Other high-bloods didn't develop their talents until puberty, although it was usually a slow, steady process.

Then there were the humans who had the potential within them, but their talents remained dormant.

And, of course, the very, very rare occasions when a talent appeared without warning.

It'd frankly never occurred to her that those spontaneous manifestations were caused by the magic of another high-blood.

"A catalyst." She tested the word, feeling it settle inside her with a sense of rightness.

"It would explain a number of mysteries," Calder said.

"Yes," she slowly agreed. "I suppose it would."

"I would like to use Molly in a few experiments—"

"Absolutely not." Lana nipped her companion's suggestion in the bud.

He might be the Master of Gifts, but there was no way in hell he was going to use Molly to discover if his hypothesis was possible or not.

Frustration tightened his sharp features. "I assure you they won't put her in any danger."

"No." Lana squared her shoulders, her magic filling the air with enough force to send papers and books tumbling to the floor. "Molly is separated from her parents and surrounded by strangers. She will be treated as a cherished guest during her stay at Valhalla, not a guinea pig in a lab."

"I . . ." Despite his frenzied need for answers, Calder was able to sense that now wasn't the time to press her. He instead grimaced before giving a nod of his head. "Yes, Mave."

Her point made, Lana turned and headed toward the door. "Please let me know if you learn anything new about Peter Baldwin."

Chapter Twelve

With a growl of fury, Stella hurled her cell phone across her bedroom. It cracked in half before falling to the floor with a satisfying thud.

She was cursed.

There was no other reason.

How else did you explain such a total clusterfuck?

She'd planned for weeks. She'd spent thousands of dollars. She'd promised her followers they were on the brink of greatness.

And when she'd crawled into bed, it'd appeared her shitty luck was about to turn. They had the clairvoyant, and soon she would give them the weapon that was going to destroy Valhalla.

Now . . .

Wearing nothing more than a silky camisole top and matching shorts, she reached to flip on a nearby lamp even as there was the sound of hurried footsteps. Seconds later the connecting door was shoved open and Peter stepped into the room, his pudgy face creased with worry.

"What's wrong?"

Stella glared at her unwelcome intruder, her lips curling

at the sight of his flabby, pasty white body revealed by the boxer shorts.

Christ. Just the sight of him was enough to remind her of what she'd sacrificed. And for what?

A big, fat nothing.

"They allowed the clairvoyant to escape," she snarled as the idiot crossed the room as if he was going to take her in his arms.

"How?" he asked, coming to an abrupt halt when she lifted a warning hand.

She felt another blast of fury as she recalled Roy's stumbling explanation.

"She was traveling with a Sentinel who supposedly managed to overwhelm the guards and take off with her before anyone knew what was happening," she ground out.

Peter scowled, his expression more annoyed than horrified. Which only proved he truly was a stupid, stupid man.

"Are they following her?"

Stella paced toward the nightstand beside her headboard. "They're searching, but she could be anywhere," she said.

"They should concentrate on the area around the nearest monastery," Peter suggested. "She'll more than likely go there to try and travel home."

Stella narrowed her eyes. She was done screwing around. She wanted that weapon, and she wanted it now.

"Or you could do another reading and tell me where she's going to be," she informed him.

Peter shoved his fingers through his hair, which looked like a rat's nest.

"I've told you it doesn't work like that," he muttered. "Now that I've had a vision the object is worthless."

"Then I'll get another one," she snapped. After the clairvoyant had disappeared from the ranch twelve years ago, Gilbert had stored her meager belongings in a safe.

That's where Stella had gotten the small silver bracelet Peter had used for his initial vision. "I think the clairvoyant left behind some clothing."

He was shaking his head before she even finished speaking. "It won't matter. I've never had two separate visions of the same person."

Sharp-edged frustration combined with her fury. She was surrounded by incompetent idiots. Keeping her gaze on his pudgy face, she pulled open the drawer.

"So you're telling me you're worthless?" she accused.

He hunched a shoulder, his expression petulant. "Hey, I gave you the information you needed to find the female," he muttered. "It's not my fault your minions screwed up."

"Trust me, my minions will suffer for disappointing me." Her voice held an edge of cruel anticipation. Once she got her hands on Roy and his merry band of fuckups, she intended to make sure they paid. And they weren't the only ones. "Everyone will suffer if I don't get my hands on that weapon."

He offered a tentative smile. "Okay, it's bad, but all we need is a new plan," he said, acting as if he had some right to tell her how to run her team.

Delusional moron

"We?"

With a smooth motion she reached to grab the small handgun she kept tucked in the nightstand, lifting her arm to point it directly at the center of Peter's chest.

Peter froze, his gaze locked on the weapon in her hand. "Stella?"

"Yes?"

"I . . ." He struggled to keep the fear out of his voice. "What's going on?"

A humorless smile curled her lips. Until she'd watched his face drain of color she hadn't been sure he could be hurt by a mere gun. God knew he'd taken endless beatings without croaking while he'd been held in the cage.

He might be a spineless coward, but he was still a high-blood, which meant he was much harder to kill than a normal human.

Now that she was certain she had his full attention, she waved the gun toward a nearby chair.

"Shall I tell you about my past, Peter?" she drawled.

"Please, do." He hurriedly moved to perch on the edge of the chair. "I'm always fascinated to learn more about you."

An addictive surge of power raced through Stella as she held the gun steady.

This was what she craved. This sense that she was in complete control of her surroundings and everyone around her.

Unfortunately she couldn't constantly walk around with a gun in her hand. So instead, she had to rely on building an empire that would ensure she didn't ever have to be vulnerable again.

"I was born in a trailer outside Vegas to a woman who got pregnant in the hopes her worthless boyfriend would marry her," she said. She enjoyed telling her story. It reminded her just how far she'd come. If she could overcome her past, she could do anything. "Big shocker, he took off before I was ever born and she was forced to make a living by stripping in a squalid club." Her lips curled in disgust. Her mother had been weak. A born victim. "My first memory is hiding beneath the stage to keep from being molested by the creeps who infested the place. By the time I was twelve I learned that instead of hiding it was far better to use the crowd of losers' lewd attentions to get what I wanted. A few smiles, a bounce on their lap, and suddenly I could buy decent clothes and a warm meal."

Peter tried to look sympathetic, even as his gaze darted toward the door, no doubt hoping he could keep her distracted long enough that he could try to escape.

"You poor baby."

"My name is Stella, not baby," she rasped. The men in the club had called her baby even as they were trying to shove their hands down her pants.

It was an endearment she wouldn't tolerate.

His gaze shifted back to her. "Forgive me."

She drew in a deep breath, struggling to hold on to her frayed temper.

"When I was fourteen I ran off with a biker who promised me paradise. What I got was a life in cheap hotels and a regular black eye." Stella grimaced. She had a dozen scars and several fractured bones from her two years in the tender care of Brodie. "One night I waited for him to pass out and then tied him to the bed. I beat the shit out of him with a whiskey bottle."

Peter cleared his throat. "You did what you had to do."

She shrugged. She wished she'd killed the bastard. That was the only certain way he wouldn't take another little girl and treat her as his own personal punching bag.

"More than that, I continued to learn from my mistakes," she assured him. "Clearly men could be used to get what I needed, but I would never again put myself in a position of weakness."

Clearly sensing he was being lumped with the other loser men in her life, Peter made an effort to distract her.

"What about Gilbert?"

"He was a pawn, like all the others," she admitted, glancing around the elegant bedroom. "He gave me access to luxury and a potential army. All I needed was a cause to unite them behind me." She stepped forward, the gun held steady in her hand. "You . . . dearest Peter, gave me that cause. And now, like Gilbert, and all the other men in my life, you've reached your expiration date."

"No." With a surge of fear, Peter jumped to his feet, his

hands held out in a gesture of pleading. "We can still get the weapon."

She arched a brow. "How?"

"Give me time to think."

"Tick, tock," she taunted, preparing to squeeze the trigger. "So sorry."

"No." Without warning, the man lunged forward. Stella took a step back, but not before he'd grabbed ahold of her wrist, yanking off the charm bracelet that was the only thing she'd kept from her life with her mother.

Instantly Peter stiffened, his eyes rolling back in his head as he dropped to his knees.

"What the hell?" Stella muttered, torn between curiosity and the urge to put a bullet in the idiot's head and be done with him.

"A vision . . ." he choked out.

"Very convenient," she muttered, her brows snapping together as he swayed, side to side. "No doubt you can now magically tell me where the clairvoyant is going to be?"

"Not the clairvoyant." He halted his swaying, his face coated in a layer of sweat. "You."

Stella lowered the gun, a flicker of hope easing her seething fury.

"Tell me."

Myst finished the last of the crisp green salad and fresh bread that Bas had waiting for her when she woke for the second time.

A part of her had been horrified to discover that it was nearly noon. She wasn't in France to lie around, indulging her desires. She was supposed to be finding the answer to her vision so she could halt the blood and death she'd seen spreading through Valhalla.

And just as important, as far as she was concerned,

was the opportunity to figure out how to be a real mother to Molly.

A larger part of her, however, was determined to savor each and every precious second of this brief respite. As Bas had pointed out, there was nothing they could do until they set up another meeting with the Keeper of Tales. And after four years of virtual isolation in the library of the Russian monastery, she surely deserved a few hours of pleasure?

Pushing away her plate, she was still torn between guilt and the tiny voice whispering she would never again have Bas completely to herself, when the gorgeous male was abruptly leaving the room with his phone pressed to his ear.

Myst grimaced, tugging the robe tighter around her naked body. She didn't need to be a clairvoyant to know this momentary bout of madness was about to come to an end.

Five minutes later Bas was returning, his unshaven jaw clenched as she slowly rose to her feet.

"Who was that?" she demanded.

"The Mave," he said as he confirmed her suspicion, the clipped edge in his voice sending a chill down her spine. Bas's tone changed with his mood. When she'd first met him it'd been cool, even aloof. The perfect businessman. When she was in his arms, it was low and whiskey smooth. Now, it was tightly controlled. A certain sign he was trying to disguise some intense emotion. "They think they found out how the Brotherhood knew where to find you."

She wrapped her arms around her waist. "How?"

"They have a male clairvoyant who has either become a traitor or is being forced to work for the leader."

Myst felt a stab of disappointment. She'd been betrayed by her family, held like an animal by the humans, and now one of her own people was using his powers to track her.

Could anyone be trusted?

"Is he someone who knows me?" she demanded. Most clairvoyants needed to be close to the person they were reading. Some even had to touch them.

Bas's expression hardened, clearly no more happy than she was at the thought of a high-blood traitor. In fact, he looked like he'd already decided the perfect way to kill the clairvoyant once he got his hands on him.

"It's impossible to know for certain," he admitted.

Myst glanced toward the window where the sun was shining brightly. If the clairvoyant had some way of knowing where she was going to be, it would make it impossible for her to hide.

"What are we going to do?" she muttered, even as she began to plot in the back of her mind.

She had to sneak away from her companion.

Bas was just stubborn enough to insist on staying with her even if she couldn't shake her tracker. She wasn't going to let him be captured by the Brotherhood.

Not because the mere thought of him being hurt made her heart race with panicked horror. Of course not. It was just . . . Molly needed him.

Yep. That was the reason.

"Wolfe is sending in Sentinels to deal with the clairvoyant."

Myst nodded, knowing there was more. "And?"

He grimaced before forcing himself to say the words. "And the Mave has set up another opportunity for us to meet with Boggs."

She felt a flare of relief. She'd feared the elusive Keeper of Tales would refuse to set up another meeting. Not that she was entirely convinced the mysterious male could help her. Still, she had to feel like she was doing something.

Otherwise . . .

A cold ball of dread settled in the pit of her stomach.

Otherwise she had to seriously consider Plan B.

Taking herself out of the equation, by whatever means necessary.

She shook off the depressing thought as Bas's eyes narrowed, almost as if he could read her dark thoughts.

"Where?" she abruptly demanded.

"An old cathedral a few miles north of here." He continued to study her with a piercing gaze. "Are you willing to take the risk?"

She shrugged. "I don't have any choice."

"There's always a choice." He stepped forward, his hand wrapping around the side of her neck with a casual intimacy. "I can take you back home."

She shivered at his gentle touch, a familiar sadness tugging at her heart.

"I don't have a home," she whispered. "I've never had a home."

"Myst."

The shimmering bronze eyes darkened with a sympathy that shook her out of her momentary bout of gloom. Abruptly she stepped back. The last thing she wanted from this male was his pity.

"I should take a shower."

He stiffened, almost as if he was hurt by her emotional retreat. Then his stunningly beautiful features settled into a mocking expression.

"Do you need help?"

She gave a shake of her head. As tempting as the thought of sharing the cramped shower with this delectable male was, she had to accept their time together was at an end.

Deep inside she could feel a growing sense of urgency. Time was running out. She had to find a way to avoid her fate or . . .

"I think I can manage." She forced herself to answer his teasing words, backing toward the bathroom.

His gaze drifted down her body, swathed in the oversized robe.

"I just want you to know that I'm here to be of service."

She rolled her eyes. "Yeah right."

His gaze returned to linger on her lips, which were still swollen from his kisses, before he reached to grab the package he'd brought back last night.

"I'm going to make sure there aren't any bad guys lurking around," he said, handing her the bag. "There are clean clothes in there."

She swallowed a small sigh. Of course he'd thought to bring her clean clothes.

The male was . . . perfect. Even when he was being an arrogant, annoying ass.

"Be careful," she said before she could halt the words.

His eyes softened to melted bronze. "You're worried about me?"

She hunched a shoulder, unable to admit the truth.

"You're Molly's father," she instead muttered. "She would be devastated if anything happened to you."

He moved forward, crowding her against the door of the bathroom. "And what about you, *cara?*" he demanded, his fingers threading through her tangled hair. "Would you be devastated?"

Her mouth went dry as she forced herself to meet his brooding gaze. He had to sense that she was terrified he would be hurt.

Why was he so determined to make her admit her unwelcome obsession with him?

"What do you want from me, Bas?"

His lips twisted as he studied her pale face. "I'll let you know when I figure it out."

She made a sound of annoyance. "Riddles."

Swooping down, he claimed her mouth in a kiss of utter possession.

"Take your shower," he at last growled, reaching behind her to shove open the bathroom door. "I won't go far."

Whirling on her heel, Myst darted into the cramped room and slammed the door behind her. She wasn't angry at Bas. No. She was furious with herself.

It was embarrassing to admit, but despite knowing she could never be like other women, she fiercely wanted to fantasize about a future with Bas.

White picket fences. Silver-haired, bronze-eyed children. And an icily beautiful assassin who turned to fire in her arms.

She dropped the robe and stepped into the shower cubicle, turning the knob to hot, although it was barely lukewarm. Only then did she allow the tears of regret to track down her cheeks.

Less than half an hour later, she had her damp hair pulled into a braid and had slipped on the pretty sundress in a pale shade of lavender. There were also slip-on flats in butter-soft leather, and delicate undies that fit her to perfection.

With her composure restored, she stepped out of the bathroom and managed to meet Bas's searching gaze with a tight smile.

"Ready?"

He grimaced. "As ready as I'll ever be," he muttered, moving to join her as she headed determinedly toward the door.

He'd changed into a pair of gray slacks and a crisp white cotton shirt that was left open at the throat, the sleeves rolled up to expose his forearms. With his pale, elegant features that contrasted with his silky ebony hair, he looked like he'd just stepped off the front of a fashion magazine.

At least until she caught sight of the bronze eyes that blazed with a power that could only belong to a warrior.

She shivered, wondering if there'd ever been a female who hadn't looked at this male and been consumed with lust.

In silence they snuck out of the small hotel, walking along the bank of the river. At a glance they no doubt looked like a young couple simply out for a stroll on such a fine, sunny day. Up close, however, the air prickled with Bas's magic as he kept his lean body close enough that she felt singed by his power.

She didn't doubt he would rip apart anything that crossed their path.

The town disappeared, to be replaced by rolling vineyards with only a handful of distant cottages. The peace should have eased the tension that clenched her muscles, but she couldn't shake the sensation of a ticking time bomb.

At last, they turned away from the river to head up a narrow path. In the distance she could see the top spire of the cathedral, but without warning Bas reached out to grasp her arm, bringing her to a sharp halt.

"He's here," he muttered.

Myst sent her companion a startled glance. "Here?"

Bas gave a slow nod, his expression wary. "Just ahead."

Her gaze scanned the nearby fields, seeing nothing beyond the grapevines and a few birds that circled overhead. Had Bas made a mistake? Boggs was supposed to be waiting for them at the cathedral, not in the middle of the road.

"I don't see him," she admitted.

Bas nodded toward a small thatch of pine trees near the edge of the road.

"There."

"Very good, assassin," a disembodied male voice floated through the air.

Bas moved to stand directly in front of her, his vibrating energy stirring the dust beneath their feet.

"Show yourself," he commanded.

An electric surge of magic clashed against Bas's power, making the hair on the back of Myst's neck stand upright.

Damn. She took a step back. She felt as if she was going to get fried.

"Not until I'm sure you weren't followed," the unseen male responded. "The last time you brought the enemy to my favorite lair."

"We didn't know the Brotherhood was able to find us," Bas said, a bite in his voice.

"Which is why I tried to alter the place of our meeting at the last second," Boggs retorted.

Myst grimaced. That explained why Boggs wasn't waiting for them at the cathedral.

Bas muttered a curse, pausing to glance around the empty countryside.

"There's no one near." He gave an impatient gesture with his hand. "Let's get this over with."

"Very well."

There was a faint rustle in the shadow of the trees before a tall, lean man walked down the road.

"Oh . . . Lord." Her stomach twisted with shock.

She'd never seen anything like the Keeper of Tales.

His features were barely formed and his eyes glowed with white power. He was a pale, hairless creature that looked more like a larva than a man.

At the moment, his body was covered in a dull brown robe that covered him from his neck to his toes. Something she was deeply thankful for. She was fairly certain she didn't want to see what was beneath the thick wool.

"Bothered, sweet Myst?" Boggs asked in a singsong voice. "I can make myself more appealing if you want."

Myst made a sound of shock as the creature moved

closer, his features smoothly transforming until he was an exact duplicate of Bas, except for the eyes, which remained a pure white.

A doppelganger.

She'd heard of them, but she'd never seen anything so . . . unnerving.

Bas hissed in anger, his body stiff as he clenched his hands at his sides.

"We're here for answers, not parlor tricks."

The creature shrugged, releasing his magic. Instantly he returned to his larva state.

"I have answers," he taunted, "but do you know the right questions?"

Myst hurriedly moved around Bas's rigid body, sensing violence brewing in the air.

They didn't have time to waste on a male pissing contest.

"I want to learn more about my vision," she announced in firm tones.

"A foreseer." The shimmering white gaze locked on her as Boggs drifted forward. "I haven't had a taste in a long time. Let me—"

In a blur of motion, Bas had his hand wrapped around the doppelganger's wrist, his eyes blazing with fury.

"Don't touch her."

The creature hissed with impatience, but he was smart enough not to struggle against Bas's hold.

"I can't see her vision if I don't touch her."

"No."

"Bas." She carefully reached out to brush her hand down his back. She wasn't excited about the thought of Boggs touching her. Not because he looked different. They were all high-bloods with gifts that made them unusual. But because his magic was strong enough to make her skin crawl. "We came here so we could see if he could help."

He didn't even glance in her direction. "No touching," he growled.

"Fine." Boggs heaved a dramatic sigh. "Give me something that belongs to you," he said to Myst.

She frowned. Everything she had on was brand new. She doubted it carried enough of her essence to help the male.

Then, without warning, Bas was loosening his hold on the doppelganger and reaching into his pocket. The sun glinted on a gold chain as he stretched out his hand.

"Will this do?" he demanded.

Myst felt her heart come to a shocked halt as Boggs reached to take the object from the male standing at her side.

It was a locket.

Her locket.

The one she'd lost in his office five years ago.

In a daze she turned her head to study Bas's elegant profile, unable to believe that he would have kept the necklace, let alone carried it in his pocket.

A dozen questions hovered on her lips, but she was forced to swallow them as Boggs pressed the locket to the side of his face, his eyes blazing like stars.

"Yes, this will do," he said in a low voice, his body abruptly arching as a cry of horror was wrenched from his throat. "No . . ."

Myst flinched. That was the same sound she'd made when the vision had seared through her.

"What do you see?" she asked.

He shuddered. "Death."

She grimaced. She already knew about the death. She needed to know how to halt it.

"Can you see what the weapon is?"

His breath hissed through his clenched teeth. "Blood."

Blood?

"You see blood?" she probed.

"The blood is the weapon."

She shook her head. "I don't understand."

Boggs lowered the locket even as his eyes continued to glow. "The blood has power."

Okay. This was getting her nowhere. Maybe she had to be more precise.

"Do you mean the Brotherhood could use my blood as a weapon?"

Boggs shrugged. "Impossible to say."

Bas made a sound of frustration, his body rigid as he glared at the doppelganger. Myst struggled to ignore him. She didn't think the Keeper of Tales was trying to screw with her.

He truly needed her to ask the right questions to bring the event into focus.

"Do I somehow alter my blood?"

"No . . ." Boggs gave a slow shake of his head. "I don't think so."

"Is it still in my body?" she pressed.

"That's all I see." Boggs lifted a hand, as if to silence her questions. "Blood and death."

Shit. He wasn't telling her anything that would help her avoid her fate.

"Are there any prophecies that would match the vision?" she asked in desperation.

"A thousand," Boggs admitted.

Myst felt her heart sink. "A thousand?"

"Perhaps tens of thousands."

Bas had reached the end of his patience. "So what you're saying is that we wasted our time coming here?" he snapped.

"No." Boggs held out the locket. Surprisingly, it was Bas who reached to snatch it from his fingers, shoving it in the front pocket of his jeans. The doppelganger stepped back, his expression impossible to read. "My role has yet to be played."

"Come on, *cara*, we have better things to be doing," her companion growled, wrapping his fingers around her upper arm.

She shook her head, not prepared to give up so easily. "But—"

"Myst, remember one thing," Boggs said, his tone suddenly urgent.

"What?"

"One man's weapon is another man's gift."

The words had barely left the doppelganger's lips before there was a crack of thunder and the male disappeared in a puff of smoke.

Myst stumbled back as the blast of magic nearly sent her to her knees.

Holy . . . shit.

Chapter Thirteen

Two hours later, Bas halted in the shadows of the stone wall that surrounded a sleepy village. Still holding Myst's hand, he studied her pale face.

During the silent trek through the countryside his fury had been honed to a lethal emotion.

The Keeper of Tales had been just as annoyingly vague as he'd expected. Hell, the entire journey had been a humongous waste of time. But it was his companion's lethargic attitude that was scraping against his nerves.

Myst was a bright, shimmering ray of sunlight. Even after everything she'd endured, she carried with her a buoyant energy that was infectious. Just like Molly.

Now it was as if the light had been extinguished, leaving her shrouded in darkness.

The very thought hurt his soul.

Stepping close enough to be surrounded by her honeysuckle scent, he palmed her cheek.

"Are you okay?" he demanded, his voice pitched low.

She sucked in a shuddering breath. "No."

"Myst." His hand slid to cup her cheek, tilting back her head so he could study her grim expression. "Talk to me."

"It's stupid," she muttered. "I knew this was a long shot. I've been searching for years without any luck. Still . . ."

His fingers tightened on her chin as her words trailed away.

"We'll find the answers," he promised, the words a solemn pledge.

"But not today." Her lips twisted with a pained emotion as she remained lost in her thoughts. Then, with an obvious effort, she smoothed her features to an unreadable mask. "You need to get back to Molly."

He narrowed his gaze. He didn't like the feeling she was shutting him out.

In fact, it frankly pissed him off.

"Both of us are going back," he said in tones that warned his plan was nonnegotiable. "Once we're at Valhalla we can decide what our next move will be."

She was shaking her head before he ever finished speaking. "Bas, you know I can't go there."

"Of course you can. It's the safest place for you."

"And the most dangerous," she said, deliberately pulling away from his light grasp.

His eyes narrowed. "Are you afraid of Lana?" he bluntly demanded. "You know I would never allow her to hurt you."

A strange emotion rippled over her face. "I'm afraid of myself."

Christ. Abruptly he realized she was worried that she was about to cause some sort of Armageddon.

"That's ridiculous," he growled.

"It's not," she insisted, her hands clenching. "You didn't see the vision, Bas. It's . . . terrifying." She gave a sharp shake of her head. "I have to stop it."

He believed her. He truly did. A seer's vision was a glimpse of the future.

But that didn't mean it was inevitable.

It was one *possible* future.

"Then we come up with a new plan," he said, barely resisting the urge to wrap her in his arms. She looked so damned fragile, as if she might shatter into a thousand pieces. Unfortunately, they couldn't risk staying in such a visible area even a second longer than necessary. Any comfort would have to wait. "But first we need to get you someplace where the Brotherhood can't get to you."

"No." The word was ruthlessly adamant even as her breath came in small pants. "I won't go there. I won't."

"Easy, Myst," he murmured, sensing she was barely in control of her emotions. Skimming his fingers down her arms, he urged her against the ivy that covered the stone wall. He felt perilously exposed as a car drove past to slowly turn through the wide gate. Who knew how many eyes were watching them? "Once the clairvoyant is captured we can leave."

She shivered, her heart pounding so loudly he could hear each beat.

"I'm running out of time."

His fingers lightly grasped her wrists, his thumbs gently rubbing back and forth in an effort to calm her. A rueful smile twisted his lips. Or maybe he was trying to calm himself.

Her barely restrained panic was starting to twist his gut with dread.

"How do you know?"

She gave another shiver. "I can feel it."

Dammit. He refused to accept that he couldn't control the situation.

"Fine, it might be near, but you don't have a weapon," he said in gentle tones. "We can still—"

"You heard Boggs," she interrupted. "He said it might have something to do with my blood."

"That idiot . . ." Bas made a sound of disgust. "He told us nothing but a bunch of cryptic nonsense."

Her expression hardened. "He saw destruction."

"It doesn't matter what he saw," Bas insisted. As far as he was concerned the Master of Tales had been nothing more than a gigantic pain in the ass. "We're going to get through this." He lifted her hands, pressing his lips to her knuckles. "Together."

"Bas." A deep yearning darkened her eyes. As if she was desperately longing to believe his assurances. Then, without warning, she was tugging her hands free and forcing a tight smile to her lips. "You're right. I'm being ridiculous."

Bas frowned, sensing the barriers she was trying to create between them.

"I'm right?"

"Yes." The faux smile never faltered. "Obviously I'm upset and not thinking clearly."

He folded his arms over his chest. "Hmm."

Easily sensing that she wasn't fooling him for a second, she cleared her throat and glanced toward the gateway leading into the village.

"How are we getting back to Valhalla?"

"We'll have to use one of the monasteries," he confessed. He'd already considered and discarded a dozen different means of transportation. They simply didn't have the time it would take to travel by traditional methods. Still, his decision didn't come without risk. "Unfortunately, if the Brotherhood have any brains at all they'll be waiting for us."

She gave a slow nod, her lack of response revealing she'd already considered the danger.

"How are we going to get past them?"

"A disguise."

"A nice thought, but I don't have your unique talent," she pointed out dryly.

He shrugged. "Then we do it the old-fashioned way."

She arched her brows. "I'm afraid to ask."

Unable to resist, he reached out to stroke back a silver curl that'd escaped from her braid.

"Wait here and I'll find something that will cover that remarkable hair," he promised, his gaze skimming down to the sundress that fit her with disturbing perfection. "And even more remarkable body."

"Okay."

He stilled. Something was wrong. Really wrong. Myst never gave in so easily. In fact, he'd already decided that she argued with him just out of a perverse need to keep him at a distance.

His fingers stroked along the line of her stubborn jaw. "You're starting to worry me, *cara*."

Her lips thinned with annoyance. "I just agreed with you."

"And that's what worries me," he murmured.

She brushed away his lingering hand, her expression unreadable.

"I don't know what you're talking about."

"Of course not." He forced a smile to his lips that was as fake as hers. She was up to something, but there was no way in hell she was going to share what she was plotting. He would have to find out by more nefarious means. "Stay here, and behave yourself," he commanded.

He'd turned away and was heading toward the nearby entrance to the village when he heard her call out his name.

"Bas."

He turned to meet her unconsciously regretful expression. "Yes?"

"Be careful."

With a nod, he disappeared through the gate that'd been carved into the stone wall. Then, with a blinding speed that made him all but invisible to the human eye, he was at the far end of the village. Bending his knees, he shoved himself upward, catching the edge of the wall so he could vault himself over.

From there he circled back to where he'd left Myst, not surprised to discover her hurrying down the road in the opposite direction.

He'd already suspected she intended to try and slip away, but the proof of her betrayal still managed to slice through his heart.

Dammit.

He'd spent centuries honing his ruthless composure. Not only during his training as an assassin, but during his years as an outlaw mercenary.

Survival meant that his emotions never, ever controlled him. But this tiny female had an unnerving ability to shatter his self-control.

Usually without even trying.

Moving out of the shadows, he stood in the center of the road, his arms folded over his chest.

"Going somewhere, *cara?*"

Intent on her escape, Myst was nearly on top of him before she skidded to a sharp halt.

"Shit," she breathed, pressing a hand to her chest. "You scared me."

"Oh, I'm going to do more than just scare you," he muttered, taking acute pleasure in the thought of chaining her to his bed.

She licked her dry lips, her gaze darting to the side as if she was considering how to escape him. At last she heaved a resigned sigh, accepting it would be insane to even try to flee.

"What are you doing here?" She sent him a frustrated glare. "I thought you were finding a disguise?"

"I haven't survived for three centuries by being stupid,

cara," he warned, meeting her glare for glare. "Plus, you're a rotten liar."

She planted her fists on her hips, her body trembling with the force of her emotions.

"Dammit, you have to let me go," she snapped.

He stepped forward, his hands grabbing her upper arms as his heart gave another painful twist.

Christ, he'd done everything in his power to protect this female. Why was she so determined to leave him?

"Go where?" he demanded.

There was a long, stubborn silence before she allowed him to glimpse the aching defeat in the depths of her velvet eyes.

"I won't let this happen," she whispered.

The truth hit him with the force of a sledgehammer to the gut, nearly sending him to his knees. She'd been running not to get away from him. But because she intended to . . .

No. He couldn't even allow the thought to fully form. Already the air was sizzling with the heat of his fury, the ground vibrating beneath their feet.

He'd destroy the world if he let himself think about what might have happened if he hadn't sensed she was lying.

"Shit." His voice was a muted roar, his fingers unwittingly digging into her flesh. "There's no way I'm letting you hurt yourself."

Her eyes filled with tears. "Bas."

He jerked her forward, wrapping her in his arms so tightly he knew it must be difficult for her to breathe.

He couldn't help it. He needed to feel her pressed against him.

So close she couldn't possibly escape.

"I told you no," he snarled. "That's final."

She trembled, her head lying against his chest. "This isn't your decision," she said softly.

His head lowered so he could bury his face in the curve of her neck, breathing deep of her sweet scent.

"I just made it my decision," he informed her.

"Then you'll condemn Valhalla to death. Including Molly," she rasped, a tear trailing down her cheek to drop onto his jaw. "Is that what you want?"

Of course it wasn't what he wanted.

But he wasn't sacrificing this female.

No. Fucking. Way.

Lana perched on the edge of the narrow bed, her fingers absently trailing through the silver strands of Molly's hair.

She wasn't sure what had lured her into the nursery at this late hour. After her meeting with Calder, she'd shared the information with Wolfe, who'd made the instant decision to attack the Brotherhood compound. He'd pointed out that they couldn't risk the clairvoyant leading their enemy to Myst. Not when she had the potential to give them a weapon of mass destruction.

Lana had agreed, returning to her own office to alert the human authorities. She tried her best to keep her dealings with the mortals as civil as possible, and once she'd explained the group was a danger to her people, she managed to get their grudging agreement.

After that she'd eaten the meal that Wolfe had sent on a tray, knowing he would come pester her if she didn't. Besides, she'd been starving.

But while she knew she should get some long-overdue rest, she found herself unable to sleep.

There was . . . something in the air.

A buzzing sense of urgency that refused to give her peace.

So instead of being tucked in her bed, she'd found herself wandering through the quiet hallways, her feet instinctively bringing her to this shadowed room.

If what the Master of Gifts had said was true, then this tiny girl had the ability to alter the course of high-bloods' history.

She would be a source of fascination for the healers and scientists. A beacon of hope for those who craved power. And a focus of hate for those who feared the magic that ran through the blood of her people.

But for tonight she was just an innocent child.

Grimacing at the biting need to protect Molly from her inevitable future, Lana didn't move when she caught the familiar scent of raw male power and heard the rumbling sound of Wolfe's voice as he spoke to the healer who was in charge of the nursery.

Then, moving with the liquid silence that marked him as a Sentinel, he entered Molly's private room to study her with a brooding expression.

"I thought I told you to go to bed," he chastised, his voice low enough not to wake the child even as it held a thread of warning.

She arched a brow, able to see the chiseled beauty of his face despite the darkness. The warm copper skin. The midnight eyes. The proud thrust of his nose.

The arrogance that was so much a part of him.

"And I thought you were organizing our . . ." She hesitated, glancing toward Molly. The little girl looked as if she was deeply asleep, but she well knew appearances could be deceptive. "Visit to the compound?"

"Done." Wolfe folded his arms over his chest. "We leave in an hour."

A sharp fear twisted her heart as she rose to her feet.

"What do you mean 'we'?" She held his dark gaze. "Do you plan to go?"

He shrugged. "I want to make sure the traitor doesn't escape."

She understood his savage desire to get his hands on the high-blood. She was itching to have him in her dungeons where she could have a long and very thorough conversation with Peter Baldwin.

But as the leader, Wolfe's place was in Valhalla.

Right?

"Your Sentinels are capable of dealing with the clairvoyant."

"True," he conceded, a hint of satisfaction easing his grim expression. He knew she was worried about him and he was enjoying the hell out of it. "But I want to be there."

She thinned her lips. "Tell me why."

"And you call me stubborn?" he teased.

"Wolfe."

He held up a slender hand, his brow furrowing with genuine concern.

"There have been too many rumors of the Brotherhood hoarding illegal weapons for me not to believe they are true," he said. Over the past weeks Valhalla had scrambled to gather information on the secretive group. The fact that they had a supply of army-grade weapons that had been forbidden by the government had been a nasty surprise. "I won't risk my men until I can be sure this is not a trap."

She got it.

Wolfe was a leader who would never send in his soldiers where he was too afraid to go. That didn't, however, ease her fierce aversion to the thought of him waltzing into such a volatile situation.

"You're the Tagos."

His lips twitched as she continued to point out the obvious. "I'm aware of my title."

"That means you give the orders and your men carry them out." She tilted her chin, trying to look as imposing as possible. Wolfe called it her "stop being a pain in my ass" face. "Putting yourself in danger doesn't help anyone."

Naturally the aggravating male simply chuckled. "I recall giving you that exact speech a few weeks ago, only to be rudely ignored."

She waved aside his accusation with an impatient hand. "That was different."

He snorted. "Of course it was."

"It was," she said, belatedly realizing she sounded like a petulant child. She gave a sharp shake of her head. "I was the only one able to keep Annie stable long enough to get her to Valhalla," she finished in cool tones.

He moved forward, invading her space and surrounding her in his heat.

"You put yourself in danger because you thought it was necessary for your people," he said, reminding her of her refusal to listen to his infuriated command to remain at Valhalla when the crazed witch had been creating chaos. "Do you expect me to do any less?"

She heaved a resigned sigh, turning to study Molly's tiny face resting so peacefully on the pillow.

"I don't know why I bother to argue with you," she muttered. "You're going to do whatever you want."

Without warning she felt warm fingers brush down the curve of her neck.

"Oh, if only that were true," he said in a husky voice.

She quivered, the tiny sparks that raced through her body an intoxicating temptation. Briefly closing her eyes, she willed herself to pull away from his light touch.

"Wolfe," she breathed, the strain in her voice revealing

how hard it was for her to deny the need that pulsed between them.

She felt the force of his frustration beat against him before he was slowly stepping back.

"Is it worth the sacrifice?" he demanded.

"Most of the time," she muttered, her gaze still on the sleeping child, a wistful longing settling in her soul.

"Does it have to be a choice?"

Her decision to break all ties with family and friends had been a personal choice, not a moral or legal necessity. But she'd never second-guessed herself.

Or at least, she'd never admitted she questioned what might be. . . .

"Yes," she said, turning her head to meet Wolfe's searing gaze.

He scowled, his expression hardening at her refusal to even consider a different choice.

"I need to get my shit together," he muttered, whirling around to head for the door.

Lana knew his "shit" meant the dozen weapons he would have strapped to his body before he traveled to the Brotherhood compound.

Once again she was struck by a strange prickle of premonition.

"I wish you wouldn't go, Wolfe" she said, the words clipped. "I have a bad feeling."

He continued toward the door, his sleek form almost lost among the shadows.

"You have your job and I have mine."

She grimaced, unable to argue. It was his decision who should be in charge of the raid on the Brotherhood compound.

"True."

He halted at the door, glancing over his shoulder with an unreadable expression.

"Lana."

"What?"

"You're exhausted. Give Molly a kiss and go to bed," he commanded.

She rolled her eyes, torn between the desire to scorch his fine ass with a blast of magic, or grab him by his hair and kiss him senseless.

In the end, she watched in silence as he walked away.

Chapter Fourteen

Kaede glanced around the group of males who seemed to take up far more space than was reasonable.

He'd gotten the text from Wolfe an hour ago that he was arriving with a few of his friends and demanding that Kaede meet them just beyond the perimeter of the ranch. He wasn't sure what he'd expected, but it hadn't been the two dozen Sentinels who were dressed in black to blend into the night.

They ranged in size from extra-large to overly massive, with enough power to send tremors through the ground and heat the air. And all of them had a variety of lethal weapons strapped to their bodies. Kaede grimaced, feeling as if he were drowning in testosterone.

The Tagos clearly wasn't there to screw around.

"Have you ever heard the term 'overkill'?" he couldn't resist taunting.

Wolfe stepped forward, the moonlight shimmering off the streak of silver in his hair.

"Don't push my buttons," the older man growled, the air prickling with warning. "If I had my way you would be locked in my dungeons."

Kaede's lips twitched. A wise male would avoid pissing

off the Tagos. Wolfe could easily have him arrested and even executed if he decided he wanted to be rid of an aggravating enforcer.

Kaede, however, had a pathological need to mock authority.

"I thought the dungeons belonged to the lovely Lana?" he drawled.

Wolfe reached out with blinding speed, wrapping his fingers around Kaede's throat.

"She's the Mave," he rasped, his fingers tightening until Kaede grunted in pain. "I hear her name on your lips again and I'll rip them off. Got it?"

Kaede gave a grudging nod, sucking in a deep breath when Wolfe released his punishing grip. Still, he couldn't resist one last jab.

"I sense a little frustration, Tagos," he murmured.

The older man ignored his taunt, his expression hard as he pointed toward the nearby ranch.

"Tell me about the compound."

Kaede instantly crouched down, his mocking smile fading as he concentrated on business.

Bas needed him to work with Valhalla.

For now, he would play nice.

"This is the bunkhouse and chow hall," he said, using his finger to draw a map in the dust. Despite the darkness, each of the Sentinels would easily be able to see what he was creating. "That's where the majority of the Brothers are located. There are six stationed guards." He moved his finger to make a series of *X*s to represent each sentry.

The men crowded around, each memorizing the layout of the compound.

"Weapons?" Wolfe at last demanded.

Kaede circled an area in the middle of the map. "In the training center."

"What kind?"

"Mostly garden variety," Kaede said. After he'd left Stella, he'd done a more thorough exploration of the area, including the locked rooms where they kept their guns. "A few high-powered rifles and a couple grenade launchers."

Wolfe cocked a dark brow. "That's all?"

"I'm not sure," Kaede admitted, standing upright to point toward the rolling hills at the north side of the property.

"There are abandoned mines on the opposite side of the lake."

Wolfe narrowed his gaze. "That must be where Myst was held."

Kaede clenched his hands. The mere thought of the delicate female being tossed into a pit like she was nothing more than a piece of trash made him want to kill someone.

Slowly, and with as much pain as possible.

"Yeah. Bastards," he muttered. "They told me it's where they keep their hostages."

Wolfe sent him a puzzled frown. "And?"

"And I managed to get close enough to be confident that there are no current prisoners," he said. "So why do they have two Brothers on constant guard duty?"

"There must be something of value they're protecting." Wolfe easily leapt to the same conclusion as Kaede. "Weapons?"

"That would be my guess."

Wolfe grimaced before turning his attention to the other possible threats.

"What about the leader?"

Kaede swept his hand toward the A-frame structure that was barely visible.

"As far as I can tell, Stella rarely leaves her house. She's more of an opportunist than a true believer."

Wolfe nodded. "How many guards?"

"I only sensed one."

"Inside?"

"Nope. He's stationed on the outside of the gate."

Wolfe looked predictably confused. "She doesn't trust her own men?"

"It could be that," Kaede said with a shrug. "Or she doesn't want any of them to guess she's using a high-blood lover as her source of information."

"True." The Tagos gave a humorless laugh. "It's always better PR to claim you have a direct link to God than admit you're screwing the enemy," he said, his voice thick with disdain. Whether it was directed at the leader of the Brotherhood or the traitorous clairvoyant was impossible to say. "Is she going to be a problem?"

Kaede hesitated before giving a shake of his head. He'd only spent a few minutes in Stella's company, but he'd sensed she was the sort of female who was willing to sacrifice others while making sure her own pretty neck was never in danger.

"No."

"What about the clairvoyant?" Wolfe demanded.

Kaede shrugged. "He was at a distance, but I couldn't detect any unusual powers. He shouldn't be a problem."

"Weapons?"

"Impossible to say," Kaede admitted. "I didn't get inside the house."

Wolfe considered his options in silence, then with concise movements he pivoted toward his warriors.

"Niko, take your crew and round up the Brothers," he commanded. Instantly a tall, dark-haired hunter Sentinel turned to melt into the darkness, taking a dozen of the males with him. Wolfe pointed toward the young male with honey curls and golden eyes. "Arel, you're on the weapons." Wolfe waited for the group of six to head in the direction of the lake before he glanced at the remaining warriors. "The rest with me."

The males instantly started to jog toward the A-frame house. Silently, Kaede fell into step beside them.

Or at least that was his intention.

He'd gone less than a hundred feet when his arm was grabbed by a ruthless hand that brought him to a halt. There was another tug and suddenly he was turned to meet Wolfe's dark gaze.

"Where do you think you're going?" the older man asked.

"I want my hands on the clairvoyant," Kaede readily confessed.

Wolfe studied his grim expression. "Is this personal?"

Kaede didn't hesitate. "Of course it's personal," he snapped. "I love Molly like she's my own daughter." He'd been a hard-ass enforcer who didn't allow anyone to sneak past his guard. But the second Bas had settled the little girl in his arms . . . hell, he'd been a goner. "I'll kill anyone who puts her mother in danger."

Wolfe's lips twitched. "Molly seems to have a magical ability to steal the hearts of others," he muttered. "Not even the Mave is immune."

Kaede gave a lift of his shoulder. "The world's a better place because she's in it."

"I can't argue with that," Wolfe said, "but—"

"Shit," Kaede interrupted, his patience at an end. He wanted to be done with the Brotherhood so he could go in search of Bas. He had a really bad feeling about his friend. "Are we going to do this or not?"

"The clairvoyant is to be taken alive," Wolfe warned.

"Why?" He didn't bother to disguise his revulsion for the traitor. Kaede might not agree with becoming an obedient soldier for Valhalla, but he would never work with their enemies. "He can't track Myst if he's missing his head."

"We need to know if the Brotherhood have any traps set for Bas," Wolfe said.

"Yeah right." Kaede gave a grunt of disbelief. "I was in the hotel room. You growled at Bas like a dog in heat every time he got near the Mave. You would be happy as hell if he walked into a trap."

"You're treading on dangerous ground, enforcer."

Kaede ignored the pinpricks of pain that bit into his skin as Wolfe released his powers. He'd been trained by the monks to endure endless days of torture.

"Tell me the real reason," he insisted.

Wolfe hesitated, then, astonishingly, he loosened his grip on Kaede and answered the question.

"If the clairvoyant had a glimpse of the future, then he might have seen the weapon that's supposed to cause destruction in Valhalla."

It was an angle Kaede hadn't considered. Probably because it was almost impossible to imagine the tiny, silver-haired female being capable of producing a weapon that could destroy the high-blood stronghold.

Now he felt a chill inch down his spine.

"Will you kill her?"

A bleak expression settled on the lean face. "Only if there's no other option." With a sharp shake of his head, Wolfe headed after his warriors. "Let's go."

Kaede followed, making a silent promise to contact Bas.

There was no way in hell he'd let anyone harm Myst. Not when it would destroy the male he'd come to consider more a brother than an employer.

By the time they reached the A-frame the lone guard was lying unconscious on the ground, and the front door open. Kaede picked up his speed as he caught the unmistakable smell of blood.

Jogging up the open staircase, he followed the scent down the hallway and into a room that might have been large for a master bedroom, but wasn't built to hold six Sentinels plus an enforcer. The air was choked with a sizzling heat and the floor groaned beneath the combined weight.

Kaede's attention, however, locked on the female with thick auburn hair tumbled around her heart-shaped face. Wearing nothing more than a satin camisole and matching shorts, she looked like a man's fantasy.

Until he caught the cold glitter in the dark blue eyes.

It reminded him of a snake about to strike.

At his entrance that flat gaze turned in his direction, the lush lips twisting.

"You."

He shrugged, moving forward. "Hello, Stella."

"I should have listened to Peter. He tried to warn me you couldn't be trusted," she sneered, acting as if she didn't notice the mountain of lethal warriors who had invaded her house.

Kaede rolled his eyes. He had to admit she had balls of steel. "Where is dear Peter?"

She glanced over her shoulder. "I'm afraid he wasn't prepared to face his punishment."

Kaede stepped to the side, gaining a clear view of the floor on the opposite side of the bed. He grimaced at the sight of the male lying face down with a large hole in his head.

That explained the scent of blood.

"You're saying he killed himself?" Kaede demanded in blatant disbelief.

She heaved a deep sigh that was as fake as her tits. "He was always weak."

Wolfe made a sound of frustration, waving a hand toward the leader of the Brotherhood.

"Take her," he growled.

Stella gave a toss of her head, not bothering to struggle

as the nearest Sentinel grabbed her by the arm and roughly hauled her toward the door.

"You can imprison me, but you'll never defeat our cause," she called over her shoulder. "The Brotherhood will eventually prevail."

Wolfe gave a shake of his head, glancing toward Kaede. "Is she always so clichéd?"

"No." Kaede shook his head, a frown tugging at his brows. Something felt . . . off.

The woman had not only watched her years of scheming come to a dismal end, but she was headed toward the dungeons of Valhalla. A place that would make the toughest criminal shit their pants in fear.

So why wasn't she crying? Or screaming? Or at least pleading for mercy?

Wolfe moved to stand directly in front of him. "What's wrong?"

"I don't know," he muttered, unable to shake off his sense of unease. "But that happened way too easy."

"Maybe I'm just that good," Wolfe taunted.

Kaede glanced toward the dead clairvoyant. "Or maybe she's plotting something."

With a shrug, Wolfe headed toward the door. "We'll find out once we have her locked in the dungeons at Valhalla."

Kaede waited until the room had cleared of Sentinels before he was turning toward the windows to make his escape. He had no intention of following Wolfe back to Valhalla. The Tagos might currently be occupied with dealing with the Brotherhood and the fear Myst might create some mysterious weapon. But eventually he would remember that Kaede was an outlaw.

He intended to be far away when that happened.

Before he could find a way to open the windows, however, there was a prickle of heat and he turned to discover

Wolfe standing in the doorway, his arms folded over his chest.

"Don't even think about it, enforcer," he growled. "For now we're all in this together. That means you're coming back to Valhalla with me."

Kaede's breath hissed through his teeth in frustration.

Well, hell.

Myst hammered her fists against Bas's unyielding chest. She wasn't usually a violent person. Actually, she didn't think she'd ever struck anyone in her life. Not even the monsters who'd imprisoned her.

But in this moment she needed some way to vent her rising panic.

"Answer me, damn you," she snapped, wishing she was strong enough to shake some sense into his thick head.

What was wrong with him? He wasn't stupid. He knew that with every tick of the clock, the risk increased she would fulfill her horrifying vision.

And now Molly was at Valhalla.

She had to put an end to it now.

So why was he shaking his head, his hands lifting to grasp her tight fists in a gentle grip?

"No." His voice was low, unyielding.

She trembled with frustration. "Because you know I'm right."

He shook his head, his ebony hair glowing with a satin luster in the afternoon sunlight.

"Because I won't be baited."

"Bas . . ." Her words ended in a shriek as he grabbed her around the waist and tossed her over his shoulder.

"This subject is closed," he informed her, heading down the narrow road.

Shocked at being so easily manhandled, Myst smacked

her fists against his lower back, grimacing as she nearly broke her fingers.

"What are you doing?" she snarled.

He tightened his hold on her legs, picking up speed. "We've attracted the attention of the locals," he muttered. "We need to get out of here."

Her anger transformed to fear as she lifted her head to see the two men who were standing in the center of the road. They were shouting and waving their hands at someone behind the stone wall surrounding the village.

The Brotherhood?

She'd stupidly assumed she and Bas had managed to shake them, but now she felt a sick fear twist her stomach.

"I think someone is following us," she rasped, watching in horror as a group of men charged out of the gate and headed in their direction.

"Shit," Bas breathed. "We need a car."

Leaving the road, Bas headed into the thick woods that had replaced the vineyards. It slowed their pace, but they were soon hidden from their pursuers.

Myst wrapped her arms around his waist, trying to keep her head from banging into his back. She was growing dizzy as he leaped over fallen trees and weaved between the thickening undergrowth, but she didn't want him to stop long enough to let her down.

Nearly a half an hour later he came to a halt, his eyes narrowed as he studied the farm that was built on the banks of the nearby river.

At a distance it was impossible to see if there were any handy vehicles, but the farmhouse, with its red-tiled roof and painted shutters, was well tended, which meant there had to be someone currently living there. And the nearby stone barn was large enough to hold an assortment of farm equipment. Surely they had to have a truck?

Obviously coming to the same conclusion, Bas lowered

her behind a large oak tree and brushed back her hair with gentle hands.

"Wait here while I check things out."

She shook her head. It was ridiculous. She'd done her best to escape him, but now she couldn't shake the fear that something very bad was going to happen if they split up.

"No. We need to stay together."

Bas pressed his fingers to her lips, his expression somber. "I can move faster alone."

Her teeth clenched. She couldn't argue with him. She might be faster than most humans, but she couldn't come close to matching his speed.

After trailing his fingers over her cheek, Bas turned to jog down the steep bank, keeping to the shadows of the river as he headed toward the arched bridge.

Myst leaned against the tree, silently willing him to be careful. The sleepy countryside might look like something out of a travel catalogue, but they were surrounded by enemies.

And worse, they were far away from any help.

She watched as he crossed the bridge, but once on the other side of the river he disappeared over a low fence that surrounded the orchard.

Wrapping her arms around her waist, she shivered as she forced herself to wait for Bas's return. It felt as if the very air was rubbing against her nerves, which had been scraped raw.

Bas would be fine, she told herself. Of course he would. He was a trained assassin who'd survived three centuries.

What could possibly hurt him?

Besides, he was too much of a pain in her ass for her to ever be lucky enough to get rid of him . . . right?

She was still desperately trying to convince herself

everything was going to be fine when the sound of gunshots shattered the golden silence.

Oh . . . hell.

Barely aware she was moving, Myst was running along the edge of the bank, crouched low to keep hidden behind the thick bushes.

The shots had echoed through the valley, making it impossible to know exactly which direction they'd come from, but she suspected they came from across the river. Which meant that either Bas had been spotted by the local landowner or the Brotherhood was taking shots at him.

All in all, she hoped it was an angry farmer.

Intent on reaching the pathway that led down the bank, Myst came to a sudden halt as she caught sight of two shadows crossing the bridge.

Crap.

She shoved herself deep inside a bush, ignoring branches that scratched her face and tangled in her hair. She would have to wait until the men had passed her before she could try to find Bas and make sure he hadn't been injured.

Barely daring to breathe, she heard the sound of footsteps climbing the steep bank, but even as she waited for them to hurry past her, they instead came to a halt less than a hundred yards away. It was only then that she realized there were more footsteps approaching from the opposite direction.

Peeking through the branches, she managed to catch sight of the nearest man, her heart sinking as she recognized him as the jackass who'd wanted to rape her in the cottage.

The Brotherhood.

Just. Freaking. Perfect.

She tensed, preparing to flee if she was spotted.

She wasn't strong enough to take on all of them. Which

meant if she wanted to help Bas, she would have to go for backup.

Seemingly unaware of her presence, the four men huddled together in the center of the path.

"Where's the woman?" one of the men demanded.

The man who'd been with her in the cottage spoke. "Hell if I know."

"Shit," the first man muttered, his breath coming in tiny gasps as if he'd been running. "Where's the Sentinel?"

"He's down."

Down? Had he been shot? Myst pressed her hand over her mouth to muffle her horrified cry.

"Dead?" the leader demanded.

There was a harsh laugh. "I won't be sure until I cut off his fucking head."

Another man answered. "That can be arranged."

"If the Sentinel was here, then the clairvoyant can't be far," a fourth voice interjected.

There was a moment of confusion as they all spoke at once, offering their opinion of what needed to be done.

At last, the first man took charge.

"Let's deal with the Sentinel first, then we can spread out and search for the woman without worrying about the bastard sneaking up on us."

"Fine, but let's hurry," the man who'd been in the cottage muttered. "I want my hands on that bitch."

There was a sound of steel sliding against leather as the men pulled out their guns, then the scuffle of footsteps as they turned to head down the pathway.

Myst grimly battled her way out of the bush, ignoring the blood that ran down her cheek from a deep scratch. It matched the others from the shattered glass the night before.

Drawing in a deep breath, she struggled to think.

She had a choice. She could run and try to find help. Or

she could try and lead the men away from Bas until she could figure out some way to rescue him.

It took less than a heartbeat to make up her mind.

There was no way she had time to find assistance before the Brotherhood could return to Bas and kill him.

Decision made, she retraced her steps, finding a spot on the bank that would not only give the men a good view of her from the bridge, but give her enough of a head start so she could hopefully escape.

Her heart was thundering as she stepped to the very edge of the steep slope, refusing to think about anything but her overwhelming need to protect Bas.

Expecting an instant reaction, Myst frowned as the men hesitated at the foot of the bridge. What were they doing? Changing the plan?

Then, it finally struck her.

It was one thing to bravely talk about killing a Sentinel. It was another to actually march up to one and try to do the deed.

They were all dragging their feet, hoping the other guy would go first.

Idiots.

Dangerous idiots, she sternly reminded herself.

Eventually the leader would herd the reluctant crew over the bridge and toward Bas. If he was hurt or somehow disabled . . .

A fresh burst of fear exploded through her at the mere thought of Bas lying helpless as the bastards surrounded him. Leaning down, she picked up a rock and tossed it down the steep bank to land with a splash in the river.

The sound at last attracted the attention of the Brothers, who turned to scan the tree line, eventually giving a shout as they caught sight of her.

"Get her," the leader shouted, pointing in her direction as she turned to disappear in the undergrowth.

Myst darted through the trees, listening to the sound of pounding footsteps. Her lips twisted. Clearly the men were far more eager to pursue her than to try and take on a Sentinel. Even if he was "down." Whatever the hell that meant.

She made a low sound of distress, trying to shut out her frantic fear for Bas.

Right now all she could do was try and lead away the danger. Once she was certain they were fully committed to following her, she could consider how she was going to lose them long enough to get back to him.

One problem at a time.

That was the story of her life.

Reaching the edge of the road, she was forced to halt as the Brotherhood stumbled through the woods behind her. Christ. They'd already lost her trail.

She stomped her feet, reaching out to grasp a slender tree and give it a shake.

"This way," a male voice at last called out. "I hear her near the road."

There was a sharp whistle as the leader took control of his floundering twits.

"Call Roy and tell him that the clairvoyant's headed back to the village," he commanded. "He can cut her off at the gate."

Assured that the men were headed in the right direction, Myst hurriedly climbed the nearest tree, balancing on a slender branch as the men rushed past her.

Watching their hasty dash down the road, she waited until they were out of sight. Even then, she counted to a hundred before she lightly dropped to the ground. Once assured that no one had the brains to leave one of the men to keep guard, she hurriedly doubled back.

This time there was no hesitation as she reached the pathway that led down the steep bank. Plunging over the edge, she struggled to keep herself from tumbling headfirst into the river. The loose ground crumbled beneath her feet, the afternoon breeze tangling the fabric of her dress between her legs.

She managed to reach the bridge, however, unscathed, and jogging across slick stones, she headed straight for the orchard.

Like Bas, she ignored the gate, instead jumping over the low fence and melting into the shadows as she moved through the straight rows of trees. There was the potent scent of apples and more distantly the stench of manure, but it was the faint hint of blood in the air that she focused on.

Damn. She darted toward the far corner of the orchard, her heart lodged in her throat as she caught sight of the male body lying on the ground.

Bas.

Her steps slowed as she reached him and dropped to her knees beside his motionless form. He'd fallen face-first onto the narrow path between trees, three gunshot wounds oozing blood from the center of his back.

Oh God. How much damage had the bullets done?

Not even a high-blood could survive three bullets through the heart.

With a trembling hand she reached out to touch his too-pale face, a sob of relief wrenched from her throat as her fingers contacted the searing heat of his skin. A Sentinel burned even hotter when he was healing.

Surely that meant he was going to survive?

Settling back on her heels, she glanced around the isolated farm.

Now that she was assured Bas was still alive, she needed to find somewhere for them to hide. The Brotherhood might not be the smartest tools in the shed, but even they would eventually realize she wasn't hiding in the village. Once that happened she didn't doubt they would come looking for Bas.

Unfortunately there weren't a lot of options for hiding places. In fact, her choices were limited to returning to the thick cover of the woods, or the barn.

In the end, her decision was obvious.

It had to be the barn since it was far closer.

It was going to be difficult enough to transport Bas a few hundred feet without causing him more damage. She'd never make it back across the bridge.

Rising to her feet, she moved to peer over the fence, making sure there were no prying eyes. Not only did she have to look out for the Brotherhood, but she had to make sure she didn't attract the attention of the farmer or his family.

At last convinced they weren't going to be spotted, she hurried back to Bas and, crouching down, she gently slid her arms beneath him, hooking them around his shoulders so she could haul his upper body off the ground. She wasn't strong enough to actually carry him, but she tried to lift as much of him as possible as she slowly dragged him toward the side gate.

Terrified she might accidentally cause even more damage, Myst was careful not to jerk him as she moved out of the orchard one painful inch at a time. Sweat trickled down her back and her muscles were screaming in protest when she finally reached the barn.

Bas was a slender male, but he was pure muscle. Not to mention the fact that Sentinels had a heavier body mass than humans. It all combined to make him feel as if he weighed a ton.

No, not a ton. It had to be closer to two tons, she silently admitted, giving a grunt as she pulled him through the open door of the barn. Still, she refused to halt until she'd hauled him across the wooden floor and into one of the horse stalls that ran along the side of the barn.

Tucking him at the very back, she carefully covered him with a horse blanket that'd been tossed over a low bench, and then gathered up loose straw to pile on top of him. Only when he was completely covered did she step out of the stall and take a close inventory of her surroundings.

It was a traditional barn.

Lots of farming implements placed in corners and hanging from the open rafters. A wooden wagon in one corner. Stacks of straw. And two tractors that looked like they should have been taken to the junkyard long ago.

What she didn't see was a vehicle that could help her escape.

Either the farmer didn't have one, or more likely, he was currently using it.

She was searching for a weapon when she heard the unmistakable sound of approaching footsteps. Fear twisted her stomach as she glanced out the window to see two men headed directly toward the barn.

Dammit.

Crossing the floor, she grabbed a pitchfork and wedged herself behind the stacks of straw. It was the best place to remain hidden while keeping a close guard on Bas. No one would be able to sneak into the stall without her seeing them.

Just seconds later she heard the men entering the barn, their breaths rasping through the thick silence.

"Do you see anything?" one of them demanded.

Myst peeked around the edge of the straw, watching as the men made a quick circle of the interior, not bothering to pull open the stalls or check behind the various tools.

They'd obviously been commanded to do a sweep of the area, but they weren't overly eager to run across the missing Sentinel.

"No, it's empty," the second man muttered.

Together they gave a last glance around before they were headed out the door and jogging toward the distant vineyards.

Releasing the breath she hadn't even realized she was holding, Myst cautiously inched her way back toward the stall, setting aside the pitchfork so she could kneel beside Bas. Carefully she brushed away the straw from his too-pale face, allowing her fingers to linger on his cheek.

He was still warm, although not as hot as before. Was that a good thing? Or bad?

Frustration blistered through her like acid.

She had no way of knowing if he was getting better or worse. Then, almost as if sensing her violent emotions, Bas gave a low groan.

"Myst?" he rasped.

Terrified he might try to move, Myst stretched out beside him, carefully wrapping her arm around his neck and pressing her lips to his cheek.

"I've got you," she whispered softly as he drifted back to sleep. "Just hold on."

Chapter Fifteen

Bas had never been a big believer in heaven, although there'd been a time or two he was convinced he was in hell. But he was fairly certain that waking to find Myst pressed close to his side, her arms wrapped around him, was as close to celestial paradise as was possible.

Of course, he could have done without the savage pain that was radiating from the center of his back down to the tips of his toes. And the debilitating lethargy that was making it almost impossible to drag himself out of the clinging darkness.

Concentrating on the feel of Myst's warm, delectable body, Bas forced his heavy lids to lift. It was a lot more difficult than it should have been, but at last he was able to take in the sight of the pale face only inches from him.

Exquisite.

"I smell honeysuckle," he said, struggling to make his lips form the words.

The tiny female stiffened, her eyes widening. "Oh my God. You're awake. I've been so . . . so worried. . . ."

Without warning Myst gave a choked moan and abruptly burst into tears.

Shocked out of his mind, Bas ignored the pain that

pulsed through him with ruthless force as he reached to gather her trembling body in his arms.

"Shh, *cara*," he murmured, rubbing his hand up and down her back. He knew he should feel regret at her emotional outburst. The poor female was clearly tired, terrified, and near the edge of collapse. The last thing she needed was to be forced to take care of him. But he couldn't deny he was ridiculously pleased by the knowledge that she'd been so worried. Pathetic, but true. He pressed his lips to the top of her head. "Please don't cry."

It took some time for the tears to slow, but eventually she gave a small hiccup and lifted an unsteady hand to lightly touch his face.

"Are you in pain?"

He grimaced. "I'll live," he said, hoping he sounded more confident than he felt. "But I need a healer to remove the bullets before I can fully get my strength back." He didn't share how severe the damage actually was or that the blood loss had critically weakened him. She was frightened enough. "How long have I been out?" he instead demanded.

"A couple of hours."

His breath hissed between his clenched teeth. He'd sensed that he'd been unconscious for a while, but he hadn't realized it had been so long. No wonder Myst had been so frazzled.

"I assume it was the Brotherhood?"

"Yes."

"Dammit, I was an idiot."

He had a clear memory of crossing the orchard. He'd been concentrating on the nearby house, hoping to avoid an angry farmer, rather than considering the possibility the Brotherhood might be right behind him. Sloppy. The monks who'd trained him would be severely disappointed.

"You couldn't have known that they would be here," she tried to soothe.

"I knew they would be spread out looking for us. I should have been more careful," he growled, then, with an awkward movement he lowered his hand to pat his pockets, realizing he'd managed to lose his phone during the attack.

She made a low sound of distress as he tried to sit up, pressing her hands gently against his chest.

"No," she pleaded, her eyes dark with concern. "Don't move."

He conceded to her demand. Okay, it wasn't really a concession. It was more a collapse back to the wooden floor as his body refused to obey the commands of his brain.

Muttering a curse, he allowed his gaze to take in the open rafters above him and the narrow wooden walls on each side. A stall, right? Which meant they had to be in the barn.

"How did we get here?" he asked, relieved when his voice came out steady. "I don't remember anything after I was shot."

"I led the men back to the village and then circled back to pull you into this barn."

He tangled his fingers in her silver curls, a strange sense of pride racing through him. It never failed to amaze him how such a tiny, fragile-looking female could have the heart of a lioness.

"Clever girl."

She shrugged, her cheeks heating at his open admiration. "They searched the barn about an hour ago, so hopefully they won't be back."

"Good."

He paused, knowing they might be safe for the moment, but eventually someone was going to find them. He needed her to leave him behind so she could escape, but how could he trust she wouldn't do something foolish to hurt herself? He would obviously have to take advantage of her soft heart. "Myst, I need you to do something for me."

"What?"

He chose his words with care. "I need you to go to Valhalla for help."

She was shaking her head before he even finished. "No."

"Myst—"

"I knew you were going to be stupidly heroic and tell me I should take off and leave you behind," she interrupted.

He gave a startled laugh, genuinely amused by her accusation.

"You should know I've never, ever been accused of being a hero," he assured her in dry tones.

"Then why do you keep rescuing me?" she demanded.

He gave her curls a light tug, savoring the sensation of lying with her in his arms. It didn't matter that they were on a hard floor in a filthy stall. Or that he was desperately trying to convince her to leave before she could be captured.

Just for a few seconds he could absorb her warmth, breathing deep of her honeysuckle scent.

"I think this time you were the one to save me," he reminded her in soft tones.

She narrowed her dark eyes. "Why does it bother you to admit you can be a good guy?"

He leaned forward to kiss the tip of her nose. "Because the villain is much more interesting."

"Fine." Her fingers trailed down his throat in an unconsciously intimate gesture. "Be the villain if you want, but I'm not leaving you here."

Stubborn female.

"Myst, you know they're still out there hunting for you," he ruthlessly reminded her. "It's only a matter of time before they return."

She refused to budge. "Then we hide. Trust me, none of them are overly eager to come up against a Sentinel."

His heart twisted with fear. Christ. Why couldn't she do as he wanted just once?

"I get that you're worried about returning to Valhalla, but imagine how much worse it will be if you're captured by the Brotherhood," he pointed out in grim tones.

She ignored his warning. "Would you leave me if I was injured?"

"If it was necessary," he smoothly retorted.

Her fingers slid into his hair, giving the strands a painful tug.

"And you call me a rotten liar," she chided. "You're worse than I am."

"Bullshit," he muttered, the pain starting to make his thoughts fuzzy and his words slurred. "I'm a highly accomplished liar who has made millions of dollars on my ability to deceive others."

"I'm not leaving," she insisted.

"Myst."

"No." She inched closer, shivering as if she was cold despite the fact it was a hundred degrees in the barn. "We'll wait until dark and then find a vehicle to get out of here."

He swallowed a resigned sigh. He was too weak to force her to go. And besides, there was a needy, illogical part of him that desperately wanted her near.

He told himself it was a reaction to his fear that she might do something incredibly stupid. How could he know she wouldn't decide to take her own life? She was convinced, after all, that was the only way to alter the future.

But he knew it went deeper than that.

Since her unexpected arrival in Kansas City, he'd developed a growing terror of her disappearing.

She'd left once and he hadn't been able to find her, despite his considerable skills and resources. She could do it again if she wanted.

Just . . . poof. And he'd be helpless to track her down.

He needed to find some way to bind her to him so she could never disappear again.

Pulling her tight against his body, he rested his cheek against the top of her head.

"You're trembling," he murmured.

Her warm breath brushed his throat. "I'm not much of a hero, either," she muttered.

"Not true," he instantly argued, quite certain she had more courage packed into her tiny body than most Sentinels. "You've been incredibly brave, *cara*."

"Not hardly." She shook her head. "I'm scared out of my mind."

His fingers stroked through the satin of her hair, something deep inside him locking into place as she burrowed closer, in need of comfort.

"You risked your life to save me," he pointed out in low tones. "You sacrificed your heart to protect your daughter. And you've devoted your life to trying to alter fate." He pressed a kiss to her forehead. "You astonish me."

She tensed, as if caught off guard by his words. Slowly she tilted back her head to meet his steady gaze.

"I didn't always astonish you," she murmured.

He heaved a faint sigh. He'd spent four years telling himself that this woman was a flighty, irresponsible female who wasn't worthy of being Molly's mother. But he'd never, ever managed to erase her from his life.

She'd haunted his dreams and destroyed any hope of him finding another woman to stir his interest.

"You did," he assured her. "I just didn't want to admit it."

There was a short silence before she at last asked the question that'd no doubt been bothering her since their encounter with Boggs.

"Why do you have my locket?"

"I found it after you disappeared," he said.

He didn't add that it'd fallen out of one of the cushions

of the couch when he'd picked it up to toss it across the room. He'd been so consumed with frustration when he'd been unable to track her that he'd nearly destroyed his entire office.

"And you kept it?" she pressed.

"At first I assumed you would return, and I intended to give it back to you," he said.

Her lips twitched. "You thought you were so irresistible I couldn't stay away?"

He arched an arrogant brow. "Of course."

She rolled her eyes. "Good Lord."

He chuckled. It hadn't just been because he thought he was irresistible, although he couldn't deny he'd always had success with women. But the passion that'd exploded between them had been so intense he truly hadn't thought anyone would willingly walk away from such pleasure.

"Later I kept it because I hoped it would help me locate you," he continued.

She wrinkled her nose. "I had no idea you would remember our . . ." She blushed as she tried to think of a word to describe their afternoon of searing hot, balls-to-the-wall sex. "Encounter, let alone search for me."

"I remembered. Even when I tried to erase you from my mind," he growled. "Then you brought Molly to me and I told myself I kept the locket so I could give it to her when she was older."

Her fingers skimmed down the back of his neck. "See, you are a good guy."

"No." It wasn't just his instinctive aversion to playing the role of hero that made him deny her claim. It might be cheesy as hell, but he wanted this female to believe he could be her knight in shining armor. But she deserved the truth. "None of those were the real reason."

Her brows tugged together. "Then what was?"

"Whenever I touched the locket I had a vivid memory of

you stretched beneath me wearing the necklace and nothing else," he admitted with blunt honesty.

She made a choked sound. "Bas."

His lips skimmed down the length of her nose, his mind easily conjuring up the delectable image. A damned shame he was too injured to actually have a repeat performance.

"You asked."

"I suppose I did." She smiled with wry humor.

His lips brushed over her mouth. "Do you want it back?"

She considered for a minute before giving a shake of her head.

"No." Her lashes lowered, hiding her eyes. "I like the thought of you giving it to Molly."

He stilled, lifting his head to study her pale face. He wasn't fooled by her deliberately light tone. She wanted him to keep the locket because she hadn't yet given up her fear that she might have to end her life.

With an effort, he bit back his angry words.

It was a waste of his dwindling strength to try and convince her there was no way in hell that was going to happen.

She'd eventually accept he wasn't letting her go.

"Does the necklace hold some meaning for you?" he instead demanded.

She hesitated, and for a long moment he thought she might refuse to answer his question. Was she still trying to keep barriers between them?

Or was the memory a painful one?

"Yes," she at last said, her voice so low he could barely catch the words. "After I managed to escape from the Brotherhood compound, I hitchhiked my way to Casper. I didn't have any money and I was starving, so I snuck into a truck stop and tried to steal a donut."

His heat blasted through the air. He was going to take great pleasure in exterminating each and every Brother who'd been responsible for holding Myst hostage. Then he was tracking down her family.

But sensing her beginning to pull away, he fiercely leashed his fury.

This was a rare opportunity to learn about this elusive female. He wasn't going to blow it with his primitive hunger for revenge.

With an effort he managed to force a teasing smile to his lips. "You were starving and you stole a donut?"

She relaxed back into his arms, her head resting on his shoulder.

"They had sprinkles."

"Well, that would explain it," he murmured.

"Anyway, I barely got it shoved in my pocket when a large woman grabbed me by my ponytail and locked me into the storage closet," she continued. "At first I thought she'd called the cops."

His fingers ran a soothing path down her back, his cheek resting against the top of her head.

"You must have been terrified."

"Not really," she surprised him by saying. "Jail couldn't be any worse than living on the street. My only fear was that the Brotherhood would find me before I could escape."

His jaws clenched. God. Damn. One day he was going to destroy those bastards.

"What happened?" he demanded.

"After Ella's shift was over, she forced me into the diner next door and fed me. Then she took me to her cramped apartment and let me sleep on her couch." Her voice softened with an unmistakable hint of fondness. "I stayed there for almost a month before I knew I had to move on."

"Ella was a rare woman," he said, feeling a deep sense of debt toward the human who'd taken in a stray girl whom most would have turned over to the authorities.

Without her, who knew what might have happened to Myst?

"She was," Myst agreed. "When I asked her why she'd been so nice to me, she told me her daughter had run away when she was just fifteen. She hoped that someone had taken her in and kept her warm when she needed it."

Ah. There were few things more powerful than a mother's love for her daughter.

As Myst had proven when she'd left Molly with Bas despite the fact it'd clearly destroyed her heart.

And his own mother . . . A wistful smile touched his lips at the memory of the woman who'd been willing to sacrifice everything for him. She'd been a poor, uneducated peasant who'd been beaten by her husband and browbeaten by the local priest. Who would have blamed her if she'd simply given in to their claim that her child was a demon?

Instead she risked everything to save him.

"And the locket?" he asked.

"It belonged to her daughter," Myst said. "She wanted me to have it. She said it would remind me that there was someone out there who cared." She tilted back her head to reveal her wistful expression. "She was the first person who ever said that to me."

His palm gently cupped her cheek. How was it possible that a female who'd been neglected and abused could still be so capable of such love and devotion?

"Did you ever go back?"

"No." Her nose wrinkled with regret. "She was too intelligent not to notice I hadn't aged."

Ah. She hadn't wanted the older woman to realize she was a high-blood. No doubt a smart decision. If Ella had started blabbing about having a freak in her home it might very well have attracted the attention of the Brotherhood.

Still, Bas didn't believe for a minute that Myst had just

walked away without trying to do something to keep in contact with the woman who'd offered her such kindness.

"But?" he prodded.

Her eyes narrowed, before she gave a reluctant laugh, accepting he knew her better than she expected.

"But I send her a Christmas card each year with a little money," she admitted. "Ella wanted to hire a private investigator to find her daughter but they charged more than she could afford."

Bas blinked, struggling to focus on Myst's face. Dammit. His body was failing in his efforts to heal his injuries. Soon he would lose consciousness.

He struggled to make his lips move. "Myst."

"Bas?" Her eyes widened as she caught sight of his grim expression. Abruptly she sat upright. "What's wrong?"

"I'm fading," he said, his words slurred. "If I don't wake within an hour promise me you'll leave me and go to Valhalla."

She shook her head. "No."

"Dammit. I . . ."

His words failed, his lashes drooping as the darkness rose up to claim him. He was going under. And there wasn't a damn thing he could do to stop it.

He thought he felt Myst move, her lips brushing gently over his cheek before she was whispering in his ear.

"I'm sorry."

But then again, it could easily have been nothing more than a hallucination. God knew he'd conjured up enough fantasies about Myst over the years.

Lana used her private elevator to travel the nine levels beneath the public rooms of Valhalla to the headquarters of the Sentinels.

She bypassed the long communal room that was made

of stainless steel and lined with high-tech computer systems and monitors directly linked in to a variety of satellites that kept constant surveillance.

Instead, she directly entered the Office of the Tagos.

Not surprisingly, the private room was a precise reflection of the current leader of the Sentinels.

Sleek. Sparse. Ruthlessly male.

Stepping out of the elevator, her gaze skimmed over the large walnut desk and two black leather chairs, and the ivory-painted walls decorated with a collection of priceless samurai swords.

Wolfe might have taken on the role of leader, but he'd always be a warrior at heart.

Her gaze shifted to the dark-haired male who was wearing a casual T-shirt and black jeans. Relief jolted through her as she relished the knowledge he was unharmed.

She'd understood his need to take charge of the assault on the Brotherhood compound, but that hadn't made the waiting any easier.

Now she allowed herself a rare moment just to appreciate the sight of his lean, chiseled body and stunningly beautiful face.

At last sensing her entrance, Wolfe turned his attention from the bank of monitors he was arranging on a narrow table shoved against the far wall.

"Lana," he murmured, watching as she crossed the wooden floor to stand at his side.

Instantly she was enfolded in his sizzling heat, the scent of raw male power teasing at her senses. Dear . . . heavens. With an effort, she forced herself to concentrate on the screens that displayed images of their prisoners who now filled the dungeons of Valhalla.

"Any casualties?" she asked, pretending she didn't notice Wolfe's lingering gaze that took in her jade sweater with a deeply scooped neckline and black leggings that clung faithfully to her slender curves.

How else could she deny the fact that she'd deliberately chosen the clothes to attract his attention?

"No Sentinels injured," he at last murmured, his slender hand waving toward one of the monitors that showed a dozen Brothers chained to beds in the infirmary. "There were a few idiots who tried to resist, but they were easily convinced to surrender." He abruptly grimaced. "Unfortunately, when we found the clairvoyant he had a bullet in his head."

Lana clenched her hands. Damn. She'd been counting on a long, highly informative meeting with the traitor. Not only to discover if he'd had a vision of the weapon that Myst was supposed to create, but to gain some insight into the inner workings of the Brotherhood.

So far they were playing catch-up with the mysterious cult.

The scribes were attempting to collect any historical references, while Wolfe's Sentinels were doing their best to infiltrate the group. But until they knew names, locations, and the various plots to destroy Valhalla, her people were at risk.

An unacceptable situation.

"Suicide?" she demanded.

Wolfe gave a shake of his head. "I would guess the female did it."

Lana arched a brow. "Why?"

He leaned against the edge of the table, folding his arms over his chest. Her mouth went dry at the sight of the thin material of his shirt stretched tight over his hard muscles.

"Maybe she realized her compound was compromised and she didn't want him sharing secrets," he murmured.

She sternly forced herself to focus on his low words. "You don't sound convinced."

He shrugged. "If she knew we were there, why didn't she try to escape?" he pointed out. "Instead she took the time to kill the clairvoyant and then waited for us to show up in her bedroom." He glanced over his shoulder at the monitor that revealed a pretty woman sitting alone in a narrow room. "Hell, it looked like she'd just put on fresh lipstick."

Lana studied the leader of the Brotherhood.

She was younger than she'd expected her to be. But then Lana leaned closer, noticing the pretty heart-shaped face that was framed by long auburn hair and enchanting blue eyes. Her voluptuous curves were boldly displayed and her wide lips set in a sulky pout.

Ah. Now she could see why the Brothers followed her.

She looked like she'd just waltzed out of the Playboy Mansion.

Sometimes males were so pathetically predictable.

Straightening, she met Wolfe's intimate smile. He'd clearly read her thoughts.

She rolled her eyes, refusing to be distracted.

"Have you searched the compound?" she demanded.

"We did," Wolfe assured her. "We found the usual stashes of drugs, alcohol, and porn." His features tightened into a grim expression. "We also found a large bunker filled with contraband weapons."

Lana felt a stab of fear. It couldn't be a coincidence that each of the individual groups had managed to get their hands on weapons that'd either been banned by the government or were still in experimental stages.

Which meant they had a high-powered connection providing them with the lethal arsenals. Either a politician or military official.

"Where are they?"

Wolfe nodded his head toward the closed door on the other side of the room.

"My techies are inspecting them." His expression remained grim. "There are a few I've never seen before, but they're all dangerously sophisticated and designed specifically to hurt high-bloods."

A chill spread through her body. They had to find the person, or more likely persons, responsible for arming the Brotherhood.

Eventually they were going to feel empowered enough to step out of the shadows and directly confront Valhalla.

Such a war might kill hundreds, if not thousands.

She would do everything in her power to prevent that from happening.

"Do you know where they're coming from?"

"I intend to find out," Wolfe promised in hard tones. "I'll start my questioning tomorrow."

"Why not now?" she asked, knowing he would have a reason for waiting.

Wolfe was very, very good at his job.

"I like to put prisoners on ice for a few hours," he explained, a humorless smile curving his lips. "They can imagine far worse punishments than I could ever dream up."

Yeah. She glanced toward the monitors where the men were pacing their cramped cells with obvious agitation. By morning they would no doubt be close to panic.

She shifted her attention to the dark-haired female. Unlike her followers she wasn't revealing any hint of agitation. Instead she was stretched on the narrow cot, her gaze trained on the camera as if aware she was being watched.

Lana narrowed her eyes. "I want to speak to the leader."

"Why?"

She turned her head to meet Wolfe's curious gaze. "She's

the type of female who is an expert at using her beauty as a weapon." The air abruptly tingled with the force of her magic. Even when she had her powers leashed they tended to leak when her emotions were aroused. "She won't be able to manipulate me."

Wolfe's smile widened. He was one of the few males who wasn't intimidated by the vast magic that thundered through her.

"Works for me."

Lana frowned, rubbing her hands up and down her arms, which prickled with a strange sense of unease.

"And have the guards doubled," she commanded.

Wolfe stepped toward her, pulling his phone out of his pocket without hesitation.

"Are you expecting trouble?"

"It's . . ." She gave a shake of her head, struggling to explain her burst of apprehension.

"What?"

"It's in the air," she whispered.

Chapter Sixteen

Myst left the barn, her heart clenched with fear.

Bas had tried to pretend he was going to be fine, but she knew he was far more gravely injured than he wanted her to believe.

He was dying. She knew it in her very soul.

She somehow had to find a way to get him back to the monastery. Once he was safely with the healers at Valhalla she could consider what she was going to do about her vision.

It was selfish, no doubt.

If she truly cared about preventing her horrific future, she would leave Bas in the barn and find some means of putting a final end to the threat.

But she couldn't do it.

She might be willing to sacrifice herself, but she wasn't going to sacrifice Bas.

Pausing at the corner of the barn, she carefully studied the farmhouse. There might be a phone inside, but who would she call?

It wasn't like there was taxi service in this remote area.

She might be able to get ahold of Valhalla. She didn't have a direct number, but surely . . .

"Don't move a muscle."

Myst froze, silently cursing at the male voice that came from directly behind her. She knew she'd been distracted, but still it should have been impossible for someone to sneak up on her.

Sucking in a deep breath, she frowned as she caught the unmistakable scent of rich earth and . . . compost?

She licked her dry lips. A farmer. Not the Brotherhood.

"Please, I need help," she said in husky tones.

"Turn around. Slowly," he commanded in a gruff voice, speaking with an obvious English accent.

Myst did as he commanded, holding her hands over her head so he could see she didn't have any weapons.

He wasn't tall. Less than six foot, she guessed. But he was barrel-chested, with the thick muscles of a man who was accustomed to working with his hands. His short hair was dark and speckled with gray while his square face was bronzed by the sun, with lines that radiated from the pale blue eyes.

At the moment he was wearing a faded pair of denims and a flannel shirt, despite the heat. But it was the shotgun pointed at the center of her chest that captured and held her attention.

There was no way she could disarm him before he could squeeze the trigger.

"I don't want any trouble," she assured him in shaky tones.

His gaze narrowed as he took in her dirt-streaked face, her tangled hair, and wrinkled sundress.

"What are you on?" he demanded. "Meth? Heroin?"

"I'm not a drug addict," she assured him. "I swear."

He shook his head, his expression hard. "Yeah, that's what they all say. Before they try to make off with whatever they can get their grubby hands on."

"I . . ." She didn't know exactly how she was going to convince the farmer she wasn't there to subsidize a drug habit, but in the end it didn't matter as she was abruptly distracted by a distinct prickle that raced over her skin. "Oh. You're a high-blood."

The male jerked, as if struck by the belated realization that she wasn't entirely human.

"So are you."

"I am," she admitted.

He warily lowered the gun. "I'm Lloyd. Who are you?"

"Myst," she said, taking a second to consider her words. Just because Lloyd was a high-blood didn't mean he could be trusted. But then again, what choice did she have? She had to get Bas to a healer. Now. "I'm here on behalf of Valhalla," she at last said.

Lloyd frowned. "What business does Valhalla have in this remote area?"

She cautiously began to back through the doorway of the barn. "I'll tell you everything, but first I need you to come with me," she pleaded. "My friend has been injured."

He stood his ground, glancing into the shadows of the barn. It seemed as if she wasn't the only one who was a little spooked.

But who could blame him?

These were dangerous times.

"By who?" he asked.

"The Brotherhood."

Lloyd's blunt jaw clenched, his fingers tightening on the gun he held at his side.

"So it's true, then," he muttered. "They're not just a myth?"

She shook her head, desperately wishing they were some ridiculous bedtime stories that high-bloods made up to scare their children.

Then she wouldn't have been sold by her own family. Or held captive in an abandoned mine shaft. Or forced to walk away from her beloved daughter. Or to consider the impossible choice between allowing her vision to occur or making the ultimate sacrifice.

"No, they're very real," she choked out.

"Bugger," he breathed, easily sensing her acute distress. He stepped forward, careful not to make her feel crowded as he entered the barn. "Let's see this companion of yours."

In silence Myst led him across the floor to the stall, her breath wrenched from her lungs at the sight of Bas. He was lying still. Horribly still. And shadows bruised the pale skin below his eyes.

Entering the stall, Lloyd bent down beside him, his fingers reaching to touch Bas's throat.

"A Sentinel," he said.

"Assassin," she absently corrected.

He made a choked sound of shock. "Well, well," he breathed. "Today is a day for surprises."

Myst was momentarily confused, then she remembered that the monks had kept the creation of the assassins secret from most high-bloods. It was only because she'd spoken with his personal staff before meeting Bas that she knew he was more than just another Sentinel.

She entered the stall to crouch beside him. "Can you help him?"

"I'm afraid I'm not a healer."

Of course he wasn't. She swallowed a resigned sigh. Nothing could ever be easy.

"Is there one nearby?"

"None that have the skill to save your assassin." With a grimace he sat back on his heels and studied her troubled expression. "We need to get him to Valhalla."

"I—" She cut off her words. Would he help them if he knew it was going to put him in danger?

"Is there a problem?"

She glanced toward Bas, then muttered a low curse. She couldn't lie to the male. He had to know the truth.

"The Brotherhood is out there searching for me," she muttered.

She didn't know what she expected. Fear. Suspicion. Wariness.

Instead his blunt face hardened with determination as he abruptly surged to his feet.

"I think I can help with that," he promised her, watching as she warily straightened. "If you reach the monastery, will you be able to travel?"

She nodded. "Yes. The monks are waiting for us."

"Good." Turning, he headed out of the stall. "Stay here."

Myst blinked, struggling to keep up with his abrupt manner. "Where are you going?"

He kept walking, headed toward the door. "Trust me," he said.

She scowled, watching as he disappeared out of the barn. "I wish people would stop saying that to me," she at last muttered, bending down to run light hands over Bas's unconscious body. She might need the farmer's help, but that didn't mean she had to trust him. At last finding the hard shape she'd been seeking, she lifted Bas's pant leg to reveal the gun he'd strapped to his ankle.

Pulling it out of the holster, she tucked it in the pocket of her sundress. She wasn't a great shot, but she could get lucky.

Keeping an eye on the doorway, she was prepared to kill anyone but Lloyd who entered the barn. She didn't think he'd gone for backup. Or to rat her out to the Brotherhood, but as long as she was the only one to protect Bas, she wasn't taking any chances.

Thankfully, she didn't have to shoot anyone as Lloyd returned. Not that she didn't consider putting a bullet through the sputtering engine of the ancient tractor the farmer was carefully backing through the wide door.

Good Lord. There was smoke billowing from a tall stack filling the air with the stench of burnt oil, and the squeak of rusted shocks as Lloyd brought the sketchy vehicle to a halt in front of the wagon.

Leaping to the ground, Lloyd moved around the back of the tractor, grabbing the tongue of the wagon and lifting it with a massive tug.

Myst's eyes widened as his muscles bulged and he pulled the wagon forward to attach it to the tractor's hitch. He didn't have the distinctive heat that surrounded a Sentinel, but he was obviously as strong as one.

Something to remember.

Working swiftly to secure the wagon to the tractor, he at last pulled a handkerchief from his pocket and wiped the grease off his beefy hands. Then, tossing aside the soiled linen, he headed across the barn.

"Go on out," he told Myst, standing at the edge of the stall. "I'll bring your male."

"Be careful," she pleaded, moving out of the way so Lloyd could bend down and scoop Bas into his arms.

"I will," he murmured, walking at a slow, steady pace.

Myst followed behind, her gaze occasionally darting toward the door. The Brotherhood had to be searching for them. Would they return to the farm?

With a shiver she turned her attention back to Bas as the farmer placed his limp body in the wagon. Then, with a gentle care that eased a portion of Myst's concern, he gathered a stack of burlap bags that'd been piled in the corner and began lining them around Bas's body. The bags were no doubt used to gather his apples, and were heavy enough to keep Bas from shifting during the journey.

Once he was sure Bas was adequately protected, he began to cover his body with straw.

Myst moved to help him, casting a dubious glance at the tractor, which continued to chug and cough and sputter.

"Don't you have a truck?" she demanded.

"Yes, but it will also attract attention," he pointed out in reasonable tones. "A farmer with a load of straw won't even be noticed." Stepping back, he glanced toward Myst. "Your turn. Crawl in."

She bit her bottom lip, her hands gripping the edge of the wagon. The thought of stretching out in the wagon and being covered with straw made her realize how vulnerable she would be.

Lloyd could drive them anywhere without her knowing precisely where they were going.

Including straight to the Brotherhood.

"I'm not sure this is such a good idea," she muttered.

"Don't worry, Myst," he urged, his eyes softening as he studied her pale, weary face. "I promise you can keep your gun pointed at my back if it makes you feel better."

She wrinkled her nose. The farmer had done nothing but try to help her. He didn't deserve to be treated like a criminal.

"I'm sorry." She heaved a deep sigh. "It's been an eventful few days."

He waved away her apology, his gaze trained on her face.

"Are you running from something?" he asked in blunt tones.

"No." A sad smile curved her lips. "I was trying to change the future."

He looked genuinely startled by her admission. "An ambitious project."

She shrugged, moving to the end of the wagon. She was only prolonging the inevitable.

Without Lloyd's help, there was no way she could get Bas to the monastery.

"More like a futile one."

Lloyd instantly moved to grab her elbow as she climbed over the tailgate.

"Let me help," he muttered, giving a sudden hiss as he jerked his hand away in shock. "Death."

Knocked off-balance, she fell to her knees in the wooden bed, her brows snapping together as she watched the color drain from his face.

"You're a psychic?" she demanded.

"I'm sorry." He scrubbed his hand down his coveralls, as if he was trying to wipe away the images he'd seen in her mind. "I didn't mean to read you, but it's very strong."

"I know." She hunched her shoulder. She didn't blame him for looking as if he'd just glimpsed a nightmare. She'd been living with it for years and it still had the power to terrify her. "Death. Destruction."

He took a step back, his eyes unfocused, as if he was still lost in what he'd seen when he touched her.

"You must face it," he muttered.

"What?"

"It's . . ." He gave a sharp shake of his head, releasing his breath on a low hiss. "I don't know why, but you must travel to Valhalla. Otherwise the evil will spread."

Shock jolted through her.

Somehow she'd assumed that the last place she should ever be was at Valhalla. After all, she was supposed to create some weapon that was going to destroy the place. Or at least cause some sort of major catastrophe.

Now this psychic was telling her the one place she'd been avoiding like the plague was the one place where she was supposed to go.

"You're certain?"

There was no hesitation. "Absolutely."

"I don't suppose you could be a little more specific?"

"No."

"Damn," she muttered.

Lloyd parted his lips, but before he could speak Bas made a low sound of distress from beneath the straw, as if even in sleep he was suffering from his injuries.

"We need to get your friend to the monastery," Lloyd muttered.

Myst reached out to lightly touch his arm as he headed toward the tractor.

"I don't know how to thank you."

He paused long enough to give her hand a light squeeze. "Be brave and know that you're not alone."

She watched as the man easily climbed onto the tractor before she burrowed beneath the straw and pressed herself against Bas.

You're not alone.

The words echoed through her mind as she pressed her lips to Bas's forehead. Despite her fear, and the sick ball of dread lodged in the pit of her stomach that told her she was making a horrible mistake in returning to Valhalla, she couldn't deny a tiny flicker of warmth.

For the first time in her life she wasn't alone.

It was . . . astonishing.

Lana studied the leader of the Brotherhood with a jaundiced gaze.

The woman was stretched on the cot, propped up by a pile of pillows like she was some reincarnation of Cleopatra. There was even a faint smile on her lips that had only briefly faltered when Lana had strolled into the cell instead of the male who she'd no doubt been expecting.

Lana leaned casually against the locked door, silently admitting the woman had balls. Maybe not literally, but Lana had seen trained Sentinels curled in a corner, pleading for mercy the moment the Mave stepped into the room.

Of course, it could be that Stella was just too stupid to realize her danger. Being a leader didn't equate to brains whether you were male or female.

Over the years she'd met kings, clan chiefs, and presidents who were as dumb as stumps.

Rising from the cot with a languid movement, Stella gave a toss of her auburn curls.

"So you're the infamous Mave," she drawled. Her voice was low, sexy. A sensuous invitation.

A pity for her, Lana wasn't interested.

She flicked a brow upward, using her superior height to peer down her nose.

People hated that.

"Infamous?"

Stella shrugged. "The Brothers are terrified of you. After listening to their stories I expected you to have horns and a tail."

An icy smile curved Lana's lips. She'd deliberately chosen to wear an emerald silk top that scooped low to emphasize her witch mark.

"They don't go with my outfit."

The woman smirked, her dark blue eyes shimmering with amusement. Once again Lana was caught off guard by her sheer lack of fear.

"Is this where we go through the tedious game of good cop/bad cop?" she mocked.

Lana pushed away from the door, allowing a hint of her magic to fill the room. Enough was enough.

"This isn't a human jail," she reminded the idiotic woman. "There are no cops. No attorneys. No rights."

Stella gave a disdainful sniff. "You can't just hold me here."

"Actually, I can." The magic filled the cell, not enough to cause pain, but as an unmistakable warning. "I've already spoken to the legal authorities who have given their blessing for Valhalla to punish you and your men."

The first hint of uncertainty rippled over her heart-shaped face. Taking a step back, Stella flicked a swift glance toward the locked door.

"I don't believe you," she muttered.

Lana shrugged. "Believe whatever you want."

"There are laws—"

"My laws," Lana interrupted.

She wasn't just trying to intimidate the leader of the Brotherhood. She truly did make the laws of Valhalla. As well as doling out the punishment.

She did her best to be fair, but in the end she always had to choose what was best for her people.

The woman gave a tiny shiver before her eyes narrowed and she was tilting her chin.

"You're trying to frighten me," she snapped.

"If I wanted to frighten you I can assure you there wouldn't be any doubt," Lana asserted. Just for a second she considered creating the illusion of spiders crawling across the floor or Stella's flesh melting from her bones, only to rapidly dismiss the petty thought. Giving in to the impulse wouldn't prove her power. It would only allow the other woman to know that she was getting under Lana's skin. "Do you think I lead the high-bloods because I won some popularity contest?" she instead demanded.

Stella stiffened her spine. "You won't hurt me."

Lana studied the woman's arrogant expression, an odd chill inching down her spine.

She understood the woman was trying to put on a brave

face. That's what she would do if she was being held captive by her enemies.

But this was . . . more.

"Why are you so confident?" she brusquely demanded.

The woman lowered her lashes, as if hoping to prevent Lana from reading her mind.

"You obviously want information from me."

Lana wasn't a psychic, but she knew when a prisoner was trying to hide something from her.

"A lie," she accused.

"Believe whatever you want." Stella threw Lana's earlier words back in her face.

Bitch.

"You haven't asked about your men." Lana abruptly changed tactics. She'd been wrong. Stella wasn't stupid. She was, in fact, very clever. It was going to take more than intimidation to force her to tell Lana what she wanted to know. "Aren't you concerned about their safety?"

Stella aimlessly paced toward the far end of the cell, pretending an interest in her scarlet-painted nails.

"Not particularly," she admitted without a shred of guilt. "The Brotherhood was a means to an end."

Lana wasn't impressed. She hadn't expected to like the leader of the Brotherhood. They were the enemy, intent on destroying her people.

But this woman was . . .

Revolting.

She briefly reconsidered the pleasure of weaving some gruesome illusion. If she had to endure being stuck in a cramped cell with the smug bitch, she should be allowed to have some fun.

Unfortunately, she didn't have time for games.

"What end?" she demanded.

"Power. Wealth." An unmistakable glint of envy flashing through Stella's eyes. "Everything you possess."

Lana shook her head. How dare the woman try to compare their positions? They couldn't be more different.

"I'm not the Mave because I hunger for power or wealth," she sharply denied. "A leader's only concern should be the welfare of her people. I would lay down my life to protect them."

Stella gave a grating laugh. "Then you're an idiot. They would sell you out in a heartbeat." She flicked a disdainful gaze down Lana's slender body. "I should know. It took one blowjob for the clairvoyant to forget his allegiance to Valhalla." Her gaze returned to meet Lana's glare. "Do you call that loyalty?"

Lana had centuries of training to keep her expression composed. There was no way she was going to let Stella know she'd hit a nerve.

She understood that not every high-blood was going to approve of her or Valhalla. There were always going to be those who resented authority, or refused to follow rules. But it troubled her that Peter would not only have turned his back on Valhalla, but that he'd be willing to sacrifice his own people.

For what?

This woman in his bed?

Pathetic.

"This is a free country," she forced herself to say, her voice frigid. "Everyone is allowed to make their own choices, even if I might not personally agree with them."

Stella snorted, no doubt able to guess that Lana was far from pleased by Peter's betrayal.

"Very democratic," she mocked.

Lana released another burst of magic. Stella needed a reminder of who was in charge. And maybe Lana just enjoyed watching the pretty face drain of color as the faint prickles turned to actual pain.

"Tell me about Peter's visions."

Stella rubbed her arms, her face flushing. She clearly didn't like the blunt proof that Lana had the sort of power she so desperately desired.

"Fuck you," she muttered.

Lana stepped forward. "It will be much easier for you if you simply tell me."

"Or what?" Stella lifted her hand to wiggle her fingers in Lana's direction. "You're going to do some hocus-pocus on me?"

Lana ignored the taunt. She'd proven her point.

"I don't need to," she informed her companion. "I have several high-skilled psychics who can dig through your brain to extract any information I need." She glanced toward the camera blinking in the corner of the ceiling. "They're waiting for my signal to begin."

Genuine fear tightened her features as Stella took a jerky step backward. Swiftly, however, she was regaining her composure. Almost as if she was telling herself that Lana wouldn't follow through on her threat.

Was the woman stupid enough to think she was going to be able to escape? Or that the men she was so eager to dismiss as necessary baggage might be able to rescue her?

"You know, we're not so different," she told Lana, her fingers running through her dark hair as she flashed a coy smile.

Lana arched a brow. "Really?"

"Of course. We're both ambitious women who've struggled to survive in a man's world."

Ah. So this was the "we are sisters" routine.

Lana might have been more sympathetic if she hadn't been born several hundred years ago. What did this woman know about suffering? Had she been bought and sold as property? Or compelled to run from angry villagers who intended to burn her at the stake?

"We're virtually soul mates," she drawled.

"Mock me if you want, but it's true," Stella insisted. "Men will never comprehend what we've been forced to sacrifice to earn a position of respect."

Lana gave a sharp laugh. No one, absolutely no one, would ever understand what she'd sacrificed over the years.

"Peter was capable of knowing where Myst would be," she said, turning the conversation back to the reason she'd sought out this woman. "Correct?"

Stella hesitated before giving a nod of her head. "Yes."

"What else did he see?"

"Exactly what you fear," Stella assured her. "That the female clairvoyant will give me what I need to destroy you."

Lana frowned. There was truth in the woman's words. The clairvoyant had foretold something that gave Stella the belief she was going to be victorious.

But there was also a hint of uncertainty. As if things weren't unfolding exactly as the woman had expected.

"What is the weapon?" Lana demanded.

Stella laughed, her expression mocking. "You can't possibly expect me to tell you."

She hadn't. But it would have saved time.

Still, there was more than one way to get the information she needed.

"Have it your way," she said with a shrug, turning toward the door. "Although, I will warn you that the extraction method is always a painful process and"—she deliberately paused, giving a tiny shudder—"on some occasions destructive."

"Wait," Stella rasped.

Lana turned back to study the woman's uncertain expression. "Yes?"

Stella licked her lips, her clever mind no doubt searching for a way to gain time.

She was a survivor.

Lana might have admired the trait if Stella hadn't been so willing to use and abuse people.

"We might be able to negotiate a deal," the leader of the Brotherhood grudgingly offered.

Lana flicked a glance around the cell. "You're hardly in a position to be making demands."

The woman's jaw tightened. She didn't like being forced to beg.

"You want something," she said between gritted teeth. "I want something—"

Her pitiful attempt to gain a compromise was interrupted as the door was shoved open and a large Sentinel with a skull-shaved head and bulging muscles stepped into the cell.

"Excuse me, Mave," he murmured with a respectful bow.

Knowing she would never have been disturbed unless it was important, she instantly turned her attention to the warrior.

"Yes?"

The Sentinel glanced toward Stella, choosing his words with care.

"The Tagos wanted me to tell you that they've arrived."

Lana frowned before realizing he had to be referring to Myst and Bas. There would be no reason to hide anyone else's identity from the prisoner.

"Good," she said, genuine relief flooding through her.

Not just because the Brotherhood hadn't managed to get their hands on Myst, even though that was obviously vital to the safety of Valhalla. But because Molly would be reunited with her parents.

With a nod, the Sentinel slipped out of the cell. Lana moved to follow him, not surprised when Stella made a sound of distress.

"No," she grated. "Where are you going?"

Lana paused long enough to send her prisoner a warning glare.

"Consider how you want to play this, Stella," she said in icy tones. "I can make your life sheer misery if you don't cooperate."

Chapter Seventeen

Bas hovered in that weird place just before gaining full consciousness.

For a minute he let himself drift, trying to figure out where he was and how he'd gotten there.

He had a vague memory of excruciating pain and a very real desire to let go. It'd only been the sense of Myst pressed close against him that'd kept him from giving in to the lurking darkness.

She needed him.

Molly needed him.

He would fight against death, no matter how painful.

There'd been a fuzzy sense of movement, followed by more pain, and then . . . blessed relief. Taking a slow, inner inventory of his body, he realized the healers had managed to dig out the bullets and close his wounds.

Which meant he had to be at Valhalla.

Fear seared away the clinging fog, and he wrenched his eyes open to take stock of the crisp white room that was filled with a combination of stainless steel hospital equipment and wooden shelves that held ceramic pots of magical potions. The high-bloods used both human technology and their own powers to heal their people.

A potent combination.

Plus, there was a newfound healer who could actually change people's DNA. It gave hope to those high-bloods born with genetic traits harmful to themselves or others.

He muttered a curse. The knowledge that he'd managed to make it to Valhalla didn't ease the fear that twisted his gut. Especially when he realized he'd obviously been in the infirmary long enough for his body to start recovering.

"Myst?" His voice came out as a husky whisper.

"Nope," a male voice replied. "It's just me."

He grimaced, watching as Kaede moved to stand beside the narrow hospital bed.

The enforcer was dressed in his familiar black jeans and tee with his dark hair pulled into a tail at his nape, but as relieved as Bas was at the knowledge that his friend was safe, he was desperate to know that Myst hadn't been allowed to slip away.

"Shit." Bas grabbed for the pad at the edge of the bed and pushed a button, levering himself so he was seated upright. He hissed as a dull ache spread through his chest, reminding him he had a long way to go before he was fully healed. "The last time I woke I thought I was in heaven," he muttered. "This time I'm fairly certain I'm somewhere much warmer."

Kaede reached to lightly touch the side of Bas's neck in a gesture of unspoken respect before he straightened to offer a mocking smile.

"Is that any way to talk to your devoted servant?"

Bas glanced around the room. "Where's Myst?"

"In the nursery with Molly."

He released a shaky breath. He'd been terrified she'd slipped away while he was unconscious.

"You're certain?" he pressed.

"Of course." Kaede frowned, easily sensing Bas's concern. "I escorted her there myself."

Still Bas wasn't satisfied. In fact, he was frustrated as hell.

He understood her desire to be with Molly. He couldn't wait to hold his daughter in his arms. But he needed to see Myst. To touch her and reassure himself that she was unharmed.

"She wasn't hurt, was she?"

Kaede shrugged. "No, although she looks exhausted."

Bas scowled. Dammit. He needed to be out of this bed. Myst refused to take proper care of herself when he wasn't watching out for her.

"You should have made her rest."

Kaede rolled his eyes. "Yeah, right. Have you ever had any success in making her do something she doesn't want to do?"

"Touché," he muttered. Myst would no doubt have insisted on being with her daughter, even if she was on the edge of collapse. "Do you know how we got here?"

Kaede gave a low chuckle. "She charmed a local farmer, who turned out to be a psychic, into hiding you in the back of a wagon and driving you to the monastery."

Bas's lips twisted. He could easily imagine Myst twisting the farmer around her little finger. Unlike most females, she had no idea just how much power she had over poor, susceptible men. Which only made her more irresistible.

"She's astonishingly resourceful," he said with a wry smile.

"Is that another way to say stubborn as a mule?"

"She is that," Bas readily agreed. For such a tiny thing, she was dauntingly persistent. He grimaced, reminded that her tenacious nature wasn't always a good thing. Not when she was convinced there was only one way left to halt her vision. "I want you to keep an eye on her until I can get out of this damn bed."

"What do you mean?"

"I don't want her leaving Valhalla."

Kaede studied him with blatant confusion. "Are you afraid she might try to take off with Molly?"

His hand unconsciously lifted to rub against the center of his chest. It wasn't his wounds that bothered him. It was the gnawing anxiety that he couldn't prevent Myst from doing something hasty.

"No. She's convinced there's only one way left to halt her future," he admitted in dark tones.

"What . . ." Kaede's words trailed away as he realized what Bas was implying. "Oh shit," he breathed.

"Keep her close," Bas commanded.

Kaede gave a solemn nod, accepting the responsibility for guarding Myst until Bas could regain his rightful place as her protector.

"I swear."

Confident he could depend on his closest friend, Bas concentrated on the next worry.

"What about the Brotherhood?"

Kaede folded his arms over his chest. "We rounded up the Brothers in the Wyoming compound, but the ones who shot you in France are still MIA."

Bas wasn't disappointed. "Good. I want to personally track down each one and have a nice, long chat."

"Why do I suspect the chats are going to involve a lot of blood and screams for mercy?"

Bas shrugged, not denying there was going to be blood and screams involved in his chat.

A lot.

"They shouldn't screw with an assassin if they don't want to get hurt," he pointed out in reasonable tones.

Kaede's lips twitched. "True enough."

"What about the clairvoyant?"

The enforcer's face tightened with frustration. "Dead."

"That's unfortunate," he muttered. He'd wanted to

personally convey his displeasure at the man for betraying Myst and delivering her into the hands of the Brotherhood.

"They have the female leader in the dungeon." Kaede's lips twisted. Obviously he wasn't a big fan of the woman. "She might be able to give information on the weapon."

"It doesn't matter," Bas assured his friend. He was done with the games. He was going to protect his family. And screw the world. "Once I'm healed I intend to take Myst and Molly away from here."

Kaede blinked, as if caught off guard by Bas's decision. "Are you certain the Mave will allow you to leave?" he demanded.

"I hadn't intended on asking for permission."

"Okay." Kaede tilted his head, studying Bas's stubborn expression. "Say that you get out of Valhalla—what's the plan?"

Bas shrugged. "We'll go someplace we can't be found."

Kaede cocked a brow. "That's it?"

Bas was instantly on the defensive. Probably because his friend had a point.

It was a shitty plan.

"You got a problem?"

Kaede didn't back down. "I'm not an expert on visions, but I don't think hiding can change the future."

"What do you suggest?" Bas lifted a hand to shove his fingers through his hair. For the first time in his life he felt as if he didn't have control. The sensation was making him more than a little testy. "That I let Myst take her life?"

There was a blast of heat as Kaede narrowed his gaze. The enforcer clearly wasn't amused by the stupid accusation.

"Is that what you think? That I would want Myst to die?"

"Christ, no," Bas breathed in regret. "Sorry."

The heat eased as Kaede studied Bas's strained face. "I can travel to the temple," he startled Bas by suggesting. "They're uncovering ancient texts every day. Maybe one of them will give us a clue as to what this weapon is supposed to be."

Bas frowned. It was possible the temple that'd been discovered by the necromancer could reveal new prophecies. Maybe even some that were related to Myst's vision. But he'd never expected Kaede to willingly offer to go there.

Not with his past.

"I couldn't ask that of you," Bas said. "If I decide it's necessary, I'll go."

"You're not asking," Kaede corrected. "I'm volunteering."

"But—"

"It's okay." Kaede held up a hand, interrupting Bas's protest. "It's time I went back and faced my past."

Before Bas could respond, the sweet scent of honeysuckle was distracting him. Turning his head to the side, he watched as Myst stepped into the room, some restless ache deep inside him slowly easing.

She was wearing a pretty raspberry sundress that emphasized the ivory satin of her skin and the stunning silver hair that tumbled down her back. Her tiny feet were bare, although there was a delicate gold chain around her ankle.

She looked like a wood nymph who'd accidentally strayed into captivity.

"I'm sorry," she murmured, glancing from Kaede to Bas. "I didn't mean to interrupt."

Kaede sent Bas a wry smile, both of them realizing that Myst had no idea the electric static in the air was because she was gut-wrenchingly gorgeous, and both Bas and Kaede were too male not to react.

"No problem," he murmured, strolling toward the door. As he passed Myst he reached to run his fingers over her amazing hair. It wasn't sexual. More a silent promise of protection. "I was headed out."

"You won't leave Valhalla until I'm out of this bed," Bas reminded his friend.

"Aye, aye, captain." Kaede turned to send him a mocking salute. Then he glanced toward Myst. "Take care of him," he requested in a low voice before leaving the room.

Myst walked toward the bed, her gaze straying back to the door where Kaede had just disappeared.

"He was saying something about confronting his past," she murmured. "What did he mean?"

Bas reached to wrap his fingers around her hand the second she was within reach.

"I'm not entirely certain," he admitted, his tone husky as his thumb stroked the pulse beating at her inner wrist. She was alive and well. Thank God. "I assume it has something to do with our first meeting."

"Where was that?"

He studied her pale face, suspecting she was trying to keep him distracted. She had a habit of building barriers the second she feared he was getting too close.

But he could find nothing but genuine interest etched onto her ivory features.

"I was sneaking out of the harem of a particularly powerful sultan," he murmured, hiding his smile as she predictably rolled her eyes.

"Why am I not surprised?" she muttered.

Bas settled his head against the pillow propped behind him. He was still weak, but having her near was easing his pain. As if she was helping to speed his recovery.

A realization that should have shocked him. Only a connection at a soul-deep level could allow high-bloods to share power.

But he wasn't shocked. He'd already accepted that this female was far more than just a transitory lover.

She was the mother of his child. The other half of his heart.

His mate.

"I didn't realize the sultan was a high-blood until he had me chained and tossed into a pit of vipers," Bas continued, grimacing at the memory.

The viper poison hadn't been able to kill him, but it had hurt like a bitch.

"Ouch," Myst said.

Bas winced as a chuckle was wrenched from his throat. She didn't sound particularly sympathetic to his plight. In fact, he suspected she wasn't at all sorry he was tossed in the pit.

"It wasn't the most pleasant experience," he assured her, insanely pleased by her reaction.

She could try all she wanted to keep him at a distance, but she couldn't disguise the fact that she was jealous at the mere thought of him with another woman.

As if sensing she'd revealed more than she wanted, Myst cleared her throat and wiped the expression from her face.

"How did you get out?"

"I'd like to say I broke the chains with my brute strength or killed the vipers by biting off their heads," he said, his lips twisting. The humiliating episode hadn't been his finest hour.

She wrinkled her nose. "Eww."

"The truth is one of the concubines took mercy on me and threw down the key to the lock that held the chain together," he admitted. As much as it grated at his pride, he'd never been more relieved when he heard the key hit the ground just inches from his feet. "I was weak from the viper poison, but managed to claw my way out."

She blinked. "You were saved by a concubine?"

He lifted her fingers to press them against his lips. "Actually, if you really think about it, I was rescued because my skills in giving women pleasure were so addictive that she—"

"Stop." She jerked her hand free, glaring at him as her jealousy overcame her determination to pretend indifference. "I would have left you in the pit."

His gaze slid over the silver beauty of her hair before taking in the delicate features and wide, velvet-dark eyes.

So stunningly beautiful, and yet so unbelievably untouched by the evil that'd tried to destroy her.

He reached to regain his hold on her wrist, and his thumb brushed her satin skin. Immediately he pondered the delicate bones. Hmm. If he gave in to his increasing urge to handcuff her to him to ensure she couldn't escape, he'd probably have to have the cuffs special-made.

"No you wouldn't," he denied.

She frowned, but she wasn't foolish enough to argue. They both knew she was too softhearted for her own good.

Which was why she needed him.

"You were telling me about Kaede," she instead said.

He thought back to the night. At the time he'd been fascinated by the beauty of the Middle East. The heat, the exotic spices, the plush luxury. The luscious women who were trained to please a man.

Now it all seemed oppressively opulent.

He far preferred the image of a sunlit glade with Myst and their daughter seated among the wildflowers.

"After I escaped I was sneaking out of the palace when I stumbled across a treasure chest," he said, leaving out the part where he'd had to kill several guards to make his escape.

Myst wouldn't be impressed.

She studied him with a curious expression, caught up in his story.

"I suppose you found enormous riches?"

"In a way." He gave a careful lift of one shoulder. "I could sense there was someone locked inside."

"Oh," she breathed in disapproval.

Bas had been equally outraged. After having escaped the pit, he wasn't about to leave another prisoner behind.

"I took the chest with me just to piss off the sultan," he said.

Myst gave a slow shake of her head. "Why can't you admit that you wanted to help whoever was inside?"

He snorted. There was no way in hell he was going to play the "good guy" card. He was a bad-ass assassin.

End of story.

"For whatever reason, I took the chest with me," he muttered. That was as far as he was going to admit he was worried about the person inside. "And when I reached the mountains I opened it to release the captive."

A man had his pride.

Her eyes widened. "Kaede?"

"Yes."

"Why was he in there?"

Bas snorted. Kaede had been like a wild man when he'd leaped out of the chest. His hair was hanging down to his waist and his skin filthy and caked with blood. He'd obviously been inside the chest for years. Perhaps decades. "He didn't volunteer the information and I didn't ask," Bas admitted. "In fact, he took off as soon as he was free. I never expected to see him again."

"Obviously you did."

"I woke the next morning to discover him waiting outside the cave I'd used to take shelter." Bas gave an amused shake of his head. He'd nearly killed the male before he realized he was there to offer help. After he'd been stupid enough to get caught by the sultan he'd been on full alert. Which meant there was no way anyone should have been able to sneak up on him. No one. "He had a hot breakfast and clean clothes for me."

"A gift for saving him?" she asked.

That'd been his first thought. But Kaede had quickly corrected him.

"Kaede's service is the gift."

"His service?" She made a sound of surprise as his words sank in. "He became your slave?"

Bas laughed with genuine amusement. "You've met Kaede. Can you imagine him being anyone's slave?"

Her lips twitched as she realized just how ridiculous her words had been.

Kaede was loyal, ruthless in carrying out Bas's orders, and willing to place his life on the line to protect his employer. But by no stretch of the imagination could he be considered submissive.

"No."

"His honor demanded that he repay me for rescuing him from the sultan, which is why I made him my enforcer," Bas said. "But he stayed because we've become friends."

She glanced toward the door, her thoughts clearly on Kaede. "And now he wants to return to that place?"

"Not necessarily," he reluctantly denied. The last thing he wanted was for her to feel guilty. "He's going to the temple that was discovered by the necromancer. He hopes the newly unveiled scripts will hold some clue to your vision."

Chapter Eighteen

Stella paced the cell.

Back and forth. Back and forth.

This was all wrong. Peter's vision had specifically seen her at Valhalla, which was the only reason she'd allowed herself to be taken without attempting to escape. But she wasn't supposed to be locked in a cell. And certainly she wasn't supposed to have her mind ripped open by psychics.

Which meant Peter had been mistaken. Or, more likely, he'd lied to her.

She had been in the process of pointing a gun at his head when he'd been struck by the timely vision, after all. It was quite possible it was his last act of revenge.

What better way to punish her than to promise her greatest desire would be found in the home of her enemy, just so he could be sure she would end up exactly where she was?

Stuck in the dungeons, at the mercy of that bitch of a Mave.

No doubt he was laughing from his grave.

But Stella hadn't survived over the years by being a naive putz.

There was no one in this world that she trusted. Certainly

not a high-blood who'd already proven his willingness to betray those who trusted him. Which was why she'd taken a precaution.

Lifting her arm, she slid slender fingers beneath her hair, locating the thin piece of metal that she'd taped to her neck. Careful to keep her back turned toward the camera, she studied the strange device.

The Brotherhood tended to be made up of bullies, fanatics, and a handful of crazies, but there were a few who had the sort of underground connections that kept them fully stocked in illegal weapons.

Most of them she left for the soldiers who possessed a weird fascination with blowing things up, but on occasion she was offered an intriguing prototype she couldn't resist. This one was by far her favorite.

Or at least, it was her favorite as long as it worked.

The Brother who'd given it to her had promised when she broke the plastic seal that covered the device it would send out a pulse that would knock out every electrical grid within a thousand feet. Even better, it emitted a high-pitched sound that humans couldn't hear, but would disable any nearby high-bloods.

Like a dog whistle on steroids.

She could only hope the disruptions would be enough to allow her to escape.

First she had to get the door to the cell open. It wouldn't do any good to set off the device if she was stuck in her cell. Thankfully, her guards were men.

High-blood or not, they could all be led around by their cocks.

Hiding the device in the palm of her hand, she allowed the strap of her camisole top to slide off her shoulder, revealing the plump curve of her breasts.

They would never fall for the "oh, I feel sick" routine.

Or the "I'm going to hold my breath until you let me out of here."

No. They needed a pressing reason. . . .

Ah. Her gaze landed on the heavy glass pitcher filled with water that had been left beside her cot. Keeping her movements deliberately nonchalant, she strolled to pick up the pitcher as if she was going to pour a glass of water. Once she had a firm grip, however, she whirled around and threw the pitcher at the blinking camera with every ounce of her strength.

There was a nerve-racking second as she watched it arc through the air, then with an explosive sound it shattered against the camera at the same time it drenched the cell in water.

Moving to stand in the center of the floor, she calmly waited for the door to be shoved open by an angry Sentinel.

"What the hell?" he snapped, shoving his head into the room to examine the broken camera and shattered glass.

"Oops." Stella smiled, leaning forward. She needed him to actually enter the room. Otherwise he might be able to shut the door before she could get out. "It just slipped out of my hands."

"Bullshit," the man growled, his gaze not even glancing toward her breasts she was deliberately exposing.

Clearly the sex kitten routine wasn't going to work.

"I need to speak with the Mave," she said, easily changing tactics.

He frowned. "Why?"

"I have information she needs."

"I'll send word to her."

"No, I need to speak with her now."

The guard's dark eyes narrowed. "She's busy."

She pouted. "Trust me, she isn't going to be happy when she learns I have the key to halting the destruction of Valhalla, but you couldn't be bothered to interrupt her."

"Fine." The Sentinel pulled out his phone but he remained too wary to actually enter the cell.

Stella swallowed a curse. She was going to have to take a chance her weapon would incapacitate the guard before he could react.

Squeezing her hand, she hissed in pain as the metal sliced into the flesh of her palm. Damn. She hadn't realized it was going to hurt. Still, she continued to press against the device, at last hearing the faint sound of the plastic cracking as the seal was broken.

And then . . .

Boom.

It wasn't an actual sound. At least, not to her. It was more an unseen explosion that rushed past her, making the cell shake and the Sentinel pitch forward. The lights flickered as she watched the guard fall flat on his face, then she was plunged into an inky darkness.

Oh, thank God. The cell door remained open.

Warily, she forced herself to her knees, crawling forward as she searched for the phone the Sentinel had been holding. She found it a few feet away, and pressing the screen, she used the light to make sure the guard was truly out for the count.

He was.

Not only was he sprawled at an awkward angle, but there was a trickle of blood running out of his ears. He couldn't fake that, could he?

Confident the weapon had worked, she rose to her feet and stepped over the guard. Heading out of the cell, she used the phone as a flashlight.

Thankfully, she'd been smart enough to keep track of their journey through Valhalla when she'd been led to her cell, so even with limited light it was a simple matter to retrace the maze of narrow hallways.

She didn't bother to go in search of her men, who'd been

placed in another section of the dungeons. Right now it was every man, or woman, for themselves. Once she'd managed to escape, she could easily find another group of Brothers. They were a dime a dozen.

Reaching the small guard room at the end of the hallway, Stella stepped inside to discover two Sentinels slumped in front of their blank monitors. For the first time she hesitated.

The weapon had clearly done its job in knocking out the computer system, which meant she couldn't be tracked by the security cameras, but that meant the elevators wouldn't work.

So how the hell was she going to get to the upper floors?

With a low curse, she searched the office, hoping to find an override for the elevator. Surely there had to be some sort of fire escape?

It took a precious few minutes, but at last she found an old-fashioned key hidden in the bottom drawer of the desk. The cells were armed with scanners that needed the thumbprint of a Sentinel to open. So what did the key unlock?

Determined to find out, she left the guard room and searched the area near the elevator.

At first she could find nothing, then, at last, she shoved aside an ugly fake plant to reveal a hidden lock set into a seemingly blank wall.

This had to be it.

Refusing to consider what would happen if she was truly trapped in the dungeon, she stuck the key in the slot. For a terrifying moment it refused to budge. She forced herself to pause, sucking in a deep breath. Panicking wasn't going to help.

Giving the key a jiggle, she managed to loosen the tumblers enough to allow the key to turn. There was an audible click before a portion of the wall was sliding open to reveal a narrow tunnel.

Stella had expected steps instead of the smooth ramp that headed upward, but she wasn't about to question her stroke of luck. The tunnel was her escape from the dungeons. That was all that mattered.

Stepping through the narrow opening, she shut the door behind her, still using the phone to battle the thick darkness.

Not that there was much to see. A smooth stone ramp. Steel walls. And an occasional door. She assumed it was some sort of emergency exit for a mass evacuation.

Hopefully it would be the last place any of the high-bloods would think to look for her.

The thought had barely managed to form when she heard the unmistakable sound of footsteps behind her. Shit. Someone was already searching the tunnel.

Stella was arrogant. And vain. And utterly convinced she deserved to be treated as a queen. But she wasn't stupid. There was no way she was going to be able to outrun a Sentinel. Refusing to panic, she continued forward, her breath hissing between her teeth as she caught sight of the doorway just ahead.

Thank God.

Not daring to slow down long enough to glance behind her, Stella grasped the lever and pressed the metal door open. There was always the chance she was about to walk into a crowd of high-bloods, but she didn't have a lot of options.

Stepping into a shadowed room, she silently closed the door behind her. Only then did she glance around her surroundings, taking in the miniature furniture and cartoon characters that were painted on the walls.

A nursery. Her heart missed a beat.

This was the place from Peter's vision. It had to be. She hurried forward. There was supposed to be a child. The clairvoyant's daughter.

Ah. Satisfaction flared through her as her searching gaze landed on the tiny girl who was happily playing with a doll in the corner. This was the key to getting her hands on the weapon.

As if sensing she was no longer alone, the girl turned her head to send Stella a radiant smile.

"Hello. My name's Molly," she said, her eyes looking oddly bronze in the dim lighting. "What's yours?"

Moving to crouch beside the child, Stella ran her fingers over the silver curls. She gave a small gasp, yanking her hand away as she felt a strange tingle race through her.

Did the child have some weird mutant powers?

She shrugged. What did it matter?

As long as she got her hands on the clairvoyant, she didn't care.

"Hello, Molly. I'm Stella," she murmured. "And I'm here to see your mother."

Finishing her call to Serra, Lana moved from her desk to stand in front of the floor-to-ceiling window that offered a stunning view of the inner courtyard. The glorious rose gardens, which were enhanced by magic, and the hand-carved marble fountains could rival Versailles. Today, however, she took little pleasure in the lush blooms or the classically carved sculptures that were arranged next to the marble benches.

Instead her thoughts remained on the heavy sense of dread that refused to be dismissed.

She wanted to tell herself she was overreacting.

They had, after all, managed to round up one sect of the Brotherhood. And so far Myst hadn't created a weapon. Maybe they'd managed to avoid disaster.

But the anxiety continued to gnaw at her, urging her to

pick up the phone and call her most talented psychic. Serra had recently left Valhalla to travel to Tibet with her Sentinel mate, Fane. The two had been manipulated by Bas into recovering his daughter from the crazed witch who'd kidnapped her, and while Lana appreciated their desire to spend time alone, she needed the woman's skill.

Once this latest threat was over they could return to their blissful isolation.

There was a soft knock before the door was pushed open and Wolfe stepped into the office. Instantly the air was filled with the prickling force of his presence, the temperature notching up several degrees.

She shivered, her heart skipping a beat as she allowed her gaze to skim down the length of his hard body, which was shown to advantage in the faded jeans that hung low on his hips and the khaki Henley with the sleeves shoved to his elbows.

When Wolfe had first arrived at Valhalla, she'd managed to fool herself into believing she would become accustomed to his raw, male impact. Now she'd ruefully accepted that was never going to happen.

Being near this male was like being struck by lightning.

Shocking, intense, and life altering.

Giving a shake of her head at her strange thoughts, she moved back toward her desk, ignoring his heated gaze.

"Did you need something?" she demanded, taking her seat with an air of casual nonchalance she was far from feeling.

"I wanted to know what happened with Stella."

Lana grimaced. "She refused to reveal anything of value. I've asked Serra to return to Valhalla to get the information I need."

Wolfe studied her in confusion. "Why? There are other psychics who are closer."

"None who have Serra's ability to get information without causing irreparable harm," Lana pointed out.

"Do you really care if the bitch has her mind crushed?" he demanded. "She had every intention of destroying Valhalla."

"True, but she was with the Brotherhood for a number of years." When Lana had first left Stella, she'd been determined to send the first psychic she could find to blast the information from the woman. Thankfully, by the time she'd reached the nursery to see Myst desperately hugging her daughter, she'd managed to regain command of her temper. There was too much at stake to be goaded into an impulsive decision. "Beyond what Peter Baldwin might have shared from his visions, she could potentially lead us to her contacts with human politicians and military leaders who share her hatred of high-bloods," she continued.

Wolfe heaved a rough sigh. "Fane isn't going to be happy," he growled. "Not with Bas lying in the infirmary. Hell, he's likely to go ballistic."

Lana couldn't suppress her smile. Fane was a six-foot-five behemoth covered from head to toe in exquisite tattoos. He was the sort of high-blood that gave humans nightmares.

He'd also pledged to murder Bas as slowly and painfully as possible.

"Thankfully he's your problem."

Wolfe rolled his eyes. He might be the Tagos, but no one controlled Fane.

"Awesome," he muttered. Then, visibly shoving away the thought of the inevitable showdown with the lethal Sentinel, Wolfe instead focused his attention directly on her. "Did you eat lunch?"

She arched her brows, well aware that he was keeping track of her.

"You already know the answer to that question."

He smiled, his expression devoid of any remorse for being an interfering busybody.

"I do. Which is why I've asked the chef to send up a tray." He held up a slender hand as her lips parted in protest. "You'll hurt his excessively fragile feelings if you don't clear your plate."

She made a sound of frustration. He wasn't lying about the chef. The Frenchman might be a genius in the kitchen, but he was a prima donna who could throw a temper tantrum that made grown men cower in terror.

"You don't fight fair," she muttered.

He shrugged, his dark gaze lowering to linger on her mouth. "I fight to win."

She squashed the urge to lick her lips, desperate to disguise her instinctive reaction behind her cool composure. Not that she was truly fooling anyone, she wryly acknowledged.

They both knew that ignoring the desire that pulsed between them wasn't making it go away.

For now, however, she was determined to focus on the very real threat to Valhalla.

"Have you interviewed any of the Brothers?" she asked.

His chest expanded as he sucked in a slow, deep breath. Then, holding her gaze, he forced himself to slip into Tagos mode.

"A few," he said, his lips curling with distaste. "They all tell the same story. Their leader abruptly died and Stella took his place with promises that they would have a weapon powerful enough to destroy their enemies."

Lana felt a stab of frustration. "No one asked any details about the mysterious weapon?"

Wolfe gave a lift of his shoulder. "She told them it was a gift from their God."

"Of course she did." Lana had lived for centuries but

she would never understand the allure of cults. Probably because she wasn't much of a follower. "A convenient way to avoid any proof that you'll deliver on your promise," she muttered.

"Most of them join the Brotherhood because they don't want to have to think for themselves," Wolfe said, his tone revealing his opinion of anyone who would prefer to become a part of a herd. His Sentinels might follow his commands, but none of them would blindly obey, or do anything that went against their morals. In fact, most of the time, Wolfe complained they were more high-maintenance than a bunch of teenage girls. "Unfortunate for us, since none of them can give us information that might help stop Myst's vision."

She leaned back in her chair. "What do you intend to do with the prisoners?"

"Once we have time I'll separate out the true fanatics and release the rest into the hands of the human justice system," he said. "If nothing else they can be charged with possessing illegal weapons."

"And the fanatics?" Lana demanded, referring to the rare Brothers who seemed to have magical abilities.

So far they remained a mystery to Valhalla, but they came from a direct line of descendants who'd battled the high-bloods since the beginning of time.

"I want the healers to study them," Wolfe told her. "If it's true they can sense high-bloods, I want to know how they can do it."

She arched a brow. Damn, she should have thought of that herself.

"A good plan."

Without warning, he planted his palms flat on the top of the desk and leaned forward.

"I have my moments," he assured her.

Entrapped in the dark promise of his gaze, Lana felt his enticing heat wrap around her.

"Wolfe."

"I could have even more moments if you would—" His words were sharply interrupted by a shrill beep. "Shit." Straightening, Wolfe reached into the front pocket of his jeans to pull out his cell phone, pressing it to his ear. "What?" he snapped, his gaze still locked on Lana's face. Then, a searing heat burst through the room as his fingers tightened on the phone. Whatever the news was, it wasn't good. Lana rose to her feet, watching as he abruptly turned to pace toward the window. "Put Valhalla on lockdown and start the search. She can't have gone far," he ordered, the power of his authority a tangible force. Occasionally, she forgot just how intimidating he could be. "And, Arel, try to do this discreetly," he warned the younger Sentinel. "I don't want a panic to complicate our search."

Lana waited until Wolfe had ended the call and slid the phone back in his pocket. There was nothing she hated worse than a dozen questions when she was trying to sort through information she'd just received.

It wasn't until he turned to meet her steady gaze that she asked the question hovering on her lips.

"What's going on?"

Wolfe stood in the center of the office, a muscle twitching at the base of his jaw.

"Stella escaped her cell."

Lana absorbed the news, carefully leashing her flare of frustration. It was a skill she'd developed as a young child. Back then she hadn't been in full command of her magic. More than once she'd caused damage, or even injured people when she was emotional.

Oddly, it was her talent to remain coldly logical in the

face of a crisis that had proven to be as much an asset in her role as the Mave as her skill as a witch.

"How?"

Wolfe didn't flinch at her icy voice. He was accustomed to working with her during times of stress.

"No one knows for sure, but she managed to knock out the electricity in the dungeon," he shared.

The dungeons were designed to hold high-bloods. How could a mere human manage to escape from her cell and cut off the electricity?

There was one obvious solution.

"Could someone be helping her?" she demanded.

"I intend to find out," he assured her, turning to head across the office. "Wait here."

With a roll of her eyes she was swiftly at his side as he moved through the door and down the hallway.

"No way," she muttered.

His long strides never faltered as he sent her a warning glare.

"Lana, right now we don't know where Stella is, or what weapons she might have."

"Exactly." She deliberately lifted her hand to touch the witch mark on her upper breast. The Tagos and his Sentinels were an overwhelming force, but she could level the entire building with one blast of magic. There was no weapon Stella possessed that she couldn't destroy. "Which is why you need me."

The lean features tightened, but Wolfe was too wise to waste energy on trying to convince her to return to her office. She was the Mave. It was her duty to protect her people.

They'd nearly reached the long bank of elevators when one opened and a large male with rich mocha skin and dark hair that had been buzzed close to his head stepped out of the nearest one and headed directly toward Wolfe.

Elias was a guardian Sentinel, although it wasn't until he was standing directly in front of them that his intricate tattoos that covered his dark skin became noticeable. Each mark was a specific spell intended to protect him from magic, psychic attacks, and mental compulsion.

From a purely aesthetic point of view, they emphasized the male's exotic beauty and the eyes that glowed with a golden shimmer in the fading dusk.

"Talk to me," Wolfe commanded.

"This is the footage we managed to retrieve," Elias said.

The male held up an electronic pad, tilting it toward them before he pressed a small button. Instantly the image of a prison cell filled the screen.

Lana leaned forward, watching as the dark-haired woman stood in the center of the floor with her back turned toward the camera. Stella. And according to the time stamp at the top of the video, it'd been seven minutes ago.

In silence they watched as the woman lifted her hand, slipping it beneath her hair. Then, slowly lowering her arm, she moved to the pitcher set beside her bed. A second later she was whirling to toss it directly toward the camera.

Abruptly the image went black.

Lana frowned, reaching out to swipe her finger over the screen. There was a flicker of light, then the video replayed. Reaching the point where Stella was lowering her hand, she pressed the screen, freezing the image.

"Look there," she said, pointing toward Stella's fingers. It was difficult to make out, but she was certain she could see a thin object. "She had something hidden beneath her hair."

"Yes," Elias murmured. "When we realized something was wrong, we went to the dungeons to discover the electricity was out and both Karl and Oshi had been knocked unconscious."

Lana swallowed a curse. Later she would consider how to punish the female. For now, nothing mattered but returning her to the cell where she belonged.

"How badly are they hurt?"

"They both had damage to their ears, but they're recovering," Elias assured her. "Karl said there was a blast of energy, as if an unseen bomb had gone off."

"What about the search?" Wolfe demanded.

Elias lowered the pad, his impatient desire to be back on the hunt obvious in the twitching of his rigid muscles.

"We've cleared the dungeons," he said. "She must have used the emergency tunnels to get out."

Wolfe hissed, the tiles beneath their feet trembling as he was forced to accept the female now had access to any floor in Valhalla.

"Was there any indication she was working with a partner?" he demanded.

"No." Elias gave a shake of his head. "There was no indication that anyone else had entered the dungeons. It looks as if she's working alone."

Wolfe reached to extract the gun he had holstered at his lower back.

"Tell Arel to continue to search his way up each floor," he ordered. "I'll start up here and work my way down. I don't want even a damned janitor closet overlooked."

"Got it," Elias assured him, turning to jog back to the elevators.

Waiting until the Sentinel was gone, Wolfe abruptly slammed his fist into his open palm.

"Goddammit," he ground out. "I underestimated her."

Lana studied his clenched jaw, knowing that the male

was blaming himself for Stella's escape. As the leader of the Sentinels, he assumed responsibility for any failures.

Regardless of whether the situation could have been prevented or not.

Lana shrugged, trying to ease his frustration. "Stella has become an expert at manipulating men."

Wolfe waved a slender hand. "I don't care if she looks like a blow-up doll," he growled. "I dismissed her as a potential threat because she's human. And now I'm paying for my arrogance."

Lana believed him. Wolfe would never let himself be swayed by a female, no matter how beautiful. Besides, she'd been equally guilty of letting Stella's lack of power blind her to the warning signs.

"You aren't the only one," she admitted.

He glanced toward her tight expression. "No?"

Lana thought back to her interview with the leader of the Brotherhood. If she hadn't allowed the woman's smug arrogance to provoke her, she would have more fully considered her sense that Stella was hiding something from her.

"When I was questioning Stella I knew she was far too complacent for a human female who was locked in the dungeons of Valhalla," she admitted. "She must have known she could escape."

Wolfe narrowed his dark eyes. "She may have gotten out of the dungeons, but there's no way in hell she can evade my Sentinels for long."

Lana shared his confidence in the warriors. Nothing could get past them. But she still worried that Stella wasn't finished with her unpleasant surprises.

"Shouldn't you warn your team she might have more weapons?" she asked.

"They'll know to be careful," Wolfe said, his body stiffening as there was a sudden shriek of an alarm. "Damn," Wolfe snarled in disbelief. "I told Arel to be discreet."

Lana yanked the phone out of the pocket of her jeans, already knowing it had nothing to do with the Sentinels. She'd allowed Wolfe to take care of the security system, but she'd personally added her own set of warnings for those dangers most warriors would never consider.

"That's not an alarm for an escaped prisoner," she grimly muttered, her heart missing a beat as she used her phone to tap into the heart of the security system.

Wolfe moved to peer over her shoulder, his muscles tensed as he prepared to face the latest threat.

"Then what is it?"

She pressed in her password, already suspecting what had triggered the shrill alert.

"The sensors have detected an airborne contaminant."

Wolfe sucked in a startled breath. "Gas?"

"Disease," she corrected.

Stepping back, Wolfe considered the various implications. "Could Stella have tripped the sensor?" he at last demanded.

Lana shoved the phone back in her pocket. It seemed the most logical explanation. After all, what better way to distract the warriors searching for her than to cause widespread panic?

But the sensors had been carefully calculated by the healers. What weapon could Stella possess that would trigger them?

"I don't know," she muttered, hurrying down the corridor. "But until we can be sure, we need to evacuate the area."

Wolfe was swiftly at her side, the gun held in one hand as his gaze scanned for any signs of danger. Lana didn't bother to tell him to concentrate on finding Stella while she dealt with the alarm.

Until she knew the extent of the danger, she wanted him at her side.

Chapter Nineteen

It took them less than five minutes to reach the offices reserved for the healers. Predictably, most of the rooms were empty as the staff was occupied with preparing their patients in case they needed to evacuate.

Impatiently, Lana moved through the reception area, which was decorated in soothing shades of blue, and down the short hall to the office at the very back. Stepping inside, she glanced toward the line of monitors that hung on the back wall. Most were used to keep a watch on the patients, but the security system was interlocked. Once the alarm went off, it should have triggered the cameras to locate the cause of the disturbance.

"Ida," she murmured as the silver-haired woman turned from the computer set on a mahogany desk. Wearing the traditional uniform of casual slacks and long white jacket, she rose to her feet.

"Mave."

Lana waved her hand toward the light flashing in the center of the ceiling. Any detection of disease would trigger the alert in this office first.

"Tell me what's going on."

The elder healer shot a wary glance toward Wolfe, who

stood a few steps behind Lana. Even with his aggression leashed, it filled the room with painful prickles of heat. Thankfully, Ida had been around Sentinels long enough not to panic, and once assured that Wolfe wasn't there to cause her harm, returned her attention to Lana.

"Something that shouldn't be possible," she said, moving across the silver-gray rug to stand in front of the monitors.

Lana swiftly joined her, studying the closest monitor. At the moment it was locked on an empty preschool room.

"Explain," she commanded.

Ida folded her arms over her chest. She'd chosen to work among humans for years, learning their technology and how it could be adapted to benefit high-bloods, before arriving at Valhalla ten years ago. It was that knowledge, combined with her crisp, no-nonsense attitude, that'd made her a perfect leader for the healers.

"The sensors detected a contaminant on the fifth floor," she said, pointing toward a middle monitor that was oddly blank.

"Fifth floor?" Wolfe muttered, taking a jerky step forward. "Shit. The nursery."

Ida gave a somber nod of her head. "At first I assumed it was a false alarm."

Wolfe sent her a confused frown. "Why would you think it was false?"

"The spells that surround Valhalla would have prevented anyone from entering who carried a potential disease," the older woman informed him.

Wolfe shrugged. "There're other ways to carry in germs."

"No." Lana gave a firm shake of her head. Over the years she'd layered and strengthened the spell, ensuring that it was capable of penetrating any container that might be used to carry in microorganisms. "The magic would have alerted me."

"We don't know what kind of weapon Stella might have with her," he reminded her, an edge in his voice.

He was still furious that the woman had managed to outwit them and escape.

"I conjured the spells myself," she assured him, using her Mave voice. It warned she wasn't going to argue. "Nothing could have been smuggled through them."

Wolfe cocked a brow. He was the only one in Valhalla who didn't twitch in fear when she used that particular tone.

"If you're so certain, then why did you add that specific alarm to my system?" he pressed.

Lana sucked in a sharp breath, her hands clenching at her sides.

She'd been so rattled by the alarm coming on top of Stella's escape, she hadn't truly considered what might have triggered her spell. Not until Wolfe asked the obvious question.

Now her stomach twisted with an icy dread.

She turned her head to meet his steady gaze. "You remember me telling you that the first Mave was dedicated to eradicating those high-bloods she considered a danger?"

He nodded. "Tough to forget."

No crap. She still woke up drenched in sweat at the nightmare of watching her friends being hunted down and slaughtered like they were animals.

"Two of those high-bloods were healers who could create diseases in people they came into contact with."

Ida made a sound of distress, her light brown eyes widening as she sent Lana a horrified glance.

"Plague carriers?"

"Yes," Lana muttered, her brain still trying to wrap around the thought.

It'd been a long time since she'd allowed herself to remember Dylan and Juliet. She'd barely known them, since they tended to remain aloof from society. Understandable, since most people were terrified of them.

Now it was a struggle to recall what she knew about them.

"They had the plague?" Wolfe questioned in puzzlement.

"Not themselves." She paused, searching her memory for anything that might help. "From what little I heard about the carriers, they could even train themselves to control their ability. They weren't any more dangerous than any other high-blood until they wanted to infect someone."

Wolfe shuddered. "They could spread disease whenever they wanted?"

"No." Lana furrowed her brow. "It wasn't like a mass epidemic. Each person would develop a completely different disease."

"Christ," the Tagos breathed. "I understand why the previous Mave was so eager to get rid of them." He held up his hand as she narrowed her gaze. "I'm not saying I approve of what she did. I'm just saying the humans would be freaked if they realized we had"—he hesitated before latching onto Ida's term—"plague carriers."

Lana couldn't argue. Especially since all humans were susceptible to the power, while only a handful of high-bloods had ever been infected.

"It gets worse," she confessed. "When the magic first manifests, the carrier can't control it. They spread infection without even realizing what they're doing."

Ida rubbed her arms, her usual calm shattered by the thought of a healer using her skills to harm others.

"I've heard of them, but I thought they were a myth," she muttered.

Lana's heart twisted with regret. If she could go back in time she would have destroyed the previous Mave the very minute she discovered the woman was killing high-bloods. Unfortunately, she couldn't change the past.

She could only learn from it and move on.

"After they were destroyed by the previous Mave their history was erased," Lana said. "She didn't want the humans fearing—"

"Germ warfare?" Wolfe completed her sentence.

"Exactly." Lana briefly glanced toward Ida, who'd paled to a pasty shade. "There was no opportunity to study why they didn't become ill or why some high-bloods were infected and others weren't."

"So instead you layered Valhalla with alarms," Wolfe murmured.

"There was always the possibility that a carrier would be born," Lana pointed out, turning her attention back to Wolfe. She was the type of woman who was prepared for any situation.

Even if those situations seemed unlikely.

Wolfe furrowed his brow, turning his gaze toward the bank of monitors.

"Is that what happened?"

"Ida?" Lana laid her hand on the healer's arm, distracting the older woman from her dark thoughts.

Ida gave a faint shake of her head, grimly squaring her shoulders. She was intelligent enough to realize the fate of Valhalla might very well hang in the balance.

"No," she said in her usually crisp tones. "There was no one who could have manifested the talent."

"How can you be so sure?"

"Because the floor was virtually empty when the alarm sounded and we set the quarantine protocol into motion."

Wolfe glanced toward the healer. "What protocol?"

"We evacuated those we could, and then sealed the floor."

Lana moved to the computer on Ida's desk, calling up the blueprints of the fifth floor.

Offices. Storage rooms. Preschool classes. And the nursery.

"Who was left?" Wolfe demanded, leaning over Lana's shoulder.

For once, she wasn't troubled by the heat that seared against her back. Instead, she savored the feel of him pressed close.

His solid strength gave her the courage to face the painful decisions she didn't doubt were going to have to be made.

Ida joined them, pointing a finger toward the blueprints. "We had to leave behind a teacher who is infected with typhoid fever and a healer who has smallpox." The healer pinched her lips together in frustration. She was a healer. Being forced to abandon the sick, even if it was only temporary, was clearly wearing on her nerves. "We couldn't allow them to leave the quarantine area until we understood how the diseases were being spread."

"What about the nursery?" Wolfe asked, his expression bleak.

Like Ida, he didn't like to leave the wounded behind.

"Most of the children were already home with their families, thank God," the healer muttered.

When a child or adolescent was brought to Valhalla, he or she was fostered by a specific family, although everyone in the community helped to raise kids.

Every day the children were expected to spend time in the nursery. It was important that they grow up without prejudice toward people who not only had a variety of powers, but on occasion looked different. And of course, it gave them the opportunity to learn to control their talents when surrounded by others.

During the evening they were returned to the apartments they shared with their foster families.

All except . . .

"Molly," Lana breathed in horror.

Ida gave a distressed nod. "She's still in there."

Wolfe straightened, abruptly pacing back toward the monitors, as if hoping to catch sight of the little girl.

"Could she be the carrier?"

Ida gave a helpless lift of her hands. "There's no way to know."

Lana pressed a hand to her thundering heart, fiercely concentrating on how she could get past the layers of magic that would have been triggered the moment the quarantine went into effect.

"Is she alone?" she asked.

"We're not sure." Ida turned to press a key on the computer. "We had her on video, then this stranger appeared and she destroyed the cameras."

The monitors were suddenly filled with a static image of Molly in the room with a familiar auburn-haired woman.

Wolfe cursed as Lana took a jerky step forward.

"Stella," Lana rasped, shock racing through her.

She'd been so caught up in the potential biological disaster, she'd almost forgotten they had an escaped prisoner.

Now she studied the pretty heart-shaped face with the cruel expression as the woman grabbed Molly by the arm and glared directly at the camera.

The woman had obviously used the tunnels to make her way to the fifth floor in the hopes of hiding until the search for her was over. Or maybe she'd even hoped to take a hostage and force Wolfe to release her.

What she hadn't counted on was being stuck in the middle of an outbreak. . . .

Lana sucked in a sharp breath, the truth slamming into her with the force of a freight train. It could be a fluke that Stella had been with Molly when the alarms went off, but Lana didn't believe in coincidences.

"She's the carrier," she abruptly announced.

There was a startled silence before Wolfe was giving a shake of his head.

"Impossible." He sent her a baffled glance. "She's a human."

Lana held his dark gaze. "She was human until she came into contact with a child capable of stirring her latent powers."

Wolfe slowly turned back to the monitor, his gaze resting on the smudged image of Molly's sweet face surrounded by a halo of silver curls. She looked the picture of innocence, but if the Master of Gifts was right, she possessed the ability to be a catalyst, stirring latent powers that Stella probably never suspected she possessed.

If the woman realized the truth . . .

Lana swallowed her curse, unable to contemplate the horror of what the immoral, power-hungry female would do if she ever learned she possessed the magic to spread disease. She'd become a monster, willing to slaughter countless humans in her desire to gain a position of authority.

That couldn't be allowed to happen.

Regardless of the cost.

"Shit," Wolfe breathed, easily following her dark train of thought. Brushing a hand down her back in a gesture of comfort, he turned his attention to the healer. "Where is she now?"

"We don't know." Ida pressed another key on the computer and the middle monitor went black. "This is the video in the nursery," she explained. "During the confusion she managed to slip away with the child."

"Stella must think she can use Molly as a hostage," Wolfe growled.

Lana nodded. "We have to find them."

Wolfe grimaced, glancing toward the computer to study the blueprint still visible on the screen.

"There're too many storage spaces on that floor that don't have cameras. She could be anywhere."

He was right. The storage rooms were the few places that weren't monitored by security.

Just their luck.

Now they not only had to figure out some way to get past the magic that prevented the spread of Stella's newly acquired powers, but they were going to have to search the entire floor to track them down.

A shame that Molly didn't have the power to contact them.

With a surge of adrenaline, Lana reached out to grasp Wolfe's arm.

"Myst," she breathed. "She has a connection to the child."

Wolfe gave a sharp nod, heading toward the door as he pulled his phone from his pocket.

"I'll have Arel start an evacuation of Valhalla," he muttered. "If things go to hell I want as many people out of range as possible."

Myst gave her phone a frustrated shake.

Of course the stupid thing wouldn't work when she needed it the most. With a grimace, she tossed it on the rolling tray set beside Bas's bed.

She'd been on the point of leaving the hospital room to return to Molly when the shrill alarm had gone off and the door had slammed shut. At first she'd only been mildly disturbed. She wasn't familiar with Valhalla, but she assumed there were any number of reasons an alarm might go off.

But when she'd moved across the room to open the door and demand an explanation, she found it wouldn't budge.

And now she couldn't reach anyone with her phone.

"Anything?" Bas demanded, shoving aside the blankets,

revealing the thin robe that covered his recently healed body.

His hair was tousled and his jaw darkened with his unshaved whiskers, but his eyes were alert and his power capable of heating the air.

He'd come a long way from the unconscious male who'd barely been clinging to life when he arrived in Valhalla. Still, she knew that he was far from full strength.

She instinctively moved toward him, anxious to make sure he didn't do anything to risk his recovery.

"No, the door is still locked and I don't have any service on my phone," she admitted, halting next to the bed.

She would physically keep him restrained if necessary.

Bas grimaced. "I forgot that the Mave placed a dampening spell in Valhalla that keeps outside electronics from functioning properly," he muttered. "I don't know exactly how it works, but it keeps visitors from covertly taking pictures or planting any sort of spy equipment."

Myst studied his beautiful face. She knew without asking that Bas had discovered the Mave's security measures when he was trying to plant some sort of spy equipment. His life as a mercenary meant he was branded an outlaw by Valhalla. He would want to know if they were plotting to hunt him down.

"Great," she muttered, even as she admired the Mave's efforts to protect her people.

Myst didn't doubt for a second that the humans were constantly attempting to probe through the outer dome that protected Valhalla, as well as sending in visitors with equipment intended to spy on the high-bloods.

"What about Molly?" Bas asked, his voice hard with concern.

Myst pressed her fingers to her temple, her head aching from her efforts to touch her daughter's mind.

"She was in the nursery, but now I can't connect with her," she said. "It feels like our bond is muffled."

"Damn." Bas swung his legs over the edge of the bed, a layer of sweat coating his face as it twisted with pain.

Myst grabbed his shoulder, ridiculously trying to prevent him from rising to his feet.

"What are you doing?"

"Obviously something happened." Bas shoved himself upright, grabbing the bar at the foot of the bed to keep from pitching forward. "We need to get out of here."

She moved to stand directly in front of him. Not that she was going to be able to stop him from falling on his face, if he continued to be stubborn. He was way too heavy for her to keep upright.

She pointed out the obvious. "You can barely stand."

His jaw clenched. "I'm fine."

"Bas."

Her plea to get him back into bed was forgotten as Bas abruptly reached to wrap an arm around her waist, jerking her behind him as the door was shoved open.

It happened so quickly, Myst didn't have a chance to stop Bas from playing the hero as the Mave and the Tagos stepped into the room.

Suddenly the heat was smothering as the two Sentinels glared at each other, the aggression prickling between them.

"What the hell is going on?" Bas growled.

Wolfe had instinctively shifted to place himself between Lana and Bas, missing the powerful witch's expression of exasperation.

"Easy, assassin," the leader of the Sentinels warned.

Stepping around the bristling male, Lana took command of the situation.

"We need to speak," she informed them, her gaze narrowing as she took in Bas's pallor. "You should sit before you fall."

Bas squared his shoulders. "No."

"Always so stubborn," the Mave muttered.

Myst rolled her eyes. That had to be the understatement of the century.

Gently, Myst smoothed a hand down his back, offering a silent encouragement.

"Please, Bas," she said in soft tones.

There was a tense pause, before Bas grudgingly moved to perch on the edge of the mattress.

"Fine, I'm sitting," he snarled, his gaze latched onto Lana's carefully expressionless face. "Now explain why we were locked in this room."

Wolfe clenched his hands, but it was Lana who answered the sharp question.

"The leader of the Brotherhood managed to escape from her cell."

Bas muttered a curse, his attention shifting to the rigid Tagos.

"A human escaped your infamous dungeons?" he rasped. "Sloppy."

Lana grabbed Wolfe's arm, almost as if she feared he might leap across the floor to smash his fist into Bas's taunting face.

She probably wasn't wrong.

Both males were on edge and ready for violence. It would take very little excuse for them to start pounding the crap out of each other.

"She had a hidden weapon that knocked out the electricity and disabled the guards," Lana explained.

Bas returned his attention to the Mave, his expression grim.

"We have to get Myst out of here," he warned.

Lana shook her head. "It's too late."

"Too late?" Bas snapped his brows together. "What does that mean?"

"Stella used the tunnels to reach the upper floors of Valhalla," the Mave admitted.

Myst tensed. The leader of the Brotherhood was on the loose. Perhaps even headed in this direction.

God. She'd known it was a risk to return to Valhalla. Especially once she realized the Brotherhood was being held prisoner in the dungeons.

But she'd been desperate to save Bas. And equally desperate to see her daughter, so she'd used the psychic's assurance that she needed to travel here to overcome her common sense.

Now her impetuous stupidity might have put them all in danger.

As if sensing her painful regret, Bas reached to grasp her hand, tightly squeezing her fingers.

"It can't be that difficult to find one human woman and return her to the dungeons," he pointed out in harsh tones.

Oddly Lana hesitated, sharing a glance with Wolfe before her gaze landed on Myst.

"We have a general idea where she is."

Myst unconsciously stepped closer to Bas, an icy shiver shaking her body. She sensed that the prison escape was the least of the bad news.

"Where?" she demanded.

Lana held her troubled gaze. "Fifth floor."

Fifth floor? Still unfamiliar with the vast labyrinth of floors that were dug deep into the ground, Myst didn't immediately make the connection.

"That's . . . oh my God." She gave a cry of horror when she realized exactly why Lana had sought them out. It had nothing to do with Myst's vision or the fear that the Brotherhood was about to get their hands on the mysterious weapon. "Molly."

"Shit."

With a flurry of movement, Bas was off the bed and

charging toward the door. Halfway across the room, however, he was brought to a halt as Wolfe stepped in his path and wrapped his arms around him. There was a short, vicious struggle that might have ended with one of the males dead if Bas hadn't been weakened from his injuries.

As it was, Wolfe managed to get Bas pinned to the wall, using his forearm across his throat to keep him in place.

Even then, Bas refused to concede defeat.

"Get out of my way, Tagos," he rasped.

"Bas, wait." Ignoring the very real potential for bloodshed, Lana moved to stand only inches from the males. Myst shook her head. Either the older woman was confident she could handle both Sentinels, or she had a death wish. "You need to hear what I have to say," the Mave insisted, her gaze locked on Bas's flushed face.

Myst wrapped her arms around her waist, her heart refusing to beat as she desperately attempted to telepathically connect with her daughter. The little girl was alive. She was certain of that much.

But a barrier remained between them.

"Molly," she breathed, her voice coming out as a croak. "Where is she?"

Lana turned to send her a glance filled with unspoken sympathy. "She was with Stella."

"Release me," Bas snarled even as Myst pressed an unsteady hand to her lips.

The enemy had her baby girl.

After all her efforts to keep her protected, her worst nightmares had come true.

"Why haven't you sent your Sentinels to get her?" she breathed.

Without warning, the Mave was moving to grasp Myst's hands, releasing a soothing burst of magic.

"Before I explain, there's something you need to know," she said in low tones.

Myst instinctively glanced toward Bas. She didn't know what she was seeking from him. Perhaps reassurance that she could trust the Mave. Or just the knowledge that she wasn't alone to face whatever the woman was about to tell her.

Easily sensing her need, Bas shoved aside Wolfe, who finally released his hold on the assassin. Moving to stand at her side, Bas wrapped a protective arm around her waist.

"What is it?" Myst at last asked, returning her attention to the woman standing directly in front of her.

"While you were gone we discovered that Molly possesses an"—the Mave halted, clearly considering her words—"interesting talent."

Bas stiffened at her side, his breath hissing between his clenched teeth.

"A high-blood talent?" he asked.

"Yes." Lana kept her gaze locked on Myst's pale face. "Calder believes she has the ability to ignite latent gifts."

Igniting gifts? Myst gave a baffled shake of her head. "What does that mean?"

"She can create what we used to assume was spontaneous manifestation," Lana clarified.

Myst parted her lips to deny the outrageous claim. Molly might be receptive to telepathy, but otherwise she was a normal little girl. Certainly she'd never been capable of affecting other high-bloods. . . .

Except, she had, Myst abruptly realized.

"Oh," she breathed, trying to wrap her head around the possibility.

"You've noticed her ability?" Lana pressed.

Myst gave a slow nod. "I gained telepathic abilities after I had her."

Bas tightened his arm around her waist, pressing her hard against his side.

"What the fuck does this have to do with getting my daughter back?" he snapped.

Wolfe took a step forward, but Lana halted any potential violence with a lift of her hand.

"We suspect she caused a change in Stella," she told Bas.

Bas made a sound of impatience. "What sort of change?"

"She had latent powers that we believe Molly managed to ignite."

Myst felt oddly numb as she studied the older woman's perfect face. Maybe it was too many shocks. There did, after all, have to be a threshold a person could endure, right?

"The leader of the Brotherhood is a high-blood?" she demanded, trying to wrap her mind around the thought that Molly had managed to turn their enemy into one of them.

It might have been ironic if the situation wasn't so horrifying.

"We believe it's possible," Lana said, her words oddly hesitant.

Bas made a sound of impatience. "What aren't you telling us, Lana?"

The Mave grimaced. "She's a carrier."

Chapter Twenty

Bas felt as if the air had been jerked from his lungs.

Not at the knowledge that his daughter seemed to have a rare, unknown ability. That was something he'd have to deal with later.

Instead, he concentrated on Lana's suspicion that Stella had become a plague carrier.

It'd been decades since he'd last heard of a carrier. Not since the former Mave had destroyed them during her crazed purge. Now he swiftly tried to recall what he knew.

At the time he hadn't paid much attention to them. The carriers were capable of controlling their powers, and the two he'd met were too ethical to use their magic to hurt others. But he seemed to recall that when their magic first manifested itself they could infect entire communities.

Hell, he'd heard rumors they'd wiped out half the human population in the olden days.

"Is she quarantined?" he demanded.

Lana gave a slow nod. "Yes."

Something in her tone sent a shaft of fear through his heart.

"How many were infected?"

Lana's pale face was hard with fury. Clearly the woman blamed herself for not being able to protect her people.

"Two that we know of."

Two? Shit.

Bas's lips parted, but before he could ask the question that was twisting his gut with dread, Myst stepped out of the protective circle of his arms to directly face the Mave.

"Molly?"

"No," Lana was swift to assure them. "The healers are able to track the diseases with their monitors and they're certain she wasn't infected."

Myst swayed, as if overwhelmed by relief. "Thank God," she said in husky tones.

Equally relieved, Bas reached out to tug Myst back against him. The female had endured one shock after another. It was a wonder she hadn't collapsed.

"Then where is she?"

Lana grimaced. "Unfortunately, Stella broke the camera in the nursery before she disappeared," she confessed. "Because of the spell we haven't been able to search for them."

Bas scowled. He understood the necessity to contain Stella now that she was a carrier, but that didn't explain why the hell they hadn't gone in to rescue his daughter.

"Explain," he snapped.

Lana carefully stepped in front of Wolfe, who looked ready to leap across the room and rip off his head. Not that he gave a shit.

Actually, a part of him hoped the Tagos would attack. His savage frustration needed an outlet. Beating the crap out of Wolfe would help to ease his smoldering rage.

A larger part, however, understood that a bloody brawl would only upset Myst. She had enough to worry about without him acting like a barbarian.

Sensing the violence in the air, Lana sent both males a warning glare.

"Once the magic has been activated it can't be lowered until the threat has been eliminated," she revealed.

"Eliminated?" He leashed his primitive urges, instead calling on the brutal training he'd received as an assassin. Cold, resolute logic was the only thing that could save his daughter. "What does that mean?"

Lana glanced toward Myst before meeting Bas's demanding gaze. Shit. Obviously the Mave was worried that what she had to say was going to upset the younger female.

"If it was a high-blood we would evacuate Valhalla and have the carrier place themselves in a specialized cell that would contain them," she at last said. "Then, they would be in a controlled environment to train to control their magic. Once we were certain they weren't a threat to others, they would be able to leave their cell and resume their normal life."

Bas arched a brow. The reason he'd agreed to work with Lana years ago wasn't just because she happened to be one of the most powerful witches ever born. She was also intelligent, rigidly disciplined, and a master chess player. Which meant she was always one step ahead of their enemies.

It wasn't like her to create such a vague emergency plan.

"That was it?" he demanded in disbelief. "You throw them in a cell and hope for the best?"

Her lips flattened, pinpricks of magic biting into his skin.

"Since it seemed a fairly remote threat, I didn't spend a great deal of time organizing what would happen once the spell was triggered."

Myst made a sound of impatience, her body trembling with the need to get to her daughter.

"It doesn't matter. I'll go in. I'm not afraid—"

Lana interrupted her words before Bas could insist that he was the one going in to get Molly.

"It's impossible," the Mave said, her expression grim.

"The carrier is capable of contaminating the entire area if her power isn't kept contained."

Bas tightened his arm around Myst, silently offering her reassurance that he wasn't going to let their daughter be sacrificed to save Valhalla.

"Tough," he growled, the word slicing through the air like the crack of a whip. "My daughter has already been used as a hostage once. I'm not letting it happen again. I don't care who gets hurt."

Lana shook her head. "You don't understand, Bas. No one can get past the spell," she insisted. "Not even me."

He clenched his jaw, trying to ignore his growing sense of dread.

"Bullshit."

Wolfe made a low sound of warning. Almost a growl, as if he truly was a wolf.

Once again, however, it was Lana who took command of the situation, using her magic to try and ease the violence vibrating in the air.

"It's true," she said, a genuine regret in her voice. "I wanted to make sure that no one could be forced to release the carrier. She could be used as a weapon if she fell into the wrong hands."

Bas understood. How could he not? Anyone who managed to get their hands on a carrier could easily use them as a weapon of mass destruction.

Moreover, he recognized what she wasn't saying. Not only that Stella could be used as a weapon by someone else, but that if the overly ambitious woman realized her potential power, she might very well destroy a huge chunk of the human population.

Bas, however, wasn't thinking like a leader of his people.

He didn't give a shit about anyone or anything but saving his daughter.

"So you intend to leave her trapped in there?" he snarled.

Lana flinched, as if he'd wounded her with his accusation.

"No, of course not." She regained her composure, her chin tilted to an angle he easily recognized. It meant she was trying to make the best out of a very bad situation. "I said we can't go in. But if Molly isn't infected, she can come out."

Bas scowled. His daughter was amazing. A vivid, joyous creature who spread happiness to everyone she met.

But she wasn't a warrior.

"Excellent," he hissed. "Now maybe you can tell me how a four-year-old girl is going to get away from a grown woman who was ruthless enough to gain control of the Brotherhood?"

This time Lana couldn't halt Wolfe from moving to the center of the room, the force of his power slamming into Bas.

Naturally Bas eased himself to stand in front of Myst, ready and willing for whatever the Tagos wanted to throw at him. The very air thickened, the floor trembling beneath their feet.

"Enough, you two," Lana abruptly snapped, stepping between them. "We can't make a plan until we know more." Her attention shifted to Myst. "Can you reach her telepathically?"

Myst shoved him aside, directly facing the Mave. "No." She wrapped her arms around her waist, her frustration etched on her pale face. "There's some sort of barrier between us."

Lana hissed, clearly disappointed. "It must be the quarantine spell."

Bas swallowed his aggravated condemnation. There was no point in slinging blame.

"Don't you have cameras?" he demanded, recalling his efforts to sneak into Valhalla three weeks ago.

He'd barely managed to slip past the high-tech security

system. How was it possible they couldn't use it to find one small child?

"Not in every room," Wolfe answered, his muscles clenched and a handgun held at his side. "Especially not the storage areas. That's why we hoped Myst could speak with her."

Of course not. Bas released a string of curses, his mind racing for a way he could find his daughter.

Any other day, he wouldn't hesitate to kick Wolfe's ass and head to the fifth floor. Whatever the Mave said, he refused to believe there was no way to get through the spell.

But it wasn't any other day. He was still weakened from taking three bullets to the chest, and while he was willing to cheat in a fight when necessary, he didn't like his current odds.

Which meant he had to figure out another way to reach Molly . . .

"Shit," he breathed, abruptly realizing how stupid he'd been. He'd had the means to reach Molly in his hands the entire time. Well, not precisely in his hands, but close. Instinctively he reached down, only to recall that he was wearing the ridiculous hospital robe and his phone was still somewhere in France. "I need to call Kaede."

Lana shook her head. "The enforcer is skilled, but not even he can get through the magic."

"I don't want him to try to slip through," he corrected in impatient tones. "He gave Molly a bracelet."

Myst glanced toward him, her expression confused. "It's beautiful, but I don't know how it will help."

"It has a tracking device," he said.

She blinked in shock. Understandable. Most four-year-old girls weren't tagged with a GPS.

"Good Lord," she breathed.

Bas shrugged. "After she was kidnapped he wanted to make sure we could always find her."

There was a short silence before Myst released a shaky breath, her fingers pressed to her lips as she struggled to hold back her tears.

"I could kiss that male," she breathed.

Bas reached to tuck a silver curl behind her ear. "No kisses," he warned her. "But he's going to get one hell of a Christmas bonus."

Lana pulled out her phone, shoving it in his hand. "Here."

He pressed in Kaede's number only to hesitate when he was struck by a sudden thought. Lifting his head, he watched as Lana moved toward a monitor built into the wall.

"His phone won't work in Valhalla," he pointed out.

Turning on the monitor, she tapped in her private password to call up the security system. A few more taps and she turned to glance toward Bas.

"It should work now," she said. "I've lowered the dampening field so you can contact him."

Completing the number, Bas turned from the expectant gazes as he pressed the phone to his ear.

There was an audible click as the call was completed, but the enforcer didn't speak, clearly suspicious of being contacted by an unknown number.

"Kaede, it's Bas," he assured his friend. "I need you to find Molly." He cut through Kaede's swift promise that he was on his way to help. "No. Just give me her location." There was a tense silence as Kaede struggled against his urge to barrage Bas with a thousand questions and instead promised to text the location to the phone. Bas cut the connection, impatiently waiting for the coordinates to show up on the screen. Once they appeared, he hastily crossed the room to show them to Lana. "This is the GPS location."

She pressed a button on the monitor, bringing up Valhalla's blueprints. Then, skimming her finger over the screen, she at last pointed to a spot almost directly below them.

"Fifth floor, Section C, room two-fifty-five," she murmured.

Wolfe moved to stand behind her shoulder, leaning forward to study the screen.

"A storage unit for the preschool," he abruptly concluded.

Bas studied the Tagos's stark profile. "Is there a camera?"

The older man shook his head. "No."

Bas clenched his hands. "Shit."

Lana slid her finger over the screen, calling up the complex schematics that revealed the building's electrical grid.

She frowned as she traced a blue line to the storage room. "There's an intercom."

Bas wasn't impressed. Dammit. His daughter was trapped with a female who'd already proven she was ruthless enough to lie, cheat, and steal to become leader of the Brotherhood.

Who the hell knew what she would do to a four-year-old child?

"How's that going to help?" he challenged in bleak tones.

Lana turned, laying a comforting hand on his arm. "We'll see if we can contact Molly. If she's hiding I can lead her to a way out," she said in soft tones. "If she's with Stella, then we can try to negotiate for her release. Either way we'll know if she's okay."

Bas forced himself to take a deep breath. It wasn't the answer he wanted, but he would have to settle for at least assuring himself that Molly was unhurt.

He nodded his head at the monitor. "Can we do it from here?"

"No." Lana shut down the screen. "We need to go to my office."

Without waiting for his response, Lana headed toward the door, closely followed by her faithful Tagos.

Waiting until they'd disappeared, Bas turned to discover Myst staring blankly into space, as if she'd just been struck by a hideous thought.

Instinctively he moved forward to wrap his arms around her slender body, tugging her against his chest.

"We're going to get her back," he murmured in soothing tones.

She nodded even as she trembled from the intensity of her inner emotions.

"I trust you," she assured him.

He pulled back to study her pale face with unconcealed surprise. This female had fought tooth and nail to keep him at a distance.

"Truly?"

She bit her bottom lip. "Yes."

He ran a hand up and down her back, trying to ease her vicious distress. Christ. She felt like she was going to shatter into a million pieces.

"Then what's bothering you?"

"This is my vision," she breathed, her eyes dark with distress.

He stilled. Had she seen something new? Something that was even worse than the first one?

"What's your vision?" he demanded.

She laid her hands on his chest, gripping the fabric of his robe.

"Don't you see?" she rasped. "When I foresaw that I would create a weapon, I assumed it would be some dangerous new technology."

He frowned, still confused by her nearly incoherent words. "You know what the weapon is?"

"Molly."

Whatever he'd expected her to say, it certainly hadn't been his daughter's name.

"Molly?"

"Yes."

His frown deepened. "Molly is the weapon?"

She licked her lips, her heart pounding loud enough that he could hear it in the thick silence that shrouded the room. Absently he realized he couldn't sense anyone near. Obviously Lana had been serious when she said that Valhalla would be evacuated.

"Remember Boggs said the weapon had something to do with my blood?" she said, her voice so low he could barely catch the words. "I created Molly and it was the power that flows through her blood that turned Stella into a plague carrier."

His lips parted to deny her claim. Molly wasn't a weapon. She was a sweet, innocent child. But he couldn't force the words to form.

Maybe she was right. Her vision had been of death and destruction spreading through Valhalla.

"God. Damn."

Stella paced the storage room, her temper at the breaking point.

For the past half hour she'd desperately searched for a way out. Granted, she held a trump card in the child. But she wanted to know that she could escape if worse came to worst.

At last she'd been forced to concede defeat and return to the storage room. Every door was locked tight. There weren't any windows. No vents. She'd had an easier time escaping from the dungeons.

Now she had to trust that Peter's vision was right and she could force the clairvoyant to get her the weapon, so she could demand release from Valhalla.

Or maybe she'd just kill them all. . . .

There was a faint rustle, then the feel of tiny fingers tugging on the hem of her camisole.

"I'm hungry," a childish voice complained.

Stella knocked away the clinging fingers and glared down at Molly's tiny face. She'd already tried to convince the kid to contact her mother. After all, clairvoyants could speak mind to mind with other people. Or at least that's what she'd been told.

But the stubborn brat refused to obey.

"I warned you, there's no snack until we find your mother," she snapped.

The girl hunched her shoulder, her lashes lowering to hide her eyes.

"She's not here."

Stella snorted. She didn't know if the child had any powers, but it certainly wasn't lying.

"Little girls shouldn't tell untruths," she mocked. "Not unless you want to be punished."

Molly took a step back, clutching a ragged stuffed hippo to her chest.

"I don't like you."

"Good." Stella leaned down until they were nose to nose. "You want to get away from me, then tell me what I want to know."

Molly stuck out her lower lip. "I can't. The magic—"

"No more about the damned magic, you freak," Stella burst out, straightening as she whirled around to resume her pacing.

Not an easy task when the large room was crammed with chairs and desks and rolled-up carpets.

"It's all around us," the little girl insisted.

Stella shivered, her hands absently rubbing up and down

her bare arms. Almost as if she could sense the magic she claimed was holding them hostage.

Ridiculous.

She gave a shake of her head, sending a glare toward the child.

"Then we wait. Sooner or later your mother will come looking for you," she muttered.

Molly stuck her thumb in her mouth, giving it a defiant suck. Stella hissed, whirling away as she realized she was squabbling with a child.

God Almighty. She was the leader of the Brotherhood. A woman feared and respected throughout the world. To be reduced to this was . . . unacceptable.

She was still pacing when a beep suddenly pierced the silence. Striding to the center of the room, she glared at Molly, suspecting she'd done something to try and piss her off.

"What's that noise?"

Molly glanced toward the wall. "The speaking TV."

Stella scowled. "What?"

"There." Molly crossed the room to point toward a monitor that was built into the wall. "See?"

"An intercom," Stella breathed, cautiously moving to stand directly in front of the screen. "How do I turn it on?"

Molly reached to touch a small button. "You press this."

There was a flicker of light, then the image of a dark-haired woman with perfect features suddenly came into focus. Stella narrowed her gaze, taking in the woman's cold, aloof expression and the elegant office behind her.

Of course she was seated in comfort, looking every inch the Mave of Valhalla, while Stella was filthy, her hair a mess, and trapped like a rat.

Fury blasted through her, along with sharp tingles of pain that felt as if she'd been stung by a hundred bees. It wasn't the first time she'd experienced that pain since being trapped. She wasn't sure what the strange sensation meant, but it had to be some reaction to Valhalla, right?

Dammit, she had to get out of there.

"Mave," she snapped, her fear doing nothing to ease her anger. "What took you so long?"

The woman smiled, looking unbearably smug. "There was no hurry," she mocked. "It's not like you're going anywhere."

Stella clenched her teeth, allowing herself to imagine the pleasure of wrapping her fingers around the smug woman's throat and squeezing.

Instead she forced a sneering smile to her lips. "You continually underestimate me. That's fine." She gave a toss of her head. "It gives me the upper hand."

"You're trapped," the Mave pointed out in dry tones. "That hardly gives you an upper hand."

Bending to the side, Stella grasped Molly's arm and jerked her up so the Mave could see that she wasn't alone.

"Ah, but I have a hostage."

The Mave's face hardened with open disdain even as there was a muffled sound coming from somewhere in her office. Was there someone there with her?

Stella hoped it was the brat's mother.

"Not even you are enough of a monster to threaten an innocent child," the Mave stated in icy tones.

Would she? Stella gave an inward shrug. The answer didn't really matter so long as the leader of Valhalla believed she would.

"I will do whatever is necessary to survive."

The Mave leaned forward, her face filling the screen. "What do you want?"

Stella licked her lips, barely suppressing the urge to back away. The woman couldn't blast her magic through an intercom. Even if it did feel as if there were electrical currents dancing over her skin.

Fiercely she shoved aside the worry she might be losing her mind. She was under a lot of stress. It was no wonder her body was so twitchy. Instead she concentrated on the Mave's question.

Her first thought was to demand safe passage out of Valhalla. All she wanted was to be miles away from this godforsaken place. But she wasn't stupid.

Even if they did let her out, they would soon hunt her down and return her to the dungeons. And this time they would make very certain she didn't have the opportunity to escape. Unless they simply killed her.

No. Her only chance to survive was to get what was promised to her.

"I want the clairvoyant," she at last informed the Mave.

Dark brows arched. "That's all?"

"For now."

"Fine." The Mave settled back in her seat. "Release the girl and—"

"Do you think I'm stupid?" Stella interrupted with a sharp laugh. "The girl stays with me until I have my hands on the clairvoyant."

The older woman studied her with an unreadable expression. She could make a fortune at poker, Stella wryly acknowledged.

"Then we are at a standstill." The Mave lifted a slender hand, as if reaching to turn off the intercom. "I won't allow Myst to come to you until I know her daughter is safe."

Tightening her grip on Molly's arm, she lifted the girl off the ground to give her a rough shake.

"Don't push me, Mave."

"Ow," Molly cried, struggling to get free.

Something dark and lethally terrifying entered the Mave's

eyes, making Stella deeply relieved that the older woman wasn't in the storage room with her. She had a terrible suspicion that she would be lying dead on the floor in that case.

"Stop," the Mave snapped. "I will see if I can locate Myst."

"Make it soon," Stella hissed, dropping Molly to the floor when the screen went black. "The bitch better not disappoint me."

Chapter Twenty-One

Myst had endured terror over the years.

The vision. Being sold to the Brotherhood. Living on the run. Discovering that she was pregnant and knowing she couldn't keep her child.

But when Molly had been kidnapped a few weeks ago, she'd learned the true meaning of fear.

And now she was forced to live through it again.

Standing near a bank of windows in the Mave's office, she trembled in the circle of Bas's arms as the computer screen went dark and the image of her precious daughter was lost.

If it wasn't for Bas's ruthless grip, she would be running screaming from the office like a lunatic.

"Dear God," she breathed, her voice choked with tears. "You have to let me go to her."

"There's no way to get you past the barrier," Lana reminded her in grim tones. "Even if we were willing to negotiate with the female."

Myst stiffened, glaring at the older woman. This was *her* child they were talking about. It wasn't the Mave's decision if they would or wouldn't negotiate to get her back.

"We have to do something."

"We will, *cara*. I swear," Bas murmured, brushing his lips over the top of her head before he was glaring at Lana. "I'm getting my daughter; I don't care what I have to do to get past the spells."

Wolfe moved to stand next to Lana as she rose from her chair.

"We are all worried about Molly, assassin," he retorted in sharp tones. "There's no need for threats."

Lana regarded them with a sympathetic expression, even as she took firm control of the situation.

"Wolfe is right, Bas. We all love your daughter, but it's not going to help to fight with each other," she pointed out in gentle tones. "We need to work together to figure out a plan."

Myst felt Bas tremble with the effort to contain his furious need to hunt down the female who'd threatened their daughter. His voice, however, was stripped of emotions when he at last spoke.

"You actually think the female can be convinced to give up her only hostage?"

Lana didn't flinch beneath his fierce glare. "The obvious solution is to convince Stella that releasing Molly is in her own best interest."

"Or we could give her what she wants," a voice drawled from the doorway.

The four of them turned in unison to discover the Keeper of Tales standing just inside the office, his odd body covered by an ivory robe and his eyes shimmering pure white in the overhead lights.

"Shit, how do you do that?" Wolfe ground out between clenched teeth, his gun pointed at the doppelganger's head.

"'There are more things in heaven and earth, Horatio, than are dreamt of in your philosophy,'" Boggs quoted with a twist of his lips.

"I'm going to staple a cowbell to your fucking ass,"

Wolfe muttered, grudgingly lowering his gun. "That will keep you from sneaking up on me."

Boggs clicked his tongue. "Always so testy, Tagos."

"He's not wrong," Lana murmured, stepping around the bristling Wolfe to stand directly in front of Boggs. "I hope you're here to help, Master?"

Boggs turned his head, his blind gaze resting on Myst. She shivered. Could he see her or did he have some other ability to sense she was near?

"I did foresee my skills would be needed when I met with the clairvoyant," he murmured.

Myst frowned. She had a vague memory of him telling her his role had yet to be played, but she'd dismissed it as a way to get rid of them.

Now she studied him in confusion.

"What skills?"

The male moved forward, ignoring warning glares from both Bas and Wolfe as he stopped directly in front of her.

"My talent for this."

There was a tingle of energy as the doppelganger abruptly shifted his appearance to look exactly like her.

Myst's breath tangled in her throat. Good . . . Lord. He'd even created the raspberry sundress she'd pulled on after her quick shower.

It was Lana who realized precisely what the strange creature was implying.

"You're suggesting that you pretend to be Myst?"

Boggs reverted back to his larvalike appearance, smoothing his hands down the front of his robe as he turned toward the Mave.

"So long as I can cover my eyes, the woman won't be able to tell the difference," he promised.

Myst allowed herself a brief flare of hope before Bas was giving a sharp shake of his head.

"That's great, but it's not going to do a damned thing if

you can't get past the layers of magic," he snapped, clearly reaching the edge of his patience.

"I can get through," Boggs assured him without hesitation.

Lana made a sound of shock. Clearly this was the first time she'd heard that someone might be able to get through one of her spells.

"How?"

Something that might have been a smile touched Boggs's unformed face.

"My power to travel will allow me to pass through."

Lana stepped forward, clearly intent on questioning him on his traveling ability, but Bas didn't give her time to speak.

"I thought you needed to be close to the person for you to take their shape?" he pointed out, his clever brain searching out each problem.

He was too much a master tactician to accept any rescue plan that might put their daughter at risk.

Thank God.

"I do," Boggs agreed, his confidence never faltering. "We need the woman who is holding the child to be near a door."

Myst didn't question how the creature knew that Stella had Molly as her hostage. Or that they needed him at this precise moment. He'd obviously seen something when they'd been together in France that had told him what was going to happen and where he needed to be.

A damned shame he hadn't shared his vision.

"I can't go through the spells," she reminded him, growing increasingly restless.

Every minute that passed meant Molly was at the mercy of a woman without conscience or morals.

"No, but as long as you're near the door, I can capture your essence."

She frowned. It was possible for her to remain in the

stairwell next to the locked door while Boggs traveled through the barrier. Stella might have gained powers, but she had no way of sensing that there were two "Mysts," one inside and one hidden on the other side of the wall.

"I . . ." She gave a slow nod. "Okay."

Her hesitant agreement hung in the air before Lana and Wolfe were surging into movement. Together they moved to push aside a panel on the wall, revealing a large map of Valhalla, softly arguing before they came to a mutual decision.

Glancing back at Myst, Lana pointed toward a stairwell at the north edge of the fifth floor.

"We need to get you here," she said. "I can contact Stella on the intercom and show her your image standing at the door waiting for her. Once she's sure you're there she'll hopefully agree to a trade."

Boggs drifted forward, moving with an oddly fluid motion. As if his feet weren't quite touching the ground.

It was . . . creepy.

"When she's headed in the right direction I can travel to a spot just inside the door," he assured them. "I won't be able to hold my shape for long."

Wolfe studied the Keeper of Tales with a narrowed gaze. "What about your voice?"

Boggs gave a wave of a too-slender hand. "I can make it sound feminine. I assume she isn't familiar enough with Myst to tell the difference?"

"No." Myst shook her head. "We've never met."

Lana turned from the map, studying Boggs with a somber expression.

"You do understand that you're exposing yourself to any number of diseases?" she asked. "Even if they're not fatal to a high-blood, they're extremely unpleasant."

Boggs shrugged. "I'm not susceptible."

"You're certain?" Lana pressed, clearly worried the powerful high-blood was putting himself in danger.

Myst bit her lip, wanting to tell the woman to shut up. Obviously she didn't want someone to suffer because they were trying to help Molly, but she was desperate. She didn't want the Mave to convince Boggs his plan was too dangerous.

"Of course I'm certain," he assured the older woman.

Keeping his arm tightly wrapped around Myst's shoulders, Bas took a step forward.

"What about Molly?" he demanded, the air trembling with the force of his barely leashed frustration. "Can you travel with her?"

"No." Boggs gave a slow shake of his head. "All I can do is keep the woman distracted long enough for the small one to escape."

Bas stiffened, but Lana hurriedly sought to reassure them.

"If Boggs can get between Molly and Stella he can push Molly through the door," she said, her finger moving to a door just down the hallway. "She'll be able to cross through the barrier. Stella won't be able to follow."

Boggs tilted his head to the side, his white gaze locked on Bas's rigid face.

"Will she obey me if I tell her to run?"

Bas hesitated before giving a jerky nod. "I believe so."

Myst wasn't so certain.

"What if she freezes?" she demanded, her mouth dry and her heart thundering. "She's just a little girl."

Without warning she felt herself being tugged back toward the windows and turned to meet Bas's searing bronze gaze.

"I know it's a risk, *cara*," he murmured softly, his hands lifting to frame her face. "But what choice do we have?"

She sucked in a deep breath, trying to ease her sudden attack of nerves. Logically she understood that Boggs was offering them their best chance to get back Molly. Her heart, however, was terrified they might be putting her daughter in even greater danger.

"None, I suppose," she at last muttered.

He leaned down to press his lips to her brow. "I'll be at your side."

She gave a sharp shake of her head. "No, I'm going to have to be alone on the camera if we're going to fool Stella," she told him.

"She's right," Lana murmured from across the room.

Bas narrowed his gaze, as if sensing there was more to her insistence than just a fear they might alert the leader of the Brotherhood that they were setting a trap.

It was true. She didn't want the male near Stella just in case something went wrong. Right now they assumed her only power was being a plague carrier, but who knew? She might have some other rare magic that would allow her to strike through the barrier.

Bas conducted an inner battle, clearly torn between his primitive need to protect her and his common sense that knew she was right.

At last he muttered a savage curse and swooped his head down to claim her mouth in a kiss of blatant possession.

"Don't you dare take any foolish risks," he commanded against her lips. "Molly is going to need you." Another demanding kiss. "Almost as much as I need you."

Myst shivered, pleasure racing through her even as she was acutely aware of their avid audience.

"Bas," she breathed in protest.

"I don't care who is watching," he growled, his fingers threading through her hair, his heat wrapping around her like a physical caress. "You need to know that you're going to help distract Stella and then we're leaving Valhalla with Molly to start our life together."

Together. A dangerous longing melted her heart. It was

a dream she'd never dared to believe was possible. Even now, she found herself afraid to think it might be within her grasp.

Hope, after all, had always been her greatest enemy.

"Are you asking me to be with you or telling me?" she tried to tease.

"I'm telling you," he warned, holding her wary gaze. "We've lost too many years already. I'm not taking a chance on wasting one more day."

Her lips twitched. "Arrogant."

"Determined," he corrected, pressing a last, lingering kiss to her lips. "Be careful."

With a slow nod she gently pulled out of his arms and turned to face the patiently waiting doppelganger.

"Are you ready?"

He immediately headed toward the door. "Let's do this thing."

"I'll contact Stella as soon as you're in place," Lana assured her. "Good luck."

Luck? Myst swallowed a hysterical urge to laugh.

Considering her shitty luck over the past fifteen years, she was overdue for her fair share.

She could only hope today was the day.

Stella was at the point of pulling out her hair when she heard the electronic beep.

Not that she was about to reveal her fear that she was destined to be forever trapped in the storage room, scratching at her skin that now felt as if it was on fire.

Not even in front of a mere child.

"I knew the Mave would come to her senses," she murmured, glancing toward the girl, who was studying her with those strange bronze eyes. "It's all about leverage, kid. I have what she wants and now she'll give me what I want."

Smoothing her hair, she waved an impatient hand toward the monitor. "Turn that thing on."

Clutching the hippo in one arm, the child reached up to press the button beneath the monitor. Instantly the screen flickered and the image of the Mave came into view.

"Stella," the older woman murmured.

Stella pasted a mocking smile on her lips. "It's about fucking time."

The Mave considered her with a cold disdain that made Stella long to bitch-slap her.

"I had to locate Myst and explain that her daughter is being held hostage by a psychopath."

"I assume she's willing to cooperate?" Stella taunted, her heart thundering.

There was no backup plan if the clairvoyant refused to cooperate.

"She is." The Mave eased Stella's surge of fear.

Stella gave a toss of her hair, suddenly far more confident.

The clairvoyant would soon be in her hands and she would . . .

Well, she didn't have a firm plan after that, but she was going to trust in destiny. She'd always known she was meant for more than the trailer-trash destiny of her mother. It had been written in her stars.

"Send her in and then I'll let you have the girl."

The Mave gave a sharp, humorless laugh. "Not going to happen," she said. "The exchange will happen at the same time."

Stella clenched her hands, the fire licking over her skin intensifying.

"Do you really think you can give me orders?" she hissed.

The Mave offered a cold smile. "Yes."

Hatred ran thick through Stella's blood. "I doubt Molly's mother would agree," she accused in venomous tones.

The Mave's smile never faltered. "She wouldn't, but she's not in charge." There was a deliberate pause. "I am."

Stella knew she was cornered. If she wanted to get her hands on the clairvoyant, she was going to have to agree to whatever the Mave demanded.

"You really are a bitch," she snapped.

The older woman arched a dark brow. "Unlike you, I didn't earn my place with lies and false promises."

Stella parted her lips only to snap them shut. The Mave was deliberately trying to provoke her. She was a fool to allow herself to be played.

With an effort, she hid her fury behind a mask of amusement.

"I'll admit to the lies. The Brothers were gullible enough to believe anything that might offer them a chance to defeat the high-bloods." She shrugged. "But my promises are about to come true."

The Mave's face was impossible to read. "You'll make the trade?"

Stella hesitated before giving a sharp nod. It was now or never.

"Where?"

"The north staircase," the Mave swiftly informed her. "Just take a right when you step out of the storage room. The door will be at the end. Myst will be waiting there."

Stella narrowed her gaze. That'd all come out far too smoothly. As if it'd been rehearsed.

"Yeah, along with a dozen Sentinels, no doubt," she accused, on the point of getting cold feet.

Being stuck in this storage room was better than a quick trip to the dungeons.

The Mave reached forward and her image was suddenly replaced by the sight of a slender woman who was standing just outside a door. The clairvoyant. It had to be. She had the same silver hair and delicate features as her daughter.

Stella leaned forward, studying the empty stairwell behind the woman, as if she could actually detect any warriors.

"There's not one Sentinel with her," the Mave's voice floated through the intercom. "I swear."

Stella stiffened her spine. She'd already decided that this was her last chance. There was no point in trying to pretend she had a choice.

"You'll be very sorry if you're lying to me," she warned, reaching forward to press the button, shutting off the monitor. Then, before her nerves could get the better of her, she grabbed Molly's arm and headed out of the storage room. "I'm going to enjoy watching that woman die," she muttered, trying to soothe her wounded pride. "As slowly and painfully as possible."

"Bad woman," Molly said, stumbling over her feet in an effort to keep up with Stella's brisk stride.

"Keep your mouth shut and stay close," she told the brat, half dragging her down the hallway. "Got it?"

A mutinous expression settled on the tiny face, but Molly was smart enough not to argue.

"Yes."

The odd pentagon shape of the building meant that it was impossible to see more than a few feet ahead of her. Which explained why Stella was so startled when she rounded a corner to discover that the woman on the camera was already standing just inside the doorway.

"I'm Myst," the female said as Stella came to a startled halt.

Stella frowned, studying the woman. In person she looked even younger. Barely old enough to have a child.

"Christ, you look like a pixie doll," she muttered, her gaze resting on the large pair of sunglasses that covered her eyes. "Why are you wearing sunglasses?"

The female held out a slender hand. "Molly, come to me."

The child hesitated, as if confused by the sight of her mother.

"But—"

"No." Stella tightened her grip on the girl's arm.

The high-blood female made a sound of impatience. "That was the deal."

Stella was desperate, but she wasn't stupid. Just having the clairvoyant wouldn't be enough.

"Not until I'm sure you can produce the weapon," she told the female.

Myst shrugged. "I'm here, aren't I?"

"And empty-handed."

There was a pause, as if Myst was caught off guard by the demand for proof that she could produce what the vision had promised. Then slowly she lifted her hands.

"The weapon isn't a human device."

Stella frowned in confusion. "Then what . . ." Her breath was jerked from her lungs as she caught sight of the dazzling display of colors that abruptly rose from the clairvoyant's fingers. "Magic?"

"I am a high-blood," Myst pointed out.

Stella felt a burst of anger, unconsciously releasing Molly's arm as she scratched at her neck. The burning was spreading.

"That's impossible," she rasped. "I can't use that."

"Of course you can," the clairvoyant promised. Slowly the colors coalesced into a ball of seething energy. "Hold out your hands."

Stella started to reach forward, only to realize her arms were now covered by a red, angry rash. What the hell?

"This is a trick," she rasped.

"Okay." Calmly pulling back her hands, Myst gave a small shrug. "If you don't want it."

"Wait." Stella bit her bottom lip, trying to think through the growing fuzz in her mind. She didn't know what was wrong with her, but she was certain that once she managed to escape, everything would be fine. "What does it do?"

"Once it's released it will spread through Valhalla like wildfire."

Stella sent the clairvoyant a suspicious glare. "And you're just going to give it to me?"

Myst turned her head toward the little girl. "I'll do anything to protect my daughter."

"Fine," Stella muttered. She held out an impatient hand. "Give it to me."

Myst took a step backward. "First, I want Molly."

Stella reached to press her hand against the girl's shoulder, wondering why the stupid brat was hesitating.

"Go to your mother," she ordered.

The little girl clutched her stuffed hippo. "She's not—"

"Molly, get out of here right now," her mother interrupted in firm tones, pointing toward the door.

Warily inching away, the little girl abruptly scampered forward, pulling open the door that had refused Stella's every effort to unlock. Within seconds she was gone, the door firmly closed behind her.

Dismissing the child from her mind, Stella returned her attention to the clairvoyant. It was time she was given what she'd been promised.

A weapon that would allow her to rule the world.

Okay, maybe not the world, she conceded, her thoughts threatening to dissolve before she could hold on to them. But her own special corner.

For now that would be enough.

Before she could speak, however, there was a strange shimmer around the woman.

Stella made a sound of shock as Myst seemed to swell larger and larger. Was this some freakish magic? She struggled to breathe as she watched the pretty young woman morph into a pale, formless creature who was staring at her with pure white eyes.

"What the hell?" she breathed, stumbling backward. "What are you?"

He, or at least she assumed it was a he, allowed his lips to twist into a smile that made her stomach clench with dread.

"I know it's tediously clichéd, but I truly am your worst nightmare," he informed her.

She agreed.

He *was* a nightmare.

A big, larvalike beast who was denying her the destiny that'd been promised.

"Where's my weapon?" she screeched, unable to accept that her glorious fate had been snatched away.

He gave a sad shake of his head. "You are the weapon."

Frustration clutched her stomach, along with a sickening sensation of doom.

"Don't screw with me," she snarled. "I was promised . . . promised . . ."

Her words stumbled to a halt as her tongue swelled, making it almost impossible to speak.

The creature stepped forward. "What were you promised, Stella?"

She blinked, feeling a wetness coming from her eyes.

It couldn't be tears. She never cried. Never.

Lifting her hand, she brushed her cheeks. They were wet. She pulled her hand away to discover the tips of her fingers coated in blood.

"Greatness," she mumbled, befuddled by the red staining her skin. A shrill warning was sounding in the back of her mind, but it was too difficult to think through the fog. "I was promised greatness."

"Greatness is earned, not stolen," the freak said, as if she were a five-year-old in need of a lecture.

"I stole nothing. I earned it." She clenched her fists, desperately trying to ignore the escalating fever that scoured through her veins. Christ. She felt as if she was being burned alive. "All those years giving my body to disgusting men. Pretending I gave a damn about the crazy-ass Brotherhood. I deserve my fate."

The white eyes blazed as the male held out his hand, revealing the ball of churning energy he'd fooled her with before.

"Fate is a fickle thing." With a wave of his hand the ball disappeared. "Seen from one angle it can look like success, and seen by another it is failure."

Failure . . . failure . . . failure . . .

The word whispered through her fuzzy mind.

"There is no weapon, is there?" she spat out. She had to get to the door. If that little brat could get out, then so could she. Right?

"I've told you, you're the weapon," the man murmured, something that might have been pity twisting his blob of a face as she struggled to take a step forward.

She blinked away the blood, trying to force her shaky legs to carry her forward.

"How could I be a weapon?"

"Easily." He shrugged. "You're a high-blood who possesses an extraordinary gift."

"High-blood?" She gave a sharp laugh, her lips cracking as she came to an abrupt halt. "That's not possible."

The creature waved aside her protest. "Believe whatever you want, Stella. But the truth is the truth. You're a carrier who must be contained for your own safety as well as others'."

High-blood. She was a high-blood.

She wanted to deny the claim. To call him a bald-faced liar. But there was more than just heat and pain that was sizzling through her body.

There was . . . a magic that was threatening to destroy her.

A wild laugh at the sheer irony erupted from her throat before it was changing to a hiss of pain as the flames beneath her skin became unbearable.

"No." She fell to her knees, the grinding agony becoming unbearable. "What are you doing to me?"

The creature's white gaze moved to study the huge boils erupting over the skin of her arms.

"It seems your powers aren't entirely stable."

"Make it stop." She glared at the freak. Didn't he realize that she was dying?

"I can't."

"Liar." She coughed, not surprised when blood sprayed over the floor. "I swear I'll be a good high-blood," she muttered, willing to promise anything to stop the torment. "I'll do whatever you say."

She thought she heard him heave a faint sigh. "It's too late."

"No." Genuine fear thundered through her. All her plans, all her plotting, all her sacrifices . . . It had to be worth something, didn't it? "Help me."

There was the rustle of robes as the man stepped backward. "There's nothing I can do."

Stella groaned, the world slipping away as she realized she'd failed.

"This isn't how it's supposed to happen. . . ." she rasped. "I was supposed to win. . . ."

Unable to leave without her daughter, Myst pressed herself against the wall, peeking around the corner.

Come on, come on, she silently urged, feeling as if each passing second was an eternity.

At last she caught sight of the little girl stepping through the open doorway, a dimpled smile lighting her face as she ran down the hallway.

"Mommy. Mommy."

Going to her knees, Myst held out her arms, her heart soaring with relief.

"Oh, my baby," she breathed, pulling her daughter tight against her as her tears fell unchecked down her cheeks.

She'd never been so terrified in her life. Now pure joy was bursting through her. Was it any wonder she was having trouble controlling her emotions?

Leaning back, Molly sent her mother a chiding frown. "I'm not a baby."

"No, you're not," Myst readily agreed, kissing the tip of her daughter's nose. "You're a very big, very brave girl."

Molly's glorious smile dimmed, her lower lip quivering.

"I didn't like that mean lady."

Myst ran a worried gaze over her daughter. The Mave had sworn that she wasn't infected, but that didn't mean she didn't have other injuries.

"Did she hurt you?"

"She squeezed my arm, but it didn't hurt. Well . . ." Molly hunched a shoulder, knowing that she was always supposed to tell the truth. "It didn't hurt much."

Myst forced a reassuring smile to her lips. "Don't worry, sweetie. She's never going to hurt you again." She tenderly brushed a silvery curl from Molly's cheek. "I swear."

Molly nodded, glancing over her shoulder. "I think she was sick."

Myst grimaced. Despite everything her daughter had endured, she still possessed that sweet, innocent belief in the goodness of others. Which meant that Myst couldn't share her opinion of the bitch who'd tried to use a child as a bargaining chip.

"Yeah, I think so too," she murmured.

"Will the healers take care of her?"

"I'm not sure she can be helped," Myst hedged, knowing her daughter's tender heart would be worried.

There was a short silence before Molly wrinkled her nose, thankfully turning her thoughts away from Stella and her ugly fate.

"I knew that man wasn't you, even though he had your face," she said, her dimples returning.

"Of course you did." Myst kissed the top of the silvery curls, fiercely grateful her daughter hadn't given the game away. "You're a very clever little girl."

Molly reached up to touch Myst's forehead. "I knew because his brains were different," she explained.

Myst studied her daughter. A new talent?

"What do you mean different?"

"They are all scrambly," Molly said, her brow wrinkled as she tried to explain. "They blink. One place and then another. As if he isn't really here at all."

Hmm. "He is . . . unusual," Myst admitted, feeling a small flare of unease. She didn't know anything about Boggs, but she didn't think he would be pleased to know that Molly could sense beneath his strange appearance. Best to keep the two of them apart. "We need to get away from here."

"Can we go home now?" Molly swiftly demanded.

"Home," Myst breathed.

Molly pulled back, her big eyes filled with worry. "You're staying this time, aren't you."

"I-"

"Yes, Molly, she's staying this time," a male voice interrupted.

"Daddy," Molly screeched, pulling away from Myst to hurtle into Bas's waiting arms. With a smooth motion he had her lifted off her feet and snuggled in his arms. "Squeeze me tight," Molly commanded.

Bas's expression was painfully vulnerable as he buried

his face in Molly's curls, his big body trembling as he pressed his daughter against his chest.

"This tight?" he asked.

Already recovered from her ordeal, Molly was swift to take advantage of her parents' overwhelming relief. Arching back, she flashed her most persuasive smile.

"Is Mommy staying with us?"

The bronze gaze moved to where Myst had straightened to stand in the center of the hallway. A fierce, shockingly possessive smile curving his lips.

"She is."

Elation exploded through Myst, even as she tried to pretend she wasn't as eager as a stray dog to be invited to his home.

"So sure?" she murmured.

A sudden heat shimmered in the depths of his eyes as he allowed his gaze to slide down her body.

"I'll handcuff you to the bed if necessary."

Molly gave a sudden giggle. "Has Mommy been bad?"

"I hope she intends to be very, very bad," Bas said, smiling with wicked pleasure at the blush that stained her cheeks.

"Bas," she protested, even as she trembled with anticipation.

"I'm hungry." Molly broke into the sensual spell that Bas could so easily weave around Myst. "Can I have a donut?"

"Come on." Bas held out his hand in silent invitation, waiting for Myst to move forward and lay her fingers against his palm. "Let's get our daughter a donut."

Chapter Twenty-Two

Bas felt like an awkward teenager.

Not a sensation he was particularly fond of, he silently acknowledged. Shifting his weight from foot to foot, he watched as Myst drifted from the sunken living room with open beam ceilings and a stunning view of the nearby lake, into the large kitchen with stainless steel appliances that the real-estate agent had insisted were "absolute musts."

Bas hadn't given a shit about appliances. All he wanted was a home that was comfortable for Myst, with large windows that offered plenty of sunshine for Molly, and isolated enough that he could easily protect them.

Now he could only hope that Myst wanted the same thing.

"Well?" he at last prompted.

"Well what?" she asked, running her hand over the marble countertop.

Bas scowled. Over the past week they'd been inseparable. They had five years to make up for, after all. And Myst had been just as eager as he had been to live as a family with Molly.

But Bas had swiftly grown tired of their cramped apartment in Valhalla, not to mention the endless parade of visitors who assumed they could drop by whenever they wanted.

He needed to be alone with Myst and Molly.

At least for the next century or so.

So he'd secretly set about finding the perfect place to live, assuming it would make a wonderful surprise for his soon-to-be wife. It had never occurred to him that she wouldn't be equally pleased.

"Do you like it?" he pressed, carefully studying her pale face.

"Of course I like it." Her smile didn't reach the velvet-brown eyes. "It's perfect."

He folded his arms over his chest. "Then why aren't you leaping for joy?"

She glanced out the window where the afternoon sunlight danced off the water in the lake. Farther away was nothing but trees that circled the property.

"This is a big change from your elegant hotels," she murmured. "Are you sure you're ready?"

His scowl deepened, an unpleasant ball of fear lodging in the pit of his stomach. He was more than ready. But clearly Myst was having second thoughts.

"The hotels were a symbol," he said, his lips twisting as she blinked in confusion. "After my mother's death I was obsessed with the need to make sure I was surrounded by enough wealth and power so I would never be vulnerable again. It was the only way I could feel in control of my life," he explained, reaching to touch the tiny locket that once again hung around her neck. "But the hotels and even the hidden safe houses I created to protect my people were never a home," he continued, holding her gaze. "Molly is my home. And now you."

"Oh." A flush touched her cheeks, but still her expression remained wary. "What about the Mave?"

Bas studied her with a flare of impatience. Surely she

couldn't think he had any interest in the Mave? Not after he'd devoted the past week to proving he was completely besotted with a silver-haired clairvoyant?

"What about her?" he demanded.

"Has she agreed to forgive your past?"

Ah. Bas grinned. Lana had spent an entire afternoon lecturing him on the importance of following the laws of Valhalla and his duty to his fellow high-bloods. All of which went in one ear and out the other.

He would lay down his life for his family, but he'd be damned if he would become a respectable member of society.

"I doubt she intends to forgive me," he admitted with a shrug. "But she has promised she won't throw me into the nearest dungeon. At least not until I do something else to piss her off."

Myst nodded, her finger drawing absent patterns on the marble countertop.

"And Wolfe?"

"He's tumbled madly in love with Molly," Bas pointed out in offhand tones. "He's willing to turn a blind eye for her sake."

Myst wrinkled her nose. "If she keeps going to Valhalla she's going to be spoiled rotten."

That was the understatement of the century. Molly's talent might be stirring latent powers, but her true magic was the ability to bring happiness to even the most hardened warrior.

Hell, he'd seen Wolfe and the tattooed Sentinel, Fane, squashing their large bodies into tiny nursery chairs so they could share an afternoon "tea" with his daughter.

"I shudder to think what would happen if we tried to forbid them from seeing her," he murmured, prowling around the edge of the counter. "It's quite likely we'd both end up in the dungeons."

Her lips twitched. "True."

Reaching out, he cupped her chin and tilted back her head to study her guarded expression. *What the hell?*

"Myst."

She shivered beneath his light grip. "Yes?"

"What's going on?"

"I don't know what you—"

"Don't," he interrupted in stern tones. Enough was enough. He was getting to the bottom of her strange behavior. "If this isn't your dream house, we'll find another one. Hell, we can find a dozen and you can choose your favorite."

"No," she breathed. "The house is truly perfect."

He leaned down, savoring the sweet scent of honeysuckle. "Then why do I sense you aren't fully committed to making this our home?"

She hesitated, almost as if considering a lie. Then, clearly realizing Bas would recognize any attempt to deceive him, she heaved a faint sigh.

"Because I'm afraid."

He sucked in a shocked breath. "Of me?"

"No, of course not," she denied, her expression horrified.

Okay. She wasn't afraid of him. Then what?

"Talk to me, Myst," he insisted.

Without warning she stepped forward, laying her head on his chest as her arms wrapped around his waist.

"I've never allowed myself to dream that I could have a real home with a real family," she confessed in a low voice that was raw with emotion. "Now I fear this might be an illusion that will be snatched away."

Oh . . . hell.

Relief and a fierce need to protect this fragile female thundered through him. He lashed his arms around her, holding her so tight he knew it would be difficult for her to breathe.

"Trust me, I'm very, very real," he assured her. "And there's nothing on this earth that's going to separate us again." He pressed a kiss to the top of her head. "Nothing."

"You swear?"

"I swear." He pulled back far enough so she could see the sincerity etched on his face. "You can believe in me, Myst."

She gave a slow nod, her wariness fading as she accepted he was never letting her go.

"Okay."

"Will you leap for joy now?" he demanded.

A small, mysterious smile curved her lips. "Actually, women in my condition shouldn't leap."

"Your condition?" His heart squeezed in instant alarm before he noticed the shimmer of absolute contentment in her dark eyes. She wasn't worried. She was . . . delighted. "Are you pregnant?" he asked, barely daring to breathe as he waited for her slow nod.

"I warned you the spell was faulty," she murmured.

Pure joy raced through him. Another baby. He felt dizzy with happiness.

"Or more likely fate is just determined to make sure we have a dozen beautiful babies," he said, firmly believing there was nothing wrong with the spell.

Destiny had created Molly. Just as it had created the new child growing within his mate.

"A dozen?" She gave a low chuckle, the last of her unease melting away. "Isn't that a little ambitious?"

His lips skimmed over her forehead. "I'm a mercenary."

She quivered, her hand lifting to cup the side of his neck in a gesture of intimate affection.

"And?"

"And I'm greedy," he murmured, his blood heating as he allowed his gaze to slowly sweep over her face. "The more I have, the more I want."

She blushed, no doubt recalling the long nights when he'd kissed her from head to toe, unable to sate his unquenchable desire for her.

"So I've noticed," she teased.

He smiled with wicked anticipation, happiness swelling through him like the most potent aphrodisiac.

"In fact . . . I'm feeling a little greedy right now," he assured her, bending down to scoop her off her feet. "Shall we discover if our new home possesses a bed?"

Her laughter filled the house with a warmth that truly turned it into a home.

"I remember when you would have been satisfied with a couch," she taunted.

He headed out of the kitchen and toward the large master bedroom at the end of the hallway.

"And I remember how you disappeared the second my back was turned," he growled, gazing down at the face that had haunted his dreams for years. "I want you in a room where I can lock the door." Bending his head, he kissed her with a promise of pleasure to come, speaking against her lips. "You're never going to slip away from me again, *cara*."

Five brave military heroes have survived the hell of a Taliban prison to return home—and take on civilian missions no one else can. They're the men of ARES Security. Highly skilled, intimidating, invincible, and one by one, tested again and again . . .

Lucas St. Clair's prestigious family had a political future neatly planned out for him—one that didn't include his high school sweetheart, Mia Ramon. Under their pressure, Lucas gave her up. But since surviving captivity, he's a changed man—and a crucial member of ARES Security. When he discovers a dead man clutching a picture of Mia that bears a threatening message, his fiercest protective instincts kick in, and he knows he must go to her.

Mia has never forgiven Lucas for breaking her heart, and she's convinced her feelings for him are in the past. But it's soon clear that isn't true for either of them. Now, determined to solve the crime and keep Mia safe, with his ARES buddies backing him up, Lucas will have to reconstruct the murder victim's last days— and follow a lethal trail that leads right back to the fate of the woman he still loves . . .

Please turn the page for an exciting sneak peek of Alexandra Ivy's

KILL WITHOUT SHAME,

coming in January 2017 wherever print and eBooks are sold!

Prologue

The worst part of being held in a Taliban prison was the nightmares. At least as far as Lucas St. Clair was concerned.

No matter how many years passed, his nights were still plagued with memories of being trapped in the smothering darkness of the caves. He could smell the stench of unwashed bodies and undiluted fear. He could hear the muffled sounds of men praying for death.

He knew that his parents assumed that his biggest regret was the derailment of his political aspirations. After all, his military career was intended to be the first step in his climb to a position as a diplomat.

From there . . . well, his family was nothing, if not ambitious. They'd no doubt seen a White House in his future.

But there were few things that could make a man view his life with stark clarity like five weeks of brutal torture.

By the time he'd managed to escape the caves, he'd known he was done living his life to please the precious St. Clair clan.

Instead he'd banded together with his friends, Rafe Vargas, a covert ops specialist, Max Grayson who was trained in forensics, Hauk Laurensen, a sniper, and Teagan Moore, a computer wizard, to create ARES Security.

He'd wasted too much of his life.

He intended to leave the past behind and concentrate on his future.

Of course, there was an old saying about "the best laid plans of mice and men . . ."

Chapter One

The *Saloon* was the sort of bar that catered to the locals in the quiet, Houston neighborhood.

It was small, with lots of polished wood and an open-beam ceiling. On the weekends they invited a jazz band to play quietly on the narrow stage.

Lucas spent most Friday evenings at the table tucked in a back corner. It was unofficially reserved for the five men who ran ARES Security.

They liked the quiet ambiance, the communal agreement that everyone should mind their own fucking business, and the fact that the table was situated so no one could sneak up from behind.

Trained soldiers didn't want surprises.

At the moment, the bar was nearly empty. Not only was it a gray, wet Wednesday evening, but it was the first week of December. That meant Christmas madness was in full swing.

Perfectly normal people were now in crazy-mode as they scurried from store to store, battling each other for the latest, have-to-have gift. Or attending the endless tour of parties.

Currently Lucas and Teagan shared the bar with a young

couple who were seated near the front bay window. Those two were oblivious to everything but each other. And closer to the empty stage there was a table of college girls. Already at the giggly stage of drunk they were all blatantly checking him out. At least when they weren't gawking at Teagan.

No biggie.

Both men were accustomed to female attention.

Teagan was a large, heavily muscled man with dark caramel skin, and golden eyes that he'd inherited from his Polynesian mother. He kept his hair shaved close to his skull, and as usual was dressed in a pair of camo pants and shit-kickers. He had an aggressive vibe that was only emphasized by the tight T-shirt that left his arms bare to reveal his numerous tattoos.

Lucas St. Clair, on the other hand, was wearing a thousand dollar suit that was tailored to perfectly fit his lean body. His glossy black hair was smoothed away from his chiseled face that he'd been told could easily have graced the covers of fashion magazines. As if he gave a shit.

His eyes were so dark they looked black. It wasn't until he was in the sunlight that it became obvious they were a deep, indigo blue.

Most assumed that he was the less dangerous of the two men.

They'd be wrong.

But while the girls became increasingly more blatant in their attempts to attract their attention, neither man glanced in their direction.

Teagan because he already had a flock of women who included super-models, and two famous actresses.

And Lucas because . . . he grimaced.

To be honest, he wasn't sure why. He only knew that his interest in women hadn't been the same since he'd crawled out of that hell-hole in Afghanistan. Not unless he counted the hours he spent brooding on one woman in particular.

The one who got away.

Lucas gave a sharp shake of his head, reaching for his shot of tequila. It slid down his throat like liquid fire, burning away the memories.

Nothing like a twelve-year-old vintage to ease the pain.

Lucas glanced toward his companion's empty glass.

"Another round?" he asked.

"Sure." Teagan waited for Lucas to nod toward the bartender, who was washing glasses at the same time keeping a sharp eye on his few customers. "I assume you're picking up the tab?"

Lucas cocked a brow. "Why do I always have to pick up the tab?"

"You're the one with the trust fund, amigo, not me," Teagan said with a shrug. "The only thing my father ever gave me was a concussion and an intimate knowledge of the Texas penal system."

Lucas snorted. They all knew that Lucas would beg in the streets before he would touch a penny of the St. Clair fortune. Just as they all knew that Teagan had risen above his abusive background, and temporary housing in the penitentiary to become a successful businessman. Teagan had not only joined ARES, but he owned a mechanic shop that catered to a high-end clientele who had more money than sense when it came to their precious sports cars.

"I might break out the violins if I didn't know you're making a fortune," Lucas said as the bartender arrived to replace their drinks with a silent efficiency.

"Hardly a fortune." Teagan reached for his beer, heaving a faux sigh. "I have overhead out the ass, not to mention paying my cousins twice what they're worth. A word of warning, amigo, never go into business with your family."

"Too late," Lucas murmured.

As far as he was concerned, the men who crawled out of that Taliban cave with him were his brothers. And the only family that mattered.

"True that." Teagan gave a slow nod, holding up his frosty glass. "To ARES."

Lucas clinked his glass against Teagan's in appreciation for the bond they'd formed.

"To ARES."

Drinking the tequila in one swallow, Lucas set aside his empty glass. There was a brief silence before Teagan at last spoke the words that'd no doubt been on the tip of his tongue since they walked through the door of the bar.

"Are you ever going to get to the point of why you asked me to meet you here?" his friend bluntly demanded.

Lucas leaned back in his chair, arching his brows.

"Couldn't it just be because I enjoy your sparkling personality?"

Teagan snorted. "If I'd known this was a date I would have worn my lucky shirt."

"You need a shirt to get lucky?"

"Not usually." Teagan flashed his friend a mocking smile. "But I've heard you like to play hard to get."

Lucas grimaced at the direct hit. Yeah. Hard to get was one way to put it.

"I want to discuss Hauk," he admitted, not at all eager to think about his lack of a sex life.

Teagan leaned forward, folding his arms on the table. "Did you pick up any intel from your overseas contacts?"

Lucas didn't ask how his companion knew he was quietly reaching out to his military connections in an effort to track down who was stalking Hauk. They were each using their various skills to discover who was responsible for leaving the creepy messages that were increasingly threatening in nature.

"Yeah." He'd received an updated report earlier that

morning. "There's been no chatter that includes Hauk or anything about our escape from Afghanistan."

Teagan nodded. Each of them had managed to make enemies during their time in the Middle East. It was war. But Hauk was a sniper who'd received a very public Medal of Honor for taking out three powerful terrorist leaders during his time in service.

That was the sort of thing that pissed people off.

"Then this isn't the work of an organized cell?"

"Nope." Lucas gave a decisive shake of his head. He'd contacted everyone he knew, including those at Homeland Security. If Hauk's name had been floating around as a potential target, someone would have heard about it by now. "It's more likely some independent whack-job."

Teagan's jaw hardened with frustration. "I don't know whether to be relieved or disappointed. If it was a cell we could keep an eye on them, but how the hell do we find some lone nutcase?"

"I have put the word out that I'm looking for information on anyone who's shown an interest in Hauk." Lucas studied his companion's grim expression. "What about you?"

Teagan reached for his beer. "I'm doing a computer search on anyone who served with Hauk during his tour in the Middle East and has left the military in the past six months."

Lucas arched a brow. Teagan was talented. Maybe even the best hacker in the States. But he wasn't a miracle worker.

"That's a long list."

"It's going to take awhile," Teagan admitted, taking a deep drink of his beer.

"Shit. I hate this waiting," Lucas muttered. The thought that some unseen enemy was hunting Hauk was making them all twitchy. "What about Max?"

"He's . . ." Teagan slowly lowered his beer as his gaze narrowed. "Did you forget to pay your taxes?"

Lucas frowned. "What the hell are you talking about?"

Teagan nodded across the room. "There's a government employee who just flashed a badge at the bartender and is now heading in our direction."

Lucas glanced over his shoulder, his gaze trained on the middle-aged man strolling in their direction.

The stranger had thinning blond hair that was ruffled from the stiff breeze. A suit that was in dire need of a good pressing. Cheap shoes. And a face that had a hint of a bulldog.

Yep. Definitely a government grunt.

Lucas turned back toward his friend. "How do you know he isn't looking for you?"

"I'm too clever to get caught."

Lucas rolled his eyes. "Christ."

"Lucas St. Clair?"

Halting next to the table, the man instantly locked his attention on Lucas. Which meant he knew exactly what Lucas looked like.

So, had he recognized Lucas because of his ties to the St. Clair clan? Or because he'd done a background check before entering the *Saloon*?

Lucas was betting on the background check.

The stranger didn't look like the sort of man to take an interest in politics.

"Yes."

The man flashed a badge that identified him as HOUSTON HOMICIDE DETECTIVE SERGEANT SAM COOPER.

"I have a few questions for you."

Lucas remained relaxed in his chair. There was no reason to get his panties in a twist. If there'd been a death in his powerful family he wouldn't be contacted by a midlevel bureaucrat.

And he hadn't killed anyone. At least, not lately.

"Concerning?" he asked.

The man glanced around the nearly empty bar. "Do you want to do this here?"

Lucas shrugged. "Unless we need to include my lawyer."

"That won't be necessary."

The "yet" hung in the air between them and suddenly Lucas was a lot less nonchalant about the encounter.

Narrowing his gaze, he nodded his head toward the chair across the table.

"Have a seat, Detective." Waiting until the man lowered his solid form into the chair, Lucas waved a hand toward his friend who glowered at the lawman with a menacing frown. "This is Teagan Moore."

"Detective Cooper," Teagan muttered, folding his arms over his chest to make it clear he wasn't leaving.

Lucas hid his smile. In his work as a negotiator, he'd learned the art of subtlety. It was easier to persuade people to do what he wanted, rather than trying to force them.

Teagan, on the other hand, was a sledgehammer.

Returning his attention to the Detective, he tapped an impatient finger on the table. He had a dozen things he needed to take care of before he could return to his elegant townhouse in the center of Houston.

ARES Security might be a relatively new business, but they were already swamped with demands for their services. And to make matters more insane, Rafe had taken off with his new bride to Hawaii for a well-earned honeymoon.

He wanted to be done with this cop so he could get back to work.

"You said you have some questions," he prompted.

The man offered a self-deprecating smile, but Lucas didn't miss the cunning intelligence in the man's blue eyes.

He was a man who liked to be underestimated.

Taking the time to pull a small notebook and pen from

an inner pocket of his jacket, Sam Cooper laid them neatly on the table.

Precise. Careful. Meticulous.

"What's your relationship to Anthony Hughes?" he at last asked.

Lucas frowned. "There is no relationship. I've never heard of—" He bit off his words as an ancient memory floated to the surface of his brain. "Wait. I went to prep school with a Tony Hughes. I don't know if that's the same guy."

"Where was the school?"

Lucas shrugged. "Hale Academy in Shreveport."

The Detective's face remained impassive, but something flashed through his eyes that told Lucas that they were speaking about the same person.

"So the two of you are friends?"

Lucas hesitated. In truth, the two couldn't have been more opposite.

He was the son of a senator. He'd lived in a fancy mansion on the edge of town with a nanny while his parents spent most of their time in D.C. Tony was the youngest of five brothers who grew up in a shack that had barely been habitable. If Tony hadn't been a six foot two behemoth who excelled at football he would never have been admitted into the exclusive private school.

And even that wouldn't have made them more than classmates.

It was only their mutual friendship with Mia Ramon that'd thrown them together.

"Not really," he said. "I haven't seen him in fifteen years."

Sam scribbled on his notepad, his gaze never leaving Lucas's face.

"You're sure? He hasn't tried to call or contact you?"

"I'm sure." Lucas felt a stab of dread. "What's going on? Is he in trouble?"

The Detective instantly pounced. "Why would you say that?"

Lucas arched a brow. "Beyond the fact a Homicide Detective is asking me questions about him?"

"Yeah, beyond that."

"It was no secret that Tony was doing drugs from the time he arrived at Hale," he admitted, not bothering to add that Tony was also dealing to make enough money to support his dead-beat dad. It wouldn't take much of a Detective to dig up that old dirt. "He was kicked off the football team when he tested positive for weed our senior year. If some unknown donor hadn't come up with his tuition he would have been forced to leave school."

More scribbling on the pad. "Were you close growing up?"

"I didn't really know him until he transferred to the academy."

"But you were friends?"

"We both played football and occasionally hung out together." Lucas made a sound of impatience. "Are you going to tell me what your interest in Tony is?"

"He's dead."

"Dead?" Lucas blinked at the blunt response. Somehow he'd already leapt to the conclusion that Tony had been arrested for murder and was desperately trying to call in favors from the powerful acquaintances he'd acquired during high school. Now he struggled to readjust his thinking. "An overdose?"

"He was shot three blocks from your office building."

A stab of regret sliced through Lucas even as he lifted his brows in surprise.

"Tony was in Houston?"

The Detective gave a small nod. "He was."

"Did he live here?"

Sam Cooper shrugged. "He was carrying a Louisiana driver's license. We're checking the address that was listed."

The air pressure dropped as Teagan leaned forward, his expression hard with annoyance. Despite his years in the military, the younger man harbored a deep distrust of authority figures.

"Why are you here?"

The Detective turned his head to meet Teagan's glare. "Excuse me?"

"If you have a body, shouldn't you be out looking for who made it dead?" Teagan demanded.

"I find it's quicker to discover the killer when I know my victim."

Lucas studied Sam Cooper. The police were clearly treating this as a murder, not a random drive-by shooting.

Interesting.

"Then you came to the wrong guy," Lucas informed the Detective. There was no point in letting the man waste his time. He felt as bad as hell that Tony was dead, but it had nothing to do with him. "Like I said, I haven't seen or heard from Tony since high school."

Sam ignored the unmistakable cue to bring the interview to an end.

"Odd that he was shot so close to your building, don't you think, Mr. St. Clair?"

"Enough." Lucas abruptly shoved himself to his feet, vaguely aware that Teagan was rising at the same time. "I've tried to be polite and answer your questions, but you're starting to piss me off." He held the Detective's steady gaze. "Are you trying to imply I have some connection to this crime?"

Sam remained sitting, remarkably nonchalant as both Lucas and Teagan glared down at him. Of course, they would have to be fucking idiots to attack a member of the Houston Police Department in the middle of a bar, plus he was probably carrying. Hard to detect beneath that hideous sports jacket.

"I think Tony Hughes was coming to see you," Sam said in a calm voice.

Lucas scowled. "Why?"

"Because of this." Reaching into his pocket, the Detective pulled out a clear baggie and set it on the table.

Lucas leaned forward to study the wrinkled piece of paper that had his name and address scribbled on it.

"Where'd you get that?" he demanded.

"Tony had it in his front pocket."

"Shit," Lucas breathed in shock.

"Still no idea why he was in the neighborhood?"

"No." A chill inched down Lucas's spine. Why the hell had Tony been looking for him after fifteen years? And who would shoot him in the back? Questions that needed answers, but not until he shook off the tenacious policeman. It was never a good idea to chat with a Homicide Detective when he had a connection to a dead body. "And we're about to take this to my lawyer's office."

"About damned time," Teagan muttered.

Sam lifted his hand, trying to look harmless. "I just have one more question for now."

"What?"

The Detective reached into his pocket to pull out another baggie. This one held a photo of a dark-haired woman with the words KILL HER OR ELSE scrawled across her face.

"Do you recognize this woman?"

Lucas reached to snatch the baggie off the table, holding the picture toward the muted light. He barely heard Teagan's low curse or Sam's protest at his rough handling of evidence.

Even at a distance he'd easily recognized the image of a stunning young woman.

Oh, her features had matured from the soft prettiness of

youth into elegant lines. And her body had filled out with curves that made his mouth water.

But he'd recognize the thickly-lashed dark eyes and soft, kissable mouth anywhere.

His stomach was fisted with a stark sense of horror that wrenched the air from his lungs.

"Mia," he rasped.

"Mia?" With a surge, the Detective was on his feet, snatching the baggie from Lucas's fingers. "Last name?"

"Ramon. Mia Ramon," Lucas said even as he was turning away from the table.

On some level he understood that he wasn't thinking clearly. Shock did that to a man. But his primitive instincts didn't give a shit. All he knew was that Mia was in danger.

Nothing else mattered.

"Wait," Sam commanded as Lucas headed toward the door. "Where are you going?"

Lucas's long strides never faltered. Not even when he sensed Teagan moving to walk at his side.

"What can I do?" his friend asked.

That simple.

No aggravating demands for an explanation. Just a sincere desire to help.

"Tell the guys I'm headed to Shreveport," he said, his subconscious making a list of tasks that had to be finished before he could leave Houston. "I don't know when I'll be back."